Praise
by Roberta Grimes

MW01144267

Cast in the form of a diary written by Thomas Jefferson's wife, Martha, Grimes's first novel chronicles the years from their courtship in 1770 to her death in 1782. Atmospheric and richly detailed, with exact accounts of such contemporary activities as leaching lye and boiling soap, the novel captures the personalities of two extraordinary people and the tumult of the Revolutionary War that consumed their lives. We view the conflict through the prism of Martha's sharply perceptive mind; the maneuvers of the era's famous men—George Washington, Patrick Henry, and Benedict Arnold—form a well-integrated backdrop to her story.

The novel also traces Martha's evolution from a self-indulgent Southern belle to an outspoken young mother with radical social views; conversations with her slave Betty on the explosive subjects of emancipation and miscegenation are revealing of the complex relationship between white and black Americans in the 18th century. Thomas Jefferson's steady rise as a lawyer, lawmaker, and statesman takes second place here to his role as husband, father, and lover, so shattered by his young wife's death that he never remarried. The moving tale succeeds both as gripping historical saga and powerful love story.

—Publisher's Weekly

My Thomas a literary tour de force

Roberta Grimes's first major novel is a marvel, a historical novel whose detail, scope and depth seem much greater than the book's more than 300 pages. *My Thomas* captures the complicated nature and depth of Thomas Jefferson's wife, Martha, who died just ten years after the couple were married and whom Jefferson mourned the rest of his life.

The novel is presented as Martha's own journal of her life with Thomas, and the hand of the author is neither seen nor felt anywhere in the book. The reader is totally immersed in Martha's life, in the person she must have been.

Grimes's mastery of the tone of life in late 18th century Virginia is complete. Her characters live, breathe, and speak with such truth and realism that the reader is drawn unconsciously into the complicated and fascinating lives of Martha and Thomas.

Not since Michael Shaara's Pulitzer Prize-winning novel of the battle of Gettysburg, *Killer Angels*, have I read such a fine historical novel.

—Daniel L. Mallock, *The Patriot Ledger*, Quincy, MA

I loved it… The greatest compliment I can pay this novel is to say I was furious when it ended. I wanted much, much more of Martha, I was so beguiled by her. I have no doubt at all this novel will be an enormous success—after all, how rare is it to find a novel so quiet and yet startling, so dignified and yet passionate, so sincere and so deductive.

—Margaret Forster, author of *Lady's Maid*

Roberta Grimes is a highly intelligent and richly gifted writer. Those with a curiosity about the American past will read *My Thomas* with delight and urge it upon their friends.

—Alf J. Mapp, Jr., author of *Thomas Jefferson: Passionate Pilgrim*

Such a different, interesting and insightful look at the family life of Thomas Jefferson. Martha was truly the love of his life yet I think there were times that in her short life she doubted that. She never failed to support him and stood by his decisions even if she did not agree. Definitely an historical novel must-read.

—Charleysangel, Amazon.com

I don't know how much of this book is factual, but it was very romantic and endearing, exciting with all the moves during the war, sad with all the children Martha lost, and had interesting dynamics between Martha and the slaves. I really enjoyed it. A great read!

—C. Lane, Amazon.com

An excellent book about the life of one of the most elusive of the presidents' wives. I would definitely recommend it for anyone interested in learning more about Thomas Jefferson, and also for anyone who is interested in the presidents' lives and their families.

—Zann A. Gibson, Amazon.com

Loved the book! So well written. I learned so much about that period of history, from the extremely vivid descriptions.

—Rebecca K. Isley, Amazon.com

Rich & Famous

By the Author

FICTION:

Rich and Famous

My Thomas

Letter from Freedom

Letter from Money

Letter from Wonder

NONFICTION:

The Fun of Dying – Find Out What Really Happens Next!

The Fun of Staying in Touch

Rich & Famous

ROBERTA GRIMES

Published by Wheatmark®
1760 East River Road, Suite 145, Tucson, Arizona 85718 U.S.A.
www.wheatmark.com

ISBN: 978-1-62787-124-2 (paperback)
ISBN: 978-1-62787-125-9 (ebook)
LCCN: 2014934986

This story is lovingly dedicated to all those who struggled and sacrificed to pass down to us their American dream, and to our grandchildren, for whom it is our legacy.

chapter one

January 28, 1988

Kim stood at her office window. The gray Indianapolis sky beyond her was flecked with snowflakes like cotton lace that flattened weightless against the glass and melted into busy dribbles. Lou watched her lift her head and set her shoulders. He could see that she was frightened. Kim was president and chairman of the board of Taste of Home, a half-billion-dollar corporation she had built around an idea that Lou had been sure would never fly. She was a marketing prodigy and a management genius, but she lacked the stomach for a dirty fight, and she was just twenty-nine. He couldn't bear to tell her everything. If she knew she was about to lose control of the company she had spent six years nurturing like an only child, she might not be able to fight anymore.

She murmured, "How bad is it?" Then she turned, and the sight of her stricken face made Lou shrink a little inside his clothes. She had the delicate skin of a genuine blonde, so the high flush on her cheeks stood out like cute clown dots. The thin white scar down the left side of her face was more noticeable than it had been in quite some time. Kim had never been willing to tell him how she had come by that scar, nor would she consider plastic surgery to correct it. She even had a habit of hooking her hair behind her ear to show it off. Now she was adding, "Can't we stall until after the board meeting?"

Lou drew a long breath and settled deeper into her sofa, eliciting a whisper of springs. He said, "City papers will have separate stories tonight. By tomorrow it's national news."

"If I get a margin call, I'm dead."

Lou had nothing to say to that. Watching her go through this was agony for him. He saw no way she could take back control of her company; the most she might do was hold on to her job. He flipped open the folder of statistics he had prepared during his hours in the air.

"Well, first the good news. Your inspiration to provide room service for hot-sheet motels is taking off there, too. Thirty-nine franchises in the Northeast is pretty good, considering we've been there just eighteen months. They're already serving a thousand motels and tourist cabins, and I picked up applications for an additional seventeen franchises. Not bad for a kid in pigtails." Kim gave him the smirk he expected as he leaned to hand her the sheet where he had consolidated thirty-nine separate statements. She came for it and looked it over as she headed back toward the front of her desk.

"They're flying, Kim. Our take this year could be fifty million dollars."

She hooked her hair behind her ear and sat against her desk, crossing her ankles, reading. Her hair was so soft that it whispered free strand by strand. She looked at Lou and said, "Do you know what's great about this? I'm used to the fact we can do it here, but having them take our procedures and do it on their own still amazes me." Again she smiled and bit her lip. This was becoming a new mannerism for a woman enjoying undreamed-of success coupled with ever-increasing anxieties.

"The only wrinkle is the Fragones own at least eleven of those franchises, and not just the two we first suspected."

"But we were careful about that! Weren't we careful? Didn't we check those people out?"

"They lied. And we were naive, I guess."

"We never should have franchised to begin with. We could have waited and done the whole expansion ourselves. Why not? Just a few years more?"

Lou leaned and sipped his cooling coffee. He had a headache coming on, but he could take some aspirin when he went back to his office to shave on his way to the board meeting.

"They're really running drugs? How long has this been going on?"

"Nearly a year in some places."

"And we're just learning about it now?"

"The locals tried to handle it on their own until the Feds decided to stick it to the Fragones. That's when they started this IRS audit, so that's when we were finally called. By the time I got there, they were setting up a multi-state raid for last night...."

"We were *raided?*" Kim bounced away from her desk and paced to the window-wall, where she stiffly stood with her hands behind her back. Her blond hair and navy-blue suit made her look like a small, dark fertility sculpture crowned in gold. "I hate this!" She turned to face him. "I can't stand being mixed up with bums!"

"It's all right. All they found was a couple of hookers who claimed they were working independently and a little cocaine in a delivery truck. The drivers said they were users. And nobody'd heard of anybody named Fragone."

"Let me get this straight. The papers are about to say we were raided because there were rumors we were dealing in drugs and prostitution? And they even *found* some girls and drugs, but nobody can link it to the Fragones? So now it looks like *we're* the crooks?"

"Not crooks . . . ."

"I hate this!" Kim paced to her desk, sat down in her chair, then immediately bounced up again.

"Listen to me. It's a P.R. problem. That happens. You deal with it."

"I don't want to deal with it! Not when there are half a dozen stockholders on my board now who turn out to have their own agendas. Sure, I own forty-three percent of the company *now*. But that's with mortgaging my house and margining my stock and putting up everything I own so I could buy back what I shouldn't have sold in the first place. If that stock falls five points, I'm going to get margin calls and then I'm dead. I'll lose everything! How could you do this to me, Lou?" Tears welled in her eyes and she tipped up her chin, looking at him.

He had seen this moment coming for the past six months, ever since it had become apparent that a pair of California investors had accumulated twenty-eight percent of Taste of Home's stock. Then a franchisee in Newark had received an audit notice, and Kim had remarked that their stockholders and franchisees were becoming more trouble than they were worth. Lou said patiently, "When you have something that works you go national or you watch somebody else crowd you out. If we hadn't gone public and franchised when we did, Intelco's Moveable Menu wouldn't be just our upstart competitor. It would be the whole show."

"I don't agree!" Kim snapped. "And now we're doing frozen food, too? We've got to do everything at once?" She fixed him with a frosty-moist glare. "This is just a game to you, isn't it? Watch your star pupil build her little idea into a not-so-little company so you can play your financial games. That's all this is to you! What do you care? You can always go back to teaching, can't you? But Taste of Home is my whole life!"

Lou tried to meet her eyes. He couldn't. He opened his briefcase and slid his folder in and fussily clicked it shut. In a tiny way, she was right. He had made it a point not to own Taste of Home stock, and he refused to be employed. A consultant, really, was all he was. His life and his pleasure for the past six years had been the development of this natural business talent and her jewel of a company that she had begun in her Aunt Dagmar's kitchen as an M.B.A. student. He had been eager for her to go public, and tickled by the complexities of a franchise operation. But, a game? He didn't think he saw it as a game. "You know I'd never dream of hurting you," he said as he tried again to meet her eyes.

"Was it deliberate? Or were you just really stupid?"

There was a wounded sparkle in her eyes that made her seem as tender as a child. The corners of her mouth tipped up a little, right on the edge of smiling. Lou loved this woman so desperately that all he wanted to do was spend forever gazing into the enigma of that crying, laughing face, but he had never been able to tell her that. There was a wall of strangeness between Kim and any man she dated that wasn't mistrust, precisely. It was more like an innate cross-gender reserve, like the grill and veiling that hide a nun. He had long ago understood that he could be her friend or he could risk their friendship for the dead-end, meaningless role of her lover.

"I've always been alone. I don't need *you*." Her eyes were moist. "Go on, Lou. Get out of here. Go screw up somebody else's company."

"You need me," he said gently. "I'm the only one in this mess who's on your side."

"Nobody's on my side! But watch me. I'll do it alone. In spite of you. Nobody's going to take my company!"

He couldn't stand the way she was looking at him, like a defiant little badger in a leg-hold trap. He knew that she was only half angry. She was working off some of her fears on him, and it pleased him to know that they were close enough for her to feel able to do that. He said patiently, "I'm sorry. I'll go with you now. We can talk about all this later."

"No. Get out of my way. It's time I stood on my own two feet."

She stalked a detour around him, then paused with her hand gentle on the doorknob while she lifted her chin and adjusted her shoulders. She opened the door with a resolute little flourish and left the room.

———◆———

Sam Denton was hunched to count off the seconds on his diamond Rolex that he wore everywhere, even on horseback and out in the vegetable fields and in the meat-packing plant. It bore a patina of unmentionable dirt that pleased him. "The bitch is now thirty minutes late," he muttered to Hicks Waverly, who sat slumped like a sack in a stiff French chair where no man could be comfortable. Hicks seemed half-asleep, with his eyes slitted and his chin sunk in rolls on his chest.

Sam saw now that Hicks was studying the woman sitting opposite him across the broad pink-marble table. She repeatedly glared at Hicks and flinched her eyes away, but he just went on looking at her and smiling with the upper part of his face. Then his mouth moved, lazily, as if he were using his tongue to count his teeth. Hicks's one big flaw was this weakness he had for women who were repulsed by him. He soon lost interest in any woman who was even neutral, but when he met one who showed him an active dislike, he would pursue her with such fervor that surprisingly often he was able to maneuver her into bed. Now Sam watched with disgust as Hicks began another pursuit. This fetish of his was such a waste of his energy.

"Think she'll show?" Hicks muttered, his eyes still on the woman, who had ostentatiously turned to chat with a sallow man sitting to her right. She was an angular creature whose winter-blue eyes contradicted the Native American look of her high cheekbones and long, dark hair.

"She'd better," Sam muttered, liking the growl of irritation in his own voice. He didn't know or care who any of these people were. And now he regretted having bothered to come to this useless meeting of a rubber-stamp board that was about to become superfluous. Sam and Hicks had spent years trying to get into restaurants on a big enough scale to make it worthwhile, and then along had come this kid with her brilliant idea that was revolutionizing the motel business. Her stock was so thinly traded that they should have been able to buy control through straws before she was even aware of them, but six months ago they had found themselves in a bidding war that had driven the price up to a ridiculous fifty times earnings. So now they were taking another tack. Hicks had thought that being on the board would be a source of inside information, but Sam knew board meetings were a waste of time when they were about to force out the major stockholder anyway and be done with it.

◆

Faith Neiquist was smoldering. If that fat cowboy with the head shaped like a pear didn't stop leering at her, she was going to stalk right out of this room. She was bored with the mouse of a man sitting next to her, so she shifted and gazed off through the window at the boxy gray Indianapolis skyline shimmering beyond the spitting snow.

"This has never happened before," fretted the mouse. "They always start the meeting like clockwork."

He was a small man in a three-piece suit with a body oddly shaped like a greyhound's: he had skinny limbs, a barrel chest, and a triangular face that seemed to be all part of the structure of his gigantic nose. His hairline was receding, which made him look as if his ears were pricked. To Faith's amusement, he fished a big gold watch from his vest pocket and took a squinting look at it.

"Have you been on the board long?" she asked.

"Two years. I'm ex-officio. Union."

Faith had no idea what that meant, but she didn't want an explanation. She slipped a Benson & Hedges from her cigarette case as she shot another glare at that cowboy who couldn't keep his eyes to himself. Faith had learned that while she wasn't conventionally pretty, she had an arresting look of wildness about her that some men perceived as great beauty. She looked at the hick as she carefully, sensually exhaled smoke through her mouth and nose. John David Neiquist was such a man. J. D. Neiquist, the textile king, had taken one look at his new public relations director and thrown over marriage and family to take up with a woman forty years his junior.

Kimberly Bonner had stolen from Faith the only man she had ever loved. Had taken him, and then had jilted him so hard that he left college and disappeared altogether. Faith couldn't say when she had first noticed Kim's success, but for years she had followed with gritted teeth all the fawning media attention that bitch surely loved. It had taken J.D. to point out to Faith that Taste of Home's foray into frozen foods was risky, since ninety percent of new food products failed. They had to get space in all the major chains to have any chance at all. So Faith had followed Kimberly's progress in *The Wall Street Journal* and *Business Week* as Taste of Home's new frozen foods were test-marketed in Columbus and Topeka. Then, "It sure would be a shame, sugar, if Higgins & Stein passed up your li'l friend's food deal," J.D. had remarked to Faith one evening as he served himself candied sweet potatoes while his butler who was also his valet stood and stiffly held the bowl. Higgins & Stein had more than fifteen hundred stores in the nine southern states. Faith had paused with her fork halfway to her mouth and looked at J.D.

"Can you do that?" she had murmured in the small, sweet voice he preferred.

"Hell, I've been thinkin' of buyin' myself a store or two. Higgins & Stein's as good as any."

———————

Paul Whist slipped his watch from his vest pocket and glanced at it again. My word, they were thirty-five minutes late. But what interested him about the delay was less the cause of it than the fact that there were ten people sitting around this table, none of whom was willing to mention the fact that they had been sitting here for thirty-five minutes. That was odd. And he loved every oddity, every break in pattern, for the insights he could draw from it and use to good effect later on. So Paul was enjoying this delay. It gave him a chance to size up the new members. There had been a surprising consolidation of stock in a few hands during the past year, and the stockholders in their wisdom had voted out the four members of the board who were up for re-election and nominated from the floor a whole new slate.

The woman sitting next to Paul he had easily dismissed as typical. She had told him she owned eight percent of the company's stock, this was her first time on a corporate board, and she lived in Charleston, South Carolina. But she had a Midwestern accent, and the stiff way she held her shoulders and smoked told him she hadn't come from money. So she was the toy of some Southern tycoon who had bought her a toy of her own. Next case.

The fat and skinny cowboys sitting across the table had seemed to be a break in pattern until Paul had assessed their expensive fur coats and jewelry and the lackeys sitting against the wall who apparently belonged to them. So they were a couple of eccentric partners who wanted to do business with the company or hoped to take it over. Next case.

The young man sitting beside the skinny cowboy had seemed at first to be typical, but Paul realized after thirty-five minutes that he was the biggest break in pattern in the room. He was a dark-haired princeling in his early twenties, a soft-faced young man in a gray chalk-stripe whose finish of buttonholes and fit of sleeves shouted that it had to be a thousand-dollar suit. Maybe two thousand. His baby-full cheeks bore a delicate flush, even though the room was just a little overheated. He was sweating so much that droplets stood on his forehead. But what surprised Paul most was the fact that he neither looked at nor spoke to anyone else. He gave the impression of being utterly alone in some strenuous and painful manhood rite. How very odd.

Paul glanced around at the others again, cultivating a carefully bland expression. He was pleased that the luck of a new slate had unexpectedly given him a lack of history. A couple of times in the past few years he had been forced to press some labor issues with the old board. Now the five older members would remember, but they had generally split on labor issues. And Bonner's mentor, Louis Pointe, was a pragmatist who would know when he was in a box.

———◆———

Dominick Ashton willed himself to sit absolutely still. His shirt clung to his back and itchily released. This had to be a trap. Why else would all these people sit here waiting for more than half an hour? There even seemed to be a conspiracy among them, a sense of shared smiles that never reached their faces. His plan had been brilliant, and if those brainless thugs his uncle had working for him hadn't screwed it up, there wouldn't have been anything so tacky as a multi-state raid. This room must be a hundred degrees. And what had it been, now? Almost an hour?

Dominick didn't realize the door had opened until there was a blur of heads turning. Then into the room walked a woman so surprisingly young and lovely that he blinked. Kim Bonner's face had appeared on so many magazine covers and television commercials and even billboards that it was impossible not to know who she was, but all her pretty photos and her tycoon image only made more arresting his first sight of her. She was lovely and slight and graceful, a mere wisp of a woman with a classic, strong-featured face. And she looked as nervous as he was feeling, with her bright-pink cheeks and her hands clasped first in front and then behind her. He was so entranced by the sight of this woman whose company he intended to dismantle that he thought now perhaps she should be part of the deal. He'd have to see. She stood at the head of the boardroom table and said, "Good morning. I'm sorry to have kept you waiting, but there have been some developments on the East Coast. I waited for details so I could report to you."

Shit! But Dominick's name wasn't Fragone. He thought they wouldn't make the connection. He watched Kim Bonner slide out her chair and sit gracefully, then watched her jump it in little hops to pull it closer to the table. He found that charming.

"Because of the extraordinary nature of what I have to say, we will deviate from the agenda before you." Her voice quaked. She paused to clear her throat. "I will declare this meeting open and go directly to items of new business. Does anyone have anything he wishes to discuss?"

Dominick glanced around the table in surprise as, one by one, every other board member raised a hand.

chapter Two

August 6, 1971

Kim had waited five years for her thirteenth birthday. When she was eight, her mother's cousin had come from Atlanta to spend the summer, and Kim had watched in mute worship as that worldly beauty with breasts and pubic hair went about all the glorious rituals of womanhood: the leg-shaving and tweezing of eyebrow hairs; the teased hair so high that it became an additional head; the strange and awful and compelling mysteries of the sanitary napkin. When Kim broke from bed to peer into the mirror on that ultimate birthday morning, she didn't look very different, but the mirror over their family dresser was missing half its silver and what was left was so full of morning that it made her squint. A better mirror might show a world of change.

Kim stepped over her brother's trundle bed to get to the closet. He was sleeping on with the same determination that Kim must have shown when her mother got up before dawn. She stood in the rich smell of mustiness and lilac toilet water that permeated all their clothing and shifted hangers on the pole at her mother's end, studying three white uniforms. What was going to be different about her thirteenth birthday was something she couldn't have imagined when she was eight. She would be spending the day working.

For Kim to care about turning thirteen seemed childish now,

when the hoped-for changes in her body had already occurred and she knew from the perspective of her thirteen years that there were more important goals to shoot for. Sixteen, when she could learn to drive. Eighteen, when she could graduate. Twenty, when her mother had had her first child. But Kim swore that her own child would have a father. She washed her face and brushed her teeth in the bathroom lean-to that had been added so long after the house was built that its floor was three inches lower than the bedroom linoleum. The naked sill of the house could be seen, and Kim liked that. She enjoyed knowing how things were put together, and this little glimpse of the bones of the house with axe marks visible and wooden pegs let her imagine all the other posts and pegs still hidden in the walls.

Kim put on her uniform quickly because the first sweetness of stove smoke was reaching her. Her mother's dress was too large for her, but still she could see the jut of breast or hip against cloth so she watched her body in the mirror as she bent and twisted, brushing out her hair. She began two braids at her temples and brought them around to the nape of her neck so she could coil them there and anchor them with hairpins. She saw now that her life would be a series of goals that would become less and less important the closer she came to achieving them; but nevertheless, it seemed to be a kindness to her eight-year-old self to feel pleased about having reached this day.

Kim's mother was in the front room, frying eggs and bacon. She had one of the stove lids out and her cast-iron pan set into the hole, so the hiss of frying was fierce and there was a blue haze of smoke above her head. "Sit, darlin'!" Darcy called as she turned things rapidly in her pan, causing brief interruptions and sputtering resurgences in the sound that could have been rain, Kim thought, as she carried plates to the table.

"Eat quick now, Kimmy. You got to get Mr. Sever's breakfast for seven-thirty." Darcy was wearing an apron made from a flowered chicken-feed bag over her best navy-blue going-to-Richmond dress.

"It's my birthday, Mama."

"Oh, I know it is, darlin'." Darcy sat down and picked up her fork. "I know it's hard workin' on your birthday, but I got to get Timmy to the doctor's. He's gettin' worse. Sometimes I'm really scared for him."

"It's just allergies. It gets worse around August," Kim said as she took a forkful of egg yolk. She was newly delighted every morning by the sunshine taste of eggs fried in bacon grease.

For as long as Kim could remember, she had yearned over her scattered, unstable mother as if Kim were the mother and Darcy the child. Darcy's constant expression was a tentative smile, as if solemnity or a full smile might be risky. She spoke in a deep twang that sounded like rural Georgia and seemed to embarrass her in central Virginia. But despite the fact that she couldn't afford a car and she heated her house with her kitchen stove, Darcy kept her long hair tidy and wore mascara and lipstick every day. Kim looked at her mother, feeling wrenched with pity by the effort Darcy had made that morning to part her hair exactly right.

"You don't mind, do you, darlin'?" Darcy looked at Kim over a forkful of egg. Then she leaned with satisfaction to envelop her food with her round red mouth.

Kim minded very much the reason why she had to work. She had been an only child until the age of eight, and she saw her little brother as an interloper who now complicated every aspect of her life. He couldn't go looking for berries in the glens below Highgrove, so Darcy wouldn't do that anymore. He had to be put down at seven, which had meant the end of Kim's reading in bed. He was allergic to almost everything. And Kim realized now that his dark hair and hazel eyes meant that he must have had a human father, but she couldn't ask Darcy who it was. Just the fact of that secret made a space of politeness between Kim and her mother that hadn't been there before. So Kim didn't feel for Timmy the love she thought she would have felt for a genuine brother. He seemed instead to be a tiny, malevolent presence in this house. But no, Kim didn't mind her occasional days of taking her mother's place in the mansion at Highgrove. Just being in those high-ceilinged, heavy-molded rooms, each of which could have held this house twice over, was a pleasure.

"Well," Darcy said after a long silence punctuated by dish clinks. "Kimmy? It's seven-ten. Mrs. Sever will be eatin', too. They're goin' to West Virginia to see to the mines. All she'll have is a fruit salad. It's right there in the refrigerator."

The path to Highgrove twisted through the swamp behind their house and up through a pasture littered with cow-flaps where sometimes there would be dairy cows that Kim eyed uneasily as she walked. Once a heifer had charged her, knocking her hard against the fence and chipping her tooth. Above the pasture was a pine wood that was scary to traverse at night, when the creaking of branches and the click of sap cooling in the trunks sounded like pursuers. The pines stopped at the foot of Highgrove's back lawn.

No matter how many times she saw this house, the fresh sight of it always brought Kim to a standstill at the edge of the woods. She stood there briefly, swiping at the moisture on her lip and catching her breath. The house was two hundred feet away, but it was so enormous on its little hill that it loomed immediately above her head. The massive shade of it made the grass look black and threw blue shadows along its veranda and into the cornices above its windows. High around its tall peaked roof, the brilliance of the sun was an orange radiance.

Kim trudged up the lawn toward the kitchen wing and let herself in at the servants' porch. She hung her mother's key on its peg beside the door and hurried into the kitchen, where she set about making breakfast with a haste of extra gestures in case someone should need to know she realized that she was late. The kitchen at Highgrove had a big gas stove that frightened Kim a little. With wood, you could see the relationship between fuel and heat, but the fierceness of fire straining against the flimsy restraints of a control knob's commands made gas cooking too miraculous to be safe.

Mrs. Sever came into the kitchen at seven-thirty-eight. She wore white slacks with loafers and a pink silk shell and a pink rayon scarf holding back her pageboy. And even though she was casually dressed for her trip to her husband's West Virginia mines, she wore gold-and-coral chains around her neck and gold-and-coral sprays of earrings. "Are we about ready, dear?" she asked in her perfectly modulated Southern finishing-school voice. Kim loved that voice. When she was tiny, her mother had brought her here while she worked and sometimes Mrs. Sever would read to her.

"Yes, ma'am. Are you sittin' down?" Kim let the gears of her accent slip, so she sounded more like her mother.

"Since seven-thirty. Ordinarily it wouldn't matter, but we promised Darcy a ride to the bus. She has to catch an eight-fifty bus."

Kim carried in the silver urn of coffee first, and then the platter of ham and eggs and the bowl of fruit, and then the orange juice, and then the grits. She filled their coffee cups smoothly before she remembered their need for cream and sugar, so she fetched that with such fluttery haste that when she flapped back through the kitchen door Mr. Sever looked up from his paper and said, "Kimmy, Kimmy, Kimmy," in the same descending tone of mild exasperation he had used when she was small and she forgot herself and ran in the hallway.

"It's all right, dear," Mrs. Sever said patiently. "We do have plenty of time now. Thank you."

When Kim carried in their plate of toast, Mrs. Sever was just saying something about a boy from Bobby's class who was missing in action. The Severs occupied all sides of the Vietnam War, with him a hawk and her a dove and their son unable to care either way, and every meal Kim had served here in the past two years had included some kind of war talk. Their daughter was in Paris for the summer. Miss Colleen shared her mother's views on the war as she also shared her voice and manners and hairstyle. Kim stepped into her place beside the door. They served themselves at breakfast, but she had to be ready to take their cups to the sideboard for more coffee or to duck into the kitchen for another slice of toast.

What money bought was space and light. This dining room was twenty feet square, with a wall of floor-to-ceiling Palladian windows to the east that made its creamy moldings and its painted mural of English castles seem luscious. The sun picked sparkles from so much heavy silver that when Kim served breakfast on sunny mornings she would be blinded repeatedly.

"You've done a fine job with breakfast, dear," Mrs. Sever said then.

"She's a hell of a cook." Mr. Sever shifted back from his plate as he picked his teeth with the silver pick that was part of his standard table setting. He was a thickset man with a heavy head who reminded Kim of a Newfoundland dog; he even had a mat of very dark hair and a patient, sagging sadness about his eyes. "You could be a cook, Kimmy." He swung his head slowly to look at her for the first time. It wasn't protocol for either of them to notice their maid, but Kim had grown up in this house so she occupied an awkward space between servant and poor relation. Mr. Sever settled against the arm of his chair, studying Kim. He added, "My, you're sure growin' up."

"Doesn't she look like her mother?" Mrs. Sever said, sounding pleased.

He pressed, "Is that what you're goin' to do? Be a cook?"

Kim knew what that was all about. She had earned a perfect record of A's since kindergarten, something her mother couldn't resist proclaiming. The Severs felt uneasy about Kim's success because their own children had done so poorly in the best private schools in the South.

"I don't know, sir," Kim said, thinking she would work the fields before she cooked for a living. She was what her art teacher called a water-color prodigy, and what she really wanted to do was paint beautiful pictures.

"We ought to go," Mrs. Sever said as she blotted each corner of her mouth precisely and laid her napkin beside her plate. "You'll be all right by yourself, dear?" Kim had been spelling her mother as a maid in this house ever since she was ten years old, yet each time Mrs. Sever was about to leave her alone there was this momentary reversion to concern for her as a child of the family.

"I'll be fine, ma'am. I'm thirteen now."

"Are you, really? My, my. J. Bob? Shall we go?"

<hr/>

After she washed the dishes and counted the silver into the vault off the back hallway, Kim had only to tidy the rooms a little and make the beds. There was no need to dust, since the heavy cleaning was done by two women who came in twice a week.

By the time Kim had worked her way into the splendid front rooms, it was after nine o'clock. On both sides of a stairway hall were formal parlors, each of them rich with moldings and solemn with the dark, dour portraits of Sever ancestors. Mr. Bobby and Miss Colleen were six and eight years Kim's senior, so they had treated her while she was growing up as a kind of clever pet. When Kim was a tot, sometimes Bobby would carry her in and deposit her in the center of a vast blue Kirman. She would stare up in horror at all those grim ancestral faces and screw her eyes tight and scream until her mother found her.

Bobby had flunked out of the University of Virginia in May, so now the big family worry was that he was going to be drafted at the age of nineteen. His mother was trying to get him accepted somewhere else. His father was goading him to enlist. Bobby himself was floating along this hot Virginia summer like an aging Huckleberry Finn on a raft, knowing that eventually he would fetch up somewhere. Darcy talked about Bobby constantly. She fretted about the way he slept until noon and went on freakish food binges, granola or Snickers bars or nothing at all. He had grown his hair to his shoulders, and often he wore a bandana around his head. He wore a fringed and beaded leather shirt sometimes, or bell-bottomed jeans with calico inserts, or sometimes a flowing purple caftan.

Kim's attitude toward Bobby had gone through many seamless stages. When she was very young she had been afraid of him, and then in awe of him, and then a worshipful eight-year-old who tagged after him for one whole summer. He was nicer to Kim that summer than he ever had been before or since. He taught her to fish, and even to sit on his lap and drive his father's Mercedes that he wasn't old enough to drive himself. Kim learned that summer what a gentle boy Bobby could be, although he had an edge of petulance that brought on irregular rages if she crossed him.

Kim hadn't seen much of Bobby in recent years, and her attitude toward him depended on how recently she had seen him last. His academic failures in the face of his lucky birth would nurse in her a fine contempt for him, a sense that he was going to need money because he was too lazy and stupid to survive without it. But then she would see him again, and the fey beauty of his face would make her yearn for him inexplicably. For a long time, his face wouldn't leave her mind: she would see shadows of it in the faces of others and confront it on the insides of her eyelids at night. She had seen him only three times that summer, but that had been enough to make her listen intently to her mother's endless chatter about Mr. Bobby's problems.

Kim paused in the broad front hall. The floor there was of gray-veined marble, and the staircase floated up to the left like a spiral in air and curled around to a landing above the front door. As a child, Kim had run laughing down that curl of staircase as if it were a slide; as a maid, she wasn't supposed to use it. She considered briefly whether using it mattered when she was alone in the house, but her sense of order made her need to go and use the servants' staircase that rose from the dim back hallway.

There were four servants' bedrooms in the kitchen wing of the second floor, and six family bedrooms in the formal part of the house. Kim opened the door off the servants' hallway and stepped out into the broad upstairs hall. Toward the front of the house, the entrance hall opened below a delicate railing. Back here, the hallway was lightly provided with Queen Anne furniture as a sitting room. Kim started for the master bedroom, her feet soft on the Turkey carpet. But even what little sound she made was heard.

"Where the hell have you been?" she heard Bobby call. She stopped at once. His room was just across from where she stood. For no reason that she could imagine now, it hadn't occurred to her that he might be at home.

"Darcy?"

"What?" she heard herself saying, softly.

"Where the hell have you been? They've been gone for hours. Come on. I've got a hard-on that just won't quit."

Kim tiptoed to his door, which was ajar by a foot and showed clothing and records scattered in the dim coolness. She peeked around the edge.

Bobby lay against his pillows with a book open on his stomach and a bowl of peaches on the sheet beside him. He had been eating them by cutting chunks with the penknife he had carried in his pocket since he was a child. There was a strange, sweet scent in the room that had a smell like old rot under it.

"I've been savin' . . . ." he said as he caught sight of Kim. His voice stopped like a needle lifted from a record. "What . . . *Kimmy*? Where's your mother?"

"She took Timmy to the doctor's."

Kim felt so strange to be seeing Mr. Bobby lying in his bed that she had to do something to cover her embarrassment. His laziness and the mess in his room made her feel self-importantly like a parent, so she bent automatically and began to pick up his clothes and records on her way to the window to open his drapes.

"It's comin' up on eleven o'clock." She felt for the cord and yanked it so hard that the drapes flourished like a pretty girl's skirt and there was a flood of radiance into the room.

"Are you crazy?" He threw his forearm over his face.

"You'll ruin your eyes, readin' in the dark like that," Kim said as she headed for the window beside his bed.

"Enough! One's enough."

Kim looked at Bobby. He was lying there studying her with his loose hair dark on his pillow. He had a pained but peaceful look about his face, like someone living on the edge of hurt. The way his eyes were taking in all of her and not politely resting on her face made Kim fidget. She went back to gathering an armload of his clothes and tidying his room.

"Leave that."

Kim looked at him again from the foot of his bed. He had eyes the color of Timmy's eyes, a very light brown. "Dirt-color" Kim had called them to her mother on the day Timmy had ripped up two of her books.

"Come here," Bobby said.

Kim walked around the end of his bed and sat obediently on the spot he patted. When he pushed at the clothing in her arms, she let it fall to the floor. He was smiling at her now, a tender smile that made his eyes seem so sad that Kim twisted her mouth and looked away.

"Can you take down your hair?"

Kim was proud of her thick blonde hair to her waist. Of course he would want to see it. She groped for the pins that held her braids and slid them one by one between her lips. She let her braids fall warm on her back.

"Can you sit on it?"

"No," she mumbled. She caught the pins from her mouth and said, "It stops below my waist."

"Your mama can sit on hers."

"I know." Kim suffered a shiver of strangeness to think he should know that about her mother. Having a grown mother who could sit on her hair was an oddity of which Kim was proud and ashamed in equal measure, so she was careful to notice that her mother kept her hair pinned up except when she was at home.

"Let your braids loose, Kimmy. I want to see your hair."

Kim leaned to place her hairpins on his cluttered side table. She grabbed each braid over her shoulder and pulled off its elastic and leaned and set those down too before it occurred to her that she was supposed to be working. If Bobby told his parents she was taking time, it might cost her mother the day. They couldn't afford to miss a day's pay.

"I shouldn't be doin' this." She leaned to take back her elastics. Bobby stopped her in mid-gesture with his hand gentle on hers. As she straightened again, he propped himself on his elbow and took one of her braids into his fingers. He ran his hand up the braid, loosening it, watching as he did it.

It occurred to Kim with a flutter of nervousness that there was an edge of propriety here that they had overstepped. She had never before noticed that edge because the position of servant was by its nature intimate and she had grown up in the intimacy of this extended family. But there was another kind of intimacy happening here. She grabbed her hair out of his hand and stood quickly.

"I think I'll get a wash in," she said as she bent to pick up his bundle of clothes.

"Kimmy?"

She looked at him. Her eyes were level with the edge of his bed.

"Shall I tell my mama you came in here an' undid your hair?"

Kim stiffened. "No! Please don't tell her." All she could think was that her mother was going to lose this job. And she didn't have a car.

"You did, you know."

"Please," Kim said as she tidied the top of her braid and re-braided the rest of it with rapid fingers.

"What'll you give me." It didn't sound like a question.

"Please, Mr. Bobby, I . . . ."

He smiled at her then. It was a smile so unexpected that Kim's busy fingers froze on her braid.

"I know. You can give me a kiss."

Kim used to kiss him pecks on the lips with both of them exaggeratedly puckering after he had teased her to tears and his mother had said they had to kiss and make up. For the last year or two, the memory of those childhood kisses had been coming to Kim at night with the image of his face, lean and dark and sad behind her eyelids.

"Come on," he said, patting the edge of his bed again. She started to sit, but then he had another idea. He reached and lifted the edge of his blanket. "Come in here."

"Please, I . . . ."

"I won't tell. Not if you come in here an' kiss me."

Kim let out her breath and crept in under the blanket beside him. She understood as soon as she had done it that this gave him something else to tell his mother about, but she was in so deep now that the only way out was through it.

Bobby took her head onto his shoulder, looking steadily into her face. Kim looked at him bravely, sniffing as delicately as a cat the dark male scent of his skin. She fitted one arm in against his chest and put the other one behind her because she had a suspicion he was altogether naked and she didn't want to know for sure.

"You're growin' up, little girl." His fingers stroked the braid at her temple and tenderly traced her cheek. Kim could smell the sweet rot of peaches on his breath. "I never guessed you'd ever grow up," he added, looking into her face with sad eyes that reminded her of his father's eyes. His fingers were drifting down her neck and over her shoulder.

Kim wanted to say, "Go ahead and kiss me," but she felt so vulnerable that she was afraid to say anything. She knew what she was doing now was worse than her taking down her hair, but anything she did to improve the situation might turn out to be worse than this. And she couldn't make him angry. Then he would surely tell. Once, when she was eight and he was fourteen, she had playfully hidden from him in a dry well near the ruins of the old slave cabins in the pine woods. He had called for her briefly, but hunting for her had been beneath him so he had told Darcy that Kimmy had been throwing rocks at the cattle. That night her mother had felt compelled to switch her.

"Hush."

Kim was whimpering high in her throat because his hand was on her upper chest. She shut her eyes tight and grabbed the sheet behind her as his fingers settled cupped around her breast.

"There now. That doesn't hurt, does it?"

"Please . . ." she managed to say.

Bobby was breathing in long, shaky breaths. He shifted his body closer to hers with a faint creaking of the mattress, and he caught her by the tail of her braids and leaned to envelop her mouth with his as that morning Darcy had leaned to devour her eggs. This was like no kiss that Kim could have imagined. Bobby's mouth was soft and wet on hers. His tongue that tasted of peaches flicked at her lips and teeth. His head and his whole body moved against hers in a slow, subtle rhythm that produced in her an agony of butterflies. She squirmed her legs together and whimpered. She twisted the sheet in her fist, desperate not to fight him.

"Oh, Kimmy," he moaned into her mouth. His hand was firm at the small of her back. He slid it down over one of her buttocks and squeezed hard enough to hurt while he moved his hips against hers. So then she fought him. She tried with all her strength to push him away. She pummeled him with her free fist while he rocked her harder against him and laughed a hoarse chuckle into her mouth.

"No!" she cried when she was able to twist her mouth free. "Get away!"

"But I'll tell." He grappled and caught her wrist while his body moved against hers, producing shivers of sensation through her belly.

"No, *I'll* tell," she snapped as she struggled to free her wrist.

Bobby stopped moving then and looked at her. "Tell what?" he asked coldly, sounding out of breath. "I'll tell how you came in here an' got in my bed. What in hell will you be tellin'?"

They looked steadily into each other's eyes until Kim flinched her eyes away.

"Please don't tell."

"Look what you did to me."

He shifted his grip on her wrist so he could guide her hand in under the sheet, where he closed her fingers stiffly around his erection. He moved a little, holding her fingers there so she could feel the loose skin and the hot solid core. He sighed.

Kim stared at his face, so honestly amazed that he chuckled

again. The only penis she ever had seen in her life was Timmy's. And she understood that something like this was what happened, but it was so much more enormous than she could have imagined that she cringed her hand away from it.

"Now I've got somethin' else to tell," he said, sounding childishly pleased.

"What do you *want* from me?" Kim wailed. Her eyes filled.

"You think you're better than me, don't you?"

"No, I . . . ."

"You always have. This little white-trash kid struttin' around as if she owns the place. I could tell by the way you looked at me you always thought you were better."

"No I didn't." She brought her hand out from under the blanket so she could brush aside the strings of hair falling into his face. "Of course not. You're my friend."

"I am *not* your friend!"

He swung over her and pinned her to the bed so fast that she gasped out a little shriek. Staring up into his face with his hair falling dark on both sides of it, she saw him again as she had been imagining him for all those nights. And beneath her surprised twinge of fear she yearned for him. Even being near him was not enough. She wanted to know him. To be inside him. To *be* him.

"You still don't get it, do you?" He had her wrists pinned to the bed on both sides, which was so uncomfortable that she struggled involuntarily. "You're just a little white-trash slut and I'm the hotshot prince of my hotshot family. You're *nothin'*, Kimmy. And I'll tell you what you can do for me. You're goin' to spread your legs for me right now so we can prove that's exactly what you are."

He settled with one of her arms pinned under him and grabbed her other wrist with his hand behind her head. He slipped his free hand up under her dress. She struggled, staring into his face.

He whispered, "I'll tell," and kissed her on the lips. His fingers were gentle on her thighs and working in under the elastic at the leg of her underpants.

For Kim, there was a dreamlike unreality to the cool light in the room and the feast of Bobby's sad, elegant face and the sense of being held down just enough so she couldn't fight him. She had to let him do this now. She knew he would tell on her otherwise. And since she had to do it, she wanted to take the experience apart and see how it was made. But she didn't mind what he had called her. He had been saying things like that all her life. When she was tiny, it was one of the ways he used to make her cry, but by the time she was seven or eight it had become just his pet way of talking to her.

He hooked her panties at her waist and had them off so quickly that she couldn't say more than, "Wait . . . !" He settled in on top of her with his legs outside of hers, resting on his elbows so his hands could gently stroke her cheeks.

"Little slut," he said softly, smiling down at her a smile so beatific that she tried to smile, too. His long weight was pressing her into the bed. She wondered whether this might be all there was to it. "I always knew I'd be doin' this. I couldn't wait for you to grow up."

"I'm thirteen today," Kim said bravely. She was finding it hard to breathe.

"*Thirteen?*" He drew away from her briefly, lightening his weight, before he settled on top of her again. "I thought you'd be a little older, though."

"Please, let's not . . . ?"

But he was kissing her so wonderfully that suddenly kissing was her whole world. He was slipping his knees in between hers, moving his body in a rhythm that called forth from her rhythms of her own. He was touching her sensitive places, but she didn't mind that. She was floating on a dreamy cloud of kissing. But then came the pain. Unexpectedly he stabbed deeper and deeper into her, hurting her more with every thrust so she struggled desperately under him, trying to move up away from him, sobbing, frantic. This couldn't be normal. It couldn't be meant to hurt this much.

Bobby was making a low moaning sound as he moved. Kim's fighting only made him thrust faster and harder until eventually he cried out a little chirp. He hesitated, his eyes closed and his face flushed with bliss, then he settled in on top of her again. "I love you, I love you," he murmured, kissing her ear. He was still moving a little inside her; the friction scraped and stung unbearably. Kim was sobbing so tightly that it took him a minute to realize that she was crying at all.

"Oh, my darlin'. It wasn't too good for you, was it? But it'll get better. And you've got no idea how good you feel, Kimmy, so firm and tight." He pulled out of her and settled on one elbow while she lay clenching her fists and streaming tears. "What? Kimmy?"

She couldn't speak. She was so sore and miserable and frightened and disappointed that all she could do was cry.

"Stop it." His voice was getting an angry edge. His face constricted as if he were holding back tears himself. "It's true, isn't it? You really do think you're better. You've always thought you were better than me, haven't you?"

Well, of course she had. It wasn't just that she knew with a pure conviction that needed no reason that girls were better than boys, but she had always been secretly glad about his unpredictable tempers and his lazy drifting because they showed he was of a weaker stock.

"You're *not!*" he shouted to jolt her into looking at him. She did. She even briefly stopped crying. "You're *trash*, Kimmy! You know it. I know it. Your mother spreads her legs for a dress or a ham but you'll do it for nothin'. You're *trash!*" His voice was thickening. "You're white *scum*, Kimmy. That's what you are!"

Kim stared at him, amazed to see that his eyes were sparkling and he was grimacing fiercely. But she was more amazed to realize he *believed* all that! She could hear it at school and not take it seriously in the safe internal place where she lived. She could hear it from him, teasingly, and believe it was another word for love. But Bobby believed it, and his belief shattered some fragile shell within her. For the first time in her life, she believed it, too.

"Nobody's goin' to have you." He started to sob like dry, hollow coughs. He wrestled her under him with a desperate strength and said, "*Nobody*, Kimmy! Do you hear me? You're mine!" He choked and sniffled and swiped at his nose before he caught her wrist again. For Kim, the sight of any man crying would have been a source of amazement. To see Bobby crying was a horror of inappropriate intimacy so great that she couldn't stand to look at him. "Look at me!" he raged, sounding frantic. He shook her body under him as if she were asleep. Moisture that must have been a tear hit the side of her face and itched there, but he had her arm pinned so she couldn't scratch it. "I'm goin' to make it so *nobody* else will want you! Do you hear me?" he shouted. Then there was a strange gleaming at the edge of her eye that made her turn toward him quickly. A pain like thin fire ran down the side of her face. Bobby leaped away from her, choking, flinging his penknife so it clattered against the wall.

Kim didn't understand what had happened. She had pain in front of her ear and pain between her legs, and there was blood (could it be blood?) on the front of her dress. And on the bed. There was blood everywhere. Bobby was cringing away from her and slipping off the bed.

Kim crept on hands and bottom to the opposite edge of the bed from Bobby and stood up foggily, feeling strange and light. What she really ought to do right now was fix her hair and pretend none of this had happened. She said, "Goodbye," and walked out of Bobby's room, fighting her persistent urge to feel the side of her face. She would clean up first. She could worry about everything else later. But she passed the upstairs servants' bathroom, walking slowly, trailing a finger on the wall. She passed the down-stairs bathroom, too. It began to seem more important that she go right home, so she stepped out across the servants' porch into the baking August heat and she stumbled, trembling, toward the pine woods.

———◆———

They didn't find Kim until after dark. She lay for hours curled six feet down in the slaves' dry well and watched the light grow pale and the shadows rise. Between bouts of hoarse, desperate crying she lay with her hands pillowed neatly under the good side of her face and listened to the wind soughing and the branches creaking and the cooling sap clicking in the trees. It sounded like complaints from the ghosts of slaves whose eyes she thought she could see sparkling overhead. Kim hadn't climbed into the well intending to die there. She had realized as she was passing through the woods that leaving her post in the middle of the day was the worst thing she had done so far, and since she couldn't go back but now she couldn't go home either, the well had been her only practical choice. By day it had seemed cozy and safe. It was only at night that the ghosts of slaves added one more horror to make her quake and tremble in the chilly dark.

She was absolutely going to hell. She had no doubt about that. She never went to church because her mother didn't have a car, but years earlier the Severs had sometimes taken Kim and Darcy to church in the back seat of their Mercedes. Kim's few minutes in church had left a forceful impression. If she messed around with boys this way, she was going to hell. And couldn't she go to hell for making her mother lose her job? Darcy had been hired as a governess when the Sever children were four and six. At that time, the house had been full of black servants, and Highgrove had been a self-sufficient plantation where life had hardly changed in a hundred years. Now they made do there with cleaning help and the fields were leased to tenants, but for Darcy it was still the gleaming center where she had arrived, poor and frightened, and been given a home.

It was Kim's home, too. She knew she wouldn't be content there forever, but she wasn't prepared to be cast out of it at only thirteen years old. (*Twelve,* her mind kept shouting. *Yesterday I was only twelve.*) Her best hope was that they would forgive at least Darcy. But if they did that, Kim would never see her mother or her little brother again. Just the thought of that brought on a spell of fresh, desperate crying that Kim tried to stifle with her palms over her face. The cut edge of her face was crisped and curling; the salt on her hands made it sting. Nobody had ever explained to Kim that cutting a girl's face was part of losing her virginity. Well, not part of it, precisely, but the two kinds of pain were so linked in her mind that she couldn't imagine one without the other.

Far off, Kim could hear someone calling her name. She had been hearing voices calling, off and on, since about the time when she could no longer make out the top of the well. She thought it might be the ghosts, calling her. Or it might be Death. The bad thing about dying would be going to hell, but even that seemed preferable to having to wander the world without any of her own people.

Light flowed and scattered through the branches overhead and was gone. Then it was there again, brighter. And gone. Kim whimpered with the shock of that and covered her face, forgetting to be careful of the left side. She hit it, and her face rang with pain. She began to cry hoarsely, trying desperately to smother her crying as the rustle of the ghosts came louder and louder. Then the light was full on her face. She could hear and feel and smell it as much as she could see it between her fingers: dusty, buzzing butter. "I knew it," she heard Mr. Sever saying from far away. He sounded sad and tired. "This is where I'd have put her. I used to play here, myself."

Kim shuddered under the merciless light. If she lay still, perhaps they would go away. Then she heard what sounded like the tenant, Mr. Auberdine, saying, "I think she's breathin', Mr. Sever."

The light probed harder and trembled away. Then there was a hurried scuffling of shoes on rock as someone clambered down the old precarious footholds. Hands turned her. The light examined her with agonizing brightness. She heard Mr. Sever saying, "Kimmy? Are you all right, girl?" The light moved away over her hips and legs. Kim could make out his face in the sudden dark. "It's just her cheek! She seems fine!" Mr. Sever shouted. He sounded glad, which gave Kim a tremble of hope. He gathered her up in his arms, being careful of the sore side of her face, and held her high enough so hands could reach her from above.

Mr. Sever carried Kim back to the house and into the kitchen wing, where he laid her down tenderly on the brown plaid couch in the servants' sitting room. The stability of indoor air and lamplight disoriented her after her long hours in the outer dark. Then she heard her mother's voice, sounding frail with shock.

"I knew he didn't kill you. He was just talkin' crazy," Darcy said from close by. Kim opened her eyes to find Darcy crouched beside her, picking pine needles out of her daughter's hair. Darcy glanced at Kim's face and winced her eyes away.

"I'm all right, Mama." Kim was so weary that her mouth could hardly form the words.

"I know you are, darlin'."

Then there seemed to be a break in time, because when Kim opened her eyes again Mrs. Sever was shaking her gently. "Kimmy? Baby? Can you wake up, sweetie?"

Kim opened her eyes a crack. Mrs. Sever was squatting beside the couch. It occurred to Kim to be surprised that she was still wearing the pink scarf and the gold-and-coral earrings she had put on that morning.

"Kim? Sweetie? You're goin' for a ride now, dear. Sully Auberdine is takin' you to stay with his people in Indiana. They'll get you help to fix your face," Mrs. Sever added tenderly, making a graceful gesture as if she were going to touch the wound, but then thinking better of it. "Come on now, dear. Can you sit up?"

Beyond Mrs. Sever's lamp-lit face, Kim could see in the gloom her mother's pale face and the sagging, sorrowful countenance of Mr. Sever.

"What?" But then the separate words assembled in her mind. They were sending her away. "No!" She struggled up to sit so fast that Mrs. Sever toppled and caught herself on her hands with a gawky gracelessness that embarrassed Kim. She couldn't stop causing these people trouble. "Don't send me away, Mama! Please! I'm sorry! I didn't mean it! I – Please don't send me away! I'll never do it again!"

"My dear, this isn't to punish you, sweetie," Mrs. Sever said, patting Kim's leg with a touching awkwardness. "Nobody blames you. I . . . ." But then a circuit completed itself in Mrs. Sever's mind that registered as a stiffening of her face, and Kim knew that they certainly did blame her. Or very soon they would blame her. And they were right. It was her fault.

"Kimmy, he is quite beside himself. The doctor has had to sedate him. He thought he'd killed you, and even after we showed you to him lyin' here he was still quite demented. You can't stay here, dear."

"Mama?" Kim cried desperately.

Her mother floated toward her. In her good navy going-to-Richmond dress and with the lamp-shadow on her hair, her face was the only part of her that Kim could see.

"Darlin', listen to me." Darcy's weariness made her accent so harsh that Kim was embarrassed for her. "He has a . . . Mr. Bobby has a . . . ."

"An obsession," Mrs. Sever put in. "It's just a phase, dear. He'll outgrow it. But until he does, you can't stay here."

"Send *him* away!" Kim blurted. But she knew that even for Darcy, Mr. Bobby's needs came first. "I'll die, Mama! If you send me away, I'll never see you again!"

"Of course you will. Don't be silly. Of course you will."

But even then, Kim was not convinced.

chapter Three

September 15, 1977

Kim was beginning her second year of college when she received the phone call telling her that her mother was dead. She had planned to buy books before she started her classes at ten and her pizza-delivery job at four, so she was already dressed and brushing her hair when the phone rang at seven-thirty. Aunt Dagmar's little pegs of feet in her stiff black sensible shoes went tapping down the hallway while Kim continued to put up her hair. That summer in Indiana had been so humid that she couldn't stand the weight of hair on her back, and since braids were beginning to seem undignified, she had come closer to cutting her hair that summer than ever before in her life. Her excuse for keeping it was that she had sworn at fifteen to wear her hair long until she was twenty, and that would be just one more year.

A cool, astringent smell in the room reminded Kim of stiff laundry fallen on the grass. She had slept with both windows open, and they had passed dark air across her bed all night. She tried to hold that subtle smell that reminded her of home, but the sun was already hot on the long porch roof. An acrid scent of tar was wafting in.

Aunt Dagmar came tapping back to Kim's room. She was a short woman with a round body and tiny hands and feet, and she always wore a good serge or gabardine dress because she had spent her life on the farm. To her, living in Oakhaven was living in the city. "Kim?" She paused in the doorway. Aunt Dagmar was too polite to enter Kim's room, and too polite to be comfortable discussing the private details of either of their lives. "Kim? You have a call. With an accent."

Aunt Dagmar's accent was Danish. It was apparent in a musicality of unexpected stresses that made everything she said sound like a spoken song.

"It must be my mother." Then Kim felt a shiver of anxiety. Her mother wrote faithfully every week, but she called only twice each year, once on Kim's birthday and once at Christmas. Kim tried to keep their conversations brief. She wanted to spare her mother the embarrassment of a big number on the Severs' telephone bill.

"It didn't sound like your mother," Aunt Dagmar said with a sniff before she tapped back along the hallway to the room where Uncle Valdimar lay, witless with old age. Kim stepped lightly into the hallway to minimize the noises she made in this house. She picked up the receiver from the table at the head of the stairs, where the Jensens' telephone reposed on its shrine as another city miracle.

"Hello?"

"Kimmy? Is that you, dear?"

It was Mrs. Sever. Kim hadn't heard her voice in six years. With it came a sense of spacious quiet and the clean scent of lemon oil.

"Hello, Mrs. Sever. How are you?"

"I'm fine, dear. But – I don't know how to say this. I'm sorry, Kimmy. Your mother had an accident last night. With her car. Forgive me. She died, dear. They say it was mercifully very quick."

Kim stared at the hand-crocheted doily where the Jensens' black phone was centered like a jewel. She had saved for six years to send her mother enough money to buy an old Chevrolet, sustained in her exile here by visions of the look on her mother's face as she sat behind the wheel of her very own car. Darcy's last few letters had been full of the unexpected thrill of complete mobility.

"Are you there, dear?"

"Yes."

"I'm so sorry, Kimmy. Believe me. This has been terrible for all of us."

Kim turned that statement over in her mind. The tone of it seemed to range beyond the edges of this unexpected death.

"Kim? Does your mother have any relations, dear? We never knew any."

But Kim was enjoying the sound of that voice so much that she hardly heard the words. She loved the home-sound of "mother" without the final "r." People in Indiana used too many consonants.

"Kim? Are you all right?"

"Oh. Yes. I just – no, not really. She has some cousins in Georgia, but she never heard from them."

"I see. Well, dear, we've made arrangements for you to fly into Dulles this afternoon and rent a car from there. You can drive, can't you?"

"Yes."

Kim always drove. The Jensens sat stiffly in the back seat like reluctant royalty.

"The tickets will be at the United counter. The rental car is Avis. We'll see you this afternoon, Kimmy. Now, you drive carefully, won't you?"

Kim hung up the receiver with the respect it deserved in this house and headed back into her room to pack. But coming through her bedroom doorway with Mrs. Sever's voice fresh in her ear and the queasy fear that her mother was dead reminded her so forcefully of the first time she had seen this room that she paused with her hand on the doorknob. She was seeing with her original wonder the oak sleigh bed meant just for her, the dresser, the mirror backed with so much silver that it perfectly reflected the wallpaper's daisies and violets. For just this instant, she couldn't see the furniture's nicks or the water-stains on the ceiling. She was looking at her room with the mingled hope and terror of a child who was without a home. Mr. Auberdine's first-choice relatives hadn't been able to take Kim, so it had been the evening of the third day before she saw this room. His wife's old aunt and uncle had been grateful to supplement their Social Security checks with whatever payment it was that arrived each month from a bank in Charlottesville, Virginia. Their son had the farm, and Kim's board freed him from having to support his parents.

The Jensens had been kinder to Kim, in retrospect, than she had had any right to expect. Aunt Dagmar fed her meat three times a day, even though her own supper was seldom more than corn fritters or cabbage soup. She was kind enough to examine each perfect report card. As Uncle Valdimar's mind slipped, he came to believe that Kim was someone he had known long ago, so he reminisced with her in gentle Danish until his mind slipped further and he could no longer talk at all.

Aunt Dagmar included Kim in all her family holidays. But Kim didn't care for Danish food, not the hard meat patties called *frikadeller* nor the stuffed cabbage called *kaldolmer*, nor even the sweet red sauerkraut the family greeted with cheers whenever it appeared. And the fact that she couldn't sing the family's songs nor laugh at what the family thought was funny made Kim feel more acutely on holidays than at any other time a desperate, physical need to go home.

Christmas dinner at Highgrove had been raisin-glazed ham with turnips and yams and lima beans. She and her mother had served it family-style so they could eat their own dinner in the kitchen while the Sever family and their uncles and cousins were eating theirs in the dining room. As a child, Kim had found an uneasy absurdity in the way the swinging door would be propped so everyone could sing carols together. But looking back now, she found a light-washed perfection in the memory of her mother's contented smile and the sounds from the next room of Bobby's high-pitched adolescent chatter and his father's rare laughter.

Still, the Jensens had been good to Kim. From the start, they had given her five dollars of her own to spend every week. They had expected her to consume it in an orgy of juvenile waste, but she had saved most of it in her bottom drawer so she could buy the car that she had imagined would finally free her mother.

——◆——

Driving down Route I-29 from Dulles, Kim kept expecting the landscape to look familiar. She was unsettled to be passing a stretch of sleazy roadside stores so much like what she had left behind that she had the sense she was infecting Virginia with Midwestern civilization as she drove along. Kim had been trying all day long to shift into an attitude of bereavement, but it had been six years since she had last seen her mother. She imagined she wouldn't feel her loss until she noticed there were no more letters coming. Instead of grieving, Kim's mind kept catching on the thought of Aunt Dagmar alone in her house. Kim had bought extra food and arranged for people to look in on her, but if Uncle Valdimar took sick or if Aunt Dagmar stumbled on the stairs, Kim's absence could mean life or death to them.

And Kim was thinking about Colin Sanderlin, who would be taking classroom notes for her and subbing for her at Pizza Pronto. He had wanted to come along. Her refusal to allow it had struck him as a repudiation of himself. Colin's high-school sweetheart had followed him back to Indiana from Ohio that fall, which had infuriated and flattered him. In his melodramatic way, he was trying to get Kim to engage in a contest for his affections, so Kim in her need for distance and peace kept failing him. She found his attitude perplexing. He kept insisting Faith meant nothing to him, then he sulked over Kim's willingness to believe him. Still, it would have been nice to have Colin with her. Mrs. Sever would have been impressed with Colin's blond good looks that had made a few people wonder whether he and Kim might be related.

And Bobby would see . . . . What did she want him to see? The force with which the thought of Bobby Sever struck Kim's mind made her throat constrict and her hands go sweaty on the steering wheel. She had tried so hard not to think about him during all these six years that he had become a permanent piece of the furniture of her mind. She could tuck her mother away and take her out for comfort when a letter came, but Bobby was always in the way. Even the look of pain he carried about his eyes had become for her a universal sorrow. Every disaster in the newspaper, every earthquake thousands of miles away made her see again the suffering in Bobby's eyes.

Kim's own eyes blurred. She was reliving with a hot stab that felt like her original pain the misery of her fourteenth birthday. For that whole day she had waited for her mother's call. The call that would forgive her and summon her home. Then after a day of waiting, the phone had rung. "Darlin'," Darcy had murmured. And Kim had heard in that single word her mother's whole vast impotence, the little constriction of her childish self over the spot where once she had had a daughter.

"Hello Mama," Kim had said, feeling like the parent. She remembered nothing of the rest of that call, but long before it ended she had wanted it over. While Darcy had talked, Kim had suddenly seen, blossoming full-blown in her mind, the perfect shiny, splendid car that would be the tool of her mother's freedom. She had fixed on that car to smother the sound of Darcy's voice and the distant, inexpressible sense of Virginia. To earn that car, she would have to stay away.

Kim had shifted from parenting her mother to parenting

herself with what seemed in retrospect to have been an absolute ease, keeping her room neat and forcing herself to make A's. Kim had been successful in high school in ways that astonished her as she sorted her memories on her long drive south. Her aloofness had made her popular, the center of a bright and funky clique. Her exotic accent and crown of braids and preference for man-tailored oversized clothes had made her a fashion leader. And the more she had tried to hide her body, the more she had attracted boys. But Kim had never dated in high school. She hadn't known what she had done wrong with Bobby, so she couldn't be sure she wouldn't do it again.

Kim's earliest memories were of warm or cold male hands, lifting her from her mother's high bed and setting her on the trundle bed. She always awakened at once but she pretended to be asleep, even when some man unfamiliar with Darcy's bedroom banged her against the bureau or dropped her on the floor. Some of the men put her on the front-room couch, but the rooms were so tiny and the walls were so thin that couch or trundle bed made little difference. Kim couldn't see what was happening. She heard only the whispers and grunting, the singing of springs, so she would lie awake and imagine her mother playing some jolly game with a gruff-voiced stranger. As she grew older, her agony of rejection and her frank jealousy made her begin to cry silently, so by the time she was five her mother had stopped entertaining men at home. Then Darcy would tuck Kim in several nights a week and leave her alone for hours, lying whimpering with loneliness and fear of the dark. Even after her rape, Kim never really connected the sounds and the separations with sex. They had seemed instead to be rejections, little abandonments that had led on with the inevitability of rightness to her final long abandonment.

———◆———

Below Culpeper, Kim turned off to head down toward Highgrove, and soon she began to see the Virginia that she remembered. There were vistas of rolling fields to plantation houses set back from the road, and here and there were poor houses with cars on blocks and perhaps a goat tethered to a rusted fender. Bent men toiled to make hay under a late-day sun that tinged every color with a wash of gold. Kim cranked down her window so she could smell Virginia, and with the sunlit tang of road dust and the dry-grass smell of summer's end came her whole emotional life at twelve years old. She had forgotten that comfortable helplessness of being poor, that simple focused need to please the Severs, that tremble of hopefulness tinged with anxiety because her life was beginning and she had just one chance to get it right. She felt like a tourist in her childhood mind.

Kim didn't recognize the town of Highgrove at first, but after passing a livestock sale barn she drove around a Confederate monument that looked familiar. Then she saw in front of her all the remembered names: High Times Good Eating, Summer Hardware, Penny Earned Variety. The buildings looked so much smaller and shabbier than she remembered them that she drove past them slowly, feeling disoriented, trying to align her memories with this strange reality. Mr. Sever's grocery store was still there beyond the tarpaper bricks of the Highgrove Pentecostal Church. It had a new front with apple-red panels and a lot of glass, and its new sign said Sever's Pantry 24-Hours.

Except during her brief career as a lap-sitting Mercedes-driver eleven years before, Kim had never approached the main house from the front. She had never seen its wrought-iron sign painted white, nor its driveway winding up through a scattering of trees to a blank foursquare whiteness with fifty tall windows and six white-painted chimneys. The house at Highgrove was gaudily beautiful from the rear, with its two-story columned veranda and its servants' porch. From the front, its only ornaments were the pediments over the doors and windows. But the perfect proportions of this three-story house and its two-story wing aligned precisely under roofs just tall enough and chimneys placed exactly right made it magnificent from the front, a poem, a whisper that sometimes clumsy mankind can emulate God in doing something wonderful. Mr. Sever's blue Mercedes was parked half on the grass of the circle in front of the door. Kim pulled in behind it, looking with wonder at the splendid bronze fountain in the center of the circle. A plump cherub bent to trickle water from a jug while grinning fish spat delicate sprays that sparkled in the sunlight.

Kim was studying the detail of carved grapes and flowers in the pediment when the door was opened, and she lowered her eyes to stare with a sense of time suspended into Mr. Bobby's face at ten years old. "You're supposed to be my sister?" the boy asked finally with mild interest. Timmy. On her drive down, Kim had tried to expand him in her mind from four years old to ten, but never had she dreamed his triangular mouth and his button of a nose would grow up to be Sever features.

"Let her in, dear," Mrs. Sever called as she stepped from the right-hand living room. "Kimmy dear, how good – Well, look at you! You look just like your mother." Mrs. Sever was pale and gaunt in her black dress and single strand of pearls. Her eyes had acquired lines that made the delicacy of the rest of her face seem like a poignant clinging to beauty long spent. "Come in, Kimmy dear. Well, look at you! Don't I wish – Come in, dear. Your mother would be so proud of you."

Timmy said, "You're my sister, right?"

"Yes." Kim turned to him, thinking she was going to hug him, but seeing Mr. Bobby's childhood face from above rather than below felt so unfitting that she could hardly make herself look at him. He looked at her and took a quick step backward. He didn't want to touch her, either.

"I'll go watch TV, okay?" he called to Mrs. Sever as he took a running jump and scampered up the staircase to the second floor.

"That boy," Mrs. Sever said fondly. "He's a pint of energy." Then she added, "Don't think ill of him, Kimmy. He's got no notion yet about Darcy. I haven't found the words to tell him. He was so fond of her."

"*Fond . . . ?*"

"Come in, dear. Let's have some sherry. You'll have to tell me all about your college."

Following Mrs. Sever into her living room as if they were friends made Kim feel so clumsy that she had to fill the silence. "I saw the grocery. It looks nice."

"That's Bobby's doin'. He went an' got an M.B.A., an' right away he's switchin' the store around. He says all-night stores are the comin' thing. Let's sit here, dear."

The right-hand living room had faded to a shadow in Kim's memory, so she was awestruck by the beauty of this thirty-foot room with its silver damask wallpaper and its furniture uphol-stered in yellow silk. She was breathing with pleasure the scent of lemon polish and the complex richness of cigar smoke and ancient furniture. Through the double sliders to the dining room she could see the table neatly set for four. It was all just as it always had been.

"Who's cooking dinner?" Kim asked as she sat down and accepted from Mrs. Sever her tiny glass of sherry.

"We've had a cook for some time. Darcy did breakfast an' lunch, but three meals was too much to ask of her. My, your face really looks fine, dear. It looks just fine."

Kim fidgeted her eyes away. The last thing she wanted to do right now was discuss her scar with Mrs. Sever.

"Where's everybody else? Colleen? Bobby?" Kim was studying the scrolling that edged the silver tray on the butler's table. She was remembering how hard it had been to polish.

"I'm so sorry. They won't be here. They've got families, you know. But they're sorry about Darcy. They were fond of her, too."

"They're married?"

"The children? Oh yes, dear. There are pictures on the piano, if you'd like to see them."

Bobby's wife was a pretty woman with dark-blonde hair and a comfortable smile. She held on her lap a newborn in a christening dress, its face puckered as if the taste of new life were bitter. And the baby had a sister about a year old who stood stiff-legged on her father's lap with his hand held easily between her legs to steady her. Kim stared at that hand. She had often seen babies held that way without finding it peculiar, but now the lean male fingers against the puffy pink diaper pants transfixed her. Bobby's little girl had wisps of brown hair that had been cutely tied into puppy-ears with fine pink ribbons that drew Kim's eyes unexpectedly to her father's face.

He didn't look like Bobby at all. Gone was the long hair, the gauntness, the lonely suffering. This Bobby had a lean and elegant face with a neat side-parted haircut; he gazed out through the photographer's lens to the middle distance with the confident air of a man who had handled life pretty well so far. His face that had been fey and tragic had changed in tiny ways to become a face so flat-out handsome that Kim looked at him with shy, proprietary pride.

"When did he get married?" She wanted to lift the picture so she could study it more closely.

"Let me see. Seventy-four, I think. Time does go by."

Kim's throat constricted. "Three years ago? Then why couldn't I come home? If he was married?" She was fighting sobs welling in her throat like hiccups. She had so many reasons for crying that she couldn't be sure what might have triggered this now, but she had learned long ago how to swallow her tears. She couldn't cry in front of Bobby's picture.

"Come home? Well, we did discuss it, but Darcy said you were happy there. You had two more years to go. High school. She said . . . ."

"Mrs. Sever, will you tell me one thing, please? Who is Timmy's father?"

Mrs. Sever's face stiffened, making Kim remember all the times she had left a room unaired or dropped a soup tureen. But she wouldn't be put off. She had a right to know this.

"It's Bobby, isn't it?" Kim hadn't expected to say that. Until the words were out, she had been thinking it was probably Mr. Sever.

"He was so young, Kimmy. And he was such a lonely child. We didn't know about it until Darcy was pregnant. Please come closer, dear. I don't like to say this across the room."

Kim crossed the rug and sat down on the sofa, concentrating on holding back her tears as if she were carrying an overfull glass. She was feeling so little shock that on some level she must have known it all along.

"Bobby told us. Darcy pretended it wasn't happenin'. Just like the first time. That poor girl never had a bit of sense. She ran away with a no-count circus tumbler. Until the day you were born, she swore it was only gas."

A no-count circus tumbler. Darcy had told Kim over and over about her father the aerialist with crayon-yellow hair who had been so much the picture of every girl's dreams that Darcy had run away with him when the show left town. That he had turned out to have a wife and three children in Winter Haven had always seemed to Darcy to be beside the point. He had shown her new places as far away as Dallas, and he had given her the wonder of a child.

"Does Timmy know?"

"Not really. He calls us Mama an' Daddy. He called Darcy by her name. I think he just doesn't care."

Kim drew a ragged breath. Her crying urge had passed. What she was feeling now was a swelling restlessness.

"We'll raise him as our own. Seein' him, it's clear he belongs with us. And so far he is our only male grandchild."

Kim stood with a snap upright that startled them both. "Mrs. Sever, may I see my mother's things?"

"Of course, dear. There'll be things you'll want to take." Mrs. Sever stood with her old Southern finishing-school grace and started for the long sweep of staircase.

The forgotten aroma of clean linens and wool and the sudden sight of the hallway furniture stopped Kim at the top of the front stairs. She stood there with her hand on the railing, looking around at the silent rooms and feeling herself at home in this house as she had been at home as a child.

"This way, dear."

Kim followed Mrs. Sever down past Bobby's room. She heard through the open doorway a television flickering the false cheer of a cartoon show.

"Timmy is in Bobby's old room?"

"Yes, dear. Come right this way."

Mrs. Sever led Kim down the hallway and through the door into the servants' wing, where the homey smell of ham baking and the under-smell of the big gas stove gave Kim an unexpected shock of pain.

"Right here, dear. She was a bit casual, I'm afraid."

Kim stepped to the doorway of one of the servants' rooms, and there on the maple furniture and pink-papered walls were all of Darcy's things. Her Buddha bank with the slot in its belly stood beside the cigar box from Kim's father and the jumping-jack between sticks and the crockery mushroom, just as they had stood in a row on the dresser in that back room at home. Four paper leis hung on the corner of the mirror as they had hung on that ancient half-black mirror. Even the circus poster that had been glued to the wall had been pried off somehow and glued on here in several misaligned pieces. Darcy had suffered from a child's willful messiness, so Kim wasn't surprised to see the bed trailing sheets nor the dresses thrown across it. She saw with a sorrow that clamped her throat that Darcy had even arranged the furniture just as it had been at home, even though that put the bed too close to the door and the dresser halfway under a window.

"Dead" was a difficult word to think. Perhaps Kim had never thought the word before this morning. And it was so monumental a concept beside the trivial words of daily thought that it produced a stuttering of the mind. Kim leaned and stroked the yarn hair of Darcy's Raggedy Ann doll that she had never been allowed to touch. She lifted the doll into her arms while she suffered a flood of fresh, agonized guilt that she had abandoned her mother to die here in the prison of herself. She had forgotten altogether the prideful shame that had permeated Darcy's life.

"She had to stay here?" Kim swallowed against the sharp constriction of her throat. "*He* got to live with the rest of you, but my mother had to stay back here?" Yet even as she said it, Kim could see her mother's face radiant with pride that Timmy was living with the family. She would have doted on him and cherished him as if he were Mr. Bobby over again, loving him more for being a Sever than for being her own blood child.

"Kimmy, people do things that seem to be right at the time. It's only later we're able to look back an' see what we might have done different." Mrs. Sever paused, then added, "We thought we were doin' right by you an' your mother, Kimmy. I hope you'll understand that."

"That's why I couldn't come back? You didn't know where to put me?"

"Sweetie, Darcy wanted you there. She really thought you were happier . . . ." Mrs. Sever touched Kim's arm with a hand that felt as cold and boney as a claw.

Kim spun and headed back down the servants' hallway to the main house, not thinking, knowing only that she couldn't stand to be there. She couldn't bear the upstairs hallway, either. She ran down past Bobby's room, slipping on the loose Turkey carpet, and down the sweep of staircase and out the front door. She remembered only when she was on the step that her purse was still in the living room, so with a presence of mind that embarrassed her, she hurried in to grab it off the floor. She hugged it fiercely with her mother's doll and rushed out of the house.

When Kim arrived at Colin's apartment late on the following afternoon, his Toyota was still in the parking lot. It was a square white car, rusted in spots, that Colin or a prior owner in some lighthearted moment had decorated with cartoon flowers painted on the fenders. Colin was a classically trained artist. Those flowers didn't look like anything he would have done. Kim's need to know how reality was put together had often made her wonder who had painted those flowers, but her contravening obsession with privacy had made her feel unable to ask him the question.

Colin lived on the third floor of a renovated Victorian house, up where the twelve-foot peaks of a former attic had combined with the cool light from northern windows to create an artistic paradise for generations of students. Kim climbed the stairs, aggravating the crampy airplane aches in her back and legs and making her long to stop and rest. But she refused to stop. By the time she reached the top, she was stiff and pale with such discomfort that as she opened his door Colin turned and blurted, "Kimbet? Did you at least get a look at the license plate?"

Kim rolled down onto a sofa that Colin had covered with a

sheet he had painted once in a failed experiment. She would rally more easily if she could take a shower, but she couldn't undress in Colin's apartment. And besides, there wasn't time. She was late for work. Thinking of that made her look at Colin, who was wearing his customary painting outfit, a spattered apron over jeans and a lack of shirt. Colin experimented with methods of applying paint, so he always looked more or less speckled. Today he had a green blob on his choirboy's forelock that gave his eyes a sea-blue intensity.

"Sponges!" He was grinning at her. "I've been getting the most amazing effects with sponges. I know, I know, sponges are old hat. But the *edges*, lovely child. The *corners*. And paper *towels*. Come see what I mean!"

"It's ten after four."

Kim realized now that Colin's habitual expression was precisely what Darcy's had been: a small, deferential smile. Darcy had used her smile to diffuse in advance the angers of the stronger-willed people around her, while for Colin smiling was just another gift that he could pass along. He saw himself as lavishly blessed with talents whose only purpose was the brightening of other people's lives.

Colin was reaching to help her up so he could show her his painting, sublimely sure that she was going to forgive him his decision not to work for her today in the face of his creative mania. And yesterday she would have forgiven him. Yesterday the loss of her job would have seemed a trivial inconvenience beside his pleasure of creation. But yesterday her job had been just a way to buy clothes without taking board money from the Jensens. From now on it was going to have to feed three people and pay her tuition besides.

Kim had spent her airport hours mentally composing her letter to the Severs, hitting just the right dignified tone as she thanked them for their help and asked for an accounting so she could repay every cent. She wasn't going to give them time to cut her off. That letter would be in the mail tomorrow. But it was only now that her fluttery exhaustion made her realize what this was going to mean in terms of pizzas delivered and classmates tutored and hurried late-night studying. The Jensens' son, Chris, had mortgaged the farm to get into hogs that kept dying on him. He had mostly stopped sending Aunt Dagmar the checks that he had promised her when he took over the farm. Kim knew that soon she was going to have to support his parents, too.

Kim looked at Colin and realized with a sense of mingled wonder and horror that his artistic intensity was a furious striving after nothing that was of any value. His life was spent creating incrustations of paint on Masonite that leaned in stacks against all the walls. He couldn't even give them away. Her chest ached with a horrible constriction. All the things she once had loved about Colin were the very things that appalled her now. And realizing that their lives had suddenly forked in opposite directions, Kim felt a terrible yearning for him. She thought that never again would she feel for anyone the pure, naive love she had felt for this soft-faced boy who once, for a moment, had been her perfect opposite. But what she said was, "Colin, do you realize it's quarter past four and you're already fifteen minutes late?"

"What are you doing here, anyway? Wasn't the funeral supposed to be tomorrow?"

"I didn't stay. I decided if she didn't want me when she was alive she would hardly miss me when she was dead." The urge to cry seized Kim so fiercely that her face contorted and she had to turn it against the sweet smell of linseed oil on Colin's sheet. "Don't touch me!" she said into the cushion. "You're paint all over!"

"Kimbet? Baby doll . . . ?" He dropped to his knees beside the sofa and reverently kissed her crown of braids.

"I'm all right," she muttered, annoyed with herself.

"Don't you think you'd feel better if you'd stayed? It can't have been all that bad."

She turned her face from the sheet and looked at Colin kneeling beside the sofa. Her own eyes were dry, but he was brimming tears that yesterday would have made him seem far better than the run of men who were too insecure to allow themselves to cry.

"I couldn't stay." She touched his cheek with the tips of her fingers. He gave her a bleary smile. She groped for the right conversational tag by which to begin an explanation, but she was so enervated by the prospect of trying to make him understand her strange life history that she sagged into silence. "I just couldn't."

"Sounds like another virginity problem. I think I can help you with that, my dear. Here, lie down on my couch. Why, you already *are* on my couch . . . ."

"You nut." She pushed him aside with the tips of her fingers so she could sit up. Colin had spent their whole time together prescribing a loss of her virginity to cure everything from a toothache to an inability to find her tube of zinc-white paint. She said, "You work on becoming the Picasso of sponges. I'll go see if I've still got a job."

By nine o'clock Kim was giddy with exhaustion. When she walked into the Pizza Pronto kitchen, she was working her hat off over her crown of braids. Joe, the owner, was ducking to gaze into a long slit of heat and rearranging pizzas with his wooden peel. Around him, six people assembled pizzas, ground cheese, mixed sauce, sliced pepperoni, and wrestled dough through the hooks of an industrial mixer, but Joe trusted only himself to do the baking. Kim was saying, "I'm going to have to quit early, Joe," as she headed for the ovens, liking the shiny rumble and clunk of the machines and the cheerful kitchen bustle.

"Six with anchovies to Restop Motel." Joe was bending to the lower oven. "They promised an extra twenty if you're there in half an hour. You can keep five for yourself."

"I'm beat. I almost drove off the road."

Joe straightened and looked at her, holding his peel cocked like a weapon. He was a short, stocky man in his fifties whose skin was a full-blush, dusky red as if it were oversupplied with blood. His coloring made him seem to be perpetually angry and alarmed. "What's this? You're an hour late so you leave an hour early? If you were two hours late you wouldn't come at all?"

"Look, I'm sorry. Maybe I can drop them off on my way home . . . ."

"Drop, shmop! You use the *van*." He bent to his bottom oven with a look of alarm. Kim had interrupted his rhythm. "It's a *billboard*, that van. Every delivery is two more calls."

———◆———

The Restop Motel was a flat slab of neon off Ferris Street below I-65. Room 119 was at the end of a wing so close to the highway that as Kim stood at the back of the van loading the pizzas into her carrying basket she could hear the racket and unearthly whine of traffic on the bridge overhead. Waiting at the door of Room 119 was a lipless fellow with his necktie loose. He stood with his forearm braced high to hold the door open, making a dingy silhouette against the smoke that hung thick and yellow in the room behind him. Kim was struck by the fact that without a motel restaurant, he was stuck with takeout pizza for breakfast, lunch, and dinner. He would likely pay more than twenty extra dollars just to get a decent meal.

Kim couldn't bear the smoke stench in the room, nor the sweet reek of liquor over the smell of too much breathing in too small a space. A coffee table had been pulled toward the end of the bed so five men could sit hunched around it, playing cards. Kim glimpsed a salad of paper bills.

"Get back in here, Rabinowitz!" a shirtless man called without turning. He was sitting so low on a hassock that he seemed to be naked, with his lean young back a long and elegant curve that Kim had to follow with her eye. She was good with charcoal, and what she liked best was sketching male nudes from improbable angles. "Get in here! You're up a grand, buddy," the young man said as he turned with taut grace and looked at them. Kim's mouth went dry when she saw how beautiful he was, with his long neck and his lean, strong-featured face. His eyes and the hair curling against his neck were nearly black. The fingers of her right hand trembled as she sketched him rapidly in her mind.

"Tell the kid to take the pizzas in the other room. Barney must be finished by now."

"Don't bet on *that*," someone said while someone else chuckled.

"Let the kid have a turn." The young man was studying Kim darkly. "He looks old enough. Would you like that, kid? A quick pop on us?"

Kim stared at him. With her substantial features and her lack of makeup, this wasn't the first time she had been mistaken for a boy in her Pizza Pronto hat and tunic.

"This way," the lipless man said in his gravelly voice. "You can dump the pizzas in here. And get Barney to pay you."

Kim's escort opened the door to the adjoining room and gestured for her to go in. She hefted her wire basket and edged it before her through the narrow doorway into a room so dark that light from its strip of high windows fell harshly across the front of the dresser. Kim closed the door behind her to keep the smoke from coming in. She looked around, blinking.

The room was a confusing charcoal scribble. Sheets lay rumpled on the bed and clothes lay draped on the chair. Then Kim realized to her amazement that there was a naked man of enormous girth lying flat on his back on the bed, apparently sleeping. Scattered light picked out details of his body in strident black shadows and shrill dull gleams. She glanced at the dresser near the foot of the bed, thinking she ought to leave the pizzas there, and gasped as the front of the dresser writhed in the white light from the ceiling-high windows. She dropped her basket with a grumble of crusts on cardboard.

"Shhh!" someone whispered.

There was a naked woman standing at the dresser. Her legs turned and rippled in the light. Kim squinted to see in the darkness a slash of hair, a slim bulk of body, an angle of elbow.

"Who are you? Pizza?"

"Pizza Pronto." Kim strained to deepen her voice. This gender confusion was a handy piece of camouflage. Her mind was catching up with the surprises of this motel adventure, and she realized the woman must be a prostitute. She tried to force revulsion, but what she was feeling instead was pity for that anxious voice and those pathetically active legs. The woman moved toward her with the jerky rapidity of a spider and whispered, "Wait! I've got to get out. Hold this while I get dressed."

Kim accepted from the woman a roll of currency the size of a fist and slipped it into the deep pocket of her tunic while the woman fumbled on the chair for her clothes. Then there was a stab of light that lit the woman's haggard face.

"What the hell is the holdup in here? Margie! Get them pizzas going. Don't dress. We like you the way you are. Come on, kid! On your way!"

The woman bent below the back of the chair and hissed to Kim, "Do you know the parking lot behind the High Style Luncheonette? Do you?"

Kim nodded, then realized the woman couldn't see her and whispered, "Yes," as deeply as she could.

"Meet me there tomorrow at noon and I'll give you half of it. Don't fail me! I'll put a hex on you!"

"Let's *go*, kid. What the hell are you waiting for?"

Kim turned to look at the rumpled man standing backlit against smoky yellow. She had formed the words, "You didn't pay me," before she realized that how-ever much money the woman had given her was probably more than forty-four dollars. She couldn't face that smoky male morass again, so she hurried to the front of the room and fumbled for the knob and let herself out the door.

———◆———

Kim parked her van in its spot beside the Pizza Pronto kitchen door and pulled the woman's wad of money from her pocket to count out Joe's forty-four dollars, but there seemed to be nothing but hundred-dollar bills slipping through her fingers. She counted them while she searched for something smaller. The last ten bills or so were fifties; Kim tugged one of these free while she counted the rest. She was holding in her hands more than fourteen thousand dollars.

After paying Joe, Kim drove to Colin's Victorian house and parked the Jensens' car in the alleyway behind it, thinking about sleeping on his couch. She was worried about alarming the Jensens by coming home so late when she was supposed to be in Virginia. Never locking his door was yet another gift that Colin could give to the world, so Kim opened it without thinking and walked into his apartment's chemical smell of paint to find him sitting cuddled on his sheet-covered sofa with Faith, his old Ohio girlfriend. Faith had taken an apartment on the second floor of this building. Colin had been upset about that two weeks ago. Kim calmly assessed his flushed cheeks and her disarrayed hair and realize they must have been necking.

"Kimbet! What's wrong? Is something wrong?"

Colin called her "Kimbet" because her full name was Kimberly Elizabeth Bonner. Kim thought as she looked at him that never again would someone care enough about her to claim her by a private name. Her chest constricted with a desperate, physical need not to lose Colin now. He and Faith had stood guiltily off the sofa, with Colin's hands hanging awkwardly as if he were aware of having hands and Faith's sulky pout of a face averted. Kim felt a little sorry for Faith. She had fine individual features, long dark hair, a magnificent chest and delicate wrists and ankles, but all her parts together had a strange asymmetry that made her look ill-bred. She had just missed being beautiful.

"Hey, Faith? I'll see you later, okay? Kim here has some problems I've got to tackle," Colin said with a brisk cheeriness that Faith couldn't resist as he edged her out the door and Kim couldn't resist as he slipped his arms around her. "What's the matter, sweet child? Is it her? Don't worry. She's just an old friend."

"But you were kissing her."

"Are you jealous?" he asked happily, looking down at Kim's face. "That sounds like *another* virginity problem."

Kim flinched a smile. Colin bent and kissed her with slow urgency and a tense pull of breathing in his throat. His hands moved on her back while his hips began a subtle rocking. Colin generally didn't reach this stage until after half an hour of kissing, at which point Kim would demurely disengage herself. He would complain with more or less good humor that she was messing up his body chemistry and ruining his metabolism, but she had always had the sense that he was glad about her virtue. This time, though, when she pulled away he said, "What *is* it with you? You want it too!"

"Colin, I . . . ."

"I love you. I've been patient with you. I'd rather die than hurt you. But do you know, that girl loves *me?* She came up here tonight and offered herself. Just simply, honestly offered herself. We used to sleep together. I won't deny that. But I swore I wouldn't do it again because it's you I love. So you treat me like this. Give me one good reason *not* to sleep with her!"

Kim stood in her Pizza Pronto tunic beside a row of Colin's cheery Masonite boards and looked at his face with his soft mouth set and his round eyes earnest. She looked at him, and she realized with a shock of pain how much she loved his gentle, larkish manner and all his foolish enthusiasms. She even loved his irresponsibility. Colin lifted her life from the burrow of duty where she tended by nature to place it. And the fact that she couldn't imagine a future with him made her love seem so poignant that she couldn't bear not to be in his arms.

Colin took Kim's desperate hugging for acquiescence. He was murmuring, "It's all right. I'll make it nice for you."

"Look, I . . . ."

"It's time now. You know it's time."

Kim really did want to do this. The loss of her mother and the strangeness of this evening and the prospect of her future without the security of the Severs made her need badly the closeness to Colin that she imagined might come from sleeping with him. She really wanted to do this now. His shirt was already off, and now he unbuttoned and unzipped his jeans. "Keep your underwear on!" she blurted.

He took her hand and began to lead her toward the bedroom that she had only ever seen from the doorway. She didn't seem able to get past its threshold. His bed and dresser were pushed against the wall because he used the floor for dripping paint onto Masonite. Sheets trailed Darcy-like on the floor.

"I can't."

Colin groaned playfully and scooped her up. He edged her feet-first through the doorway while she pummeled his shoulder with a fist. He carried her across the room and dropped her playfully onto his bed. But Kim was gagging. She couldn't breathe. She struggled out from under him and ran in panic into the outer room. Colin came stalking out of his bedroom, looking perfectly balanced between anger and alarm.

"What is the *matter* with you?"

"I can't. I'm sorry. I can't."

"And you know why, don't you? You don't love me. I worship the ground you walk on, but you've *never* loved me. Are you capable of love? Are you?"

"I do care for you." Kim was edging herself uncomfortably toward the door. As she would have expected, Colin's face was contorting against impending tears, but now the sight of all that emotion repulsed her.

"You're all I think about! I thought someday you'd love me, too."

"I'm sorry. Really. I wish you could . . . ."

"I won't be here when you get back!" he shouted after her as she hurried down his dark stairs.

———◆———

Driving toward her meeting with the prostitute the next day, Kim examined that ghastly moment in Colin's apartment as if it were a beam she had exposed in the hidden framework of her mind. She realized with an abstract wonder that she had been assuming some weirdly contradictory things. Her belief that sex was slimy and painful but women in love were glad to do it was a ridiculous notion. She didn't want to do it. No matter how much the thought of Colin made her tremble with a terrible yearning, not even for that prostitute's fourteen thousand dollars would she let him do a thing like that to her. The shame of it appalled her. The pain and degradation. The messy unpleasant details of it, the hideous embarrassing intimacy made her stomach clutch with revulsion as she drove up the sun-bright highway. So it was just a male trick, after all. No matter how men tried to paint this dross of sex and make it look like pleasure, it wasn't pleasure. It was horror. Fourteen-thousand-dollar prostitutes were proof of that. Kim's eyes stung as she thought of all the women deceived through all the generations. All those Darcys and Aunt Dagmars and Mrs. Severs seemed pathetic to her now, bravely making their barters of sex for a roof and food and a bit of laughter.

Kim sat in the Jensens' car at the edge of the High Style Luncheonette parking lot until her dashboard clock said ten minutes after two. She had arrived a little late, at twelve-oh-three, but she thought this clock was a few minutes fast. And even if she had been terribly late, she couldn't believe a woman who had worked so hard for her money wouldn't have hung around all afternoon waiting to claim it.

Eventually Kim started her car. She would just put the money in the bank on Monday and worry about what to do with it later. What she had to do now was make amends to Colin. She could perfectly well explain to him that she was too smart to buy all that male sex propaganda, although to say it without hurting his feelings would require a more delicate turn of words than she could manage at the moment. But still, she had to comfort him somehow. She had to let him know she did love him. If he wanted never to see her again because she wouldn't give in to this male sex thing, that was up to him. But she wouldn't feel right until she had told him she was sorry.

Colin's flowered Toyota wasn't in its customary spot at the front of the house. Kim pulled in beside where it should have been as she thought about how he might actually laugh at her. He would likely think this situation was funny; she could see his face even now. He would look around from trying to paint a portrait with a slice of cabbage, and he would laugh the put-on giggle with which he rewarded all her efforts at joking. He considered Kim's sense of humor to be so fragile that he nurtured it like a baby.

Colin's door was open. Daylight from his brilliant apartment splashed out into the hallway. Beyond his door was a chaos of smashed Masonite against the walls, and on the sheet pulled awry on the battered sofa his old girlfriend, Faith, sat hugging her knees and keening. Kim looked at her and whispered, "What . . . ?"

Faith looked terrible. Her hair was in knots around a crumpled face so red that it seemed to be stripped of skin. She was whimpering a shrill whine through slitted lips. "Get out," Faith said without a break in her wailing.

"Where's Colin?"

"Get out. Get out! Haven't you done enough?"

Then Faith was crying in earnest, grabbing a fistful of sheet and stuffing it into her mouth to stifle her noise. Kim was spellbound by Faith's crying. She hadn't cried this way since all those hours spent in the old slaves' well that she remembered so clearly in the face of Faith's crying that the smell of turpentine in the room was the clean pungency of Virginia pines and the sun was a flashlight full in her face.

"Where's Colin?"

"Gone! He left! All because of you!"

Gone. Before Kim could tell him she was sorry. She took a long look at his ravaged front room where they had done their first-year assignments together, all those still-lifes and sketches and sculptures in plaster. Her love for Colin was all bound up in her love for color, for the joy of strokes that created on paper such a perfect replication of reality's moment that eyes could see flat what they were too jaded to see in depth. How Kim had loved her years of useless, pointless painting. And how she had loved Colin. She blinked, smelling those pines and hearing Faith's crying like night sighs in the trees. Colin and all her old childhood dreams. They seemed to her now to be one and the same.

chapter four

September 16, 1981 - March 26, 1982

Professor Pointe was spending his first lecture trying to convince a hall full of numbers buffs that marketing was the key to business success. "Product *development* is marketing!" His gesture unbalanced him to the left, so he stalked a few steps away from the podium to the left. "Employee *relations* is marketing!" involved a sweep to the right, so off he went in that direction while he never stopped his earnest room-wide efforts at eye-contact. Kim liked him. He was a squarely-built man about six feet tall who moved with a touching toy-like stiffness. He spoke in a deep and musical voice that connected his words like notes and gave an impression of effortless volume, as if his body were as hollow as a cello. She was enjoying Dr. Pointe's tender passion for his subject, but the girl sitting next to her whispered, "I wish he'd get to the *Pointe!*" and snickered.

Kim attracted people. She didn't understand why that should be so when she thought of herself as cool and aloof, but in new groups she always found herself collecting the ill at ease and the out of place. She hunched away from the girl and planted her chin on her hand while she gazed up at Dr. Pointe on his stage, trying through the intensity of her attention to give him the encouragement he deserved.

"The best organization in the world means *nothing* if you're making what nobody wants to buy!" he was booming to sum up what must have been a brilliant argument. Kim hadn't precisely heard it. She realized then that she was listening more to the weight and shape of his words than to their meaning, so she sat up to force her mind to focus. Dr. Pointe noticed her motion and looked at her, and something about the way she was looking at him caught him as he was beginning a sentence. He cleared his throat with a self-important cough and began again.

"Marketing people have to be involved in *every aspect* of the management process," he was saying while he began another pace to the left. Kim sat there in the front row, taking notes. As he turned he gave her a careful look, as if he were confirming his first impression. "So this semester we will consider the *whole range* of corporate decision-making." He pulled himself back to his tracking across the stage. "We will go from the original idea for a product or a service *right through* the marketing steps you'll take when you are Mister or Miss Corporate America. Now the hour is up. Are there any questions?"

But people were already chatting politely and sliding sideways out of the tiers of seats, leaving Dr. Pointe looking deflated as he watched their leave-taking. Partly because she wanted to jettison her first-day clique and partly because he looked forlorn, Kim gathered her books in a hug against her chest and walked along the front of the stage to speak with him.

"Dr. Pointe?"

He looked down at her from his two-foot-high stage. Then he hopped down beside her. "Hello there, Miss . . . ?"

"Bonner. You know, I really liked what you had to say today. It made a lot of sense."

A professor at his lectern has an aura of celebrity. To be talking with him face-to-face made Kim feel shy.

"Thank you." He gave her his creased and crooked smile. His face was rugged with lines and planes that with his steel-gray hair had made him look much older from a distance, but Kim could see from the texture of his skin that he must be something like thirty-five years old. Her mind automatically reclassified him from the comfortable fatherly age group, but still he wasn't young enough to be a nervousness-making contemporary. As people generally did when they first met Kim, he was noticing the scar on the side of her face and wondering briefly what it was before deciding it was none of his business. Kim had learned to read through every separate stage in a stranger's face. And she found their reactions so tedious that she gave new people an immediate good look to get this awkwardness out of the way.

Catching his eyes with hers, she said, "I loved it because you see, well, I just started my own company last Tuesday, and I . . . ."

"You what?" he blurted with another grin.

"Started my own company. And right now I'm . . . ."

"Hold on a minute! I've got to hear this."

Dr. Pointe stretched around and unbalanced his folder of notes from the podium into his fingers. He put a hand at the small of Kim's back to start her moving up the series of walks and steps out of the empty lecture hall.

"I've really just incorporated it," Kim explained, feeling shy again. Her business idea had seemed brilliant to her as she had developed it over the past four years, but now that she was in the presence of an expert it seemed unbearably naive and foolish.

"So, what are you selling?" he asked pleasantly.

Kim liked this man's cozy molasses aroma of pipe tobacco over a clean steel smell like pencil leads. She liked his relaxed step beside hers and the way he pushed the door open for her with an effortless politeness.

"It's a little hard to explain . . . ."

"Animal? Vegetable? Mineral?"

"Well, a little of each."

"This I really have to hear. Do you have a lunch break now? Would you like to grab a bite?"

"A bite? Oh. Gee. Well, I'm . . . ."

"I'll pay. Just promise to include me in your first group of investors."

He was giving her his crooked grin again, but he didn't seem to be talking down to her. And his offer of lunch was tempting because her budget wouldn't allow her more than the apple that was waiting for her in a bag on the seat of Aunt Dagmar's car.

"Well, okay. But I don't know where you'd like to eat. This is just my first time in this building."

"At least you know the campus. This is my first day here. I'm fresh in from Boston yesterday."

"You used to teach in Boston?" Kim asked as she led him through glass doors that gave onto a strip of student shops.

"Boston University. I'm here for two years on an exchange program. I was traded for a professor of paleontology." He chuckled to himself.

Kim had stayed at Indiana University for her M.B.A. because she had to live with Aunt Dagmar in order to be able to afford to go to school. Anyway, Aunt Dagmar needed her even more now that Uncle Valdimar was gone and Aunt Dagmar's left side had been partially paralyzed by a stroke. But Kim had briefly dreamed of going to Harvard, of buying the best M.B.A. in the country, so to hear that this man had taught in Boston and would be returning to Boston gave him a reassuring aura of higher quality.

"Let's see." Dr. Pointe was standing in the sunny courtyard like a rock in a stream to study the row of shops from under his hand while students crowded past them on either side. "Pizza, do you think? Say, what's this? Do I see something called the Jiffy-snack Vitamin Celebration?"

It was a crystalline mid-September day glowing brilliant with colors and sweetly smelling of pungent dying grasses. They took their sprout-salad pita pockets and their carrot-and-apple-juice shakes down the lawn to the grassy embankment that ran along a highway cutting like a stab of reality through the haven of this campus.

"I couldn't resist that," Dr. Pointe said as he settled with a grunt on the battered grass. "What a great name. They break every rule and it works just fine."

Kim dropped cross-legged at a polite conversational distance. She wasn't worried about grass stains on her jeans, but he was sure to stain his lecture pants and even his unfortunate green-tweed jacket. She glanced at his hand and confirmed that he wore a wedding band, which meant he had a wife at home to scold him.

"I'm breaking the rules too, you know," he told her as he set down his drink and unwrapped his pocket. "No fraternizing, they said. Whatever that means. I asked them how they expect me to teach if I can't talk to students." He licked a couple of fingers like a greedy child and leaned to bite a corner from his pita pocket. "So tell me about this animal-vegetable-mineral idea you have," he mumbled after he had chewed and swallowed half his mouthful.

Kim's teacher seemed less self-important now, sprawled grace-less on the grass with a line of Russian dressing and two sprouts marking his cheek. She took a nibble from one lip of her pocket and chewed and swallowed and said, "There are lots of motels without kitchens, right? People stay there? So I used to deliver pizzas to these poor souls who were stuck with nothing but pizza for breakfast, lunch, and dinner. Then it occurred to me what I ought to do was work out a way to bring them real food instead."

"That's it!" he crowed through a mouthful of food. He chewed impatiently and added, "That's *exactly* what I was saying today! *You* should be teaching that class, not me!"

"What . . . ?"

"Market-driven! The whole thing is market-driven! You didn't say, 'I'm a great cook so I feel like selling food to motels.' What you said was, '*They* want a decent meal.' You studied the donut to look for the hole!"

"Oh. Well, I guess so . . . ."

"That's great!" He took a sip of his vitamin shake and set it down again. "Not bad," he remarked in an aside to himself. "That's a great idea, Miss. I admire your idea. I wish like hell there was some way to make it work."

"What do you mean? Of course it'll work!"

"It's too bad." His sandwich hand was drooping to the grass under the weight of his despair for her idea. Kim had the warm sense that he felt some personal responsibility for her impending failure.

"Why won't it work?"

"Well, for one thing the logistics are impossible. You could never get the food there hot enough . . . ."

"I'd use a van with warming ovens. We had one at Pizza Pronto."

"And then there's convincing the motels to try it . . . ."

"They love the idea. I've talked to four already. I was thinking of giving them a cut, but maybe that won't be necessary."

"Oh. Well, then what about the liability problem? Your exposure would be tremendous."

"It won't be so bad. I've talked to the people who insure Pizza Pronto. If my kitchen is inspected and I keep to their rules, they'll just base the premiums on my volume. And besides, Professor Pointe, I'm judgment-proof. I don't have a penny to my name."

"Call me Lou. Please. When women call me Professor Pointe all my bones creak. How do you think I got so gray?"

Kim smiled at that and took another polite nibble of her sandwich. The day was so warm that boys higher on the embankment had taken off their shirts, but it was cool and earth-smelling down where they were sitting.

"And where did you pick up a term like judgment-proof?" he asked after he had taken another drink. He ate and drank as if he had a physical need to do it. Kim thought his wife must surely find a great satisfaction in cooking for him.

"Oh, I read a lot. I've been working on this for four years now. I even took a year off after college so I could try out managing a restaurant."

What Kim didn't add was that she had also been saving her money. Sending the Severs fifty dollars every month for the past four years had been a considerable additional drain, what with her need to support the Jensens, too. For six months the Severs had sent her checks back. Then it had been another year before they had begun to cash them.

"I was going to finish business school first, but I'm twenty-three already. So I filed the corporation papers last Tuesday."

"You're kidding. You are kidding, aren't you?"

"I'll just do breakfasts and dinners for now. And only for one motel. Do you know the Restop Motel? In Oakhaven? They think it's such a great idea they've threatened to set up their own food service if I don't do it first. I can deliver their breakfasts at seven and still get here for my first class at nine. And I've arranged my schedule so I'm through by three. I'll do dinners at six. No problem."

Lou gave Kim a look of surprise and then a slow, contrived double-take backward onto his hands that upset the last of his vitamin drink into the grass. He glanced at the drink and sat up again, dusting bits of clinging grass from his fingers.

"A prodigy. What we have here is a genuine business prodigy."

"Actually, what I am is a water-color prodigy. But I haven't painted a stroke in years."

"Can we use your business for our classroom model? Maybe we can wake up those calculator-brains if they see a real business in action."

"Oh. Well, actually, I'd rather not. I'm probably about to do everything wrong. I'll stand a better chance of succeeding if I don't realize how wrong it is."

"Wisely put. I'll drink to that." He saluted her with his empty cup before he stuffed it with the wrapper of his pita pocket. "I guess I'll use video phones again. Or manufactured housing. Every time I teach that course, I ask the students to choose a product, but they make such a production out of it I end up having to do it myself." Lou took Kim's wrapper and waited politely while she finished her drink. He had a smooth veneer of natural manners that was missing from her generation, but his light, childlike zest made him seem to be younger than Kim was herself. She had noticed the way teachers tended to remain forever somewhat adolescent. And this man had Colin's old knack of lightening her mood. She was sorry their picnic was about to end.

"Ah, Dr. Pointe? Lou? Do you have a secretary? You know, to do your copying? Because I'm looking for odd jobs. To raise some capital."

He smiled at that. His smiles were so frequent they had marked his face with well-worn merry creases, and they crookedly broke a little to the left, as if he couldn't keep them under control. He stood and extended a hand for her as he said, "My dear, it will be an honor to have you do my copying. I hear people every day talking about how they're going to start a business, but not one man-jack in a hundred ever actually does it."

Kim took his hand and stood and brushed off her seat. She stooped to gather her books and notebooks close against her chest, while Lou bent with one leg cantilevered behind him to snatch a napkin that had been left by prior picnickers. His hair in the dappled light held strands in every shade from white through black. He had so much hair that was so unruly he had given up any hope of styling it, so it fluffed at will, it lifted in the breeze and fell in wisps onto his forehead. Kim thought his wife must have fallen in love with his hair.

"So, what is the name of this Xerox of the future, may I ask?"

"Taste of Home. I called it Taste of Home, Inc."

"And you picked the name because . . . ?"

"Well, that's what everyone wants, isn't it? A little taste of home?" They began to walk up the embankment as she added, "I'm thinking of offering some regional specialties. You know, like for the South I'll have ham and eggs and grits, with maybe *oevos rancheros* for the Southwest and some granola thing for California. Cranberry muffins for New England. That kind of thing. People will like seeing something familiar, but since they're traveling they'll try something new."

"I love it. A marketing genius. If you need my help, just ask for it."

"Well, do you know how to make *oevos rancheros?*" she asked, and he laughed.

———◆———

It wasn't until just before Christmas that Lou insisted on intervening. On a snowy Thursday morning he walked to Kim's end of the stage as she was gathering her things to leave. He hunkered to her level and greeted her with his usual, "How's business?"

"Look, I'm sorry about falling asleep. It really was interesting. Really."

"How many motels is it now?" His sweet cello voice had an edge to it.

"Five. And they're filling up for Christmas. Who'd want to spend Christmas in *Oakhaven?*"

Lou took a long step down in front of her and stood inside her personal space until she was forced to look up at him. She straightened with her notebooks against her chest and gave him what she realized was a guilty child's defiant look.

"I want to see your books."

"Thank you, no. This is *my* business. I've got to do it my way."

"Dear child, you must hire people now. There is no human way one little person can serve a hundred meals a day and still go to business school. You can't do it! Do you have any idea how many businesses die because their owners can't manage growth?"

"I'm handling it. I'm fine."

"You are *not* fine!" he boomed in his lecture-hall voice.

Kim winced and glanced around to confirm that they were almost alone. Three girls who had paused inside the doors turned to stare briefly, then hurried away.

"You've lost weight. You've got circles under your eyes like saucers. Tiger's love-scratch looks a mile deep. You're going to crack unless you get some help, and I couldn't stand to see you do that."

They had become friends enough for Lou to ask Kim how she had gained her scar, and he had willingly seized her explanation that her childhood cat had done it. One of the things Kim liked about Lou was his refusal to treat her scar as something too shameful for polite mention.

"I'm all right. Really. I'm just still not making enough money to hire any help."

"But that's my *point!*"

"Keep your voice down."

"That's my point. You should be making enough to hire help and rent yourself a real kitchen. Either your pricing is wrong or your costs are fouled up or there's money there and you don't know it. I'll make book they're about to close school for the snow. What you and I are going to do is take a ride to Auntie Dagmar's and look at your books."

"They're going to close? Really?" Kim asked with a frail hope that made her wince with embarrassment. A party of senior citizens was staying at the Bide-a-Wee. There was a family gathering at the Restop. Despite the fact that Kim's dinner order was seldom more than eighty, tonight she would be serving almost two hundred people.

Lou's face went slack with exasperation. He muttered, "That does it," and grabbed her notebooks from her arms. He hurried her with a hand on her back up the long course of lecture-hall walks and steps.

"You can't come to Oakhaven! What about your wife?"

Lou's wife had come to class last week and hidden at the back of the hall to catch him coming up the walks and steps telling Kim a funny story about his three-week stint in advertising. Kim had barely glimpsed a dark-haired woman as thin as Mrs. Sever before Lou had spotted the woman, stepped away fast, said a mumbled few words to another student, then feigned great surprise at meeting Carolyn here. Kim guessed that stories about Lou's friendship with a student must have gotten back to his wife, and she was sensitive to that. She didn't want to cause him trouble.

"Won't she mind?" Kim stopped and looked at him.

He smiled to the left and said, "Not if I don't tell her."

Their drive to Oakhaven took more than an hour, what with the falling snow and the stops they had to make to gather door tags from all five motels. Kim's tires were so bald that she had to creep around corners and skulk along the highway with her hands frantic on the steering wheel. She kept glancing into her rearview mirror to make sure Lou's red Volvo was still behind her. After ten years, Kim still wasn't used to these Indiana winters that locked down hard right after Thanksgiving and could pile snow ever deeper into March. Snow was dashing against her windshield in a perfect fireworks burst of white that had her squinting against the glare and the relentless impending collision of it. She had never seen snow like this back home.

And the Christmas coming up was going to be just another holiday on the farm, with horse-drawn sleighs and home-fattened goose that even the fourth-generation tots called *gasesteg*. With long rolls of pastry called *wienerbrod*. With *julekage* and *snegle* and custards and puddings and more of that cheers-producing red sauerkraut. The Jensens were very good to Kim. They were so grateful to her for caring for their matriarch that they had given up their rude chattering in Danish. Kim had even learned some Danish songs, different songs for different holidays, and Aunt Dagmar's daughter-in-law and granddaughter had become something surprisingly close to friends. But it wasn't home. And it wasn't Christmas.

Kim had been forcing Virginia out of her mind for so long that she had moved beyond her obsession with it to a loose old distant nostalgia that gave her a pleasant pang as she wrote out the Severs' checks. She managed whole days when the thought of Bobby Sever was only a vapor at the back of her mind. But now, driving through this curse of snow while back home there might still be garden spinach and salmon-colored geraniums, Kim felt again a stab of her old off-center misery of loss and yearning. Her eyes blurred foolishly. She pinched them, hard. How stupid she was to be missing Virginia when she wouldn't still be there at twenty-three, anyway. She couldn't imagine a lifetime spent with Darcy polishing andirons and baking peach strudel for an ever-older Mr. Sever. If she had grown up there, perhaps she would have remained forever a child like Darcy.

So perhaps they had done her a favor. That notion never had occurred to her. Kim couldn't imagine now what her life would be like if she hadn't been cast out at barely thirteen, and thinking of that made her want to enumerate all the blessings that had flowed from her banishment. Perhaps no one who looks back on a life can imagine it unfolding in any other way. But still, Kim missed Virginia. She missed it as an arm misses its shoulder after an amputation, or as a grown cat misses its mother's teat and suckles at anything in the dark.

—◆—

Aunt Dagmar's house was flaking paint from its stucco front. The flat roof over its porch and its low-browed second floor had patches of mismatched shingles that Kim herself had added over the years. Kim had thought this cottage was lovely once, with its trellised porch and its picket fence enclosing a patch of dark-green lawn, but in the pure snow it looked faded and shabby. She was embarrassed for it before her teacher.

Kim always saw Aunt Dagmar as soon as she got home. Aunt Dagmar's mind was good, but at eighty-six and after her stroke, she spoke in barely intelligible cryptograms that Kim had to interpret for the rest of the family. Kim went up to Aunt Dagmar's room and spent her usual twenty minutes there, telling her about Marketing class and how it had felt to drive in the snow and then sitting through a stumble of sounds that was something about mice in the dishwasher.

When Kim went into Aunt Dagmar's kitchen, she found that Lou had scattered the contents of her file pocket on the kitchen table. That was forbidden. If the health inspector happened by now and saw all those papers and germy bills, he would shut her right down. Kim had been forced to borrow a thousand dollars from Chris Jensen so she could repaint and lay a linoleum floor and buy a dishwasher so Oakhaven would license this kitchen for food preparation.

She could have borrowed instead from the prostitute's funds. After four years she was sure the woman was dead, perhaps killed by the man with the beautiful back, and she had stopped carrying that bankbook with her so she could hand it over. But she didn't want to touch the money. Over four years' time it had been transformed by the alchemy of possession into something even more precious than money: it was permanence, security, a haven as real and stable as a parent. When Kim was panicked sometimes by the night-terrors of not enough money or a bad grade, the awful awareness of her heart beating and the hollow ache of being without Virginia, she would take from the back of her closet her bank book and Darcy's old Raggedy Ann. Cuddling the money and the doll, feeling soft and foolish, she could comfort herself to sleep.

"You're all over my workspace," Kim complained as she hurried in to whisk her apron from the drawer and turned on her oven. She used that table for packing the styrofoam containers that provided the only means she had for transporting food in the Jensens' car and keeping it more or less hot.

Kim dragged her heavy kettle of spaghetti sauce out of the refrigerator and pulled the oven door open with her foot and slid the kettle in. It would take a good hour to heat up properly. She had deliveries scheduled for every half-hour from five o'clock until seven, but with the snow to delay her she ought to get started a half-hour early. And she still had all those sandwiches to make.

"This is a *disaster!*" Lou was stabbing dollar bills and receipts onto piles with the stiff bursts of energy he displayed at his lectern and almost nowhere else. Kim glanced at the back of his head as she sorted her door tags quickly by main dish. They were color-coded for each motel, so she sorted them while she was preparing food and then separated the colors again.

"Is this all you've got? No records? Nothing?"

"I've got no time for records," Kim mumbled as she washed her counter down with food-grade soap and began to lay out her first course of sandwiches. She offered just one hot dish at night, a different dish every night of the week, so two-thirds of what she served for dinner consisted of her half-dozen sandwich specialties that her regular customers liked so well they often ordered extras to take along. One salesman who came through every few weeks ordered six head-cheese-on-rye sandwiches made with the red Danish sauerkraut and home-jarred sours that Chris's wife, Hilda, supplied to her.

"No *wonder* you're in a mess!" Lou sputtered while Kim laid out Canadian bacon and wondered whether this was going to hurt her grade. "Let me see one of those tags." He was creaking around on his chair and gesturing. She handed him a tag from her current pile. He sputtered, "This is insane! Look at these prices. Where in creation did you get these prices?"

"I made them up."

"*What?*"

"I made them up! Okay? You've got no call to go yelling at me!"

"I'm not yelling."

"Of course you're yelling."

"Look at me."

Kim glanced at Lou over her shoulder.

"These people are cheating you. Here, this man has ordered eight – What *is* this? Crabmeat and bacon?"

"It's my own invention. It's pretty good."

"Well, he has ordered eight of them, Kim, and you're not telling me he's got eight people staying there. He's going to live off these sandwiches for *weeks*, my dear, because you're charging less than the cost of the ingredients."

"I buy in bulk." She felt shy now, having him see her lack of records, having him sit in her kitchen watching her cook.

"We're going to double these prices across the board."

"You can't do that! Nobody'll buy!" Kim spun to look at Lou, feeling panicky.

He gave her an unexpected crooked grin. "Do you know the biggest argument there is against trying a new idea? It won't work because if it could work someone else would have done it first. But here you are doing something so obvious a hundred people must have thought of it first, and because you don't know

76

it can't be done you're doing it. You've got a gold mine here. If you'll listen to reason and run it like a business, it's a bloody gold mine."

"But not *double*. How can they afford to eat?"

"Double. Trust me on this." Lou was locking eyes with her, willing her to give in.

He had eyes a little lighter than his hair and slightly upturned behind his glasses, one more than the other. Every feature of his face was pleasantly a little bit out of kilter.

"One and a half." Kim turned back to her sandwiches. She had to hurry. She would never make it at this rate.

"Double," he insisted as the telephone rang. "Did you design these tags yourself? Did you draw the pictures?"

Kim grabbed a sandwich bag and used it to pick up the receiver. She wouldn't have bothered with that if Lou weren't there. "Hello." It had to be a Jensen relative. Hardly anybody else ever called here.

"Kim Bonner?" It was the desk manager at the Oakhaven Inn. He had a high, irritated voice.

"Yes. Hi."

"Are you giving up on us, or at least are *you* still working?"

"No, it's only three-thirty. I'll be there. If my tires hold out."

"Finally *somebody's* working. We've had a bus come off the road because of the storm. Do you think you can pack us a hundred extra sandwiches? On short notice?"

Kim tried to meet Lou's eyes through the fluorescent shine that had appeared on his glasses. He smiled at her with just the left side of his face. Looking at him, biting her lip, she said, "Oh. Well, I guess so. If I can get the fixings. But, you know, I'll have to charge you double."

———◆———

It wasn't until March that Kim felt ready to move into rented quarters. By then Aunt Dagmar's furniture had been covered with sheets and pushed against the walls so her front room could accommodate tables where four of Kim's classmates assembled sandwiches. They were serving two meals a day at seventeen motels, with a waiting list of twenty more. The public-health inspector wasn't pleased. He was a portly retired veterinarian who knew Aunt Dagmar from her days on the farm, so his visits were more frequent and more lenient than they might have been otherwise. He dropped by every week or so and went upstairs to visit, stepping over crocks of pickles and sauerkraut and seventy-five loaves of bread. Kim would tidy her apron quickly and try to smile, but she could see that his beak of a mouth was working. When Dr. Thurston came downstairs again it was with Aunt Dagmar's deterioration further souring his outlook.

"Miss Bonner, you *can't* have an electric cord crossing the door this way. And what's this? How long has this meat gone unrefrigerated? And *this?* And look at your hair. You've got to cover your *hair.* And for the love of mercy, girl, *when* are you going to put that poor woman in a home?"

"But she's fine," Kim mumbled as she tried on tiptoe to balance the meat-slicer extension cord on top of the door case. With her free hand she was catching her braids and twisting them nervously. "It's just talking that's a problem. And walking, too, lately," Kim added as she maneuvered an armload of liverwurst between Ellie Walters and the sheet-covered sofa. The fact that there was no room in the refrigerator was a discovery she wanted to spare Dr. Thurston by making this distracting show of moving the extra meat onto the kitchen counter.

"You don't leave her alone like that, do you?"

Kim couldn't stand the thought of Aunt Dagmar in a nursing home. Chris and his sisters thought it was time, her doctor had made arrangements, but Kim did the driving and she every day managed to find other tasks that were more important. It wasn't just that Aunt Dagmar didn't want to go. It wasn't even that Kim didn't want to lose that prim old lady who drooled drips from one corner of her diagonal mouth onto the front of her gabardine dress. No, what knotted Kim's stomach and dried her throat was envisioning Aunt Dagmar's anguish at that moment of final removal from her own home. Without wishing the old woman ill at all, Kim had come to hope that she would die soon. How could she be forced from this city house she still loved so much that she dragged herself on her walker every day to dust the upstairs and straighten the doily under the hallway telephone? For Aunt Dagmar to die in her own clean house would be a final grace note to a life well-lived. Kim saw her passive resistance to this nursing-home idea as a gift whose meaning she and Aunt Dagmar both understood perfectly.

"You can't go *on* like this," Dr. Thurston muttered as he bent to stack shiny streams of bread that he had inadvertently toppled. Kim was selling seven or eight hundred sandwiches a day, so she had bread piled in drifts against the walls.

"Tell you what," he added as if they had been haggling and this would be his final offer. "The Chow Down is going under, but I don't know if I can get you in there. That's asking a lot. You're really twisting my arm here."

———◆———

The Chow Down was a failed steak house just a mile south of the Restop Motel. It was in a poor location for a restaurant, too far from the interstate and too far from town on a square asphalt bite out of a cattle pasture. Over the past ten years, a succession of restaurants had bloomed and died there, so the canny owner of the farm was tickled to sign another sucker to a three-year lease.

The building was perfect. It had a broad kitchen open to the dining room, a walk-in refrigerator and a walk-in freezer, two six-burner stoves and a grille where the Chow Down had barbecued its ill-fated ribs and steaks. The dining room had been brightly tiled for a former Mexican restaurant, so the walls and floors could be washed down clean. Classmates could come in after school to assemble sandwiches and drive the four new Taste of Home delivery vans.

Kim had been gone from school for a week before Lou came looking for her. She hadn't meant to drop out of school. She just had taken time to haggle back-ended leases on the restaurant and on the vans, and to wash the place down and complete the move while she kept up her daily deliveries. But after a week, she had added four morning employees and six more motels. She was planning a formal dinner menu and a luncheon trial at the Restop. She didn't know how she was going to find the time to go back to school.

Jerry Case had been taking notes for Kim. He was the first boy she had dated more than twice since she had broken up with Colin Sanderlin four years before, and she liked him for the same reasons she had liked Colin. He had an air of impractical cheerfulness that made her smile. He was as obsessed with cost-accounting as Colin had been obsessed with his art. And he was willing to neck to the point of pain without insisting they go farther than that.

Ellie Walters drove Jerry down from Indianapolis every day at three. He was, as he liked to put it, between cars: his pattern was to buy antiques and restore them until they began to bore him. He had sold his '57 Chevy when he bought a '59 Cadillac in November, but since he had joined Kim at Taste of Home, he hadn't done more to it than take it apart all over the floor of his father's barn.

"Hey, Hero!" he called as he banged in the door.

He called Kim "Hero." She loved that because there was no reason for it. He just had remarked once that her business made

her the hero of the first-year class, and then he had called her Hero
forever after. Kim downplayed it all by insisting she was only the
hero of hero-sandwiches.

"Hey? Where are you? Hero?"

Kim was wrestling a hand-truck out of the refrigerator. Her
afternoon help arrived at three, and she couldn't stand the thought
of not being ready.

"In the back! Can you help me with this?"

"Aha!" Jerry said as he came tapping into the sweet wine smell
of beef stew over lemon pastries. He wore just jeans and a fish-
erman's sweater because it was warm for the end of March. His
green eyes and rusty hair and the boyish tilt of his freckled nose
made him look no more than eighteen years old, a rugged Tom
Sawyer forever adolescent.

Kim glanced up at Jerry from the irritation of her overbur-
dened hand-truck. He smiled catlike with the corners of his mouth,
a naughty pleased expression that thrilled her. She had thought
that after Colin she never again would find a man she could love,
but here she was falling for this unlikely farm boy who smelled like
grass and wore a rime of permanent grease under his fingernails.

"What do you have *on* this thing?" Jerry made a self-important
show of yanking Kim's truck over the inch-high threshold, one
stubborn wheel at a time. After each lift, he leaned to receive from
her a peck on the lips. "Pointe asked about you today," he remarked
as the truck rolled free. "He asked the class if we knew where Miss
Bonner was. Stubby told him with a snicker he'd better ask me.
You wouldn't believe the dirty look I got. Now I'll flunk. I took the
teacher's pet."

"Did you tell him where I was?" Kim was piling loaves of bread
on top of her fifty pounds each of ham and cheese and roast beef
and hog's-head cheese, her ten pounds of butter and her case of
pickles.

"Sure. Didn't you tell him you were moving?"

"No. I've got to do this all by myself now."

Ellie was seated at the front desk. She was so good with numbers that for the past few months she had been keeping the books under Jerry's direction. Jerry glanced at the passive back of her head. Then he caught Kim's wrist and pulled her into his arms. "Time for love, my leetle sausage." He kissed her neck with nibbles that erected hairs and made Kim shiver. He chuckled and caught one of her braids to tip her head back so he could kiss her. Kissing Jerry, hearing his breathing and feeling the ripples of pleasure his kissing produced had become a secret delight for Kim, something separate even from her feeling that she was falling in love with him. She could close her eyes and listen to him, feel his body tight against hers and the trembles in her belly like delicate wings and be filled with a bliss associated somehow with childhood, with Virginia, with every fine and fragile happiness of her life bound together. And Jerry had learned early that she wouldn't go farther, so he was willing to kiss her this way until he was frantic with his frustrated need.

From outside came the dim concussion of doors slamming and the muted babble of arriving workers. Kim's friends had arranged their schedules so they were through with school by two most afternoons. She had gotten her workers started and washed her hands and sat back down to her tray of butterflied pork chops when she developed a sense of eyes on her. She glanced up. Lou was standing there beyond the long serving counter. His face was unreadable, as it was in class before he pivoted and made some gigantic point.

"Hi." The sight of him produced in Kim an annoying twist of guilt because she had made all these changes without him. It was only thanks to Lou that she had even survived December, thanks to him that she had enough money now to grow into rented quarters and to pay Aunt Dagmar's new companion besides. But this wasn't Lou's business. It was her business. She went back to twisting chops and spooning in stuffing to show him she was too busy to talk.

"Nice place." He was using his clipped and boomy classroom tone. At the sandwich table, heads turned with mild interest.

"Why don't you come in here?" Kim mumbled, intent on her pork chops. Lou stepped to the right through the flapping doorway, moving with his jerky classroom quickness. Kim had learned by now that he also moved this way when he was upset.

"Have a seat. Please."

Lou snapped out a chair across the table from hers. As he sat down, he said, "When were you going to tell me?"

Kim glanced up at Lou's dear misshapen face, at his eyes bright and active behind the shine on his glasses. "This is *my* business." She went back to her stuffing. "I'm grateful for your help, but I think it's time for me to be on my own."

Lou didn't say anything to that, so after a moment Kim lifted her head and looked at him. He smiled his crooked smile at her, something so unexpected that her spoon drooped toward the table. "I love that," he said as he picked up a knife and studied the tip of it. His hands were always busy. "It's so like you, and it's so terrific. You're going to succeed in spades."

"*What* are you talking about?"

"This independence. I'd rather see you run headlong in the wrong direction than sit there waiting for success to happen. Or come crawling to ask *me* what to do next."

"What do you mean, the *wrong direction?*" Kim blurted. Then she realized from his broadening grin that this was the reaction he had wanted. She clamped her jaw and bent fiercely to her pork chops.

"I've got something to tell you," he said as she was finishing her last pork chop. "I don't think you'll care, but still I'd like to be the one to tell you."

"This is *not* the wrong direction," Kim insisted, feeling sulky.

She stood and levered open the refrigerator door so she could carry in her tray of pork chops. The Restop delivery would be made at six, so these wouldn't go into the oven until just before five. "Where else could I get a setup like this? All this space?" Kim asked as she lifted one of the stew lids, releasing a fog of fragrant steam. "All this equipment? For eight hundred dollars a month? And I even got him to back-end that, so it's six hundred now and a thousand in the third year."

"All right. It's only partly the wrong direction. But you've got too *much* here, Kim. There's a limit to how big a radius you can cover with a single kitchen. What you should be doing is looking at kitchens in new areas. Gary and Fort Wayne. And what you really should be doing is getting to the coasts before somebody notices and beats you to it."

Kim turned to Lou with soft wonder. She had spent her week happily mapping the theoretical limits of this kitchen's service area. Never had she dreamed the giant dream that she was seeing now behind his eyes.

"Would you like some stew?"

"Sure. Lay it on me." He settled back with a creaking of his kitchen chair. They had developed an ego-saving discussion dance of advances and retreats that generally involved her feeding him.

Dr. Thurston's whiney voice rose in the sandwich room, ordering some hapless worker to cover her hair. Then, "Miss Bonner. There you are. Nice place you've got here." Dr. Thurston was edging his round belly sideways through the kitchen doorway. He spoke in brief exclamations without exclamation points, and whatever he said covered layers of meaning that would have Kim going over his visits for days afterward. Now the tone of his voice expressed pride in his having suggested this place and disapproval of the noticeable infractions, and underneath it all a sulky rage at Kim's having hired Aunt Dagmar's companion against his advice.

"Oh. Hi. Dr. Thurston, this is Dr. Pointe. He's a corporate

doctor," Kim added by way of explanation as she ladled Lou's stew and set it on the table in front of him. Then what she had said struck her as funny. She gave one stifled nervous giggle.

"Miss Bonner, *look* at your hair." Her giggle hadn't pleased him. "How would you feel if you found a hair that long in your dinner? How would you like *that*, Dr. Pointe?"

"Oh, for crying out loud. You don't like my hair? Fine. Just fine. I'll cut it." Kim took from Lou's hand the filleting knife she had used to butterfly her pork chops and held it to the root of her left braid. She hadn't intended to do this now, but the blank, stricken looks on the faces of the men gave her a feeling of silly inevitability. Oh, what the heck. She was twenty-three. And it was such a perfect gesture. Briskly she tugged her braid out taut and sawed it off.

"*Kim!*" Lou stood fast, as if she had maimed herself and he was desperate to stanch the flow of blood.

"Just relax. Eat," Kim said calmly, studying the cut braid in her hand. Her head felt lopsidedly light. Lou sat down slowly, staring at her.

Kim found it harder to saw with her left hand. Her head felt so oddly airy that she thought her knife might slip. When she realized she was wavering against the edge of the table, she said, "Lou? Can you help me with this?"

Lou stepped around the end of the table and snatched the knife from her hand. She met his eyes, willing him to see that what she needed from him was not shock or anger but a calm, sure hand on the knife. His face firmed as if she had spoken aloud. He gripped her right braid and placed the knife with a close-focus concentration she could see through his glasses, and gently, hair by hair, he cut it off.

Kim said, "There. Is that short enough? Or would you like it shorter?"

She shook her head, feeling free and light. And grown up.

She should have done this years ago. Dr. Thurston liked to grab the last word at every visit, so Kim imagined he must be inventorying his own body now for something he could cut in return. Finally he snapped, "Use a hairnet!" Then he hurried through the kitchen doorway so fast that his belly bounced against the jamb.

Lou had laid Kim's braids on the table. He was aligning them reverently, straightening the blue cords she had tied that morning as if he were dressing a corpse. He blinked several times, looking at them.

"Eat. It'll get cold," Kim said calmly, going to stir her stew. That she could cut her hair for the first time in twenty-three years and have its loss mean so little to her was mildly amazing, a revelation about herself like an extra hand that she wanted to examine to discover its uses.

"He wasn't worth that." Lou wasn't looking at Kim.

"Of course he wasn't. I did it for me. And it's no big deal. Stop acting like I died or something."

He roamed around the table and sank into his chair. Someone in the sandwich room was telling a joke that brought a ripple of laughter from the line of backs. Slowly Lou picked up his spoon and began to eat.

Kim turned on the ovens for the pork chops and the baked potatoes. Teddy Cavendish would be back any minute from his final room-tag round. Kim had stuffed eighty chops because she had forty orders from the two-o'clock trip, and the final round generally meant as many more. This gourmet idea seemed to be a hit. The desk clerk at the Restop had kindly told Kim their business was up twelve percent this month, and management was guessing her fancier dinners might be the main reason.

"Tell me. Gary and Fort Wayne and both coasts. Tell me what you're thinking."

"This is terrific," Lou said, talking about the stew. His voice still had that stiff, clipped flatness.

"Look, forget the hair, will you? I should have done it years ago."

"It's not the hair." He sounded grumpy.

Kim stood against the stove, combing her hair with her fingers and testing the astonishing sharp flatness of the ends. "Tell me," she said again, enjoying the sight of him relishing her food like a man starving. Lou glanced at her askance, as if he were afraid to see her. Then he lifted his head and gave her a long, full look. Kim was relieved that the new self she was seeing reflected in his face wasn't all that ugly.

"We've got to develop a business plan," Lou said, chewing. "Forget the major cities. Target maybe a dozen markets with lots of small motels. Either you're in those markets within two years or you'll see them taken by someone else. I mean that, Kim. Good news travels fast. You might be able to generate your own growth money, but my guess is you're looking at a public offering."

"No way. I won't give up control."

"You won't have to. We'll rent or do limited partnerships for the real estate. Once we've got some visibility, we'll offer stock in maybe forty percent of the company. Enough to get listed on a regional exchange. I'd rather be in Boston since I know the terrain, but I'll shop around out here and see what we've got."

"Oh, great." Kim forced a frown while delight swelled against her diaphragm. A public company. She was going to run a public company.

"I'm taking in a lot of money." She was speaking slowly so she could taste the wonder of it. During all her four years of planning, she never had grasped what twenty-three motels times fifty or sixty meals a day would mean in terms of actual dollars.

"We'll gross two hundred thousand this month. Can you believe that? Although we're still paying last month's bills with this month's income. Luckily we're a cash business and vendors give us thirty-day credit. That's a break. And it's nice the people tip so well we hardly have to pay the delivery kids. But there's nothing left for capital, Lou. I keep thinking there will be. Although I've got, you know, a little put by. About seventeen thousand dollars by now."

"Peanuts. One TV ad. What we ought to do is franchise. You know, this is terrific stew. Could you make it centrally and ship it out? Would it reheat?"

"It's already reheated. What do you mean, franchise? If we do that I won't have to sell my stock?"

"You've got to do both. That'll give you the leverage to bloom nationwide within four or five years. You'll be unstoppable, Kim. The IBM of a whole new industry."

Kim hid her grin behind her fingers and turned to begin another round of stirring. This was all so much more than what she had envisioned. But she could picture it. With Lou sitting there calmly framing the dream, it was believable.

"I've got to tell you something." Lou's voice sounded flat and stiff again.

Kim turned from her final stew kettle and said, "Will the name work nationwide? Taste of Home? Do you think?"

"Sure. Listen to me. You're going to hear this, so I'd rather have you hear it from me." Lou sighed and said, "Carolyn's left me."

"What? Your wife? Why?" Kim was so stricken that she sank into a chair, staring at Lou helplessly.

"No reason. Every reason." Lou slumped with his elbows on either side of his bowl. He grabbed off his glasses and rubbed his eyes. "She hates it here. She has no friends. She had tests that show she probably can't have children."

"Well, adopt!" Kim said with spirit. "Move back to Boston. What's more important?"

"Ah, there's the rub," Lou said with a wan left-sided smile. He replaced his glasses. "I've had to ask myself what's more important. You've never been married, but sometimes you realize it's you or the marriage. It can't be both. And over and over I've chosen the marriage. I think this time maybe I'll choose me."

"This has happened before?"

"She spends her life giving me ultimatums. I've been married ten years, and it's only lately I've come to see that no matter how many hoops I jump through, she'll never be satisfied. The lack is inside her."

"Oh, Lou. I'm so sorry."

"I wanted you to hear from me that it's really my choice. The rumors are saying otherwise. And . . . ."

A good-natured cheer erupted in the sandwich room as Teddy Cavendish burst through the flapping kitchen door. He dropped his bundles of tags in front of Kim with a rustling of nylon parka and a puff of the cold air cocooned around him, said, "'Night, boss! I'm outta here!" and was gone.

Kim picked up the first of her twenty-three bundles and slipped off the elastic and began absently to sort the tags by main dish. "We're going to run late," she remarked. She was surprised to realize how little that mattered. With Lou sitting here and without her braids, somehow her need to please wasn't so desperate.

"Let me tell you what you're going to hear," Lou said to his folded hands. "You're going to hear I've been having an affair with a student. It's not true, but denying a rumor just makes it worse."

"Who do they say it is?" She had never seen Lou with anyone.

He gave Kim a faintly sheepish look. "I want you to sit right there and not say anything for a full minute. Agreed?"

"Agreed. Sure. It's none of my business anyway."

"You know I've been spending a lot of time with you. I've helped you get your business going. The students see a lot of us together. So," he said with a long sigh, "Carolyn decided finally we're having an affair. You and me."

"That's ridiculous!" Kim could feel the beginnings of a roaring blush.

"You promised," Lou said, sounding hurt.

"That's crazy! Tell her it's crazy. *I'll* tell her it's crazy!"

"I've told her. That's not the point. My worry now is they'll have me up on discipline. Them and their damn fraternization rules. Oddly enough, my friends tell me the separation helps. They like to think I'm already being punished."

"But you didn't *do* anything!"

On impulse, Kim leaned and touched Lou's hand. It was larger than she had expected it to be, firm and square and warm. She drew back quickly, feeling redder still.

"I can handle it. They've got no proof. I'm only here for another year, anyway. With Carolyn gone and with us ignoring them, soon it's going to be yesterday's news. But you've got to ignore them. One word of denial and they'll be at you forever."

Kim folded her hands to match the way Lou was folding his. She pursed her lips in a tiny smile. She saw Lou as a fond and comfortable mix of wise father and goading older brother, so to envision him briefly as a sexual man made her feel shy before him. Studying her hands, she gave a little involuntary chuckle and said, "Everyone thinks I'm such a prude. It's nice to be a tainted woman for a change."

chapter five

May 6, 1983

Trying to finish business school while she opened six distribution kitchens and designed new packaging and rented additional offices and did five million dollars worth of business in 1982 was a chore Kim had found hideously frustrating. She couldn't maintain her precious A-average. And to have professors whose only contact with the business world was the books they had read scrawling, "Impractical!" or "Lacks IMAGINATN" across her essays was so infuriating that a hundred times she had thought about dropping out. But she hadn't dropped out. Her M.B.A. would be confirmation that she was capable of doing what she was doing. Kim finished her second-year final exams on the first Thursday in May. She drove to her office on Friday morning, trying to see this as the first morning of the rest of her life; but what she was thinking instead was that she had misread Lou's exam question about market penetration. If he didn't just give her an A anyway she was never going to speak to him again.

When it had become obvious late in the previous summer that she couldn't have four clerical workers typing in Aunt Dagmar's front room, Kim had rented office space in a brick Victorian block downtown. That had seemed to be a tremendous stretch, but by the end of the year she had taken a second suite in the same building. Then in February, her accounting department had replaced the

Oakhaven School of Creative Dance on the first floor. By May, she was occupying twelve thousand feet of space in four locations in that creaking building, and she had hired a high school boy for the summer to run errands among her scattered offices.

The previous January, Kim had marked this day off as the point when Taste of Home would change from a student's hobby to a real business run by an M.B.A. Over the months, she had dreamed today into such a daunting red-letter event that as she parked Aunt Dagmar's car in front of her "K. Bonner, *Pres.* *T-H*" sign she felt a sense of sinking dread. She should have planned just to take the day off.

Kim's office was on a third-floor corner. There was a marble fireplace carved in vines and flowers on an inner wall; exposed pipes and wiring in the corners were painted the same chalk-green as the hammered-tin wainscoting. Kim loved her office despite its musty smell because from its windows she could see two Taste of Home motels standing beyond a plain of roofs that held Aunt Dagmar's cottage among them. A wisp of highway along the horizon was an umbilicus running south and east. And right below her, edging the parking lot, was a weed-lined creek called Three-Ladies River that reminded her of Redrabbit Run. For the first time since she was a child crossing the pasture and climbing the hill to Highgrove, Kim felt in her office that blessed sense of being centered on a sturdy base.

The main thing on Kim's agenda that morning was a two-hour presentation by Harvey, Oldfield, Westlake and Sharon, an Indian-apolis advertising firm. Kim had never before seen a presentation by an advertising firm, and it surprised her to realize how much she resented it. While four officious people flipped charts and played jingle tapes and showed mock-ups of packaging and ran a projector against an inner wall of her office, she tented her fingers and chewed her cheek to keep from saying anything. Finally the plumpish woman in a pink silk dress who had been coordinating the presentation snapped off her projector and finished with a flourish as she said, ". . . after that we'll start on the *foreign* markets!" Then they all looked at Kim expectantly.

Kim and Jerry and Ellie glanced at one another. Kim said finally, "that was impressive."

"Thank you." The woman sat down with a fuss of pink skirt over widely rounded hips. Kim liked her very feminine dress that seemed courageous on a professional woman. She felt a special reluctance to hurt her feelings.

"Ah, Miss Westlake? Did Dr. Pointe tell you we already have packaging?"

"Call me Connie."

"Oh, and call me Kim. But we've spent a year working on the packaging until we've finally got it right. Anyway, I don't think orange is really the image we want to convey." Taste of Home's packaging was in bright pink with large cartoon flowers. It was happy. Orange was garish.

"That's just the point," Connie said with a graceful rearrangement of her skirt on her chair. "You've done well locally, but Dr. Pointe feels you're going to need something powerful to go nationwide."

"This is his idea? He's seen all this?"

"We've discussed it."

"Oh. Well, and race-car drivers? That's really not the image we're looking for."

One of the men said, "Miss Bonner, Vic Engstrom is the hottest driver on the circuit. He's just twenty-eight and he looks like a rock star. This year he'll make a million dollars just from endorsements."

"I'll do *more* than a million dollars." Kim felt a faint internal amazement. Ellie had just revised her 1983 projections to show a gross of fifty million dollars. The bottom line after expenses looked like something over a million of that, and since Kim hadn't revoked her Subchapter-S election it was all going to hit her personal tax return. She had decided while she was botching Lou's exam that her only sane option was to leverage into some business real estate so she could pay rent to herself and offset it with depreciation. But she would have to revoke her Subchapter-S election next year so Lou could do his public offering, and then maybe the SEC would say she was self-dealing if she owned the real estate.

"Miss Bonner?"

"Oh. Sorry. I guess I'm just tired."

"I said he'll be at our Mr. Harvey's party tonight. Did you get your invitation?"

The advertising people were studying pink door tags, ordering lunch, when Lou came ambling in. He was wearing his usual teaching tweeds and smoking the pipe he must have been dying for while he proctored over the past two hours. "Crabmeat and bacon. Make it two," he said as he dropped onto the sofa beside Ellie. Kim looked at him sitting slouched into the sofa with his head back dreamily so his dying pipe was tilted at the ceiling. He had sensed the tension in the room, so he was pretending to be somewhere else. But with Lou sitting there, taking up space, suddenly Kim was in an equal fight.

"What's this with orange? And some Indy driver? And now I've got to move to *Indianapolis*, for heaven's sake? And they're letting *Time* come to my graduation? I don't want reporters at my graduation! What *is* all this?"

"You *are* your company," Connie said patiently. "You're the symbol . . . ."

"It's news when a student starts a fifty-million-dollar business," Lou said in his laziest voice. "*Time* just wants to do a profile. I think it's a good idea."

Kim knew from the bland way Lou was talking that he was trying to interpose himself between the factions. Anger made him so uncomfortable that he was a compulsive peacemaker.

"It's important you have the right home. The right friends. The right offices," Connie's assistant said, glancing around with a sniff. He was a gaunt fellow who held his head at a tilt, as if every sight and smell offended him.

"Look, I live with my aunt. She's eighty-eight. I'm the only one she'll talk to. And she's the only relative I have in the world, so until she dies, I'm not going anywhere." Until the words were out, Kim hadn't realized how badly she needed to see Aunt Dagmar through to a decent death.

"This is never going to work," Connie said in an aside to Lou.

"It's her company." Lou took his cold pipe from his mouth and studied it as if he had never seen it before.

"We're trying to create a persona," said a quiet man of about Kim's age. "You're a beautiful young woman, and you're talented. You're one of maybe a dozen young people who really are national news. If you play this well, you can be your own best corporate asset."

Kim snapped Lou a look. "That's you talking."

"Let's just say they agree with me."

"I think you'll like it," the gentle man went on. Kim remembered now that his name was Fred and he was from the firm's public-relations arm. "It's fun to be at the right parties and know the right people. It's fun to be recognized. To be envied. It's fun, Miss Bonner, to be famous."

"And you're going to make me famous?" Kim asked lightly. She was feeling the giddy, amazed sense of stretching that happened whenever she glimpsed another vast new possibility.

"*You're* going to make you famous." Fred's grin was unexpectedly white and toothy. "You're going to do it. All we'll do is point."

"Fine. But can't you point at me the way I am?"

"Well, yes. Pretty girl runs – What did you call it, Lou? A fifty-million-dollar business? That's what it's worth?"

"Could be." Lou smiled at his pipe. "At a hundred and fifty motels right now, we're grossing a hundred-thousand dollars a day. By the end of the year we'll double that figure. And we're negotiating to buy our central kitchen. We'll soon own most of our satellites, too. With all that in place and the California franchise operation coming on line, I think you could say we'll be worth at least fifty million dollars."

"Oh. Wow. I could point to that. But so much of it is image, Miss Bonner. Suppose you show up at the party tonight with Vic and I have a photographer take your picture. Suppose the wire services pick it up. A beautiful young couple. Rich. Successful. *That* would be national news."

"Now you want me to go *out* with this guy?"

"He's willing. It's good for him, too."

Kim glanced at Jerry sitting there beyond Ellie at the far end of the sofa. He had been her boyfriend for a year and a half, giving her whatever support she needed but never asking for more than necking and always careful to keep out of her way. Kim was fond of Jerry. He was as comfortable and familiar as a bodily appendage.

When the advertising people had gushed their goodbyes and Kim had nodded to Ellie and Jerry to let them know that they could go, too, Kim and Lou were left alone in a vast silence. Lou glanced at her. She said, "I blew the second question. Just give me an A."

"You hated it."

"What, them? No. They just need some breaking-in. They'll be fine."

Lou chuckled. "I told them you were the one to please, but they kept believing it was my show. So you took them apart. They deserved it."

"They'll be okay. We need someone to handle all that. We just won't give them much leash. Orange packaging. Moving me around and finding me dates. How ridiculous."

"Kim?"

She looked at Lou.

"If I tell you something, will you promise not to shoot the messenger?"

"Rats. What is it now? Who quit? Who died?"

"It's not that."

"You're leaving."

"It's not that, either. Although I've just had my last paycheck."

"So, come work for me."

Kim had been dreading for months this moment when she would find out whether she could talk Lou into staying after his two years of teaching at Indiana University were over. It was only as she had begun to contemplate having him gone that she had come to realize how central he was to whatever this was that she was building. He held no position at Taste of Home, he came and went in these offices at will, but she wasn't sure that she even could go on without him. Lou shifted straighter on the sofa, moving bone by bone while he looked at Kim. He had a loose, animal way of moving when he wasn't thinking about being a professor that seemed friendly and familiar. Kim's throat constricted.

"Look, you're getting divorced, right? So, what do you have to go back for? What's in Boston?"

"I'm a teacher. That's what I do."

"I'll make you a vice-president. I'll pay you whatever you ask. How can you leave me now?"

"Well, for one thing, I'd lose my tenure," Lou said so lightly that Kim realized with a swelling of her chest that he was leaning toward staying.

"Anything! Money? Stock?"

He stood off the sofa, looking thoughtful. "Would you mind

if I wrote a book about Taste of Home? I called the chairman of
my department a few weeks ago and asked for a sabbatical to write
this book. It's irregular, but your story fascinates him."

"How long? How long will they give you?"

"Two years. That's what I asked for. By then you ought to be
on your feet. And I don't want a position. Just make me a consultant. This has to be your baby."

Kim stood with so much energy that it carried her around her
desk and across the room. Lou felt big in her arms, even bigger
than Jerry, big and rough and wonderful. "Thank you, thank you,"
she whispered.

"Is this part of the job? If I'd known that, I'd have told you
sooner."

Kim gave Lou a final squeeze and leaned back to smile up at
his dear crooked grin, then slipped away from him. She felt so
carefree all of a sudden that she realized his leaving had been a
big worry.

"Kim? Now that you're in a good mood, I think there's something you should know. It's about Jerry. It's, ah, a little hard to
say."

Kim stood before her chair while she sorted piles of letters to
be signed. Without looking at Lou, she said, "He's sleeping with
his secretary?"

"You know?"

She glanced at him as she sat down in her chair. She hadn't
known. She had suspected. "Is this the big news in the hallways?
They're afraid I'll find out and dying to have me find out?"

"I wouldn't put it that way . . . ."

"Thanks for telling me. I can't say that I blame him. What I
don't understand is why I don't seem to care."

———◆———

Kim had read about Graham Harvey's house when it had first been built two years before. *The Indianapolis Star* had run an architectural supplement that had been little more than a collection of magnificent pictures of this house. Kim had thought at the time such a story must mean it was the most fantastic house in Indiana; she saw now that it had just been more of an advertising man's self-promotion. The house was set into a hillside in one of the richer Indianapolis suburbs. From the street it was a sleek white marble slab sparked strident with lights and backlit by a lake that was visible beyond it as a flat shine purple in the twilight.

What had been most impressive about this house in that Sunday spread of pictures had been its three-story great room with a thirty-foot-high wall of windows facing the lake. Even though it was almost dark outside, the sudden dip beyond the foyer into that deep vault of marble was so dramatic that Kim and Jerry stepped ten feet to the brass-framed railing and looked down. The marble was white, the sofas were white, the fixtures were brass or crystal, but the trees and ivy everywhere made the place seem as friendly as a garden. It had a cool, clean smell of marble and of the chlorophyll in all those leaves.

"Some spread," Jerry murmured.

"His mother was scared by the Parthenon," Kim remarked.

Jerry led Kim around to the left toward a course of steps that ended at a sloping walkway. He leaned and said, "You'll have a spread like this, too, Hero. Mark my words." Kim looked away. Jerry kept bringing up her success in terms of what it could buy her, placing a wedge between them that he acknowledged by the way he excluded himself from his speculations about her future. But still, he couldn't stop talking about it. After seeing those fifty-million-dollar projections, it seemed he could talk about little else.

They started down the walkway toward a bar shaped like a marble whale. Jerry was holding Kim's hand, and she found she was uneasy about that: people were looking at them. There were perhaps a hundred people in evening dress standing and sitting in groups on the course of descending walkways, and more and more of them were glanced their way as Kim and Jerry approached the bar.

This was brand, brand new. There had been an article about Taste of Home in the Sunday *Star*, and Lou had warned Kim that Graham Harvey would let his guests know she would be coming. *Big deal*, she had thought when Lou had said it. Lots of clients at Harvey, Oldfield, *et al* were famous. But they weren't new. They weren't *hot*. Kim glanced around quickly, looking for Lou. She felt naked here without him. He had promised to come when she had insisted, but he had promised in such a way that she knew he would find some last-minute reason not to come. He didn't own a tuxedo. He wouldn't have a date.

"I feel as if my slip is showing," Kim said to Jerry. She let go of his hand so she could make a little show of straightening the shoulders of her dress. She could see now that her dress was all wrong. Every other woman wore a dignified slink in some dark color and state of semi-undress, while Kim wore what she thought of as a party dress. This was a party, wasn't it? So she wore a square-necked confection with big puff sleeves that was patterned in pink and magenta flowers.

"Strawberry daiquiri, honey?"

"I'd better not. One more bit of pink and someone will mistake me for dessert."

Jerry looked at Kim directly then. He had combed his willful ruddy hair, and with it tamed he seemed older. Leaner. His freckles and the tilt of his nose were less cute and more handsome. No wonder his secretary wanted him.

"What's wrong? Are you nervous?"

"Tell me all those people aren't looking at me."

"Which people?" he asked with a glance around.

"Oh, shoot. Really? It's all in my mind?"

"No. But it's better if you think so."

Kim poked Jerry with her elbow then, such a natural gesture between them that she was able to lift her head and glance around. A few heads turned to avoid her eyes, but most of these people weren't looking at her. She probably wasn't famous enough to worry about making a fool of herself.

"That's him," Jerry whispered. "Picture a face like that over our friendly flowered lunchboxes."

Kim turned as Jerry made an eyes-up gesture. She didn't know at first who he was talking about, but then she spotted the best-looking man she had ever seen in her life. He stood on the walkway below theirs in a little knot of people who had all aligned their bodies in obeisance to his. His head was at the level of Kim's waist, and he was barely twenty feet away; she could see the clean planes and angles of his face and the carefully casual drape of his crayon-yellow hair. *Crayon-yellow.* Kim had heard her mother use that phrase a hundred times, but never had she seen a real person with crayon-yellow hair. That man could be her brother.

"Who is it?" she hissed to Jerry. The man was bent politely to listen to the woman next to him. Kim heard him softly laugh.

"Vic Engstrom. The stud who wants to date you for publicity reasons." Jerry said it with a light, resigned bitterness that made Kim realize he already knew he wouldn't be keeping her. No matter how hard he worked, she had gone so far beyond him now that even standing here she felt oddly like a horse in double harness with a cow. He might have turned to his secretary out of despair.

"I'll have a daiquiri, after all."

As Jerry handed Kim her drink, she spotted Connie Westlake threading toward them among the groups on the walkway. Connie was a dark, vaguely ethnic woman who seemed to wear her extra weight as a fashion statement, neatly hugged and draped by a white one-shouldered dress. Kim smiled when Connie caught her eye and smiled. She found that she was starting to admire this woman.

"Kim. I'm so glad you're here." Connie took Kim's free hand in both of hers. "And Jerry. Good, I see you've got your drinks. Let me introduce you around."

Then Connie's eyes slipped upward to Kim's right, and Kim heard her name spoken as lyrically as a line from a poem: "Kimberly Bonner." She turned. She was looking full into the face of the beautiful man with crayon-yellow hair. There he was, with his lean, fey face and his sad eyes that she had to call a crayon-blue. But for his coloring, he looked like Mr. Bobby when young. He looked as Kim had all her life imagined her circus-star father must have looked. Like a rocker. Like a bemused and cynical angel. She had never in her life seen a man so beautiful.

"Kim? This is Vic Engstrom. Have you met?" Connie asked while Kim and Vic stood and looked at one another.

"You saw my picture in the paper, right?" Kim asked in a quavering voice she couldn't believe was her own.

"No. I recognized the flowers."

Kim glanced down, flustered. He laughed an easy, friendly laugh that both acknowledged the inappropriateness of her dress and somehow told her he thought it made her all the more wonderful. Unless she was imagining all that, coming from a laugh. She looked up into his eyes again.

"Have you seen the rest of the house?" Vic asked in a voice meant just for her. It crossed her mind to think it was rude for him to be excluding Connie and Jerry, but she had the simultaneous thought that she didn't care. About anything.

"Come on. I'll show you around," he said easily, taking her hand and nodding a brief "Excuse us" to Connie and Jerry.

"He's my date," Kim whispered to Vic as they walked together up the ramp.

"He doesn't deserve you."

———————◆———————

Eventually they sat down on the bed in what must have been the master bedroom. On three sides of the room were backlit glass shelves of Graham Harvey's collection of pre-Colombian art, shedding a glow that made everything look either pink or charcoal-gray. Vic's eyes were as dark as cinders. He wore his hair longer than was normal, and it was straight and fine, so it lay curved above his forehead and ears in a casual perfection that Kim assumed must be some sort of cutting-edge hairstyle for men.

"Do you have a house like this?" she asked, making conversation.

"Don't you think it's awful?"

She did think it was awful, but it seemed impolite to say that. And the house had so overwhelmed her that until this moment, she had thought her taste must be wrong and this house was probably wonderful.

"I hate opulence," he was saying in his soft voice that carried no farther than Kim's ear. "I grew up on a farm. That's the human way to live. I bought a farmhouse on six hundred acres of land."

"I grew up on a farm, too." It felt good to be able to say that. He had had a childhood something like her own. Then she realized with a swell of joy that this man had had a life exactly like her own so far: he had grown up poor and become successful and rich very young. He had gone through just what she was going through now. Kim had been feeling an ever-stronger sense of isolation because everything she said now, every fear or complaint, seemed to be a shabby form of bragging. But she realized with delight that here was someone she could talk to.

"I was dying to meet you." Vic ducked his head with what Kim thought was a put-on shyness. "My agent suggested I take you out because he'd seen your picture. I hadn't. What I wanted you for was your *food*."

Kim liked the way his voice rose and fell, making everything he said sound like poetry. After just a half-hour, his voice was familiar. She was used to the drape of his hair. And his complex scent like spices and machine oil was as comfortable for her as breathing. She wondered whether this sense of owning the details of him might be what was meant by falling in love.

"Do you know, it's gotten to the point where my friends won't stay at my house anymore? They stay in your motels. They can't get enough of the food."

"They're not *my* motels," Kim mumbled. She was feeling briefly awestruck to be sitting here talking with somebody famous. If it weren't for Taste of Home, would a man like this even look at her twice?

"It really is wonderful. Your food. My favorite is that sandwich with pastrami and red sauerkraut. But you're not everywhere, are you? Just in Indiana?"

"Mostly Indiana. We've got some client motels across the borders. But we're at a hundred-fifty now, and we think by this time next year we'll be at something over six hundred motels. In five states," Kim added, loving the taste of her words. Talking to Vic, they didn't feel like bragging. "We're going to California, too. It's taking some time. The regulations are wicked. But we think by the end of 1985 we'll have five hundred motels in California alone. We're franchising. There's a limit to what you can do with your own money."

"Take in some investors." Vic was watching his foot scuff a pink sheepskin rug with a sparkling shoe.

"I guess we're doing that, too. I'm fighting it. I hate to give up stock."

Vic had lifted his head. He was studying the side of Kim's

face. She realized then with soft amazement that for the first time she hadn't thrust her scar at someone new, daring him to be put off by it. Slowly, shyly, she lifted her hair and hooked it behind her ear. Vic reached and traced her scar with a touch so delicate that Kim could feel his finger trembling. "How did you get this?" He was studying her scar. In the dim light of this room it must look enormous.

"My cat."

"No cat did that."

"Well, what do you think did it?"

"A jealous lover."

Kim gazed into eyes as deep and sad as Bobby Sever's eyes had been. It seemed to be an event forever ordained when Vic cupped her cheek with his hand and bent to give her a little kiss on the lips. He murmured, "I'm sorry he hurt you."

Kim wanted to protest, but looking into Vic's eyes she felt unable to say anything.

"Well," Vic said then, standing off Graham Harvey's bed, "I've had it with this place, haven't you? How would you like to see my house?"

"What, now?"

"Come on." He took Kim's hand with a child's naughty grin and led her out of the wing and along the balustrade above the party.

"*Wait* a minute," Kim said as they reached the balcony that served as a foyer. From below them rose the cheerful murmur of a party far enough along to produce dish-clinks and peals of loosened laughter. "We haven't even eaten!"

"We'll eat at my place. I know you can cook."

"But what about Jerry?"

Vic stopped his forward motion then and turned and looked at Kim. He was elegant in his tuxedo, the satin lapels sleek and the tiny shirt-studs real gleaming mother- of-pearl. Kim was so impressed by the fact that Vic's tuxedo wasn't rented that her resistance to him was faltering.

"Who is this Jerry, anyway?" Vic asked, sounding annoyed. "Is he the one who gave you the scar?"

"No! No. He, ah, works for me. We're kind of going together."

"Which seems to thrill you."

Vic smiled at her. His smiles were like Lou's smiles, gleeful transformations of his whole face. Looking at the sadness of Vic's passive face, it was hard to imagine the delight with which he could smile. "Come on, Kimberly. You know you're dying to take a ride with me."

That was true. She was.

"Come on, baby. When was the last time you tooled around in a Ferrari with an Indy winner?"

"But what about Jerry . . . ?"

Vic switched the hand holding Kim's from his right to his left so he could seize a champagne glass as a tray of them was carried by. He took a sip and said to the waiter under the tray, "Tell Jerry . . . what's his name, baby?"

"Jerry Case."

"Tell Jerry Case I'm taking his date home. She'll call him tomorrow," Vic added, replacing the tulip on its tray.

"He's not going to like this," Kim was saying as Vic hurried her out the tall double doors into a night very cool and bright and black and smelling of hyacinths.

———◆———

By the time Vic drove into his garage more than an hour later, Kim couldn't imagine a time when she hadn't known him. Standing holding his hand under the white canopy while a teenager fetched his black Ferrari, she had wondered briefly whether this might be a Harvey, Oldfield, *et al* publicity setup. She had expected flashbulbs at any moment. But Vic's car had arrived, glittering under the outside lights as his shoes had glittered against the sheepskin rug, and Vic had opened the door for Kim himself. Then three boys and several guests had stood awestruck and watched Vic Engstrom fold into his car as they would have watched Rostropovich caressing his cello. Vic had leaned and buckled Kim's seatbelt while she was trying to get used to this semi-reclining position with her feet thrust forward. Then he had said, "Hold on, baby," and roared out of the driveway.

Kim thought she had read somewhere that race-car drivers were cautious to a fault. But she gripped the door on one side and the edge of her seat on the other while Vic hit ninety and a hundred miles an hour on residential streets. When she shouted, "Slow down!" over the roar of his speed and her own demented fear, he said calmly, "Relax. I do this for a living." He slowed finally to eighty when he hit the entrance to I-69. "Wasn't that fun?" he said to her.

"Fun? You must be out of your mind!"

They talked then about his racing, how he drove poised on an edge of fear where his reflexes were perfect and his senses so alive that driving a race felt like making love. *Oh*, Kim thought, finding that profound. Sex and auto-racing were both male passions that she found inexplicable, so to hear that they were connected made sense to her.

Then they talked about Taste of Home. Kim tried to describe how it had felt to grow a business from the days when she had made every sandwich herself to this amazing worry that a million dollars was about to hit her personal tax return. She even told him that. And he had paid taxes last year on more than nine hundred thousand dollars, so he took her hand and kissed it playfully and said he'd be glad to retire and let her support him. They talked about dreams and worries and this strange loneliness of their extraordinary good luck. So by the time Kim stepped out into Vic's garage that smelled like grease and dog fur, she felt that she had never in her life been closer to another human being.

"Are you hungry?" he asked as he unlocked his door and they entered his dark front hallway. Kim was charmed by the simplicity of his old farmhouse that smelled of bottled gas and ancient dinners. And when he flicked on the hallway light, she smiled to see his old marble-topped table that looked like Aunt Dagmar's hallway table. It was buried in a cascade of mail. "Or would you like some wine instead?"

"Just wine. I left my stomach in Carmel."

Vic led Kim into his dark-paneled living room and walked around lighting candles here and there with a lighter he took from his pocket. Kim wondered then whether he smoked. Smoking would be okay; she was used to smoking, with Lou always smoking and chewing his pipe. Vic brought in two glasses of wine from his kitchen. They settled together on his gray-velvet sofa, where he laid his arm behind Kim and told her a story about racing in the heat during a water shortage that made her laugh out loud.

"Is your hair dyed?" Kim asked as a perfectly irrelevant break in her laughter.

"Is yours?"

"I asked you first."

"No. But the whole rest of me is dyed." He slipped his arm behind her and poked her side, which made her squirm.

"Was your father in the circus?" Kim asked, fighting the squirm. That poke had been too much intimacy.

"My dear Miss Bonner, my father is many things, but a performer isn't one of them."

"He's still alive?"

"And my mother. And my four sisters. And my eighty-year-old maiden great-aunt."

"I've got an aunt, too," Kim said, liking the coincidence of that. "She lives with me. She's a complete imp. Sometimes she talks as if she thinks I'm still just going to school, then the next minute she'll get a sparkle in her eye and say, 'Take 'em apart, Kim. You're better than a man any day.' At eighty-eight and barely able to talk, she can still say a thing like that. It makes me wonder what she's *thinking* all day long."

"Look out, world." Vic sipped his wine.

Vic seemed to be nothing so much as a playmate. He reminded Kim so much of Bobby Sever, with his lean height and the way his face caught the light in planes and angles and the way he gently teased her. She imagined as she studied the perfect drape of hair above his ear that she had known him all her life.

"You don't live rich." She liked that as another bond between them.

"I'm fighting it. That mausoleum of Harvey's makes my skin crawl. So I've got money in maybe seven banks to keep under the hundred-thousand-dollar limit. Quick, how much money is that?" He leaned and kissed her.

This kiss of Vic's was like no kiss that Kim had ever imagined. He began it with subtle moving while he took her wine glass from her hand. He even broke the kiss briefly so he could lean and set both glasses on a table. Then he settled back and drew her to him and kissed her with a delicate suction and a primitive rhythm of his head that gave her violent flutters of arousal at once. She pulled away. He brought her back. He obeyed her fumbles that insisted he stop moving his hand on her waist. He kissed her into a glow that had them both out of breath before he broke the kiss to lick a tiny cool spot onto her ear and murmur, "Let's go upstairs."

"What?" Kim was feeling delirious with his kissing. But then she looked at him and registered his meaning. "What – Of course not! No. I'm sorry if I gave you the wrong impression." She was tidying her hair and sitting up.

Vic lay against the back of his sofa, looking at her. "Do you really think you can just stop now?" He laughed a bitter chuckle and sat up, too.

"I really am sorry. Really."

What happened then was too fast for Kim to anticipate or counter. Vic grabbed both her wrists and tipped her onto her back on the sofa and began kissing her and moving his hips against hers in a rhythm she remembered as if it were yesterday. "No!" she sputtered. But she couldn't breathe. She could hardly make an audible sound. All she could think to do was bite his lip, so she did that desperately. He released a wrist long enough to slap her so hard that her ear rang; she heard his slap more than she felt it. She was so frightened that her whole body fought him while he forced her against the springs of the sofa in that infernal, sickening rhythm.

"Stop it." He lifted and slammed her upper body against the sofa.

"*Please!*"

"Don't bite," he said as if he were instructing a child. He bent and began to kiss her again.

"No!" Kim tried to say. But the way he was kissing her and moving his hips, the way he had her pinned so she couldn't fight him gave her a rush of such intense sensation that she was floating delirious above the velvet. Then unexpectedly Vic stopped kissing her and stepped off onto the floor politely, straightened his tuxedo jacket.

"*Now* we'll go upstairs."

Kim looked up blearily. She took his hand so he could help her sit up.

"Take me home."

"Come upstairs first."

"*No.*"

He said patiently, "Kimberly, you are two miles from the

nearest house. You'll do as I say." She lifted her head and looked at him. He couldn't have said what she had just heard.

"I will *not* sleep with you." She accepted his help to stand. She was so giddy with arousal that she teetered briefly. Oh, he was good at kissing.

"Why not? You want it, too."

"I do *not* . . . !"

"Just come upstairs. I want to show you something."

"Take me home."

"Come upstairs first." His voice was light and musical and playful.

"Promise?" Kim sniffled. "Promise you'll take me home?" She realized then that she had more or less been crying.

"I promise." Vic looked so friendly, so warm and kindly, that Kim thought with relief she must have misunderstood all that sexual business on the couch.

He led her by the tips of her fingers up the stairs, then down a hallway and into an old Victorian bedroom where one lamp burned. The tall, carved double bed was unmade. Clothes and books lay in piles on the floor. He left her and went to rummage in his closet.

"Your problem is you're inhibited," he said as he reappeared with a gaudy fistful of ties. "But that's a problem we can fix." He caught Kim's wrist and pulled her to the head of his bed, where he began with careful concentration to tie her wrist to his bedpost.

This behavior was so strange that Kim didn't even fight him. Her impulse was to express irritation and simultaneously to giggle.

"Come *on*, this is ridiculous!"

He tugged her wrist to test his knots, then toppled her in front of him onto his bed. He crept politely across her to the opposite side and began to tie her other wrist.

"*Stop* this! Are you crazy?" But she was feeling an exquisite

111

stimulation, a physical joy in his tying of her wrists and his tender determination. That her body so deeply relished these feelings felt even more shocking than her fear.

Vic pulled her shoes off. And while she was still preoccupied by the weird helplessness of her splayed arms, tugging, sinking into her feelings, he ran his hands up under her dress and eased off her pantyhose and her panties. Kim remembered to kick too late.

"What? Stop it! I'll scream! I'll sue you for everything you've got!"

That sounded to her like an effective threat, but she could hear him chuckling as he tried to tie her first ankle to his footboard. "I don't think so," he said under his breath. Kim was kicking her remaining foot, straining to scrape him away from her ankle. He dropped her ankle then. Both her legs were free.

"Stop it. Lie still."

"No!" She was kicking like one demented. The air on and between her legs made her feel excruciatingly naked; the thrill and the fear made her wild, delirious.

Vic dodged around and sat on his bed in front of her legs, where all she could do was try to hit him with her knees. "I'll give you one more chance to give in," he said in his soft and musical voice. For answer, Kim managed a clout that unbalanced him forward onto his hands.

Vic righted himself and slapped her hard across the face. Then he slapped her from the other side, so hard that her brain rang with concussion and tears started in her eyes. She looked at him, and all at once she suffered an excruciating surge of pleasure. It was less physical than it was emotional, spiritual; it felt as freeing as the release of soul from body. Kim yanked at her wrist ties, frantic to escape these peculiar needs she was finding in herself. And he was finding. She saw from his small, tickled smile as he studied her that he knew pretty much what she was feeling. She twisted her face away.

"Look at me."

She looked at him, askance. Her cheeks stung.

"Have I made my point?" He reached and tenderly freed some hairs that had stuck to the corner of her mouth.

"Please . . . !" She had to get out of this. She had to think.

He slapped her again from the right. Not hard. She looked at him through the blurring and bit her lip.

"Do you know how they break a horse? They tie him up and touch him all over his body. If he resists at all, they beat him. It always works. The man always wins. And it's always the best ones that fight the most." He gave her a brief peck on the lips. "Any fight left? Would you like some more?"

"Please untie me."

"Later. First I'm going to enjoy every inch of you. And there's not a thing you can do about it."

Vic's words stabbed Kim with genital pleasure, appalling feelings that made her choke and squirm. She realized with a calm edge of her mind that she wasn't really afraid of him. She knew he wouldn't hurt her; his life was too important to him. He simply was playing some perverted game in the misguided belief that she was enjoying it, too.

Vic stood off the bed while he studied her dress. He bent and rummaged in his bedside drawer for a pair of enormous sheers. "Wait! Stop it!" Kim shouted as he began to cut her dress up the center of its skirt. She flailed her legs just a little. She was afraid he would slip and cut her skin.

"I hate this dress. I'm going to want to see you in red. Or black."

"*What . . . ?*"

"Come on, Kimberly, you know you're in love. As soon as we get past this shyness bit, I'm going to be in love, too."

"*Shyness . . . ?*"

He cut her sleeves and slip and then the front of her bra. He

eased her clothes out from under her with an impersonal politeness that made her willing to shift her hips and make it easier for
him. Then he stood in his tuxedo with its loosened tie and looked
at her.

Kim tried to watch Vic's face, but his eyes on all her skin made
an intimacy so unbearable that she squirmed and twisted helplessly. This situation was arousing her so much that she wished
she could just enjoy the sensations as she used to enjoy them
during innocent kissing on the front seat of some boyfriend's car.
But this wasn't innocent. This was genuine, hideous, male-made
sex. Despite all her care, it had gotten her, too.

"You're really loving this, aren't you?" Vic sounded amused.
Kim looked at him and tried to still her legs. She had been squeez-
ing and squirming them tight. He was undressing with the care
that accompanied everything he did, setting each stud on his
dresser and aligning the creases before he tossed his pants over
a chair.

"Please don't. Please stop."

"You little slut." He was smiling as he kicked off his underwear. "You really get off on being tied to a bed."

"Please." Kim was pursing her face against tears. The need
to beg him to stop was bubbling in her mind, but begging would
have cost whatever was left of her dignity. And anyway, she didn't
seem to want him to stop. She found an undreamed-of titillation
in this loss of control, a thrilling helplessness. This time, truly, it
wasn't her fault.

Vic had a lean and fluid body. She could have sketched him a
hundred times and never tired of the play of muscles under his
skin, the clean line and weight of his silken bones and the elegant
way he moved. But she looked away fast. He had a purple erection
that swayed when he turned and made his beauty into hideous-
ness. Even drawing, she had never sketched the genitals. Her
classmates had teased her about her lovely male nudes with their

blank white pubic spaces. Vic eased onto the bed with tenderness and began to kiss Kim as he had kissed her downstairs, ignoring her struggles until she kicked his leg with her heel.

"Stop it. The game is over."

She hadn't meant to kick him. This sensation of being so well kissed while she was helpless to prevent it was so unexpectedly delicious that she thought she wanted him to tie her legs, too. But she couldn't say a thing like that. So she kicked him again. Vic slapped her hard on her naked thigh, which hurt so much she whimpered. He kissed her cry away. Then he kissed her rapidly all over her face, he kissed her cheeks warm from slapping and her salty eyelashes and her scar and her ears and her neck and her throat before he slipped down in the bed and began to kiss the tops of her breasts. Kim couldn't stand that. The sensations were unbearable. The hideous, embarrassing intimacy panicked her. "No!"

He lifted his head and slapped her face. Then he bent to tongue her nipples, which made her squirm desperately under him and brought her another spank before she was able to lie still without complaining. Vic's mouth on her nipples was producing intense genital sensations. As he went on sucking and exploring her skin, thrills of light flowed outward, radiant, until after the briefest hesitation her lower body convulsed in contractions of the keenest pleasure. Kim choked out a cry and brought her legs up fast. He was going to hit her again, but she couldn't help it. She twisted under him, desperate to escape his slap, trying to hold these exquisite sensations that were flowing away through the tips of her fingers. It crossed whatever part of her mind was still functioning that this must be an orgasm. She had assumed those ripples of warm feelings she had felt when Jerry kissed her were orgasms, but such naive nonsense embarrassed her now. She wanted to throw her arms around Vic and thank him that his craziness had produced this wonderful moment.

Vic was saying something she caught just the end of, something about how only a complete slut can climax from being tied down and kissed. But she thought the way he said it sounded kindly. He was uncurling her and kissing her, edging her legs apart and his body between them. Kim had known this was coming. But after what he had done for her, perhaps it was only fair. And it was time, really; it was long past time. Her orgasm, still glowing, made her think her whole concept of sex was up for reevaluation. But this moment was the difficult part. She squinted her face and gritted her teeth and gripped her ties so she would be able to get through it.

Vic lifted himself on his hands and entered her smoothly, producing a stab of remembered pain and then a continual friction of stinging that was all bound up with orgasmic pleasure. Kim was both shrinking from it and moving upward to meet it. She was gazing into Vic's face, watching in wonderment as it tensed with building pleasure.

"Move! What's the matter with you?"

It never had entered Kim's mind to think she should be doing anything. "I've never done this before. Tell me what to do."

Vic startled when she said this, and just then his orgasm overtook him so his eyes rolled shut and he shuddered, babbling what must have been a comeback. He grabbed her hard around the waist with one arm while he went on moving inside her. He eased out and fell onto his elbow with uncharacteristic clumsiness.

"You're kidding," he said. Then he smiled.

chapter six

April 16 - June 20, 1984

During that final year of Aunt Dagmar's life, Kim spent most of her free time with Vic. They used Kim's bedroom over the porch, and Aunt Dagmar had so little hearing left that Kim thought she never knew when he spent the night. The nurses knew, so Kim silenced them with an escalating series of bribes. Kim almost moved out of Aunt Dagmar's house at the height of summer, again in the fall, and then again just after Christmas; but each time she would begin to pack, Aunt Dagmar would divine it somehow and develop heart palpitations or even pneumonia. Kim had been suffering an ever-stronger sense of being trapped, but sitting there on that final April morning she was grateful for Aunt Dagmar's sweet dependency.

The thin dawn was as diffuse as vapor. It had risen so gradually that Kim was startled to realize that for some minutes now she had been able to make out the network of spidery wrinkles on Aunt Dagmar's putty-gray cheek. The hand in Kim's was cooling imperceptibly. Kim had thought she would hold Aunt Dagmar's hand until the undertaker came, but he had said he had two other pickups so he might not be there until nine o'clock.

Aunt Dagmar looked more like herself in death than she had in her final months, when two strokes and her deepening coma had contorted her face with life's own hideous struggle against its ending. Now her face was relaxed and her mouth was open, an untidiness Kim was pleased to see. It made Aunt Dagmar seem more her own, somehow. Kim thought she should be feeling relief at this lifting of her burden, but what she was feeling mostly was a soft sadness. She didn't regret this good ending. She just wished they had been closer in age so they might have had one another longer.

Chris and his sisters had left at four, a decent ten minutes after the death and a heroic eight hours after they had gathered at Kim's summons. The doctor had thought Aunt Dagmar might last another week, but Kim had known by Sunday afternoon that she wouldn't last the night.

Kim had shifted on her chair, so feeling was returning to her bottom after her long hours of sitting, giving her a tingle of pins and needles that made her think of Vic. She blushed a little in the cool white silence, as if Aunt Dagmar could hear her thought. She was studying Aunt Dagmar's face as she had been too polite to study it in life. Aunt Dagmar had been a small, tight woman, tight with her money and her time, tight with everything. It was a legacy from the thirties, when she had been so desperate to help Uncle Valdimar save the farm that she had hired out to do whatever grinding work she could find, scrubbing floors at the insane asylum or pulling a plow like a mule. She had starved herself and her children so much that her older daughters had died of pneumonia when they were seven and nine years old. Chris had been an only child then until the Depression ended, and Aunt Dagmar had gone on to bear two more daughters when she was close to fifty. She had been a tight woman, but in her later years she had disciplined herself to perform acts of kindness that went so much against her nature that Kim marveled at them now, sitting there studying that empty profile.

Aunt Dagmar used to make goulash and give it away to one of the poor families her church had adopted, telling Kim when

Kim asked why the Jensens didn't eat it themselves that they were used to their simple suppers. She would crochet baby sweaters for rummage sales and buy clothes and furniture for burned-out families, and Kim realized that even the taking in of a stray child from Virginia had been another forced act of kindness. Aunt Dagmar had saved most of Kim's board money and given it to her after her break with the Severs so she could afford to finish college.

Kim had always been embarrassed by the effort it had taken for Aunt Dagmar to do anything kind. A compliment on a report card or a gracious word to a high-school friend would come from a grim face and pursed lips that used to mortify Kim when other people were around to see how mean-spirited Aunt Dagmar was underneath. Yet Kim saw now that these kindnesses of Aunt Dagmar's wrung from a soul that was tight by nature represented a triumph for her, a widow's mite of goodness worth more than all the easy, mindless giving of someone who was naturally generous.

Colin Sanderlin used to give away his jackets and shoes, books and paintings and the answers to exam questions as a flower gives off fragrance, shedding himself mindlessly into the void of other people's needs. Yet he had been raised by Bible-belt Christians who routinely gave themselves to others, so where was the triumph in that? It was so hard to live against the grain of one's own nature. And perhaps that was Darcy's explanation. Kim had thought more about her mother in the past few months than she had in the six years since Darcy's death, seeing in Aunt Dagmar's dying an echo of that long-ago summer. It was as if she had absent-mindedly forgotten to mourn. She was only beginning to do it now.

Darcy had been a child, weak and willful, playful and gay, so absorbed in her own narrow life that she could be charming and mean-spirited in a single gesture. That doctor's appointment made on Kim's birthday with the excuse that she could buy a gift in Richmond had been typical. But what if that were just Darcy's nature? What if she were made of weaker stuff than Aunt Dagmar, so she couldn't overcome the handicap of who she was? It seemed to Kim in a flash of insight that Darcy's being true to who she was had been no more a sin than Colin's kindness had been a virtue. And then there was Vic.

After almost a year of being obsessed with Vic so she had trouble thinking of anything else, Kim was still being surprised by quirks that made her realize she didn't know him very well. She wanted to know him utterly, to be inside him, to *be* him as she had not wanted to be anyone since she had loved Bobby Sever more than ten years before. Yet by now she knew quite a lot about Vic.

Vic had four sisters and a cowed mother and a bull of a father so sharp and cynical, so disapproving that Vic had been a sprint-car champion at nineteen because his father had once remarked it took some guts to drive them sprint cars. But even his sprint-car championship, earned after a concussion and a broken arm, hadn't won his father over. So Vic had gone on to stock cars and then to Indy cars, steadily escalating the speeds and the stakes in an effort to get some paternal reaction. He should have known it was hopeless. Even winning the Indianapolis 500 hadn't done it. Indeed, his father was in a permanent snit because he couldn't get through the crowd to Victory Lane on the day Vic won the Indy. He hadn't attended a race of Vic's in three years. Yet Vic went right on trying. He didn't realize he was doing it for his father. He had been enraged once when Kim suggested that possibility. Now another Indy was coming at the end of May, and already Kim's stomach was knotting at the thought of it.

The month of May last year had been a giddy round of parties and practice laps and sexual frenzy while the absolute conviction grew in Kim that Vic was going to die at the end of the month. She had tried to be brave, but by the last week in May she had been begging him to pull out of the race. It came to a head at the dinner that was given on the Thursday before the race to honor the pit crew whose driver had qualified with the fastest time. Winning the pole position was an honor almost akin to winning the race itself, and since the pole-sitter that year was Derek Anderson, Vic's closest friend, Vic was in high spirits. Vic himself had qualified seventh fastest, which put him on the inside of the third row of the thirty-three-car grid. Two senior drivers were the favorites that year, but Derek and Vic and a couple of others were thought to have excellent chances to win.

Kim's first weeks in Vic's world had been an overload of amazing discoveries, not the least of which was Vic's fondness and even his reverence for his crew chief. Here was a greasy-haired buffoon in his forties whose hands bore a permanent rime of dirt, yet Vic catered and deferred to him. They had been together for six years, through two car owners and innumerable sponsors. Vic had even said a couple of times that if Jelly quit racing then he would, too. Jelly was between wives, so the three of them sat together at the pole mechanics' dinner. Kim didn't say much while they were eating. She concentrated on the speeches. But the first thing she said when she turned to Vic afterward was, "You know you don't need the money. Why, I'd even *pay* you if . . . ."

Vic said to Jelly, "Straighten her out, will you?" and snapped out of his chair to go and look for Derek. Kim picked up her teaspoon, blinking to see it. All she could think was that Vic had three more days to live.

"You've never seen him race, have you?" Jelly was straining his beer-swilling voice into a gentleness that made it waver and crack.

"I saw him qualify. That was enough."

"He's good."

"He's crashed before."

Jelly picked up his own teaspoon in hands that were oddly paw-like, thick and flat with short, blunt fingers. Like Lou's hands, Jelly's were always busy.

"Do you know why he's good? He's got the sense to be afraid. He's scared out of his mind. So he goes through all these rituals. No sex for a week. Like that. Then he goes to Mass the morning of the race even though he's not Catholic. He gets in that car completely at peace an' drives the hell out of it."

Kim gave Jelly a brief, shocked glance and ducked away, blinking at her spoon. She and Vic had not been able to stop having sex last Saturday night, so he had decided finally it would be all right as long as he didn't climax. He had continued to make love to her in every way but intercourse, joking about his discomfort and what he was going to do to her next week, until finally last night he had misjudged and come anyway. He had been so upset that he had gone home right away, although by tonight he had gotten over it somehow. Now Kim was afraid it would happen again. Unless once was enough all by itself to jinx him.

"It's not them rituals that does it, honey. If he makes a mistake that don't mean nothin'."

So Kim realized Jelly knew they were sleeping together. Everybody knew they were sleeping together. That people knew about the things Vic was doing to Kim was such a keen new humiliation that tears throbbed hot behind her eyes. She lifted her chin to keep the tears back and looked off away from Jelly, trying to spot Vic in the cheery crush. Between two bickering drivers she glimpsed him with Derek's sister, Janice, dancing without music with his hands clasped loosely behind her back while he talked to her. Vic had dated Janice off and on for years. He had insisted to Kim that they were only friends.

By Sunday, Kim had made peace with herself enough to go to the Speedway for the race, although she wouldn't sit with Derek's family. She took a seat high in the grandstand with Vic's youngest sister, who was the only family member willing to defy his father and attend the race. Hannah had Vic's thin blond hair and his gentle, graceful mannerisms that Kim assumed must have come from their mother. She kept darting glances behind her, as if her father might surprise her at any moment.

From the top of the grandstand the cars looked like flat toy missiles inside four thick tires. When the singing ended and their engines were started, they set up an unearthly whine over a roar of guttural power that made Kim tremble and grind her teeth with building terror. She hadn't seen Vic that morning. Now she would never see him again.

Vic's car was easy to spot because it was the only black spider on the track. There it was on the inside of the third row, moving with thirty-two others as they accelerated toward a hundred miles per hour while they were still in grid formation and inches apart. Kim gasped as the colorful lines of cars zagged fast around the turn below her. She had heard one of the drivers saying proudly that this was the most dangerous moment in all of sports. The track was two and a half miles around, so huge that the cars were just dull specks as they floated along the far side. Kim took a shuddering breath.

When they came around for the first lap after the green flag fell, there were six cars fiercely bunched, battling at almost two hundred miles per hour for the lead position. Kim made out Derek's car, gold and red, and Vic's car right behind it. She took another breath and let it out. She lifted her chin and adjusted her shoulders.

"He likes to lay back at first." Hannah was fidgeting and twisting her hands.

The leaders were gone again, trailing a gaudy dust of non-contenders. All around Kim, people were sitting down, chatting and scratching, settling in happily for three hours of this, so tightly packed in the stands that they gave off a gamey, humming smell of life. Kim felt ready to bolt at any moment. She heard the leaders again before she saw them, a rising whine and then a rumbling roar that had some crazies down in front whooping and clapping. The cars were still bunched in a frantic clump, and Vic was right in the middle of them, streaking along inches above the track as if he were steering a bullet.

"They're going to crash," Kim murmured. As she said it there was a high, thin crack followed by a long shriek of metal and screaming. Those in front stood, but Kim stood faster. She saw three cars spinning into the corner, a fiery vortex careening off the wall, spewing pieces and bouncing tires. The black car behind them seemed to flip like a coin in surreal slow motion to land on its tires sixty feet away.

"Oh lordy, lordy," Hannah moaned above four hundred thousand collective gasps. It was the last thing Kim heard before she started to scream. Nothing could quiet her, not the arms of strangers nor Hannah's pleading nor the pageant of horror on the track below. They had red-flagged the race so they could clear the track. Kim stared down at the ambulances and wreckers and the swarm of people, the two drivers on stretchers and a third who limped from the husk of his car to the thin cheers of spectators. That they weren't taking Vic out of his car was the greatest horror of all, an indication that he was already dead. Then Kim noticed Jelly in the crowd down there, spitting and gesturing furiously.

"They're startin' his car." Hannah held Kim's hands in hers while she craned like a bird. Then Kim heard the single tiny roar.

124

She trembled into silence as the knot of men parted and the flat black spider scurried off toward the pits. Then soon there were cars on the track again and Vic's car was among them, blipping past in a black blur amid the streaks of color while the announcer said something kindly about Vic Engstrom's courage. Over the busyness of chatting and scratching came a ripple of applause.

That crash flamed in Kim's mind and roared in her ears. She watched every lap in an agony of terror, as if all that kept Vic's car on the track was the force of her own eyes. Vic had sprained his back, but he went on in pain to finish the race and come in tenth. What pleased him about the Indy that year was the spur it gave to his reputation for luck, something prized by drivers even above courage and talent.

Vic's legend had begun three years ago, the year he won the Indy. As a green driver with just one prior Indy start, he drove around two crashes late in the race to overtake the leader, Silvio Fascetti, who was nursing a car with mechanical problems. "I never saw him," Fascetti was quoted as saying good-naturedly, giving Vic the name he had carried forever after. Most of the drivers kept their nicknames secret from the public, but Vic was so proud to have been named by the legendary Fascetti, the greatest driver ever, that all his cars carried a tiny scrawled "Phantom" on their doors in place of his name.

Kim had managed in the past year to encapsulate her fears, to attend and even to enjoy the 500-mile races in Michigan and Pocono where Vic had won and come in sixth. He had seemed to float in those races on a cloud of safety. She hardly feared for him at all. But the Indy was another matter. It might have been the awful size of the track, the nervousness of trying to win on home turf, or simply that God's-eye view of what might have been the last moments of his life. But it was spring again. Another Indy was weeks away, and Kim knew with a certainty that dried her throat that this time Vic wouldn't be so lucky.

———◆———

When the door-pull clanged, Kim assumed it was the undertaker. She went down the stairs and opened the door to find Lou standing on Aunt Dagmar's step. He was glancing over his shoulder at three women with toddlers who were staring from beyond the picket fence; since *People* had run an article about Kim and Vic in January, this house had seldom been without its gawkers.

The familiar sight of Lou made Kim feel alive and normal after her week spent losing her battle with death. And she was charmed to notice that his mannerisms were those of a man much taller: he ducked his head and restricted his arms and took tiny steps inside Aunt Dagmar's house, as if he felt too large for it.

"She's gone," Kim said as she helped him off with his raincoat. "I'm waiting for the undertaker."

"Oh. I'm sorry."

Kim wanted to say, "No you're not. One more week of playing president would have driven you right up the wall." Instead she said, "Thank you. She didn't suffer."

Lou adjusted his shoulders inside his jacket as he looked around at Aunt Dagmar's low-ceilinged hallway with its yellowing pink-sprigged paper. He said, "The packet came from California. And Harvey sent ads and press releases. I thought you'd like something to do."

Kim took a Federal Express envelope and two manila folders from Lou's hands. "What's this? You've got the first quarter's numbers?"

"Take a look," Lou said with a crooked smile. "We grossed fifteen million in three months even without California. We'll show a loss, but it's just depreciation. They're great numbers, Kim. I say offering forty percent of the company for ten million dollars is aiming too low."

RICH AND FAMOUS

"Good. Let's sell less."

"Let's raise more."

They exchanged puckish smiles, although their days of play-fighting about this would soon be over. The work on the stock offering was almost complete, with little left to do but fix the price.

"So what's the final total for California? How many franchisees balked at the changes?"

"None. We'll be starting with all fifty."

"Well, that's good news," Kim said as they headed up the stairs. She hooked her hair behind her ear and slipped from its folder Harvey's sheaf of ads for California. They had never advertised in Indiana, but with their franchisees paying fifty thousand dollars as well as hefty sums for food and supplies they had decided to spend half their initial fees on a California advertising campaign.

Lou stopped in Aunt Dagmar's bedroom doorway. His Adam's apple rose and fell. "Come in." Kim glanced at him as she sat down in her chair. She was liking the trend of these ads, which featured business people and families choosing their motels for the small "Taste of Home" signs and the bright pink doortags. Their first task in California would be to sign up motels, which were the ads' main targets.

"Aren't you supposed to – you know – cover her up?"

"What, you mean with a sheet? Don't tell me you're afraid of her."

Lou was such an imposing man, with his craggy face and gray hair and his expansive way of moving, that Kim was always freshly surprised to see how tender he was. He said, "Believe it or not, I've never seen a body without the makeup."

"Have a seat. Keep me company. It won't be much longer. Hey, look at this – did you see this one for TV? All the cars and trucks piling in off the highway, and here's this cowboy leading his horse? Isn't that cute?"

"It really doesn't bother you, does it?"

"What, that she's dead? Of course it bothers me."

"The body."

"Oh. Why should it? She looks the same, only paler."

"You amaze me," Lou said softly from behind Kim's shoulder. "I keep thinking you're this vulnerable child, but you're tougher than I am."

"Something does bother me, though." But then the fact that she was going to speak it aloud made Kim's throat catch.

"What?" Lou asked when she didn't go on.

"Do you know, I never told her I loved her? Not once?" The horror of that made Kim's voice crack and her eyes fill so quickly that even tipping up her chin couldn't keep them from spilling. She had never told her mother that she loved her, either. There had been some need in her to hear it first. "If I'd *said* it, I'm sure she'd have said it, too," she insisted through lips so stiff that she could hardly make out her own words. A sob caught her like a sharp hiccup.

Lou drew Kim out of her chair, crushing the ads between them. He hugged her, whispering, "She knew, she knew," while Kim tried to swallow her crying.

"Hello?" Vic said from the doorway. He stepped gracefully into the room, looking long and elegant in the leather jeans and jacket he had worn on the plane. His face as he glanced from one to the other bore its usual expression of fey sadness, but Kim read amusement in the set of his cheeks as he gravely shook Lou's hand.

"Vic! You're home!" she babbled foolishly as she rushed into his arms. He kissed her a public kiss and then stood holding her, studying her face. She looked up at the perfection of his clean planes and angles, his bright-blond hair curved precisely by his helmet, his pink nose and cheeks from his week in the sun. Even the droop of weariness under his eyes and his golden stubble were beautiful. After a year, she still couldn't get enough of looking at him. "Vic just got back from Phoenix," Kim said to Lou while she looked at Vic. "He won the first race of the year. Now he's going for the championship."

Vic had always limited himself to stock cars and 500-mile Indy-car races, but this year he was trying to win the PPG-Indy Car World Series, which would mean a dozen races all over the country between now and the middle of October.

"Don't *say* that." Vic gave Kim's rump a playful slap that might have been a prelude to lovemaking. He insisted he wasn't super-stitious, but it seemed to Kim that he was so extremely supersti-tious that even to admit it would have been bad luck.

"Congratulations," Lou said smoothly. Kim glanced at him. She was saddened to see that Lou really could not abide Vic. To see Vic touching Kim could actually make him squirm. For her sake, he showed Vic a cold, stiff pleasantness that carried beneath it so much tension that Kim kept them apart as much as possible.

Vic looked at Lou, then at the bed. He released Kim, studying Aunt Dagmar's face, and caught Kim's index finger with his in their private gesture.

"I tried to get back in time. How are you doing?"

"Fine. I'm fine."

"The real relatives never showed up?"

"They were here."

Lou cleared his throat and said, "Kim is a real relative."

Vic glared at Lou. Kim watched his mind framing a retort, but the edge of menace in Lou's voice seemed to freeze him. The bell-pull clanged while Kim was nervously looking from face to face. She blurted, "That must be the undertaker!"

"I'll get it." Lou turned while he held Vic's eyes. Kim let out a breath as she watching him leave the room.

"Everybody's okay? Nothing happened?"

"There was a coming-together at the start. A rookie hit the

wall and took Derek with him. They're both okay, although Derek's new Penske was trashed."

"That's all?"

"That's all," Vic said woodenly. Kim knew he hated the way she insisted on hearing about the crashes. Other wives and girl-friends kept their fears to themselves.

Vic and Lou waited downstairs while Kim helped the under-taker and his son arrange Aunt Dagmar on their stretcher. All the way down the stairs she was giving them directions. "Just finger waves. She never wore it fancy. And no makeup – I mean, she never wore makeup. But she was plumper, you know? This dress won't fit."

"They can handle it," Lou said as she reached the first floor. He drew Kim away from the stretcher with an arm at her waist, but Vic caught Kim's hand and pulled her out of Lou's arms and into his.

"It's over, baby." Vic hooked her hair behind her ear so he could kiss her temple and her long, pale scar. "You were perfect. But it's over."

The hearse and Vic's Ferrari had attracted fifty or sixty housewives and retirees. There would be photographers there, too. During the past year, Kim had developed a paranoia about photographers that made her fix her face in a stiff smile whenever she ventured out of doors. "Not now! There's been a death!" Vic snarled at two women trampling the tulip bed beside the door while they waited to ask for autographs.

Lou slipped in front of Kim to clear the way. She heard his polite, "One side, please. Excuse us," as Vic rushed her toward his car.

This level of fame was brand new. Ever since that January *People* article had named Kim and Vic "The Couple of the Eighties," it was impossible for either of them to go anywhere without being mobbed. Sitting there waiting for the death last night, Chris Jensen had even said it might be better if Kim didn't come to his mother's funeral. Kim had thought that being famous would be fun. She had imagined respect and adulation, people smiling and being nice to her. But fame was turning out to be crowds who didn't care about Kim at all. What they were starved for was this intangible aura that clung to her like a lucky smell, and she thought they would be willing to tear her limb from limb to get it.

Vic's Ferrari was a 1973 Daytona, at eleven years old already appreciating in value. It looked like a racer with its sleek air of rapid motion, and its doors bore the tiny word "Phantom" in gold script. There wasn't a soul in Indiana who wouldn't know whose car this was, Kim realized as Vic opened her door against the legs of people standing there. Then he stepped fast around the front of his car as if he were moving through a swarm of insects and opened his door so wide that it hit a woman standing at a respectful distance. He started his car with a roar that shocked the bystanders away from it and drove off as they scattered before him like chickens in the dust.

———◆———

"*Twenty*," Kim insisted.

"You're dreaming," muttered the officious lawyer sitting two seats away down Kim's brand-new marble boardroom table. Although she had seen him at three prior meetings, she couldn't remember his name. She thought that might be because no self-respecting name would have him.

"Kim dear," Steve Vorovich said patiently from the seat next to hers, "your company is barely three years old . . . ."

"Not *even* three," the other man muttered to his pencil. He was a tiny young attorney, a caricature in pinstripes and hornrims who spoke with a booming bluster that seemed to be a way to make himself feel taller.

Steve cast the man a warning glower. Steve's firm was the lead underwriter for Kim's stock offering, so he held the higher rank. He said, "I'll admit we're seeing some aggressive things now. Companies going public with a good idea. But in a way, it's easier to ask the moon for a stock like that than it is when you've got some track record."

"*What* track record? For the first six months she lived in a shoebox! We had to footnote the hell out of the whole first year, and *still* the accountants had trouble signing."

"But they did sign. Lay off, Jim."

Jim. That was his name.

Kim gazed to the left away from them, out over downtown Indianapolis. Tall glass boxes reflected so much strident light on this mid-May morning that she had to squint. Perhaps Vic's crew had already solved the problem with his right front wing. He might be out there even now, strapped in, taking his practice laps. And thinking of Vic reminded Kim that her period was now ten days late. Ten days. That was all she needed.

". . . so it seems only reasonable you give these brave new partners of yours a good price. They deserve to make a profit, too."

"What? I'm sorry. What did you say?"

"Look," Jim broke in with exasperated patience, "you're going to have two and a half million shares. You sell a million for ten dollars apiece, that's ten million dollars. That's a heck of a lot for forty percent of a bright idea, don't you think? And if you ask *twenty* dollars a share, you're saying this company is worth fifty million dollars. *Fifty million dollars*, Miss Bonner! Can't you see the craziness of that?"

The door opened then and Ellie came in, stepping stiffly across the rose-tweed carpet. They had been in these city offices for barely a month, and it seemed to Kim they were all still being too polite to the furniture.

"Here she is. Steve? Jim? You know our executive vice president, Ellie Walters?"

"Miss Walters," Jim muttered, nodding.

Ellie was tiny and desperately thin, her upper arms as frail as wrists. Kim had been trying since the day they met to put some weight on Ellie, who wore Darcy's old habitual half-smile for more or less Darcy's reason: she seemed to live each moment expecting another blow from somewhere.

"Gentlemen, Ellie has just revised the numbers," Kim said as she slid Ellie's sheaf of computer sheets across the pink marble toward Steve. She flipped through them quickly, craning to see. "Look, Steve. Look here. We'll do a hundred million dollars worth of business this year."

"Irrelevant!" snapped Jim.

Steve said, "Kim dear, listen to me. You can say you've suddenly discovered you're going to do a billion dollars of business this year, but the red herring – the preliminary prospectus – has been out for three weeks. The agreements are signed. We're taking checks. If you're going to need that ten million dollars to fund your summer expansion, I'm afraid you're going to have to go with the price that's set."

"But what if we've got to raise more money later? What then?"

"You'll do what everyone else does, dear. You'll sell more stock."

Kim was coming to hate the paternal way in which so many men dealt with her. Even Lou, although he was less than ten years older than she was. His prematurely gray hair and professorial style had from the beginning made his role in her life seem to be more supervisory and even parental, but he really wasn't that much older. And now he had maneuvered her into doing this stock offering. Good idea or bad, it was a railroading.

"I won't lose control." Kim gathered Ellie's computer sheets in front of her as if to protect them.

"It's ten dollars or nothing."

"*Jim . . . .*"

"That's okay, Steve." Kim was studying the numbers on that final sheet, mindlessly checking the computer's arithmetic. "I called you here today to see these numbers. I really think the numbers should make a difference . . . ."

"You'll be glad to know we think we can raise the money," Steve interrupted her kindly. "You've still got a lot of debt, but our brokers say there's interest after that article in *People*. You shouldn't have told them about the offering, but you did, and you'll get away with it. Now Harvey's planning another splash for the Indy. He says we'll have features in *Life* and *Newsweek* that skirt the 'quiet time' rules. You're selling this offering yourself, my dear. We're just taking the checks."

———————

Kim had been trying for months to lure Lou out to see her new house being built. Ellie and Jerry were always glad to come, but Kim felt more and more as if sharing this thrill with them was showing off. They couldn't afford a two-million-dollar house, and Kim could afford one largely thanks to their combined efforts. Lou had been spending so much time in the air, meeting with brokers to push the stock offering and holding the hands of California franchisees, that it wasn't until the third Wednesday in June that Kim talked him into making a visit. He had promised to give her that whole afternoon, but the offering was so close to being subscribed that he lingered in his office until after three, making calls to brokers.

Kim waited in her own office, feeling sulky, refusing calls from *Newsweek* and *The Indianapolis Star*. She was propping decorating boards against her desk to catch the window light and walking around to see from every angle her decorator's notion of colors and fabrics for her new house. But it was all wrong. She had told that man just what she wanted, down to the crystals and

Hummels and the yellow cord for the drapery tiebacks. Yet he persisted in trying to talk her into these sleek, perfectly-decorated rooms that weren't *her* at all. Kim was crouched behind her desk, writing comments on the boards, when she heard her door whisper open. She craned up. Lou was standing in her doorway, puffing and smiling. "You can stop praying now," he said around his pipe stem.

"Oh. No. I'm just straightening out this decorator." Kim stood up quickly. She felt compelled to gesture at the boards, so Lou crossed her office and stepped around her desk to look at them.

"Pretty classy. That's for the house?"

"But it's wrong. It's awful. That's supposed to be silver damask on the living-room walls, but he gives me this *blue* he says goes better with yellow. What does he know? And look at the yellow. A sickly lemon. I said *yellow!*"

"It looks fine to me," Lou said, puffing. His smoke was a sweet male breath on the air.

"Are you ready to go?"

"Aren't you going to ask how the offering went?"

"Of course it sold out. Who wouldn't buy stock at fifty cents on the dollar?"

Lou looked at Kim. He took the pipe from his mouth. "The first thing you ever said to me was you didn't want to know what was reasonable because you were about to do the impossible. Kim, three years ago you didn't have a penny to your name. Now you've got a net worth of fifteen million dollars. Can't you even act surprised?"

"I'm surprised you're finally giving me an hour. That surprises me."

"Can I help it if the boss spends all her time decorating? *Somebody's* got to work around here."

———◆———

Kim had bought her seventy-five-acre farm for its wooded hill set back from the street. It was forty-five minutes from the city, on a quiet road lined with developing subdivisions of formal homes on spacious lots. She turned Vic's red pickup onto her new access road, driving past the cellar hole of the farmhouse and the beams of the barn, explaining as she drove that those buildings were coming out and these trees would be thinned to improve the approach.

"You knocked down a house?"

"It was a funny little shack. You should have seen it."

The hill wasn't tall enough, the trees weren't large enough to give Kim's house the approach it deserved. And now the wing didn't look right. She had insisted the framing be altered four times as they strived for perfect proportions, but now that the siding was on she could see it still wasn't exactly right.

"Good lord," said Lou.

"This will be a circle with a fountain in the middle. A cherub with a water jug. It's being made in Italy."

"What is all this costing?"

"Too much." Kim slid from Vic's truck while she studied the roofline and the brand-new pediments over the windows. From this angle it was looking better. She came around the truck and gave Lou a hug, loving the thick bearish feel of him. "Thank you for working so hard. Now come see. I'm dying for you to see." She unlocked her front door as she added, "Hey, the big rumor is your ex-wife just remarried. Is it true?"

"It's true."

"Are you glad?"

"Glad?" he asked lightly as he stepped into her foyer. "The joke is she married some plumber because professors don't make enough money. But I'm making twenty times what I made as a professor. And maybe twice what a plumber makes," he joked with a sad smile.

"That's what she gets for not believing in you." Then Kim was struck by the thought of Lou married, as a child will suddenly realize a parent has an independent life. Lou kissing a wife, sharing private gestures, making love to a wife as Vic made love to Kim. To kill that vision she blurted, "Look at this floor, will you? I said gray-veined marble. They've got it all wrong."

"It's gray."

"But it's not *veined*. It'll have to come out. I don't know what's wrong with these people."

"This is unbelievable. I've never seen anything like it. What holds up that staircase?"

"Isn't it great? You can run right down as if it were a slide."

"You're going to spend a million dollars on this house."

"More," Kim said lightly, glancing around, loving the clean smells of new wood and plaster and fresh-cut marble.

"You're spending too much." Lou sounded peevish. "Too much on yourself. Too much on me. It kills me to take these enormous fees when the company is running a deficit."

"Come on, sailor. Don't be a crank. We've earned it."

Kim had taken to calling Lou "sailor" after the previous summer's company picnic, when he had stood to help her out of a boat and capsized them into the water. She had meant it as a dig at first, but now she used it to try to cut through their working formality to the man himself. Like Bobby Sever's old taunts, it had become a way to express feelings too complicated to name. She glanced at Lou, liking the way his presence made her house feel like a home. He filled it with his cozy normality, letting her envision appliances humming and the comfortable ticking of clocks. But he looked so tired. His cheeks were hollowed and his moist eyes blinked too often behind his glasses.

Kim had spent the months since Aunt Dagmar's death working on her house and playing with Vic as she turned her mind with wonder toward the changes in her body. It had been a respite from her ten years of working eighteen-hour days. And she had lately begun to wonder why she was working so hard, just what it was that she was trying to achieve; she even had wondered, feeling abashed, whether she was still trying to please her mother even seven years after her mother's death. She didn't know what she had been trying to achieve, but whatever it was, she thought she must have achieved it. So Kim had slacked off over the past few months, and the more she had pulled back, the more Lou had felt compelled to take her place. And now he was feeling sad about his ex-wife, too. Kim couldn't bear to see him sad.

"Come on! Be happy!" She grabbed his hands on impulse and pulled him in circles across her foyer, grinning, willing him to give her his crooked smile. "Look at that fireplace! Those big windows! Isn't it the loveliest house on earth?" Lou grinned around his pipe stem in spite of himself as he play-stumbled with Kim into her right-hand living room. "See the dining room? Those big windows? That's for sunlight in the morning. Oh, come on, love it with me! California is taking off. We'll be in fifteen states by the end of the year."

"But why so much *space?*"

"I love space."

"What do you have in this house? Fifty rooms? How many children do you plan to have?"

"At least one." Then Kim bit it off. She hadn't mentioned the baby to anyone. Keeping it a secret had made it feel more precious, somehow; and anyway, she didn't know what to say. People would expect her to talk about plans, things like setting up a nursery and marrying the father. But she had no plans. Lou was giving Kim a level look that meant that he was reading her mind. If he hadn't been away so much, he probably would have guessed her secret weeks ago.

"Tell me."

"Tell you what?"

"Whatever is putting that little pinch at the corner of your mouth."

Kim stepped away from him, making sharp echoes in the empty house. She thought as she did it that she was moving out of his striking range. "I'm pregnant." Saying those words to Lou was so easy that Kim felt a thrill of relief, as if he were shouldering for her yet another burden. But she saw his face go slack and then tighten. He spun away, taking an audible breath.

"How far — how far along are you?"

"Two months. More or less."

Kim couldn't talk about details with Lou. That felt like too much intimacy. She realized now that her pregnancy was proof of all the things she and Vic had been doing, and she couldn't bear for Lou to know about that. But still, he must have known.

"You're going to have it? The baby?"

"What, abortion? You're suggesting abortion?"

"You're going to marry him, then?"

"He doesn't even know. Look at me, Lou. It's not the end of the world."

"He doesn't *know?*"

"He's been doing all these races. There's never been a good time to tell him. But I will tell him. Tonight I will. He failed to qualify in Portland, did I tell you that? It's the first time in three years. Jelly let his nephew work on the car. Vic is furious. He's coming home tonight."

"Are you going to marry him?"

"Boy, can you picture Vic as a father? I keep seeing him giving the baby these go-carts before he can even walk. That's the thing about auto-racing. It runs in families."

"Auto-racing is what you do when you've got more testosterone than brains!" Lou shouted. His voice echoed in the empty house. He stomped into the dining room, seeming to relish his noise. "It's crazy! *He's* crazy! You can see that, can't you? Even in love? You can see the man is crazy?"

"Watch it."

"I hate all this! I hate everything about him, and now you're *pregnant?* For the love of sense, didn't it occur to you to use protection?"

"Enough!" Kim couldn't bear to talk about this with Lou. He was filling her dining room with ringing steps that echoed in the vast silence and made her feel panicky, as a child feels panic when she glimpses any weakness in a parent.

"It won't make any difference. Probably we will get married. Sure. He's talked about it."

"That's just what he wants! Can't you see that? The baby? It's a trick to get your assets."

"Oh, is that what this is about?"

"Don't marry him."

"He doesn't need my money. He's a millionaire. That's why we're The Couple of the Eighties. We're equally successful in two different fields. That's why the . . . ."

"He's not even *close!*"

"But he just won the Indy for the second time! He's leading in points for the championship! He's going to make *two* million dollars this year, which is more than I'm taking in salary now . . . ."

"He's beneath you," Lou said in the deep, gentle, melodious voice that made Kim think of cellos.

"And he's . . . ."

"Don't marry him. Have his baby if you must, but don't marry him." Lou stiffened as he said that, as if he were accepting an expected blow from behind. There was a sad drawing-down of his cheeks and the up-tilted outer corners of his eyes. Kim had to fight her need to run and hug him.

"He's the father."

"Don't marry him!"

Kim couldn't bear to see Lou's distress. She ran into his arms, a clatter of shoes and a deep, enveloping, smothering hug that smelled of sweet tobacco. Hugging Vic was all tautness and titillation; hugging Lou felt safe and protected and loved.

"I want a baby."

"I know." His hand trembled as he stroked her hair. "I understand. I know."

———◆———

Vic's German shepherd was barking his dispirited chirps below the bathroom window. He was an old mountain of a dog with a tiny voice that should have belonged to a Chihuahua; Vic teased him about it sometimes, ridiculing him with cuts to his maleness while the dog hung his head in misery. He was too old to accept with grace the fact that while Kim was living there he had to sleep outside.

Kim was soaking in Vic's footed tub under the open window, sorting with little sniffs the complex smells of the night. Under sweet whispers of flowers and drying hay she caught the pungency of the dog and the far-off musk of a skunk. The smells reminded her of Virginia, so she could close her eyes and imagine she was soaking in the lean-to tub and smelling hay drying in the sloping field that led down to Redrabbit Run. After the first cutting, Mr. Auberdine would turn his cows in there because the field was too poor to take a second cutting.

Vic should be home any time now. As the minutes passed, Kim's swelling anticipation was making her feel ready to burst. Never could she have imagined how complex sexual feeling was, how fear and rapture, pain and pleasure blended like trumpets and violins to create such exquisite music. But now she understood the Mrs. Severs and the Aunt Dagmars. She couldn't imagine their men doing these things, she blushed to imagine them submitting, but oh, lying there naked and waiting for Vic, she surely did understand them. She ought to be in bed when he got home. If she were in the bathroom she might whimsically feel the need to fight him, and that might tip him beyond the line between titillation and genuine anger. A few times before he had crossed that line. Kim wondered how other couples dealt with these problems.

As she leaned for her towel and stood from the tub, Kim tried not to speculate about where Vic might have been for the past three days. Race day was Sunday. He generally came home on Monday, but now it was Wednesday. When he had called to say he was coming home tonight, she hadn't asked him where he had been. She realized now that she hadn't wanted to know.

It would be easier if they were married. Kim couldn't imagine a future without Vic; just the thought of it was a knot in her chest. She should marry him now, while she still could fit into a wedding dress. The press would have a field day when the baby was born, but that would be later. Still, the thought of marrying Vic was as discomforting as the thought of losing him.

Kim left the bathroom and rounded the corner into the bedroom while she told herself her panic was just bridal jitters. It wouldn't change anything. What could it change? They were already living together. She climbed into Vic's bed, enjoying the cool slide of the sheets, and lay still while she strained to listen for the un-muffled rumble of his airport car. He couldn't leave his Ferrari in a parking garage, so he kept for these trips the Impala he had been driving before he became a success. Maybe he would come right out and tell her where he had been for the past three days. Kim got up and went to choose a book from the four stacks she had made in the corner, and no sooner was she out of bed than she heard Vic's key in the lock downstairs. She scooted back into bed, out of breath and giggling. She had planned to pretend to be asleep, but she couldn't delay her first sight of Vic.

He walked in with a firm stride that showed his distress, all long, lean elegance and primary colors. Although he generally wore denim and leather, tonight he had on a pair of red golfing pants and a blue T-shirt that bore an obscene legend. But he was so beautiful, with his yellow hair and his sad eyes and his elegant grace. The sight of him was a shock of pleasure like candy in the mouth. Vic gave her the barest smile as he dropped his suitcase and crossed the room to kiss her. "Don't ask," he said in his musical voice. Kim watched him lever his T-shirt over his head to expose his back while she wondered, *Don't ask what? The clothes? The race? Or the three missing days? Had he been reading her mind?*

"It was Jelly's nephew. That little turd. Jelly lets him screw up the car, then he has the nerve to say I was stroking. *Stroking.* When I stood on that throttle with both feet! There was nothing *there.*" Stroking. Loafing around the track. There had been showers for the race in Wisconsin two weeks before, and a sweet-faced boy of twenty-three had hung his car on the wall. Kim hadn't been there, but she remembered the boy. He used to follow Vic around like a puppy. She remembered the way Vic's voice had trembled when he called to tell her about the crash.

"Where did you get those clothes?"

"These?" he said bitterly, kicking off his pants. "A joke. You had to be there." He was rummaging in his drawer for pajamas. Pajamas? After ten days away?

"Where have you been since Sunday?"

Vic straightened and looked at Kim. The lamplight on his back and buttocks and legs made one long, sinuous line.

"Derek led for ten laps and blew an engine. We went up to his cabin to forget about racing."

Derek had a lodge in New Hampshire that was little more

than a wooden tent. Kim and Vic had gone up last fall with Derek
and his wife to see the foliage. What Kim remembered best was
the flimsy blanket strung between the beds and the embarrassing,
appalling sounds of Derek's lovemaking.

"You went to New Hampshire? Without me?"

"Well, if you had come to the race, my pet, you'd have been
there for the party, wouldn't you?" This was the edge of a fester-
ing argument that Kim didn't want to get into now. She caught
her breath, but Vic spun to face her and bored right in. "You know
I can't race without you there! I've got a *right* to have you there!
How do you think it makes me feel, having nobody there at all?"

"Did Janice go?"

"What? To New Hampshire? Sure. I popped Sandy while
Derek had his sister. Don't change the subject."

"She *was* there, wasn't she?" Kim sat up fast in bed.

"You think you're hot stuff, don't you? Following the circuit
is beneath you?"

"I've got responsibilities . . ." But then Kim decided this wasn't
a good time to tell him about finishing the stock offering.

"So, *sell* the stupid company! Give it away! Start acting as if I
matter to you!"

Kim swallowed a little bubble of joy. She wanted to turn to
Lou and say, "See? He does love me!" But her temples were throb-
bing. "Was Janice there?"

Derek's sister had a worshipful crush on Vic that Kim had
seen that he enjoyed feeding, whispering to her sometimes and
meeting her eyes with a look whose intimacy Kim would find
chilling.

"Was she there? Of course! She's always there! *She's* the one
who's there for me when I climb out of that car. So, sure, baby,
you'd better believe I took her to New Hampshire."

Kim had kept this fear of hers squashed down so tight that
its sudden confirmation was a physical shock. "You bastard!" she

shouted while the light paled and the walls shimmered. "Get out
of here!" She fumbling away, clutching the blankets while Vic
advanced on the bed. "Go away! Leave me alone!"

He caught her wrists and twisted them behind her, gazing at
her face. He pulled her against him and toppled her under him,
stabbing her pinned arms with unbearable burning. He kissed her.
She tried to bite. He twisted her wrists together under her so he
could free a hand for slapping, but instead he tenderly stroked
her scar while he kissed her in nibbles all over her face. "I love
you. Shhh. I love you," he whispered as Kim struggled, fighting
thrills of pleasure. The thought of Vic with Janice was an agony
so intense it was arousing her unbelievably. Janice looked like her
brother, short and thickset. Derek was a sexy imp, but his face on
Janice was as serviceable as a compact car. Janice's drabness made
Kim's jealousy feel like a manageable pain.

"Why?" she whimpered.

"Shhh. Kiss me."

Kim looked up into the earnest face of this man who was
willing to drive at two hundred miles per hour but was afraid to
take showers because when he was small his father had held him
under a shower and nearly drowned him. The dear curve of his
lip, the perfect almond roundness of his eyes, the droop of yellow
hair onto his forehead made her gasp.

"I did it for you, baby. You know you're loving this. Kiss me."

Kim was agonized by Vic's awareness of all these quirks
of her psyche, these shameful thrills she couldn't have known
were part of herself until he found them out. He threw back the
blankets and kissed her all over her neck and chest, sucking at her
skin, making her squirm and whimper as he moved down over her
belly and parted her legs.

"No." She couldn't stand this. Sometimes he would use his
tongue until the pleasure was so unbearable she would be thrashing and moaning.

"Stop it. Behave yourself." He was forcing her legs apart with an impersonal politeness, as if she were a balky patient. His calmness made her feel silly about not submitting; she relaxed her thighs under the pressure of his hands. He settled in and began a rapid, furious licking so intensely pleasurable that she shrieked as the contractions began and she was flooded with waves of bright sensation.

The orgasm wouldn't stop until he did. She pushed his head away and clamped her legs. "Very nice," she heard him murmur while she curled tight, holding the feelings. Vic's enjoyment of her pleasure was a peculiar shame. She closed her eyes tight so she couldn't see him smiling. Then there was a soft motion beside her as he eased down into his place on the bed. He punched up the pillows behind his head. She opened her eyes and looked at him.

"My turn," he said. Two clear, pure notes. Kim's mind was so fogged with pleasure that it took her a minute to realize his meaning. "No! I can't. You know I can't." Vic had never found a way to force her to perform oral sex on him. Not that he hadn't tried.

"Do it." His voice was flat. "I've been going down on you for a year. It's time you returned the favor."

"Please, Vic . . . ."

"Shall I tell you how well Janice does it? Prompt that Bonner competitive spirit?"

"*No!*"

"What *is* it with you?" he shouted as he curled up to sit. "Every woman is willing to give some head, but you're too good to do even that?"

"No. No. No," she whispered, groping for the covers, rocking with misery and panic.

"*Do it!*" he shouted.

"You don't understand . . . ."

"*Now!*" Vic waited. Then he said frantically, "You selfish bitch! You make me feel like dirt! You make me feel . . . !"

Kim's eyes were squeezed shut. She didn't see it coming. But suddenly, inexplicably, she was flying through the air to fetch up hard against the front of Vic's dresser. The corner of his pajama drawer rammed her stomach with such searing agony that she felt ripped open. Kim dissolved onto the floor, doubled and retching, clutching her belly to protect her infinitesimal baby. She had never in her life dreamed of pain like this. Perhaps she was going to die. Then Vic was there, gathering her into his arms, cooing and kissing her, rocking her, whispering, "Kimberly? Baby? I'm sorry. I love you."

He cradled her, smoothing hair out of her face, using pajamas to wipe the acids welling in her mouth. Kim looked up at him through her black fog of pain to see his face constricted in anguish and real tears sparkling. She focused on his tears in wonderment as she realized with mingled relief and panic that he loved her. Only love could make him behave this way. He loved her. She tried to dwell on that. She wanted to feel love for him in return; she was desperate to believe he hadn't meant to hurt her. He was as helpless in his way, and as innocent, as Darcy had been when she had banished her daughter. He loved her, but Kim understood now that she couldn't love him in return. She looked up into his love-struck face, and she realized that in fact she nearly hated him. Their sex life was the only thing about him that she found appealing. But it seemed to her now that in some ways Vic had come to own a part of her life. She was realizing she never could send him away.

chapter seven

October 16, 1985 - August 9, 1986

Kim spent the year following the close of Taste of Home's first stock offering dreading the moment when she would have to agree to the second. Of course there would be a second offering. The men around her discussed it too easily, as if her remaining interest in her own company were a bank into which they could dip at will. And she watched with grim satisfaction as the after-market tripled the price of Taste of Home's outstanding shares, thereby validating her own judgment and putting into investors' hands the twenty million dollars that might have made a second offering unnecessary.

The price of the stock tripled in less than a year because the company did more than a hundred and twenty million dollars worth of business in 1984. That brought a lot of press notice. The cover of *Forbes* for March 18, 1985, was a witty overview of a motel with its roof removed to show every guest eating from a flowered pink box. The accompanying article predicted heavy pressure from three competitors started during 1984, but it concluded by saying that Kim Bonner was a motel-food prodigy who wouldn't let a little thing like competition stand in her way. And the price of the stock, already up sixty percent, doubled almost overnight.

This was all despite the fact that growing from fifty thousand dollars worth of business in 1981 to sixty million in 1983 and doubling every year thereafter had cost everything Kim could take in or borrow. All the kitchens were mortgaged. The trucks were leased. The bank account from which she met her three-million-dollar monthly payroll sometimes had as little as five thousand dollars in it. But she found that she couldn't increase her prices to accumulate cash because 1984 had finally brought the curse of competitors Lou had been predicting all along.

A food conglomerate named Intelco introduced Moveable Menu in the Washington, D.C. suburbs as the first Taste of Home stock was being offered in June. And before the California franchisees were solvent that summer, startup companies in Los Angeles and Sacramento were using Taste of Home's advertising to promote themselves as cheaper, more efficient alternatives. The better-quality motels and the chains still opted for the industry leader, but the marginal ones did not: by November of 1984, the California franchisees were reporting that they were losing one sale out of three. Kim saw that as blatant theft. She responded with a flurry of meetings to consider price reductions and sales contests, but in fact her pricing was already so tight that she couldn't do anything without compromising her Three Guarantees of delivery time, quality, and temperature. After a night spent hugging her pillow and talking it over with Vic, she ceded to her competitors the bottom third of the California market.

The frozen-food project proved to be the final financial straw. So many letters had been received asking for frozen entrees to be eaten at home that Jerry spent the first part of 1985 exploring the possibilities. Kim liked his ideas at first. Shipping the food in bulk seemed more efficient than making six daily trips to each of two thousand client motels. Her board approved the project in June on the strength of Jerry's preliminary numbers, and by the time his consultants reported in August that a full-scale project could cost eighty million dollars, they felt too committed to back out. By the morning of the October board meeting, it was obvious there would have to be a second offering.

———◆———

The Taste of Home board of directors met on the third Wednesday of every month, spending the morning sampling foods that scented the room with spices and wine while Kim worked her way through a loose agenda. That October board meeting felt deceptively usual, with people murmuring as they sampled the food while sunlight picked sparkles from the crystal-flower centerpiece that Kim's employees had given her for her twenty-seventh birthday. Kim shifted and sat back in her chair to see whether a change in posture might make her calmer. What the board did today would determine whether she kept control of her company or gave it up.

"I've got an announcement to make," Kim said as Connie Westlake noted the final routine vote. "You're surprised to find Lou still here after we gave him that farewell party in August. Well, Lou liked his party so much he's just signed another two-year contract. It's not that B.U. didn't want him. But he decided teaching was pretty dull after his years of clowning in the real world."

Kim's effort to be funny sounded so strained that all she saw were blank faces. Lou saved her by adding easily, "I told them I'd been making half a million dollars a year. Of course I assumed they could meet that salary. Imagine my surprise when I found they couldn't. So, what could I do? A man's got to eat." He smiled. A few of the others chuckled.

The common-knowledge story was that Lou had spent two days teaching before he walked out and quit. The reality was more complicated. After three weeks of missing him, Kim had flown to Boston and sat in on one of his classes with her hair in stubby braids, and by the end of the day he had negotiated another two-year sabbatical. Kim had been hoping he would quit altogether. Now she was going to have to do the same thing over again in 1987.

"Welcome back, Lou," she said while Marshall Cavendish, the skinny attorney, stood and shook Lou's hand across the table. Marshall was a tall and balding man with buck teeth and no chin whatsoever. And he liked Lou. With his constant patient efforts at peacemaking, Lou gave even Marshall the impression that he was on his side. Lou functioned as a special consultant to the board of directors, so he attended every meeting in his own name-plated chair.

"Now, on to the first item on our agenda. Are we going to do a second offering so we can expand into frozen food? I assume you've read the proposal Jerry sent around." Nine morning faces turned to hers, while Vic stood with his boot on the window ledge and gazed down at the shadowy city. Sunlight gleamed on the shoulders of his blue silk suit and flamed in his yellow hair. Vic was so claustrophobic that he spent these meetings pacing off whatever screaming childhood memories the room brought to mind; yet he was able to drive a three-hour race crammed into a carbon-fiber tub so tight it functioned as a second skin. He even seemed to relish the womb of that tub as a protection from his more complicated terrors.

"I want to thank Jerry for his work on this. He's done a great job. Do you want to talk about the numbers, Jer?"

Jerry was Vice President of Operations. Kim trusted him. She had discovered about herself the fact that she much preferred to promote from within, even though she thought that Jerry still was relying too much on Lou. Kim and Jerry had thoroughly discussed this project, his eagerness for it and her worry that it was going to cost her control of her company. Now her bland praise mottled Jerry's cheeks with the farm-boy flush that he had never outgrown.

He said, "As you know, we closed our year in September with a gross of two hundred twenty-four million. And we made maybe fifteen million of that, even with expanding as far as Las Vegas, where it seems we're already taking off. So this proposal for a second offering isn't so much to fund our expansion. It's mainly for the frozen-food project and to put some cash in the till. Eighty million for the frozen food seems high, I know, but that's if we have to flog it. And now – ah – are there any questions?" Jerry took a careful breath.

The discussion was brief and supportive. Kim listened with a rising sense of inevitability that tightened her throat and chilled her skin. Then Vic said, "Wait a minute!" He was standing at the far end of the table in an elegant blue chalk-stripe that made him look like a movie star playing the part of a businessman.

Kim had nominated Vic to her board last December in an effort to bring them closer after her miscarriage the previous summer. She had been furious at first, refusing to have anything to do with him while he had borne her anger with gentle patience. She had thought she was going to break up with him. For awhile she would have done it on the least excuse. But he had absorbed her fury in a bland acceptance that gave her nothing to push against until it began to seem excessive and foolish. Officially Vic was a consumer advocate. But he had spent his whole nine months on her board as an advocate for nothing but Kimberly Bonner, building goodwill between them like a debt she didn't want to have to repay.

Vic was saying, "As I read this sheet, it seems to me we're dropping our majority stockholder to thirty percent. She'll never agree to that. The whole thing is ridiculous."

"Kim?" Steve asked politely.

"Well, I might." Vic's advocacy tended to push her toward the center.

"Is it even possible?" Marshall asked. "Can we really raise a hundred million dollars? Steve?"

Steve Vorovich was president of Taste of Home's lead underwriter. He cleared his throat and said, "I think it's possible. I've put out feelers to brokers. They say the company's hot. You're raising the money for a speculative venture, but you're doing it right. It'll probably fly. We'd need a contract with Kim. They all say that. The fear seems to be she's cashing out. But if we time it right, if we price it right, I think it'll fly."

Vic had moved around to stand behind his chair. Kim read from his graceful slump a feeling that he wanted to be sitting down, while his face showed a gaunt claustrophobic panic that showed he was barely able to stay in the room. That face. Whenever Kim considered breaking up with Vic she would look at his face and see so many faces: little Timmy's neediness and Bobby's pain, Colin's joy and Darcy's self-caressing. Vic's beautiful, sensitive, transparent face seemed to carry within it every loved face. She couldn't bear to send him out of her life. She was gazing at him, no longer listening as her board's quiet discussion continued; but then Connie as Secretary restated the motion.

"Moved that we authorize an offering of two and a half million shares. As Marshall notes, that doubles our size. We expect to raise about a hundred million dollars."

Hearing it put that starkly began a wave of chilly nausea in Kim's belly. She looked around the table, counting votes. "So you're telling me it's six to two? If we took a vote now, I'd lose? What are my options, Lou? As majority stockholder? What can I do to prevent this?"

"Call an emergency stockholders' meeting. Recall the board. As a practical matter, we'll be taking the offering before the stockholders in December and you can vote it down then, anyway. But if you're going to say no, do it now. Don't air our dirty laundry."

"So it really is up to me? It's my choice?"

"Of course. You know that without my saying it."

"All right, then. Listen to me. No matter how many times

people tell me I can control this company with thirty percent, thirty percent is not *control.* But what you're making this come down to is it's me or the company. Faced with a choice like that, I have to give in. I love this company. If I wouldn't deny it food from my mouth, how can I deny it money if what it needs is money?"

"Kim . . ." Lou started to say. Her lifted hand silenced him.

"I'll do it, but on *my* terms. Do you hear me, Steve? I wasn't too with-in the last time, but I'm smarter now. If I sell more stock, it'll be at *retail.*"

"I never said . . ." Steve started to say.

"Let me finish. I happen to think a hundred million dollars isn't nearly enough. What we're going to do is raise a hundred and *fifty* million dollars, and the extra fifty is going in the bank so we'll never again be in this position. Is that clear? Steve? Everybody?"

"So you're selling, what? Four million shares?"

"No. We'll ask more for the stock."

"You *can't. . .*" Steve blurted.

"We'll do a three-for-one split and ask twenty dollars a share. That makes each existing share worth sixty. If they want our stock, they're going to pay what it's *worth.*"

"Kim, there is no human way you can ask a fifty-percent premium for a second offering."

"I say the price will be sixty by spring. It ought to be sixty now."

Marshall growled, "So you're saying, chick, you'll let us spend several hundred grand preparing an offering and scotch it if the underwriter won't meet your price?"

"That's exactly what I'm saying. I want a guaranteed offering, too. None of this best-efforts nonsense we had the last time. If your firm won't do it, Steve, we'll find one that will."

"We'll do it. If you're willing to pull the offering on our advice, we'll do it."

"Okay, then. You've heard my terms. Now you decide whether Taste of Home should take the risk. Would somebody care to make a motion?"

The board members glanced at one another. Some of them shifted in their chairs. Then Paul Whist, the union representative, said, "I move we offer two and a half million shares at a price to be approved by the majority stockholder."

Those were a lot of words from someone who had hardly ever spoken before. Everyone looked at Paul while Kim said, "Thank you. Is that good enough, Lou?"

"That's good enough."

"Fine. Then is there a second?"

"I'll second it," said Rodney, the bank president.

"Thanks. All those in favor?"

Five hands rose. Five voices mumbled, "Aye."

"Opposed?"

From his place by the window, Vic snapped, "Opposed!"

"One opposed."

"All right. Do we need a motion on using Steve's firm?"

"So moved."

"Seconded."

"All in favor? Connie, see Lou about the wording of these motions." Kim was feeling a swell of elation that trembled in her voice. It seemed the painful part had been agonizing over whether to let it happen, but now she was safely off the cliff and falling. The moment she had been dreading for more than a year had come and gone.

Vic was looking down at the street again, his lizard-skin boot on the window ledge and his forearm on his thigh. Kim studied him, loving the way his hair curved above his ear and curled in baby wisps behind it. Vic had cried for hours by her hospital bed the night Kim lost their baby. Something about the sunlight on his hair made the sound of his crying come to mind. He had driven her to the hospital in a panic, babbling to her to keep her alive, and when doctors had told him the pain and the clots were from nothing more dangerous than a miscarriage, he had wept for the baby as if it were a full-term child. Now he wanted Kim to conceive again, but just the thought of going off the birth-control pills her doctor had advised made Kim suffer a trapped and desperate sense like Vic's discomfort at being in this room.

She said, "Next agenda item. I called it 'Go after the restaurants?' I've been thinking about all the motels with bad restaurants where nobody wants to eat. I asked someone to look into it, and twenty calls brought twelve expressions of interest. So in places we're saturated, like here in Indiana, I think we should go after all those bad motel restaurants. And we should look at home deliveries, too. To my mind, those are our next horizons."

———◆———

Kim found the circumstances of Derek's crash so peculiar that all the way to the hospital she couldn't stop talking about it. "He goes two hundred and fifteen miles an hour. He qualifies *second* for the Indy. Then he gets in his street car and racks it up. I can't *believe . . . .*"

Vic stabbed the intercom button and said, "*Step* on it, Tucker! Do you want me to drive?"

"It's the traffic." Kim reached for Vic's hand. He slid his fingers from under hers and leaned to flick on the television.

". . . no further word on his condition. Anderson was on his way to the airport, minutes after his front-row run. Ned Millett, winner of this year's pole position, said . . . ." Vic kicked the control button with his toe.

Kim remarked, "You know, I heard him telling Derek he drove too fast. Ned Millett. I think it was last year's mechanics' dinner. He said . . . ."

"I could *walk* to the hospital faster than this!"

Derek's wife had reached them in the limousine as they were heading for one of the dozen parties they attended during the month of May. It had taken the Indiana State Police three hours to find Sandy in the Kansas City hospital where she had just given birth that morning. Then it had taken Sandy another hour to locate Vic.

"We could call the hospital and see how he is," Kim offered.

"I promised Sandy I'd *be* there."

"We'll go, of course. We just ought to find out . . . ."

Vic gave Kim a look of animal panic. She reached to stroke the hair above his ear and at the base of his skull while he turned his head against her fingers. He settled into the leather seat with a sighing of cushions, slipping his eyes shut, easing his body while his fingers gripped the seat, long and taut and white. He said, "It's not the pink car. I don't blame you, baby."

The bad-luck color for Indy cars was green, but Vic had been saying if there was a worse color than green it had to be Taste of Home pink. He had complained right up until Derek's pink March had won its first race at Phoenix in April. Then Vic's pink car had won Long Beach, and today pink cars had qualified second and third for the 1986 Indy. Kim had just been remarking that now half the cars were going to be painted pink, when the car's phone had rung and Sandy had asked for Vic in a voice of soft, strangled terror.

———◆———

Reporters and fans stood thick at the front doors of the hospital, so Tucker drove around to the service entrance. Tucker had been Kim's chauffeur and bodyguard for most of the past year. He was a patient, somber giant of a man who seemed to possess neither emotions nor gender.

A crew-cut teenaged orderly in a white coat led Kim and Vic through a corridor lit by dusty bulbs to the doors of a freight elevator. There he pressed the call button and turned to study these celebrities. "Kim and Vic! You are! I wunta believed it! Can I have your autograph?"

Kim and Vic. Thanks to Harvey, Oldfield, *et al*, by now they were on a first-name basis with everybody in America. Kim fumbled a pen from her purse and wrote, "Best, Kim Bonner," on the pocket of the orderly's jacket.

The Intensive Care Unit was a hub of monitors from which beds radiated in three directions. Two women in white stood with a white-coated man, sharing conversation in breathy whispers. Vic stepped up and said, "Where's Derek Anderson?" Three heads turned.

"Kim and Vic!"

"But you can't go in . . . ."

"Just family . . . ."

Vic caught the lone male by his white lapels and said, "I'm here for his wife! Where is he?" While Kim did what she saw as the sensible thing. She went looking for Derek. She was choosing between two forms wrapped in white, both tangled and clustered with tubes and equipment, when Vic hurried past her toward one of them. Kim followed him reluctantly. She had the peculiar sense that Vic couldn't see Derek except through her own eyes.

There was a sweet metallic smell by Derek's bed, a whisper of motors and a quiet hushing. Derek lay in a cocoon of bandages, his limbs as stiff as the limbs of a doll whose child-friend had made a mummy of it. Derek was such a dynamic man that Kim was surprised to see how tiny he seemed in that enormous bed. His chest moved to the even demands of the respirator tube in his throat; his face was a red and sooty square. Indy drivers wore fire-proof Nomex clothing and sat strapped into carbon-fiber tubs in cars designed to disintegrate. If Derek had crashed at the track, this would have been nothing at all. Kim heard a rasp of in-taken breath and looked at Vic. He was studying Derek with eyes dark and wistful, his head barely cocked, his long jaw working.

"We just brought him up from surgery," a man's voice said from behind them. "Now we'll have to see."

Kim pressed the doctor out from between the equipment and the bed. She couldn't let Vic hear this. "You're Kim and Vic, aren't you?" the man said with interest.

Kim hated being recognized. She saw her fame as one more sacrifice that she had made for Taste of Home. Her response had been to withdraw into a circumscribed life where she seldom met a stranger, so when she was thrust into the world this way and she saw again how much she had lost, she felt horrified and disemboweled. She didn't know how Vic felt about his fame. They never discussed it, except to share a laugh when something embarrassed them, but she suspected that he relished being famous. He was finally getting his father's attention.

"What's wrong with Derek?" Kim whispered harshly.

"Head injuries. Spinal fracture. Second-degree burns. We've relieved the pressure on his brain for now, but . . . ."

"Will he live? Is he going to be all right?"

"I don't know. He's lucky to be alive. They clocked him at a hundred and twenty."

Kim looked at Vic. He hadn't moved. He stood with his familiar gentle grace, one hip advanced, one hand in his pocket. The lights in the room made his hair gleam white. Kim squeezed in close beside him again and slipped her hand into his. She couldn't look at his face, but over the hush of the respirator she heard his labored breathing.

"Excuse me?" the doctor whispered from behind her. "His sister's outside. She's been waiting three hours."

"Send her in," Kim whispered over her shoulder, although Janice was the last person she wanted to see.

"One visitor at a time," the doctor replied. He was a tall, thick, gray-haired man. Like Lou. Kim's impulse was to like and trust him.

"Then ask her to wait. We'll leave in a minute."

For a long time, for too long a time, Kim had pretended not to care about Janice. She had seemed to feel simultaneously that Janice was no competition at all, but if she forced Vic to choose then she might not win. So she had stopped attending Vic's races, yielding that part of his life to Janice, until the tabloids had begun to run stories with titles like, "Can Kim Keep Vic?" and "Vic's New Love – First Pix." So Kim had given him an ultimatum, and now she attended all his races. She sent office equipment and an armored limousine ahead on a transporter truck and flew in with several employees and Tucker on the company jet.

Kim had never examined her relationship with Vic. It had seemed too unlikely, too impossibly fragile to stand much scrutiny. To the extent that she thought about it at all, she imagined he reminded her of Bobby Sever. And living with Vic felt very much the way living with Aunt Dagmar had felt: they had so little in common that they hardly talked beyond the mechanics of their life together, so Kim could put between them a safe and familiar moat of privacy. And she loved being with Vic. She couldn't get enough of looking at him, of the crackles of excitement and pleasure and danger he produced in her so easily. But Vic's affair with Janice had shifted the seam that connected the structure of his life with Kim's. She could see the sill, and it made her wonder about the rest of the framework within the walls. In spite of herself, she wondered why she had been willing to permit his cheating, why his abandonments had thrilled her with such titillating pain that she used to think of him with Janice a hundred times a day to produce a predictable agonizing rush. It seemed to be bound up with her mother somehow, bound up with needs buried even deeper than any that Vic had yet ferreted out.

Ellie had begun to go out with Jerry at about the time that Kim discovered Vic's affair. Given her past relationship with Jerry, Kim thought she should find this situation embarrassing, but she remembered their time together as just a dry fact devoid of emotional content. All she felt about Ellie and Jerry now was intense curiosity.

Over time, Kim had come to suspect that the way she and Vic were making love wasn't normal. She had told herself that probably people did these things to one another all the time, until the shock of Vic's cheating had slapped her into a kind of deeper sanity. One morning during May of the previous year, she had managed to ask Ellie some of the questions that were starting to fester in her mind.

"Jerry's a sweet guy."

"Oh, Kim, I feel so bad. He says I shouldn't. He says it was over between you years ago."

"Of course you shouldn't! Don't be silly."

"You really don't mind?"

"Jerry's like a brother to me, Ellie. Believe me. Ah . . . but he's nice, isn't he?"

"Oh, he's wonderful!" Ellie lifted eyes that sparkled with genuine stars.

"Oh, Vic, too. But he, you know, he gets excited sometimes."

"Jerry does, too!" Ellie bubbled, her face alight.

"Men are funny, aren't they?" Kim went on, prodding Ellie to talk. "About sex. You know what I mean."

"Oh, very funny," Ellie said, smiling. "Sometimes Jerry, he . . . I shouldn't say this . . . ."

"Please do. This is fun. Just between us."

"Well, he . . . like last night. We – you know – we did it all over again in the *shower.*"

The single time Kim and Vic had done it in the shower, she had been washing the blood from cuts he had given her while he was trying to shave her body. She had thought it was fun at first, the gentle sensations and the water dripping, but again and again he had deliberately nicked her with his razor. After a half-dozen cuts, she had been angry enough to stalk off to the shower. She had assumed he would never join her there, but the bloody water had excited him past the constraints of his old phobia.

"Don't you love it? When they get that way? All desperate?" Ellie said eagerly. "It's kind of scary. But it's so nice, too."

"I'll say it's scary," Kim agreed as she turned back the cuff of her pink silk blouse to show Ellie a purple and yellow bruise on the knuckle of her wrist. "Police handcuffs. I told him they'd leave a mark."

"*Handcuffs . . . !*" Ellie clamped her hand on her mouth.

So now Kim knew for sure that the way she and Vic were making love wasn't normal. Over the past year, she had tried to convince herself to make some changes, but she had found to her faint internal disgust that she didn't really seem to want what was normal. Vic never actually hurt her. What he did was play titillating games with her mind, very playful and creative games: he knew with masterful certainty all the things that were going to thrill her most. But Kim didn't want to be abnormal, either. So, as much as she clung to Vic, as much as she loyally still tried to love him, the space that she had always felt between them was filling now more and more with her vague awareness that something was deeply wrong.

"We should let her come in," Kim finally whispered to Vic over the hushing of Derek's respirator. Derek had been furious when Vic broke up with Janice. He had thought that Vic really loved his sister but was living with Kim for publicity reasons, so for months after Vic had ended his affair they had hardly spoken while Derek sulked and Vic brooded. It really had only been after Taste of Home had offered Derek a contract that he had made his peace with Vic. Now Vic was standing here, holding Kim's hand, probably wracked with remorse over having chosen fame and living with Kim over his closest friend.

———————

The 1986 Indianapolis 500 should have been a triumphal moment for the Taste of Home team and the Garrett-Smith Racing Company. Peter Garrett had been a factor in Indy-Car racing for thirty years. His cars had won two Indies and sixty-odd other races by the late seventies. But in recent years, success at racing had become ever more dependent on money spent, so Garrett had been forced into partnership with an insurance tycoon named Tobias Smith. And even with all the money Smith could be coddled into spending, they hadn't been able to win at Indy since Vic's freakish victory in 1980.

Vic had moved on in 1982 to a more successful car owner, but Jelly had remained friendly with Garrett and had talked Vic into returning to him for 1985. Now Garrett-Smith's drivers were first and third in championship points. They had qualified second and third for the 1986 Indy. And those pink Marches with their cartoon flowers that people used to snicker at had appeared not just on *On Track* and *National Speed Sport News*, but even on the covers of *Life* and *Newsweek*. Indy-Car racing was finally becoming a mainstream American passion, and thanks to his connection to Kim and Vic, Peter Garrett was right at the front of it. But then had come Derek's accident. On race day, Peter was pacing the pink-and-silver Taste of Home box, looking foolish in his rose-pink suit, while Kim and Jerry and Ellie and Lou sat behind him watching the start of the race on television.

Peter was ranting, "Vic couldn't even break two hundred! What makes you think he's going to do it now?"

Vic had spent most of the past two weeks at Derek's bedside, coming to the track just for practice and stroking so badly he had turned in laps slower than the greenest rookie's. Derek's car was down there on the track right now, alone and empty in front of Vic's car in the center of the first row. Behind it, the gaudy grid of cars seethed with brightly-colored crewmen. The television camera panned the field and came to rest on Derek's car while the announcer recounted the story of Derek's accident.

". . . So before we enjoy this day and the greatest event in all of sports, let's pause and remember Derek Anderson, one of the bravest drivers and one of the nicest guys it was ever my pleasure to know." The announcer paused. Kim bowed her head and began to think the Lord's Prayer, while from the corner of her eye she could see Lou's lips moving. That startled her. She had come to imagine God as a kind of president of the mind who collected prayers, perhaps, as thought taxation; so she gave Him the Lord's Prayer sometimes. She was glad to do it. But for Lou to be talking aloud to God as if He were a person was so unsettling she lost track of her words. What came to mind instead was the way Derek had walked, with a saunter at once sexy and tough and cute. And his laughter. Derek was always laughing, not chuckling like Vic but laughing out loud. Connie Westlake had told him one of her goofy stories at Kim's last Christmas party and he had whooped with laughter, fallen onto a sofa with laughter, roared with laughter until he lay there grinning and swiping at the tears on his cheeks.

"Our prayers are with you, Derek," the announcer said finally. "You'll always be a winner." Then he introduced the National Anthem while an honorary crew of four retired drivers came onto the track dressed in Taste of Home suits and wheeled Derek's car into the pit lane.

"He's going to be fine," Lou said as a soloist began to sing, "Back Home Again In Indiana."

Behind them Peter was ranting. Jerry was saying, "Relax. It's only a race. Have a seat. Here, have a beer."

Kim said to Lou, "But the doctors say . . . ."

"Vic. He'll be fine once the race starts."

"He didn't go to Mass," Kim said shortly.

She and Vic had hardly spoken since Derek was hurt. He had lost all interest in lovemaking, and the lack of that had created such a gulf between them that she couldn't think of anything to say to him. But the few times Vic had spoken, he had patiently insisted there was no way around it. His career was over. If he raced again, he would wind up like Derek.

"He didn't go to Mass. He always goes to Mass. He didn't see the point when he was about to die, anyway." Kim's mind kept catching on that. She could see Vic saying those words that morning, sitting pale at the head of the table while the red sun rose behind him, and she had felt in that moment a strange elation at the thought of his neat and tidy death. She had found it hard to imagine what their life would be like if Vic quit racing, but until that morning she hadn't imagined she might be hoping that he would die. She was fascinated, as she always was fascinated to glimpse a hidden facet of her own psyche.

Lou put his hand over Kim's on the arm of her chair. His hand was large and warm, with a satisfying weight to it. She looked up at his face, feeling faintly amazed. His crooked smile was exactly right: supportive, not cheery. Everything Lou did was exactly right. He wouldn't be sitting back there like Jerry, telling a man whose life had been lived for this moment that the Indianapolis 500 was only a race.

"Vic is stronger than you think," Lou said while Kim looked at him, loving the upward tilt of his eyes that gave him a youthful, playful look. His eyes were no longer the shade of his hair, which was gradually going silver.

"Why are you sticking up for him all of a sudden? I thought you couldn't stand him."

"He's what you want. It took me awhile to accept that."

Kim studied her hand under Lou's. Slowly, wondering

whether she really was going to do this, she turned her hand and slipped her fingers in between his. He closed his hand on hers. It was so large that all she could see were the manicured tips of her fingers.

But now she couldn't look at Lou's face. His hand was warm and intense in hers; an energy was flowing, a gender awareness. Never in all his posturing and his brutal playing had Vic made her so aware of his maleness as she was aware now, sitting there, that Lou was a man, and aware of her.

Through the window, she glimpsed gaudy cars accelerating around the track in an irregular grid. Some were trailing. Some were weaving like restive horses while they warmed their tires for additional speed. Vic was doing what he was supposed to do, holding his position between Millett and Fascetti while he worked on his tires.

"I don't know if he is," Kim said softly after too long a silence.

"What?"

Behind them, Peter Garrett slammed his beer mug down on a table and shouted, "Green flag! Get ready to jump out front!" at the tiny cars on a television screen.

"I don't know if he's what I want. How are you supposed to know?"

"I'm a great one to ask."

Kim lifted her eyes when Lou said that. To be holding his hand and looking at his face made her cheeks glow warm.

"And what do *you* want?" she whispered.

"I want . . . I still want a family. I guess what I've always . . . ."

"That's it! That's it!" Peter Garrett shouted. "He's out there! Here they come!"

The field was streaking into the second turn, filling the window with riotous colors, pink first, then white, then yellow. "He did it," Kim said under her breath.

Vic survived Fascetti's attempt to pass him on the second turn.

They roared down the backstretch, thirty-three cars, while Jack Henry's cheerful, homey voice droned on, calling the race for ABC.

"He's doing fine." Lou shifted his hand to put Kim's fingers together. Now they really were holding hands. Kim was sitting there holding Lou's hand as if she held it all the time, while through their contact of skin on skin came a sexual energy so intense that she was fighting her need to pull her hand away. Then suddenly she couldn't bear it. This wasn't just another man. It was Lou. Sexual tension between them felt as obscene as that awful, forever-remembered moment when Bobby Sever had made her touch his penis. She jerked her hand away as Henry blurted, "Engstrom's in trouble! He's slowing down! He's heading for pit lane after one lap!" Kim stood to cover that embarrassing reclaiming of her hand as she craned to see what was happening almost a mile away.

"Here, Kim. The monitor."

A close shot of Vic's car filled the screen. He was bumping down the cement pit road and stopping for the pink "Vic" sign. His crew hurried in around his car, but since it had just gone out they didn't know what to do to it.

"No word yet on what's wrong," Henry was saying. "It might be a transmission problem. Team Garrett has had to replace . . . Whatever it is, Jelly's not too happy about it." Jelly could be seen there on the screen, sweeping his arms and silently shouting.

"That's Jerard Piscatelli, Team Garrett's crew chief. Legend has it he got his nickname from his physique. Let's see if we can have a word with him."

Kim could see that Vic was trying to remove his steering wheel while Jelly was trying as fiercely to hold it in place. A microphone appeared beside Jelly's ear.

"Can you tell us what's wrong?"

"Nothing's wrong! Can you give us a damn minute?" Jelly shouted as he jabbed an elbow at the microphone.

"He's a little crusty," Henry said, sounding abashed. "Well, Vic took Derek's accident pretty hard. His practice times have been way off the pace. Maybe he didn't feel ready to start."

Kim looked at Lou and said, "He quit."

"No, he . . . ." Lou started to say, but Jack Henry's eager voice cut him off.

"Here's Tony Mitchell, one of Engstrom's pit crew...!"

"He really did it," Kim said with slow amazement as she sank into her chair. On the television, Vic could be seen walking away with his familiar grace, the sunlight brilliant on his yellow hair. Jelly appeared beside him. He slipped an arm around Vic's shoulders.

Then Kim realized that this might possibly be a wonderful moment. Vic's success had made him selfish and arrogant. He had spent two-thirds of his time on the road. Perhaps his retiring now would give them a whole new start.

———◆———

The second stock offering had been delayed until the second week in July to take advantage of the Indy. Taste of Home couldn't seek publicity during the "quiet period" that had begun when it had decided to offer stock, but it wasn't responsible for news stories that might appear without its courting them. Steve Vorovich had thought when the timetable was set that the Indy might give the offering a boost. But no one could have anticipated how this Indy's double tragedy was going to seize the public's sympathy, nor how many pictures were going to be published of those two pink Marches without their drivers. The price of the stock had hit fifty-four before it split three-for-one at the end of May. By July eighth, the day the offering opened, it was at twenty-two dollars a share.

Having been right about price and timing made Kim feel so much better about the offering that she decided on the fifteenth of July to hold a closing party on the ninth of August. Steve insisted the ninth was too soon. The second quarter had ended with a loss; the prospectus numbers ought to make investors wary. But he had reckoned without the souvenir factor, which let them sell a lot of single blocks. And he hadn't counted on a California company named Lion's Paw that bought up a quarter of the offering.

Lion's Paw had filed notifications with the Securities and Exchange Commission and with Taste of Home, indicating it was buying the stock for investment purposes and this wasn't the start of a takeover bid. But Kim wasn't comforted. Having anybody owning thirteen percent of Taste of Home was so distressing to her that she wanted to undo it all right now. Hang the expansion and the frozen food.

"We've got nothing to worry about," Steve kept insisting. "They're just a couple of farmers with a food conglomerate. They think we're going to quadruple in size. They want to be around for the pop."

"They're trying to take me over," Kim fretted. But she couldn't call off her party. By the time they were having this conversation, bushes were being planted behind her house and lights were being installed and a bandstand and a row of shops were being built at the foot of her long back lawn. She had planned a turn-of-the-century party. Guests would come in period costume and serve themselves from Victorian shops while a band in pink-striped jackets played "Daisy" and "In The Good Old Summertime."

———◆———

The evening of August ninth was so warm that Kim could feel perspiration trickling down her back as she hurried from shop to shop. Everything was ready. Guests would choose each separate course in the gaily-colored gaslit shops and dine at the round wrought-iron tables that surrounded the gaudy bandstand where the band was tuning up. The mingled scents of food, the shrills and toots, the close blue twilight sparkling with lights combined to produce such a swelling of delight in Kim that she paused as she started up toward the house and turned with a swirl of skirt to give it all another look.

The house was enormous at the top of its hill, washed with light that cast shadows on its long veranda and made the pediments over the windows stand out in bright relief. Kim crossed the veranda and entered the library through its tall French doors. Never once in the two years she had lived in this house had she entered it through the servants' porch.

"Can I help you, Miss?" someone said from behind her. Kim turned. Rosalinde said, "Oh! I didn't know it was you, ma'am. You look so different!" Rosalinde was Kim's downstairs maid. She worked weekends and evenings, fetching things and answering the telephone and the door.

"We'll be greeting people in here, Rosalinde. Offer them drinks, then suggest they head down toward the party."

"Yes, ma'am. And you do look lovely."

Kim was wearing a white bustled dress trimmed with ribbons and tucking and lace. It was accented in black and in Taste of Home pink. Atop her dark wig with its Gibson knot she wore a stiff white hat with a pink ostrich feather.

"Thank you. Have you seen Mr. Engstrom? Is he ready?"

"I think so, ma'am. It's almost eight."

The party was set to begin at eight. Depending on his mood, Vic might be ready at any time between now and midnight. Kim had last seen him shaving a half-hour earlier, standing naked and rosy from his bath; she had thought he was in a good mood then, but she never knew for sure.

"Here he is, ma'am," Rosalinde said, indicating the door that opened into the hallway.

This room was thirty by sixty feet, which Kim realized now was a great deal bigger than the library had been at Highgrove. The whole house was bigger, and she had gotten the proportions wrong. She had resisted for a long time the notion that she was replicating Highgrove, telling herself all she was doing was building a house the way a house should be built. But she could see now that what she had created was a caricature of Highgrove, every detail more fantastic, more grand and enormous. And still it didn't seem to be enough.

Vic was crossing the room in a bright-blue jacket with white pants and shirt and a celluloid collar. His cravat and the ribbon on his hat were striped in brilliant pink. Kim's couturier had designed his outfit to complement hers, but Vic had hated it when he saw it. And he had been right. He looked like a cartoon. People were going to kid him.

"You look great, babe," he said to Kim. "I like a lady with a little extra ass." He ducked beneath the brim of her hat to kiss her a friendly peck while he stroked her bustle.

"Cut it out," Kim whispered, indicating Rosalinde with her eyes. Rosalinde was setting glasses on a bar thirty feet away. Kim was trying to train Vic to decorum when servants were in the room.

"No ass." He glanced disdainfully at Rosalinde. He held one of Kim's hands up by the fingers while he stepped back and looked her up and down. "You know, that's very sexy. I thought Victorians were supposed to be repressed."

"They did it less but thought about it more."

Vic had remained in his panicky, desperate depression until the plug was pulled on Derek at the end of June. Kim had thought he would be even worse after the funeral, but instead the funeral had marked an ending for Vic, as if he had already done his grieving. He had soon gone back to driving his Ferrari. He had returned to making love, not as the bodily function it had lately become but as his old perverse, pleasurable art form.

But there was a manic quality to Vic's behavior now, a sense of having shifted to a higher gear. He was fresher and sillier and faster and wilder. Vic and Derek had been such intense friends for so long that they had molded one another: Vic had been the straight man, and Derek the clown. Kim had thought while Derek was alive that each was doing some living through the other. She thought now that without Derek, Vic was struggling like an adolescent to learn who he really was. But his dramatic retirement and Derek's death had made him a bigger media star than ever. A studio and a publishing company had bought the rights to his life story, and he was being asked to endorse everything from antacids to sneakers to cars to soap. He was in a very good mood.

———◆———

Lou didn't arrive until after ten.

It had turned out to be a terrific party, the best so far of Kim's lush theme parties that had caused a *Chicago Tribune* columnist to remark that Kim Bonner was becoming the hub of Indianapolis society. Most of the hundred-fifty guests had come in costume, and the first hour had been a happy posing of folks in bustled dresses, celluloid collars and derby hats while pictures were taken for articles planned for two newspapers and three major magazines. The little shops and the bandstand were a hit. And the fun of strolling and nibbling in costume had people saying by ten o'clock that this had to be the most wonderful party since this style of clothing had first been in fashion.

But still Lou hadn't come. He had told Kim he was going to be late because he was bringing Connie Westlake, and Connie had to appear at another party first. To hear that Lou was bringing a date had been a shock for Kim. She told herself he was giving Connie a ride, he was doing her a favor; but Lou had been careful never to let himself appear to be paired off. No blind dates. No dinner-party matchmaking. So his casual mention of Connie's name had been so out of character that Kim felt as if he had blared from a bullhorn a sudden, dramatic interest in women.

To have Lou absent from her party, and to have him (could she imagine it?) actually dating felt so unfitting that whatever Kim was doing she kept turning to scan her long back lawn.

Most of the guests had eaten all their courses by ten o'clock. Now everywhere Kim could see people engaged in her planned gay-nineties pursuits. Rodney Ralston and his wife and Nelson Baldwin, the mayor of Indianapolis, were playing croquet under rippling light with the tall bald stalk that was Graham Harvey. Jerry and Ellie were among those fishing for orange carp in a temporary pool. Marshall was wobbling crazily alone on a bicycle built for two, startling the horses that were giving guests rides around the grounds in a shiny black phaeton. Concealed lighting created an intimate daylight. A soft breeze had risen with the half-full moon. Except for a few mosquitoes that had escaped all efforts at control, it was the sort of night when being outdoors was all by itself a pleasure.

Kim had paused to chat with Steve Vorovich at the entrance to the shop called Sweets For The Sweet. He was working on a Taste of Home peach strudel, his fourth dessert of the evening, while he told her again that Lion's Paw was nothing to worry about.

"You should see these guys. Mutt and Jeff. One is a big, fat guy who never says more than two words at once. The other is a skinny little thing who never stops talking. And they wear *cowboy* clothes, Kim. I guess they started on a ranch somewhere, so they like to think of themselves as cowboys."

Vic was ambling down the lawn from the house with Reuben, Jelly's mechanic nephew. Vic seemed to need another man around for reaction and reinforcement, but Kim wasn't pleased to find him choosing Reuben. Vic had loosened his ascot and lost his straw hat. His disarrayed hair was shining in the moonlight. And Kim could tell by his ungainly walk that he had had quite a lot to drink.

"Kim?" Steve had expected a smile at his description of the California cowboys.

"I'm sorry. I know you're not worried. I just . . . ."

"Hey, Steven!" Vic called as he approached them. "What do you think of my lady here? Don't you think she should dye her hair?"

"You look very nice," Steve said to Kim.

Vic slipped an arm around Kim's waist, feeling stiff and distant through her corset, and ducked and kissed her just in front of her ear. "They're taking pictures all over the house. Is that supposed to happen?"

"That's *Metropolitan Home*. They wanted some pictures at night."

"Dye your hair, babe. That black wig is a wicked turn-on."

"It's brown," she said after him as he and Reuben moved on lazily toward the pool of carp. "Useless," she muttered, watching them go. "He's supposed to be the host."

"Kim?"

She looked up at Steve's grave, pleasant face with its brow marked by rows of perfect lines and its two deep grooves down his cheeks. Steve's face was as wise as a dog's face. It seemed too intelligent to be human. And thinking of that made Kim picture J. Bob Sever with his heavy face that had carried within it every bit of wisdom, every shred of pain.

"Kim dear, this is none of my business. Shoot me down. Please. But are you sure that's the kind of man you want?"

Kim glanced after Vic in time to see him stumble. He never used to drink; he had said it affected his driving reflexes. She almost said, "I love him," but she was less and less sure she even knew what that meant. What she said was, "We belong together. Neither of us has a family. And he'll be all right. He's getting over Derek."

Whenever Kim considered leaving Vic, she saw the awful

public interest that move would generate. They were paired in the media like blond bookends. And she couldn't bear to lose the sight of Vic, nor to lose his perfect understanding of things she didn't want to begin to understand about herself. Besides, could he live without her? Wouldn't he die?

"Uncle Louie!" she heard Marshall call from the path in front of the appetizer shop called First Things First. In typical Marshall fashion, he was still trying to ride alone on a bike that was meant for two people.

Kim paused in mid-stride with her skirt in her hands. Lou was coming down the lawn with Connie. They were in plain evening dress, Lou in the tuxedo Kim had given him so he could act as her sometime escort and Connie in a long white dress that Kim recognized and knew was backless. Connie was saying something to Lou, and he was laughing. Kim heard his familiar laughter from a hundred feet away. And Connie was holding his hand. They were swinging their hands between them like children. Kim dropped and smoothed her skirt. She had spent the past hour telling herself what a nice thing Lou was doing, escorting Connie to parties so she wouldn't have to attend them alone. But that laughter and those swinging hands told her that Lou was loving being with Connie. Kim lifted her chin and swallowed against a dry throat.

"Kim! I didn't *know* you!" Connie called when they were twenty feet away. "Lou said it was you. Did you dye your hair? My, don't you look wonderful!" She kissed the air beside Kim's cheek. "I'm sorry we're in civvies. We had to show at Silas Ogilvie's party. Do you know him? He's in infants' clothing? I mean, he *makes* infants' clothing!" She added this last with a giggle while Kim looked at Lou. He was smiling around his pipe stem his crooked, amused, delighted smile.

"This is *wonderful*," Connie gushed. "You're so clever! Look, Lou. Isn't it great? Even horses? And what are those little shops?"

"That's where you get your dinner." Kim was watching Connie's hand playing with Lou's big fingers. She had just begun to make a friend of Connie, who was funny and brash and bright. Kim had begun to have lunch with her sometimes, to ask her opinions and confide in her. Now Kim was floundering back through all their conversations, hoping she hadn't said anything that she wouldn't want Connie to repeat to Lou.

"You look beautiful," Lou said to Kim. "You didn't dye your hair, did you? That's a wig?"

"It's a wig," Kim said grimly. The sight of that small dark hand in that familiar large pale one rocked her with almost hysterical feelings, horror and anger, fear and loss, so many harsh emotions that she couldn't bear to lift her eyes and look at their faces.

"Are you all right?" she heard Lou ask.

"Just tired." Kim was remembering with a chill of recognition the way Lou and Connie would whisper together, his head bent to hers and both of them smiling. When Connie said something funny, Lou's laughter was the loudest. When Kim had lunch with Connie, Lou's name was always coming up. But was he really dating Connie? Would he sleep with her? Kim had a ghastly flash-image of Lou's dear face hardened into Vic's grim set of pleasure. Lou's big hands, patient and tender and cruel. Even though Kim understood that the way she and Vic made love wasn't normal, she wasn't sure how much of it might be normal. And she couldn't bear to think of Lou doing any of those things. Not any of them.

"Do you want to lie down? We can take over for you," Lou offered gently.

"I . . . no. Thank you. I've got to see to something. Excuse me. Please help yourselves. I mean, if you're still hungry."

chapter eight

March 25, 1987 - January 25, 1988

The price of Taste of Home's stock rose so gradually that it wasn't until the final Wednesday in March of 1987 that Kim really saw what was going on. Her company was listed on the American Stock Exchange, and she had acquired the habit of checking its price as she had her midmorning cup of coffee. Thirty dollars a share. The price had been at twenty-nine and an eighth just yesterday.

Kim rattled the pages around and folded the paper so she could take a closer look at that amazing price. She rocked forward in her chair while she sipped her coffee from a gift mug that said in block letters, "Be Nice To Me. I'm The Boss." At thirty dollars a share, her four and a half million shares were worth, what? A hundred million dollars? More. She shifted her mug to her left hand so she could do a calculation in the margin of the stock page. A hundred and thirty-five million dollars. After the second offering last summer at twenty-two dollars a share, the value of Kim's stock had stood at ninety-nine million. That fact had briefly thrilled her, but then she had forgotten about it.

A heavy rain was falling beyond the window wall to Kim's right, giving her office the cozy atmosphere of a winter evening. She rocked back, feeling buoyant with wonder, and glanced around at the sparkle of chrome and the neutrals gone yellow in the lamplight. She studied the brown-and-gray painting of angles over her sofa while a ghastly suspicion swelled until she was trembling with panic. Kim called Steve Vorovich. Then she spent a further half-hour doodling circles in the margin of her newspaper or gazing out her window into blue lines of rain until he called her back.

"Thanks, Steve," she said before she stabbed her intercom button. "Karen? Ask Lou and Ellie and Jerry to come to my office. Right now."

They came in all together, as if for protection. Kim noticed that fact with light amazement. After five years, she still felt apologetic and foolish about being the boss. She hated the slavery of power. Being the boss made her feel like the property of each of Taste of Home's four thousand employees, as if the pyramid were standing on its point.

Ellie carried a steno pad for taking notes. She wore Darcy's tranquil expression of a woman who had given her life so completely to others that she had nothing to fear: whatever was wrong, Kim would fix it. But the men exchanged reinforcing looks.

"Sit down. I hope I haven't interrupted anything."

Lou dragged a chair with a leather seat from its place against the left-hand wall, parking his pipe briefly in his mouth to do it. He was trying a technique to quit smoking that involved his constantly holding his pipe in his hand. "Is something wrong?" he asked politely as he sat down. Jerry and Ellie had pushed the guest chairs closer together for mutual support. Their fingers, lying on the arms of their chairs, seemed to be straining to touch one another.

"We're at thirty dollars a share."

"Wow," Jerry murmured. "Are we worth half a billion dollars yet?"

"Pretty close," Lou said.

"That's not good news!" Kim blurted, feeling panicky.

"Sure it is," Jerry argued. "If we do *another* . . . ."

"There'll never be another offering! We're not *worth* half a billion dollars. I'd like to think we are, but we're not." She paused, considering that. Half a billion dollars. "Do you know where all the buying pressure is coming from? Does any of you know? Anyone?" she asked, babbling on while she consulted her notes in the margin of her stock page. "Here it is. Three-quarters of the buying is being done in California, most of that in Monterey. Do you know what town Monterey's near, Jerry? Does anybody know?"

"Salinas," Lou said quietly.

"Bingo!" She gave Lou a fierce look. "Does anybody think this has nothing to do with the California cowboys?"

"No," said Lou.

"Thank you. I'm not crazy after all."

Kim looked at Lou, trying to rearrange her grim expression into something more tender. She badly needed their old comfortable intimacy. But she was so aware now of a husky male intensity in the way Lou moved and spoke, even in the way he breathed; she found herself hanging on the details of him, on the way he used his fingers and the lift of his brow. But she was getting over it now. She was.

"I've done some calculations," she said, talking mostly to Lou, trying to feel more at ease with him. "If half the shares traded since last summer went to people fronting for Lion's Paw, it already has eighteen percent of the company. Steve saw my point. He's looking into it. He says they're buying slowly to keep from pushing up the price, so if it really is a takeover bid, we ought to be able to stop it."

Karen's voice whispered from the intercom on Kim's desk. "Miss Bonner? I'm sorry. There's a woman on the phone who insists you'll take her call. I said you're in conference."

"Who is it?"

"Colleen Drake. She says you'll know her as Colleen Sever."

Kim gazed over Lou's head at the hard brown angles some

artist had thought she should see every day while she felt again the weight of hair on her back and smelled the sweet pungency of sunlit tar. Someone must have died. And if she didn't take this call, she could avoid ever knowing who it was.

"I'll take it, Karen. Excuse me, folks. She's, um, a distant cousin." Then, "This is Kim Bonner," she said into her receiver.

"Kimmie? Darlin'? Is it really you?"

Kim had carried a memory of Colleen Sever for fifteen years that was revised in an instant by the reality of that breathy Southern voice. She recalled how Colleen's voice would go soft and she would call Kim "darlin'" when she wanted something.

"Hello, Colleen." Kim had almost said, "Miss Colleen."

"Kimmie. Darlin'. Somethin' terrible's happened. Daddy's died." Colleen's voice went husky.

"I'm sorry," Kim said, feeling light with relief. She had worried that it might be Bobby. Her life was still tied up with his by her childhood crush, by her thirteenth birthday, by all the shames that clung to her closer the harder she tried to fling them away. She was going to have to face it all sometime, and her mother was gone where she could be of no help. Kim needed to know that Bobby was still alive somewhere.

"It was cancer," said Colleen, not pronouncing the "R." "It was not altogether unexpected. But Daddy was like a father to you, so I thought you'd want to know when the services are. You can stay at the house, of course."

"Oh. I – look, Colleen, it's been so many years . . . ." Kim was seeing with perfect clarity that drive up to Highgrove and the house floating weightless beyond the pines.

"Kimmy, please. Mama tells everybody you're kin to us. It would mean so much to her. They're gettin' Taste of Home at Foxy's now, an' Mama tells *everybody* . . . ."

There was an irony in that so unexpectedly sweet that Kim sagged on her elbows, savoring it. The Foxhunter Inn was a pillared bed-and-breakfast on the road between the plantation and the town of Highgrove. Kim used to announce to her mother the out-of-state plates as they were driven by.

"Kimmie? I *said please.*"

Kim was feeling so completely like a child in Highgrove, Virginia, that when she noticed Lou watching her she startled and sat back off her elbows. She was living on the phone a vivid dance of rivalry. The most important thing to her right now was provoking Miss Colleen to tears.

"I – well, perhaps I can come," Kim said slowly. Images of home were flitting through her mind with such urgency that she was astonished to realize how long she had been away. But all she had been waiting for was a summons home. And this was a summons. She was going home.

"When is the funeral?"

"Saturday," Colleen said, making the word two syllables.

"Oh. Well, I suppose I can come on Friday."

"You'll stay at the house?"

"I think not. I travel with six people. But you might make us reservations at Foxy's. Four rooms? Their best?"

Kim had never even stepped inside the Foxhunter Inn. She used to look at the brass kickplate on the bright-red door, the sparkle of chandeliers through the windows at night, and imagine herself grown up and rich enough to drive down to Foxy's from another state.

"Mama'll *want* you to stay at the house," Colleen was whining.

"I'm sorry. I'll make the reservations myself. Now, tell me, are they still using the Saddletree Airport?"

"It's private. You've got to go to Charlottesville. Or Richmond."

"But will the Saddletree take a Learjet, do you think?"

"I wouldn't know about *that.*"

Kim was smiling as she hung up the phone and met Lou's eyes. He said, "I'm guessing you just lost your worst enemy."

"No. Just a dear old man. My goodness, he must have been more than seventy." Kim pressed her intercom button and said, "Karen? I'm leaving Friday at noon for Highgrove, Virginia. That's H-I-G-H-G-R-O-V-E. There's an airport there called Saddletree, but it might not take a jet. Charlottesville is next closest. And we'll need reservations at the Foxhunter Inn. I'll be gone just the weekend, so all we'll need is a fax, I guess. But ask Merry to come. And have Tucker send the Mercedes, will you, please?"

Kim had just leased a custom-built armored Mercedes that was worth a quarter of a million dollars. She had intended to travel with an older limousine and keep this new one for commuting, but if she was going home now she wanted to do it right.

Kim and Vic did so much promotional traveling that it had become automatic. The car and equipment would be sent, reservations made, the plane made ready, all without Kim's having to think about it. They traveled with Merry, Kim's original secretary, who had finished college on a Taste of Home scholarship and become her personal assistant. And they always brought Clara, Kim's personal maid. So with Tucker and the man who drove the transporter and also two company pilots, Kim and Vic routinely traveled with six other people. But Vic wouldn't be coming along this time. He had been raffled off by a Taste of Home franchisee in Oregon as part of its opening celebration, so he would be spending Saturday cutting ribbons and having dinner with the winner.

"I can see why you're worried, Kim, but I don't think it's a problem. Really."

"What?" she asked, looking at Lou blankly.

"Lion's Paw. They're not as big as you think. Even at twenty-two dollars a share, eighteen percent cost them sixty million dollars. That taps them out. There's no way they can buy control."

"I'm sure you're right."

The knot in Kim's stomach was gone. She felt as if she had

stepped back higher up a hill and glimpsed so much world beyond Taste of Home. She sat looking at Lou and feeling amazed at the un-guessed hold that Virginia still had on her mind. She should have made this trip long ago.

Kim's assistant had once been a coltish student, but she had become at twenty-two a woman almost unutterably beautiful. She even had the long, lean body of a model, although she moved as if it had grown so quickly that she hadn't yet learned to operate it well. She giggled and sparkled and shifted in her seat. When Vic was along, Merry generally rode on a jump seat, but today she was sitting in Vic's place, gazing out the window at the city they were skirting. Kim tried not to look. She had been to Charlottesville just once, when the Severs had taken her with their own children to Monticello. But her memory was of a hot, quiet town with a few more streets than Highgrove. This Charlottesville was a building city.

"Look at the *mountains!*" Merry craned down so she could look up. "It says Monticello. That's Thomas Jefferson?"

Kim had forgotten about the mountains. She was so used now to seeing flatlands. But Virginia had soft, velvety mountains covered in forests of ancient pines. Monticello was right on the top of a mountain.

"Let's have another letter to answer, Mer. We've got a long drive still ahead."

Merry leaned to pick an envelope from her briefcase on the floor. It was so quiet inside the car's armored skin that Kim heard the whisper of paper on paper.

Kim had received her first death threat more than three years before. It had come in the mail, and she had been so alarmed that for two weeks she had hired guards to shadow her and watch Aunt Dagmar's house. She had received two more threats about a year later, and that was when she had decided that she needed an armor-plated car. But the Lincolns had seemed to sway too much, and their motors had set up a faint vibration with the ground. Kim loved the leather-scented hush of this new Mercedes.

". . . so I think you should deliver cigarettes and condoms. It would make extra money, I am sure. Sincerely, John M. Johnson," Merry read in her lovely voice.

While Kim pressed the button on her dictation unit and composed a response about the difficulties of running a delivery service, she gazed out her window at the first plantation she had seen in almost ten years. The road frontage had been sold off for house lots, but beyond the cottages Kim could see a three-story white mansion on a hill. She said to Merry, "We should do statistics on these suggestions. This is one we've gotten before. Next letter."

Tucker had some trouble finding Highgrove, Virginia. Kim kept seeing things she thought she recognized and directing him by intercom to turn corners or even to turn around until Merry said, "Kim? Don't you think you're too excited to drive?"

"I'm not excited." She wasn't. She felt something like dread of this homecoming, combined with an electric sense of coming-together like magnets aligning. She left Tucker to find his way alone, and soon the town of Highgrove was slipping ghost-like past smoked windows: High Times Good Eating, Summer Hardware, the Highgrove Pentecostal Church. Beside Sever's Pantry, Penny Earned Variety had been replaced by a drug store called SeverCare; Kim leaned quickly and followed it with her eyes. Kim pressed her intercom button and said, "The Foxhunter Inn is ahead on your left. The house is a mile down on the right. You can drop me there and go back to the Inn."

Western sunlight slanted yellow through the pines as Kim's limousine turned up Highgrove's driveway. With the partition in place, she couldn't see ahead. She pressed her cheek to one side window, then the other, while Merry giggled and leaned back out of her way. Kim caught just glimpses of the house as the driveway drifted left and right, until Tucker began a slow turn around the front circle.

Kim rested her fingers on the glass, trying to touch the house. How small it was! It couldn't be more than a hundred feet from end to end. Beside her memory of her house in Indiana, for which she hadn't yet thought of a grand enough name, Highgrove was a delicate doll of a house. The western sunlight painted it orange and cast long blue shadows beside the pediments, making it appear to be wracked with suffering. This was a house of death. That was a new thought for Kim, and she focused on it as Tucker stopped her car beside what must have been Mr. Sever's last Mercedes. It was a metallic gray-blue not unlike the color of her own Mercedes, and noticing that made Kim wonder whether she had copied the car as she had copied the house.

"I'll be here a few hours. I'll call when I need you," Kim said as Tucker handed her out of the car. He drove in a tuxedo with a flat peaked hat, and he moved with the stiff grace of automation. Kim felt a brief thrill to imagine the Severs watching from the windows as she commanded this huge and splendid man like a monkey on a chain.

Kim hadn't realized before that this place had a smell compounded of pine and boxwood and the syrupy scent of blooming magnolias. One breath made her twelve years old again. She clung to Tucker's hand, held gracefully for a moment at shoulder height, while she looked around, adjusting to the sights and scents.

"Are you faint, ma'am?" When Tucker spoke at all it was in a quaint shorthand.

"No. I'm fine."

The front door opened as Kim was reaching for the bell.

"Oh, Kimmy! Darlin'!" Colleen gushed while Kim took in the stiff pageboy and the thirty extra pounds. Although Colleen couldn't be more than thirty-six, her face had begun to melt like wax into the drooping sadness of middle age.

Kim turned and said, "Thank you, Tucker." The chauffeur touched his cap and went back around the limousine, and Kim watched Colleen's avid face as he started the car and drove away.

"Is your mother here?" she asked finally.

"Oh! Yes. Yes she is. Come on in, Kimmy. My, I don't know where my head is today. Terrible thing. Terrible."

Colleen shuffled backward, staring at Kim in her blue cashmere suit and her single strand of pearls. The foyer with its floating staircase was a charming miniature of Kim's own foyer. Without gold leaf, it looked as plain as a black-and-white picture.

"I believe she's in the library. Why don't you . . . ?" Colleen was saying, while Kim looked into the right-hand living room and saw Bobby standing beside the grand piano.

He hadn't aged at all. He looked as he had looked in that family portrait, as if he had stepped down off the piano to visit with his brother-in-law from the other picture. Colleen's husband had aged. Kim could see that from thirty feet away. But Bobby had a young and confident face and a cocky tilt to his chin that Kim remembered now from the years before he had outgrown being happy. She was in the living room before she realized she was moving. Her mind floundered among all the things she wanted to say to find the perfect retort, the slap to reach back fifteen years.

Bobby was talking with animation and tossing his forelock out of his eyes. That was something else he had done as a boy, before he grew his hair to his shoulders in the sixties. He seemed taller than Kim remembered him, and she had forgotten some details: his high cheekbones; the way his lips quivered at rest as if they were mirroring what he was thinking. There were a half-dozen other people in the room who seemed to have flattened against the walls.

Bobby didn't notice Kim until she was a few feet away. He looked at her, then he grinned with unaffected delight. "Look who's here," he said in his gentle drawl. Kim's roil of emotion at seeing Bobby had given way to an icy calm. Slowly, carefully, gazing into his eyes, she hooked her hair behind her left ear. Bobby calmly studied her face, smiling. He had a cool excitement about him, a gentle zest like blue electricity that she had altogether forgotten.

"You take after Darcy," he said finally. "Archie, you recognize Kim Bonner? Taste of Home? Kimmy, this is Archibald Drake. He's Colleen's husband. Their kiddies are around here somewhere."

"Hello." Kim barely glanced at the short rodent-faced man who was staring at her with his close-set black eyes. She added, "Bobby, don't you think you've got something to say to me?"

Bobby startled, then chuckled one chuckle. He caught Kim in his arms and cuddled her in a presumptuous hug while he said close to her ear, "I'm not Bobby."

Kim felt knocked off-balance. She pushed away, but he was reluctant to let her go. He held her with his hands on her shoulders while he grinned down into her face. "You don't know who I am? You really don't know?"

Kim wasn't thinking well enough to do the calculations. "Timmy?" she whispered.

"Will you tell this guy I'm your brother? Nobody ever believes me. I say I'm your brother. I say I'm Bobby's son by a servin' wench, an' nobody *ever* believes me!"

"*That's my mother!*"

"Mine, too," Timmy said easily. He reached to take a half-full glass from the grand piano. "Believe me, if she were here she'd be the first one to call herself a servin' wench."

Kim had hardly thought of her brother in fifteen years. When people had asked, sometimes she had told them she had a brother living in another state, but sometimes it had been easier to call herself an only child. She was so used to being without relatives that the sight of this beautiful brother of hers stunned her with lightheaded amazement.

"Hold on! Are you all right? Here, sit down."

Timmy eased Kim into a chair while she concentrated on the firmness of his fingers through her sleeve, the sweet whiff of alcohol on his breath. "How old are you?" She was squinting up at him as if he were the sun.

"Twenty. I'm a sophomore at Harvard. An' I mean it. *Nobody* believes me."

"That I'm your sister? Should I write you a letter?"

Timmy laughed a soft, relaxed laugh that wasn't like Bobby's laugh at all. How could she ever have confused them? She saw now that while Bobby's cockiness had had a desperate edge to it, Timmy had the easy self-assurance of someone at peace to his core.

"Do you still have allergies?" She felt desolated to realize that was almost all she could remember about Timmy. Allergies and blowing bubbles in the sink and chocolate ice cream all over his face.

"Just a little hay fever," he said as she was adding, "Do you still blow bubbles in the sink?"

Timmy threw back his head in a shout of laughter. Someone across the room said, "Timmy! Please!"

"I remember that," he said to Kim, bending so they could speak privately. "You put dish soap in the sink an' gave me a straw. An' wasn't Darcy rippin'?"

"We got it all over the floor."

Kim nearly said, "You." She had always blamed Timmy for making a mess that day and spoiling their fun, but in this single instant she forgave him. For everything.

"I'm sorry about Mr. Sever," she said as Timmy hunkered on his heels beside her. Kim noticed the way he did that, the folding of one leg in advance of the other, the way he pinched up his pants to spare the creases. She felt as if she had suddenly been given the world's most miraculous toy, and she was desperate to learn all there was to know about it.

"He had cancer for two years. Lungs an' liver. It was a blessin', really."

"Oh. Poor man. And poor Mrs. Sever. I guess I should go now and pay my respects."

"She's upstairs restin'. We just got back from the wake. We've got to go again tonight. You're stayin' for dinner, aren't you? They're countin' on that."

"Oh. Sure. I guess so," Kim said distractedly. "Hey, something occurs to me. How would you like a summer job?"

"Doin' what?" He glanced at her with a conspiratorial twinkle.

Kim wanted to say, "Just being my brother," but she didn't know him well enough for that. Instead she said, "We're expanding into the South. We've got lots of jobs."

"Thanks. I'd like that, but Bobby'd be rippin'. He counts on me to manage stores. I spell the managers on vacation."

"What does he pay you?" Kim asked, and Timmy smiled. "I mean it. I'll double whatever he pays," she said in a voice so desperate she shriveled a little at the sound of it.

"Take it up with him," Timmy said with a shrug that made Kim realize how delicate his bones were, like the bones of a bird. "When your brother is also your father, he tends to think he owns you."

————◆————

Kim and Timmy were huddled near the western windows. The setting sun gave his skin a rosy caste and picked sparks of gold from his light-brown eyes. Kim asked him whatever questions came to mind, just prompting him to talk, while she watched the fading play of light on his face. She couldn't believe she never had wanted to know her brother, when the reality of him, his voice soft in her ear and the tremble of his earnest lower lip, thrilled her with a delight almost physical. She had an urge to smooth back his forelock and tuck his errant tie inside his jacket. From behind them Colleen said brightly, "Kimmy? Darlin'? Mama can see you now."

Timmy startled and stumbled to his feet. "Let her rest. She can see Kimmy at dinner." He paused, looking into the middle distance. From where Kim sat, he was Bobby completely. He swung down and slipped an arm around her shoulders and said, "I don't know what happened with you an' Bobby. They tell me stories. I can guess. I don't know how you're gonna feel about this, but you'll oblige me if you'll go say hello." Timmy drew her to her feet with his eyes and indicated the sofa and chairs behind her, where older people were murmuring over coffee. Kim turned, face first.

For an instant of time he was Mr. Sever sitting there. He had the same heavy hair, the same patient face full of tragic understanding. Kim saw him stiffen visibly and set down his cup.

"He didn't want you here. He fought with Colleen about callin' you," Timmy murmured while Kim looked at Bobby. "Colleen won. She brags about you all the time. But past is past. Go say hello."

Kim took a step. Bobby stood from the sofa, and his wife's hand went up after him. The grace of that supporting hand snagged on Kim's mind. It seemed to be a shout in Bobby's defense that he was a husband, valued and loved. Bobby was still a handsome man. He had a quiet, settled look at thirty-four, and his cheeks were developing his father's fullness but he still had the same fey, delicate face that Kim used to see behind her eyelids at night. He stepped out around the butler's table that Kim recognized with a catch in her throat. He waited for her, his face pinched and tight, then steered her into the foyer with a hand on her elbow. Bobby was heading for the library, but Kim stopped and faced him under the head of the front staircase. She thrust her chin, glaring into his eyes, breathing fiercely while she struggled to assemble the perfect thing to say. She lifted her hand and flicked her hair behind her ear.

"Why did you *keep* it?" Bobby twisted away.

"Look at it! Bobby . . . !"

He lifted his head and looked at her from the edge of his eye. Slowly he faced her, moving his eyes over her face with the same wistful pain that Vic had shown when he first saw Derek in the hospital. "I saw it in a magazine. *People* or somethin'. You told them a cat did it." Bobby dared to lift his finger and bring it so close to the top of her scar that Kim could feel the warmth of his hand on her skin. "Why did you *keep* it? Can't they fix it?"

"I don't know," Kim said to both questions. She found she had no heart to punish Bobby now, and that realization annoyed her. It had taken her years to build a healthy anger out of her misery of shame and loss, and then she had spent further years believing that someday she was going to have it out with him. But she couldn't do it. Her righteous rage seemed to be one more thing that he had taken from her. Realizing that made her angry enough to blurt, "I was a child! You were a grown man!"

He was looking at her with an expression that Kim remembered well, as if he were shouldering some monstrous sadness. It was a trick of the way his eyes were set, and something about his mouth; she realized, seeing him as an adult, that he wasn't sad at all. He was looking at her with the possessive intensity of a camera lens. "Not a day has passed that I haven't remembered." His voice faded with a sadness that was no more real than the sadness in his face. "Do you know how sorry I am? Do I have to say it?"

"Why did you *do* it? And why did you let them punish *me?*"

Kim saw a flicker then of genuine pain. He swung away from

her and lifted his head as if he were studying the construction of the staircase. He said, "I was glad."

"Glad they *punished* . . . ?"

"I had you once. Then you were gone." He paused. "You were beautiful. I was in love with you."

"It was *my life!*"

"Hush! Come in here." He tugged her through the library doors and closed them past a sticky spot that Kim recalled so vividly that she was surprised she hadn't built it into her library doors at home. Kim stood looking at remembered walls of books and breathing their scent of ancient musk. She was reeling, struck by the sudden awareness that they had all been victims, all three of them, the servant and the child and the lonely boy. What must Bobby have suffered then, pining for a girl beneath his station? And when had Darcy first seduced him? How far back went the cycle of pain?

Bobby's arms were stiffly bent, as if he were preparing to defend himself. "You want me to be honest. I owe you that."

"You owe me . . . !" Kim started to say. But her mind was wrestling with the calculations. My God. Darcy must have slept with Bobby when he was only thirteen years old.

"Do you want to try to understand this now? Or would you rather yell? Or hit me. You can hit me." Bobby straightened his arms to his sides with a visible effort.

"Of course not." But then Kim realized that was exactly what she wanted to do.

"I used to fantasize we'd find out your father was a prince. My mama'd insist I marry you. How's that for a confession?"

"You should have married me anyway. I grew up to be rich."

Then Kim realized with the same foolish amazement she had felt about her refusal to know her wonderful brother that if she hadn't been sent away she would be fixing dinner now in the Severs' kitchen. She and Darcy. They might well be sharing Bobby's bed with his wife and feeling grateful to do it. Kim had

had this thought before, but the immediacy of it in this room while she was looking at Bobby rocked her with the impact of truth.

"Why did you keep the scar?"

"I don't know."

She didn't. It seemed as much a part of her as the rest of her face.

"Perhaps they can . . . ?"

"I think it was the only thing I had from home. From you and my mother. It was all I had left. It made you part of me," Kim said in a rush, thinking that was actually true. "Every time I looked in the mirror I could remember who I really was."

"I'm so sorry."

"It's all right." She lifted her chin. "I forgive you. I never thought I would, but I do." She just wanted all this to be gone from her mind. She was weary of her long anger. Forgiving Bobby felt like a physical lightening, as if she had been carrying a rock around for fifteen years and she had just set it down on the rug at his feet.

"I'd do anythin' to make it up to you. The sad thing is, I've got nothin' you want."

"What about my brother?"

——◆——

When Timmy arrived in Indiana at the end of May, he was like an explosion of color on a black-and-white screen. Kim had designed for herself the perfect life: successful business, lovely home, glamorous lover. She was as famous for her lifestyle as she was for founding Taste of Home. When she gave interviews, most of the questions centered not on Taste of Home's expansion but on her parties and her house, on her cars and her plane and what it was like to live with Vic Engstrom. And when she was going to marry him. She was hearing that question more and more. But then Timmy came, with his gentle irreverence and his constant infectious delight.

Kim had written to him weekly in the intervening months, and he had sent her scribbled notes that each centered on some improbable theme. *Toxic Waste*, he would write at the top of the sheet. Then he would free-associate on the subject and its relationship to his own life in a tone at once poignant and gleefully funny. Kim had to be alone when she read his notes because they made her laugh aloud, and sometimes they made her run tears.

Kim liked to categorize new people in terms of people she had known before. She thought at first that Timmy reminded her of Colin Sanderlin, whose pleasure in the details of living used to make Kim feel more alive herself. Or perhaps he reminded her of Darcy's best qualities, her friendliness and her sweet simplicity. But after Timmy arrived, Kim realized within hours that he was an original. Nobody else had ever been so gentle and irreverent, so languid and frisky, so playful and wise. All Kim wanted to do in those first days was sit by the hour and talk with him. They talked while sprawled on sofas in the library. They talked sitting cross-legged on his bed. They were up doing that until two o'clock on the night he arrived, until Vic's little string of patience ran out and he stormed in and confronted them.

Vic had reacted to Kim's announcement that her brother would be spending the summer very much as she might have reacted if he had told her that Janice would be moving in. He hadn't known that she had a brother. He didn't believe it now. He thought Kim was prolonging a fling for which the funeral had been her cover, and he referred to Timmy as "Kim's little stud" during the two months they waited for him to arrive.

That Vic thought Kim would even dream of sleeping with Timmy made her queasy with revulsion. Kinship aside, she loved him too much. She couldn't stand to think of Timmy being sexual any more than she could think of Lou being sexual. But she couldn't say that without hurting Vic's feelings. So she didn't say anything beyond muttering, once, that if Vic didn't like it he was free to move out.

———◆———

That first night Timmy was in the house, Kim really did mean to go to bed. He drove up at ten in his silver Volvo, having been delayed by Speedway traffic, and she spent two hours helping him unpack and giddily helping him raid the kitchen. At midnight, she said "goodnight" and left him.

Vic was nursing a cold that Kim was sure was a psychosomatic response to the first-year anniversary of his decision to quit auto racing. She had thought when he first quit that it was just a temporary loss of nerve and he would go back to racing, if not in '86 then surely in '87. But now she realized that what had happened to Vic was less a loss of nerve than it was a breakdown of his whole covenant with God: if he raced again he was going to die. The distractions of his increased popularity had carried Vic through his first year of retirement, but this spring was another matter. It was impossible to avoid the Indy in May if you lived in Indianapolis, and as the month wore on, the buildup of reminders from newspapers and television had weighed him ever more heavily into a depression that had culminated in this wracking cold.

He was asleep when Kim entered her bedroom. He was graceful even in sleep, making a long S under the pink silk quilt with his arm flung naked across her pillow. Kim could hear the stuffy whistle of his breathing. She tiptoed into her closet and then into her bathroom, meaning to join him in bed; but by the time she had brushed her teeth, the lack of Timmy had become unbearable.

Timmy was asleep, half out of the blankets, wearing knee-length blue pajama bottoms covered in red hearts. When Kim knocked and then opened his door, he sat fast upright. "Hey, do

you know what I noticed?" he said foggily. "It's the same house."
He fell back against his pillows. Kim groped to close the drapes
on both windows so her security people couldn't spy on them. She
turned his lights halfway up with the dimmer and went to perch
on the edge of his bed.

"Do you feel like talking some more?"

"Oh. Sure." He pushed himself up to sit on his long, thin arms.
The blanket fell from his narrow chest and the fine corrugation
of his ribs.

"We've got to put some weight on you!"

"That's what Mama says. She's at me all the time. Don't you
start! Two fathers, an' now two *mothers?*" He made himself a
cross-legged nest against the padded headboard. Kim clambered
around him to the other side of his bed and did the same. They sat
there, Buddhas side by side, and smiled at one another.

"I figured it out. This would be my old room at home. But it's
so big! Bobby'd fall right over if he saw all this."

"Why don't you call him Daddy?"

"He's my brother. Like Darcy was a funny big sister. Did you
know we moved to the big house right after you left? I lost a sister
an' gained some parents. It seemed a fair deal at the time." He
picked up and studied the frayed ends of his pajama drawstring.
"They're good to me. Especially Daddy. I've cried my eyes out,
but I can't want him back the way he was. But look at what he
did. Prep school. Harvard. He even left a trust to pay for medical
school."

"Give it back. I'm making you president of Taste of Home."
Kim realized only as she spoke that was exactly what she was
going to do.

Timmy smiled. "You'd better see me in action first. A bull in
a china shop. When I come to town, they close the banks an' lock
up the women an' children."

"Did you ever think about me?" Kim asked lightly, not sure she wanted to hear his answer.

"A lot. I was lonely growin' up. Then you came back, but you took one look at me an' right away left. I know I acted stupid, but after all that time I didn't know what to say." Timmy's face wore a loose, open, wistful look. Kim's chest clutched with pain as she looked at him. She had been so involved with herself on the day she had gone back for Darcy's funeral that she hadn't thought to wonder what she was doing to that little boy.

"I'm sorry." She leaned to slip an arm around his bony shoulders. He let out a calm breath and lifted his chin. She slid nearer to him, thinking she would keep her arm around him, but she felt so awkward that after a moment she took it back.

"Then by the time you started to be famous I was at Choate. Try tellin' those guys some famous blonde who doesn't look like me an' doesn't have my name is my sister? Forget it. I wondered, too. I never heard from you. I thought you'd written me off."

"I had," Kim said lightly, watching the articulation of his lips in profile as he spoke. Every detail of him was as remarkable as if there never before had been eyes or teeth, never been skin that smelled like sunlight nor breath oddly scented like the skin of apples. Yet each new detail of him sparked in Kim a shiver of recognition, as if she were being reminded of things she must have known long ago. She couldn't believe there ever had been a time in her life when she hadn't known him. She said playfully, "You wouldn't let me read in bed. When you got water on the floor, *I* got switched for it. You'd better believe I wrote you off!"

Timmy gave her a twinkling smile. "Ah, Kimmy. I've dreamed about showin' up at your door. What you'd say. If you'd be glad to see me."

Kim slipped her arms around Timmy's waist and rested her head in the crook of his shoulder. She had never hugged anyone but Lou without a sexual undercurrent to the moment, but now the frail strength of Timmy's arms and the warm resilience of his skin produced a tremble of delight in her that was nothing like sexual arousal. It seemed to be a primitive joy of the body, as if her very cells were thrilling to have found their kin. They were sitting back from this hug when Vic kicked the door open. Kim didn't hear him try the knob; there was just an explosive crack and the door rang hard against the wall.

"What the hell is going *on* here?" Vic shouted.

In that moment of shock, Kim took in Vic's blue satin robe and Timmy's bright jams and her prim white nightgown with its long puffed sleeves. It was her virgin's nightgown. She wore it when she and Vic played deflowering games. He assumed that was what she was doing with this delicate boy.

"We're talking." Kim gave Vic a deliberate, stone-calm look. "We're catching up on fifteen years."

"*You weren't talking!*" Vic shouted. He picked up the chair that matched the cherry secretary beside the door and threw it at the wall, where it shattered in a series of crisp, dry cracks that Kim heard individually.

"No. We were hugging."

"Who *are* you?" Vic ranted, advancing on the bed. Even though Timmy had insisted that all he had now was a little hay fever and, yes, maybe a bit of asthma, there was a frailty about him that made Kim feel Darcy's old need to protect him. She grabbed her nightgown in a bunch and stumbled on her knees to put herself between them.

"He's my brother."

"Half-brother," Timmy added so pleasantly that Kim had to swivel and look at him. "You see, Vic . . . may I call you Vic? Our mama was a servin' wench who gave out comfort with the break-fast toast. She had Kimmy by a circus star an' me by my brother. My *adopted* brother. I'm the one who's adopted. By my father's parents. My grandparents, I mean to say. Does that make it any clearer?"

Vic was so nonplussed by this speech that he stalled a few feet from the bed. His cold reasserted itself with a ragged sneeze. "You don't think I believe one word of this, do you?"

"Frankly? I don't care whether you believe it or not. He's my brother. He's spending the summer here. Now I think you should respect your cold and go back to bed." Kim thrust her chin at Vic in what she realized was becoming a new mannerism, the stubborn assertiveness of a woman who had the power to push people around.

Vic's autobiography wasn't selling. His TV project had just been scrapped. Nearly all his recent advertising had been done for Taste of Home. Kim watched him thinking through the implications of all that as plainly as if she were seeing behind his face. Then with a poignant dignity that made her need to bite her lip to keep from calling after him, he shuffled a graceful turn on the carpet and walked out of the room. Kim let out a breath she hadn't realized she had been holding. Vic was fighting for her here as hopelessly as he fought for her on the board; he couldn't win, but just the fact of his losing made her feel a sickening moment of pain. She supposed she had known all along how this was going to come out.

———◆———

The August board meeting would be so climactic that Kim couldn't wait through a half-hour of approvals of minutes and reports. She intended to get right to the meat. Board members were shaking hands and smiling through tales of each other's vacations while they glanced inside their directors' folders.

Then Timmy came in, preceding Lou, telling over his shoulder some languid story of the sort he told Kim, where the humor seemed accidental and there were poignancies to catch on the mind for days afterward. It sounded like the one about trying to reform a cheater by feeding him incorrect answers, only to have him pass the answers to other cheaters until the wrong answers were such common knowledge that even honest students began to think they were right.

For Kim to assign Timmy to be Lou's assistant for the summer had been a mistake. They had become intense friends, perhaps because they were so much alike: they were cheerful, good-natured people with such secure egos they seemed to have no egos at all. Kim was realizing that she had a greedy need to own each of them individually, but now here they were, betraying her with one another.

"Please sit down." Kim tapped her gavel on its tablet.

"Did you see the price today, chick?" Marshall asked happily. "Thirty-nine and an eighth? How does it feel to be stinking rich? And why didn't I buy at twenty?"

"Please sit down. I've got an announcement to make."

Lou had stopped to talk with Connie at the far end of the table, where she was ducking to study a chafing dish of experimental curry beneath its lifted lid.

After a year of dating half a dozen women, Lou was spending more and more time with Connie. Kim knew that because Connie often called and talked a giddy streak about the places they had gone, the things he had said. Last week Lou had even made dinner for Connie. He had been telling Kim that his apartment was so shabby he didn't want her to see it, yet he had entertained Connie there amid his cement-block bookcases and futons on the floor.

Hearing Connie describe Lou's apartment had been alarming for Kim. He was still refusing to put down roots. He had arranged for one more year of sabbatical, but he had been told that would be the absolute limit and Kim knew that money wouldn't make him stay. He cared so little for the fees he had already earned that they were piling ever deeper in twenty banks, and he had begun to remark to Kim that he was going to have to take a cut because he was running out of banks.

"*Spend* something. Enjoy yourself," she had urged him.

Lou had lifted his gaze from Ellie's spreadsheets and said reflectively, "You know, the best thing about growing older is learning how many things you don't need."

Kim was going to miss Lou's plain wisdom, his honesty when nobody else would be honest. Last month she had gone through a period of disgust at the type of person she was becoming so she had asked a number of people to tell her whether she was turning into a rich, spoiled jerk.

"Of course not!"

"How could you even ask?"

"You're completely down to earth!"

"You haven't changed at all!"

Then she had asked Lou. He had said gently, "You're going through the worst thing I can imagine. Too much success too young. But all you need is one little failure. Have patience. It'll happen sooner or later."

Perhaps it was happening now.

"I'm going to open this meeting with an announcement and a request for a vote. As Marshall points out, the price of our stock is up to thirty-nine and an eighth despite the problems we're having getting started in the South. Steve and I think the run-up in price is due to a covert takeover attempt by a company called Lion's Paw, which we estimate now controls as much as twenty-five percent of our stock. We've protested to the SEC, but the California boys have covered their tracks. It seems we're on our own."

Kim looked around at six bland, friendly faces and two tense ones. None of them but Steve and Lou understood what this was going to mean. As she paused, Marshall even said lightly, "Call them up, chick. Form a coalition. You'll have your majority after all."

Kim took a calming breath and said, "On Monday I filed a notice of intent to buy a controlling interest in Taste of Home. I'll need three million shares, which means spending about a hundred and twenty million dollars. I've begun the process of margining my stock and mortgaging my home. I'll sell everything, if that's what it takes. I want my company back."

There was a long sound as each of them let out a breath. Lou's craggy face tightened. Kim hadn't mentioned this to him because she had been afraid he might talk her out of it.

"Surely there's another solution," Rodney said, sounding uncomfortable. "Why don't we look for a white knight who'll let us keep our autonomy?"

"No!"

Steve said wearily, "I've made inquiries. Nobody wants us. The price is so inflated they'd be paying twice what the company's worth. We've got lots of debt. Very little cash. We're the opposite of what the big boys want."

"It won't be easy," Kim went on as if she hadn't been interrupted. "Our stock is thinly traded, so no matter how carefully I buy I'm going to drive the price up even more."

"You'll pay retail and watch it crash," Marshall said dryly. "How to flush a fortune in one easy lesson."

"Have you thought of just selling and walking away?" Connie asked from Kim's right. "A hundred and some-odd million dollars makes a nice retirement fund."

"It's not my money. It came from Taste of Home. Now it's going back to Taste of Home. I don't care if I wind up penniless."

"You can have my medical trust," Timmy said brightly.

Kim felt her face soften as she looked at him, her tense cheeks going tender. He was leaving for Virginia in less than a week, so she was studying him all the time now, trying to fix his details in her mind.

Lou said, "Forty percent should let you keep them from controlling the board. If you try for a majority, you'll have so much margin the least drop in price will kill you."

"I'm going to have to take that chance."

Lou's building a relationship with Connie was making Kim feel as rejected as a child with a remarrying father. Not that his marriage would have to change anything. Jerry and Ellie had been married in July, and they had remained her devoted friends. But Lou had belonged to Kim so completely for so long that his shift in loyalty felt like a personal betrayal.

She said, "What I'd like now is the board's consent to my takeover of the company. I'm going to do it anyway, but it would be nice not to have to go hostile. Discuss it if you like. Or someone make a motion."

"There's no need to discuss it," Rodney said. "I move we invite Kim Bonner to buy a majority position, and I'm only glad she's willing to do it."

"Second," said Marshall.

"All in favor?"

Seven hands rose, not reluctantly but all at once. Kim's chest swelled. "Thanks. That's what I wanted to know."

———◆———

Since Ellie had no local family, Kim had for years been giving her birthday dinners. In 1987 her birthday fell on Friday, November thirteenth, and Vic grumbled about the stupidity of doing *anything* on a Friday the thirteenth, but he dressed for the party because that was what Kim wanted. Whenever he complained now, just a look from her was enough to silence him.

Kim had long been the actual boss while they both had pretended that Vic was in charge, but she was becoming unwilling now to pretend anything at all. She was feeling a fine impatience with Vic, an anger she couldn't pin down beyond noting how miserably he failed to compare with Lou on so many levels. She was coming to feel as if being with Lou always had been like hearing a symphony, while Vic had never been more than one note. Why had she never noticed that before? Her anger with Vic at his failings and at herself for having been blind to them was driving her now to humiliate him in subtle ways, and to what she saw as their mutual surprise, he put up with it. Oh, he had money enough to leave. Kim thought he must have several million dollars. But his fame now came mostly from Kim, and he hungered for public attention as surely as she shrank from it.

Kim had invited just Ellie and Jerry and Lou to this little birthday dinner, but Lou had insisted she include Connie, too.

"What, now you're Siamese twins?"

"Come on, you'd make me go alone?"

There was so much tension between herself and Lou now that Kim was even picking fights with him, doing anything to provoke interactions, to draw him closer while she pushed him away. She was aware of what she was doing, and embarrassed by it, but still she didn't seem able to stop. She would blush with shame as she said things like, "Connie was married twice. What does that say about her?"

"I've been married, too. She doesn't seem to hold that against me."

Kim was so worried about his marrying Connie that a couple of times the question slipped out. "Lou? If you were getting married, you'd tell me, wouldn't you? I wouldn't have to read it in the papers?"

"What makes you think any paper would print it?"

"Lou . . . !"

"I'll tell you if you'll tell me."

"But you're not, are you? Not right now?"

"What makes you think any woman would have me?"

Hearing the word "woman" in Lou's voice was unexpectedly titillating. Kim bit her lip and looked away.

———◆———

Ellie's favorite meal was a chicken fricassee with carrots and peas and little pearl onions that Darcy used to make. It wasn't dinner-party fare, but as one of seven courses with salmon in aspic and artichoke salad and borscht, with stuffed potatoes and apple-cheese tarts and chocolate-frosted rumcake, it made an adequate meal.

"This is great!" Connie said when she tasted the salmon. "Isn't it great, Lou? Can the company offer it, do you think?"

"Oh, I don't think so," Kim said crisply.

There were two-foot tapers lined the length of the table, so faces were dreamily lit from above. Lou and Jerry were at Kim's end, while the female guests sat on either side of Vic. Jerry and Ellie were so caught up in their brand-new marriage that every conversation Kim started with Jerry would falter as he included his wife, and Vic had a similar problem at his end of the table. So he talked mostly with Connie, and Kim with Lou.

"How much did you buy on the downtick?" Lou asked as the salad was being served. Rosalinde and Kim's butler, Johnson, were wraiths beyond the island of candlelight.

"Almost fifty thousand shares. All I could get. It seems the California cowboys dropped out at fifty-five, and the dip to forty-eight didn't bring them back. Now the analysts say we're going south, which should bring even more stock out of the mattress," Kim added, feeling a surge of relief. It looked as if her crisis had already passed.

"So now you've bought . . . what?"

"A million and a half. I'm halfway there."

"That should be enough. That's close to forty percent. Don't tap yourself out."

"It's exactly forty percent. But I'm going for broke. Fifty-one or nothing."

This salad had been invented by Taste of Home's senior California chef. It was such an odd combination of flavors—artichokes with endive and goat cheese, lime bits, and sun-dried tomatoes—that it made Kim think of an orchestra combining to create one perfect note.

Lou said, "You know, if you run short of cash, I've got a little in the bank."

"Thanks, but we're really pulling in our belts. We're down to two gardeners and one limousine." Kim stifled a smirk at the wry look on Lou's face.

"When I first saw you in class in a flannel shirt and those long braids . . . ."

"A flannel shirt? Really? How embarrassing."

". . . I pegged you for a natural rich person."

"I'm a natural, all right." Kim let her voice trail off as she caught what Vic was saying at his end of the table.

"I just wanted a pool. One little pool. She wouldn't even consider it. Now, suddenly, we're building a *pool* . . . ."

Kim hadn't wanted a swimming pool to spoil the line of her long back lawn. Highgrove didn't have a pool, which had been reason enough not to build one here. But after seeing Highgrove again in March, it was her home's resemblances to Highgrove that made her uncomfortable and not their differences. Then one muggy day Timmy had remarked that what this place really needed was a swimming pool.

Lou said, "Do you know what you should do? You should take a cruise."

Lou and Connie had taken a Hawaiian cruise in September. Now they were even vacationing together.

"There's a luxury ship called *Sea Goddess*. I hesitate to say it's like having your own yacht, because the next thing I know you'll be buying one."

"Do they come in pink?"

"*Kim . . .* !"

"I guess not." Kim sipped her wine and added, "Do you want to know something? I'm starting to get tired of pink."

———————

Kim changed for bed in her closet, which was a dressing room with a Queen Anne chaise. She was holding for as long as possible the essence of this evening, the resurgence of her old sense of identity with Lou, that feeling she almost wasn't sure where he left off and she began. For the first time in a long time, she hadn't felt uneasy around him. She hadn't resented his talking with Connie, nor found him too intensely male. She was slipping her nightgown on and thinking with relief that her problems with Lou were over, too.

Vic didn't like it when Kim dressed in her closet. He wandered in and out, making remarks. She answered him in monosyllables while she hugged to herself the gentle pleasures of this evening.

"That poor old goat just spent another night drooling over what he can never have," Vic remarked from the doorway. He was wandering naked while he used his cordless electric razor. And the fact that he was shaving again meant that he was going to want to make love. "Do you think he'll ever get tired of it?" he pressed when Kim didn't say anything. "Decide it's time to get on with his life?" She lifted her head and looked at Vic. There was a thin, angry edge to his voice.

"Lou?"

"Don't give me those big eyes, lady! You know he's dying to get in your pants. And you love it. You never get sick of the game. But what gripes you is he's finally found a woman to take the edge off. You can still give him a hard-on, but now he's got something to do with it."

"You're *disgusting!* All you think about is filth! He's not like you. He's a decent man. And he doesn't sleep with Connie. They're just friends."

"Dream on, baby," Vic said without interest as he wandered back out of the closet. Kim followed him. For Vic to believe something made it seem to be true.

He was ducking gracefully to see inside his top drawer. "What I love is the way you keep teasing him." Vic's voice was stiff as he shaved his cheek. He reached a careful hand to probe the drawer's corners as his voice went high. 'Lou-ou, is my slip showing?' 'Lou-ou, is my seam straight?' 'Lou-ou, wouldn't you love a little nookie if only I'd give it to you?'"

"I've never said anything like that!"

"No. You pretend you're talking business. But all you have to do is bat your eyes and the poor guy almost wets his pants."

"That's not *true!*" To Kim's horror, tears were blurring her eyes.

"Of course it's true. Have you seen my gold chain?"

"Look in your bathroom," Kim mumbled. She was seeing Lou's gentle crooked smile, his face sweet and wise and kindly. The thought that he might have sex on his mind made her skin shrink with horror.

"It's not there." Vic was wandering out of his bathroom. "Have them look for it tomorrow, will you?" He paused in mid-stride and said. "Don't take it so hard. We're all used to seeing it. Nobody cares. Oh, I did care at first, but I can see the last thing you want is Uncle Louie in your bed. Then the game's over, baby. You give it to him once and the game's all over."

"Stop it!" She was so careful to keep decorum for the sake of the servants that the sound of her own shouting made her wince.

"I don't blame him. What rips me is you. *You,* lady, are the horniest woman I've ever met in my life. But you pretend you're so reluctant, you're so damn pure, and when you find out you love it that's a big surprise. *Every time* it's a surprise! Do you think I'm a fool?"

"*Stop it!*"

Vic would never dream of talking this way outside their bedroom. With her consent, he was master here. But she had to set limits. She shouted, "You will *never* talk about him again! You're not fit to lick his boots!"

"No, but I'm fit to lick something else."

"Shut up!"

"*You* shut up!"

"No, *you* shut up!"

He wheeled and snapped a look at Kim that dried her throat and stabbed her groin with sexual feeling. "It's time you learned some manners." He grabbed her wrist and yanked her toward his closet. She struggled, feeling aroused against her will by their conversation and by this new intensity in a man who had seemed to stop caring about anything.

Vic had bought her leather handcuffs for their first Christmas, with ropes attached to tie her to the bed. Kim hadn't seen them for two years at least.

"Vic, I really don't think . . . ."

He was buckling on the cuffs, holding her wrists one by one in the air between them. Kim watched, feeling an odd combination of detachment and titillation.

"Look, why don't we just . . . ?"

"Do you think he'd do this for you?" Vic muttered as he tugged her toward the bed. "Do you think he'd play games with you? Tie you up? Do you think you wouldn't *disgust* him?"

Kim planted her feet and yanked the ropes out of his hands. Vic was so astonished that he stood, staring blankly. He wasn't used to more than symbolic resistance.

"You're getting too full of yourself, my love," he said in the patient voice he used to adopt at these moments, the voice that made Kim feel like a child for whom an adult was doing these difficult things for her own good. His gaze on her hardened as he added, "It's time somebody put you in your place." He stalked off past her back into his closet.

Kim knew he had a whip in there, a horse-riding whip about three feet long he had hit her with a few times, lightly, symbolically, as part of some particular game. Even those little taps had hurt quite a bit.

"Vic . . ." Kim started to say. But she was swaying with the force of memory.

Darcy used to cut a switch off the forsythia bush that grew beside the road. Suddenly Kim remembered as if it were only now happening the way Darcy would take a knife from the kitchen drawer and lead Kim out there by the hand. They would come back together across the yard and cross the porch, and Darcy would sit down on one of the kitchen chairs. Kim was remembering intensely that feeling of creeping across Darcy's lap. There had been a peculiar thrill to it that she realized now must have been sexual; she had thought at the time it was a need to go to the bathroom. Sometimes Darcy used to let her run and do that, although sometimes she insisted Kim was stalling.

Those had been the only times that Darcy had touched her daughter on purpose. If they ever had hugged, Kim had been too young at the time to remember it now. So she used to thrill to the feeling of her hand being held. She savored the solid comfort of her mother's thighs under her hips and chest, and the furtive touches of Darcy's hands as she lifted a skirt, pulled down shorts and pants. Darcy had had Vic's manner about her at those moments, that sense of patiently hurting Kim for her own good. And from the time she was tiny, Kim had loved the stinging of that switch. She could admit that now, hearing Vic's muffled rummaging in his closet while she wondered how she was going to talk him out of this. Oh, it had hurt, she had cried, and if Darcy hit her more than half a dozen times she used to struggle from a primitive panic at having her body damaged. But she had loved being switched. Sometimes, as she grew older, she would misbehave on purpose just to have the comfort of correction. The touching and the pain were bound up together with the heart-swelling certainty that Darcy wouldn't bother to do all that unless she loved her.

Slowly, watching the closet door, Kim unbuckled the leather cuffs. She caught them by their ties and set them on the bed so she would remember to put them away. She wanted to spare her servants the confusion of finding them.

"Pay attention now," Vic was saying as he fumbled out through his closet clutter. "I'm going to prove something to you once and for all."

"No, you're not."

He stopped in the doorway.

"Put it back," she said with such level firmness that he hesitated. Then she heard a dim clatter as the whip and something else hit the floor. He knew that he had overstepped. His face wore a strange, half-sullen look of mingled anger and supplication. She said, "Now you get out of here. You're never going to touch me again."

But even as she said it, she knew she wasn't going to put him out. No matter how much she yearned now for a day when she might be free of him, she couldn't bring herself to put him out.

———◆———

Kim stood from her desk and wandered toward her wall of windows. Bits of snow were flitting, hanging in the air, wheeling and rushing like schools of fish in the errant winds whirling among the buildings. This was the end of a two-day storm that had closed the airport until an hour ago. Kim had fretted on the phone with Lou all weekend that the storm would prevent his getting to Newark in time to attend the IRS audit of a franchisee. Now what she was fretting about was the danger of his flying in the snow.

The January board meeting should have been held the day after tomorrow, but Kim had postponed it until Friday so Lou could be there. She couldn't face alone the four new members who had unexpectedly voted themselves onto the board at the December stockholders' meeting.

The California cowboys.

Some guy from New Jersey.

Some woman from South Carolina.

Her double doors clicked, sounding so loud in the snow-blanketed quiet that Kim whirled defensively. There was Lou, setting down his briefcase. "Great day to fly," he remarked. She studied him hungrily, needing the sight of him.

"Should I be doing anything? To get ready for Friday?"

"Kim, it's not a disaster. What can they do? Even if they're acting together, you've got four votes to match their four. Then you'll break the tie. What can they do?"

"I'd feel better if you were a member." Kim rubbed her upper arms through their sleeves. She was feeling a chill more abstract than cold.

"I'm better for you off the board. You've got the votes, anyway. Steve and Marshall. Paul and Vic."

"But what if I lose even one of them? Vic? What if he moves out again? And what happens when they're all up for re-election, too?"

"This will be long gone by December." Lou smiled at her wanly in the clean white light, breaking his face into planes and creases. Seeing his smile, Kim felt a rush of tenderness for him, a welling so intense that she choked and swallowed.

"I should be back by Thursday night," Lou was saying. "A day or two in Newark, then another day with the rest of the troops. But frankly, this smells like a fishing expedition. I'm only going because the franchisee is green enough to do something stupid."

Kim was feeling consumed by her need to be close to him. She crossed the room, her heels loud on the parquet floor and muffled on the carpet, and put a hand shyly on his arm. The tweed was rough and nubby, warm and alive, as if she were feeling the energy of his body through the cloth. She took back her hand.

He said, "I'll fix it. I promise."

chapter nine

January 28 - April 16, 1988

The board meeting was over in half an hour. The tense and frantic staff meeting that followed it lasted for most of the afternoon, and for all that time Kim watched the side of Lou's face. She was so distracted by him that she kept losing track of what was being said by all these people who were desperate to save her corporate life.

Kim had hurried into her office to escape the impotent shouts growing louder in the boardroom, and Ellie and Jerry had crowded in after her like children made frantic by parental strife. Then had come Fred Fletcher and Raul Mendoza. Kim had hired Fred away from Graham Harvey to handle her corporate communications soon after he had stood over her desk and vowed to make her famous; and his friend, Raul Mendoza, was Taste of Home's in-house counsel. Kim spun at her desk and blurted, *"Well!"* Then she bit her lip. She didn't want to further alarm her people. What came out after she had taken a long breath was a bright, "Everyone's here. Now all we need is Lou."

Ellie sank onto the office couch, giving Kim a panicky look. Kim tried to feed Ellie calm reassurance, eye to eye, while what she was feeling was a fluttery sense of reality settling around her like dust in the air. It was as if the past sixteen years had been a single night's dreaming. Now the shock of that board meeting had jolted her awake to become again just Kimberly Bonner, small fatherless waif, airing rooms and making beds and serving breakfasts to a Mr. Sever who was no longer there.

Ellie had gotten pregnant on her honeymoon, and at six months along her formerly hidebound frame was plumping wonderfully. Kim looked at Ellie's luminous hair and skin, her radiant eyes, and she tried to remember the heavy contentment of her own lost pregnancy. She thought she would never be pregnant again. She couldn't imagine ever again trusting so much.

"Where's Lou?" Kim clenched her teeth at the note of panic in her own voice. He was out there placating the upstart directors who had minutes earlier tried to oust her from the management of her own company. "Jerry, ask Karen to send Lou to us as soon as he's free. Then please close the door."

The shouts were coming from the hallway now. Kim heard snippets of Marshall's belligerent bellows of "*How* can you think you can . . . ?" "*What* the hell *right* . . . ?" above the murmurs of Lou's patient peacemaker's voice saying, ". . . I'm sure we can work it out . . . we just need some time . . . ." Kim listened through Marshall's shouts and the growls of those evil strangers for the distinctive rise and fall of Lou's voice. Even such a faint hint of him thrilled her with a private comfort so familiar she must have been feeling it all along, although now it seemed brand-new. She had owed him so much before this morning, but now she owed him everything. If he hadn't joined the meeting when he did, if he hadn't known just what to do, she might very well at this moment be packing the things in this office that didn't belong to Taste of Home. It had been that close.

"We've got some talking to do," Kim began as she closed her double doors, creating an immediate hush. She walked around her desk and sat down in her chair. "I don't know how much you were able to hear, so I'll tell you what just happened. Two of our new directors control twenty-eight percent of the company through

their own company, called Lion's Paw. They're claiming I've mis-
managed the business and misappropriated funds. They've called
for my immediate ouster." Kim paused for the expected gasps.
"They even offered me a million dollars' severance pay. But I'm
not going anywhere."

"Can they *do* that?" Ellie wailed.

"Lou saved the day for us. He forced an adjournment to buy
some time. Now it's up to us to use that time wisely."

"But what can we *do?*"

Kim knew Ellie was worried that both she and Jerry might
lose their jobs just as they were becoming parents. She said gently,
"Trust me, Ellie. There's no way on earth they're going to take
my company away from me."

The door opened then, and Lou came in. He winced, looking
around at the senior staff sitting in the chairs that each preferred
for meetings. "Oh. This isn't a good time, Kim. Call me when
you're free."

"Sit down!" Kim stood like a hostess. "Here, Lou. Sit here." She
was remembering why Lou might not feel welcome. Earlier this
morning, in her agony of worry over facing all those new directors, she had shouted at him horrid and insulting things, doubting
his motives, refusing his help. She hadn't meant those things, even
as she was saying them. Now the realization that he had come to
her office expecting to be fired made her cheeks glow with shame.

———◆———

Repeatedly during that afternoon, Kim tried to catch Lou's eye,
but he sat facing the others and he never looked at her. Kim
watched and watched his face in profile throughout that panicky
afternoon, loving its every detail, willing him to know what she
was going to blush and stammer to have to tell him. She was
sorry. She was grateful. This wasn't his fault. As she watched
him calmly dealing with her crisis, she began to speculate about

when Louis Pointe had been transformed from just her mentor and friend to the entire center of her emotional life. When had that happened? She could see no beginning more recent than their long-ago first picnic in the grass. Even then, this man had delighted her. Even then.

Meetings of the Taste of Home board had always been casual gatherings of friends operating under a relaxed set of rules. Kim had made a fresh beginning for her new board by giving up the informal sampling of foods, but still she had had no clear idea of the way a real board meeting should be run. Sam Denton of Lion's Paw and his advisers had used her inexperience to claim the floor for fifteen minutes, citing sin after sin committed by Taste of Home's management all documented in spiral-bound booklets that Denton dropped with a snap before each director. He moved like what Kim thought of as a balding and bow-legged little Vic, glancing out the window in mid-sentence, pausing to clutch the backs of chairs. Vic stepped out of his way whenever he went by. Vic was wearing a carefully bland expression that mixed amusement with a swelling anger and, Kim thought, with a measure of satisfaction at her distress. Twice in the past two months, Vic had packed up and moved back to his farm, only to return when Kim's worry over his welfare had made her go after him. Things between them were not going well at all.

Kim was shut off whenever she tried to interrupt Sam Denton. She was forced to listen to his diatribe for fifteen minutes, biting her lip, tipping up her chin to hold back tears. When Lou came in, she suffered a chill of horror to have him witnessing this greatest shame of her life; but after he had listened for several minutes, Lou wrote a note and passed it to Steve Vorovich behind the sweaty young fellow in the slick dark suit.

"I object to the consideration of this question," Steve read from the note.

Kim grabbed up her gavel and tapped it and said, "Lou? Is

that in order?" Denton's attorney stood and bent to confer with Lou briefly; then he stepped back. Lou nodded to Kim. She took the vote, but it was tied and a two-thirds majority was needed to drop the issue. So Sam picked up his rant from a standing start, until almost at once another note found its way from Lou to Steve behind Dominick Ashton. That was the man's name. Dominick was staring at Kim, then seeming to stare at nothing, then looking at Kim again. A film of perspiration gave his face the glittery look of a fine-sprayed fruit.

"I move we lay this motion on the table," said Steve.

"Lou?" Kim asked, reaching for her gavel.

"Now, *wait* a minute!" Sam shouted. "Greg? Get your ass in here! Earn your fee!"

This time, the attorney objected with an indignation that Kim heard as a series of rapid hisses. Then he stepped back, reseating his horn-rims with one finger.

"Mr. Denton's attorney takes the position that debate has already begun, which makes Steve's motion out of order." Lou sounded as if he were thinking as he was speaking. "Has a motion to remove the president been made?"

Kim couldn't remember having heard such a motion. She thought she would remember something like that. But the board splintered into private arguments that she had to gavel into silence while she noticed freshly the woman on her right, the one from South Carolina. There was something familiar about the way she held her head, as if she were pushing against the sky. The whine in her voice carried the smell of paint and the old, small worries of college life.

"We were *shocked*," Denton blurted, winding himself up again. "We thought we were buying an investment. This isn't an investment! This . . . ." Denton's voice feathered involuntarily as he watched yet another note make its way behind sweaty, smiling Dominick Ashton.

"I object to the right of this board to consider this matter," Steve said, reading.

"Of all the . . . *Gregory!*"

This time the lawyer's conference with Lou was longer and angrier. Eventually Lou said, "We can't agree. Just note Steve's objection in the minutes." Against the wall to Kim's right, Karen scribbled in rapid shorthand. Kim tried to read from Lou's eyes some sign of how this was going, but he looked away from her, drawing a rapid breath.

"So, anyway, we don't have a *choice*," Denton huffed, resuming his rant as he prowled past Vic's empty chair. Vic was standing at the window, boot on the sill, gazing down listlessly into the street. "We have a responsibility as *directors* . . ." Denton was saying. Another note was on its way. "We have a *duty*," he insisted, trying to talk his way past whatever Steve was about to say.

"Ahem!" Steve said loudly. "In view of all this confusion, I move we adjourn until we can sort things out."

"Out of the question!" Denton shouted.

"Second," said Vic from the window. His eyes met Kim's down the length of the marble table.

"Oh. Well. Lou?"

"That's a motion."

"*Wait* a minute! Greg? Where's your two cents?"

The attorney stood from his chair. "We object. Mr. Denton has the floor."

"This board allows a motion to adjourn at any time. Take the vote, Kim." Lou's eyes were steady on hers.

"Okay. That's a motion to adjourn. All those in favor?" Kim sucked in her breath and looked around the table as Steve's, Marshall's, and Vic's hands rose at once. Then Paul's hand rose. He was giving Kim his unreadable look, as flat and bland as the eyes of a fish.

"Okay. Good. Thank you. Anyone else?" Kim looked at

Dominick Ashton, who was staring at her. Carefully, willing each muscle to act, she managed a thin smile, and he lifted his hand. "That's five. Great. Thank you. Is anyone opposed?"

"I'm opposed! Hicks! You idiot! Do something! Raise your hand!"

Hicks Waverly had been studying Kim with such tiny eyes so deeply set that they didn't give off the heat of contact that made being looked at feel uncomfortable. Slowly he lifted one wrist-thick finger.

"Opposed!" snapped the woman sitting on Kim's right. "How dare you railroad this meeting!"

"Finish the vote," Lou prodded.

"It's five to three. Now, um . . . Lou . . . ?"

"Adjourn the meeting."

"This meeting is adjourned." Kim stood and left the room.

Lou spent the better part of that long afternoon talking with the staff. "You've got to answer their points. Ellie can do that. The most they've got is the plane and Kim's security, but we have the plane in a lease program and she's had death threats." Lou sat back with a softening of his body that made Kim see how tired he was. "Then you'll feel them out individually and arrange a compromise before the next meeting. There's a provision in the bylaws for written approvals of minutes and reports, so you've got a month to work things out. That five-to-three vote was a positive sign. Only a couple of the new directors are troublemakers."

"But what about the Fragones?" Fred Fletcher asked. They had only just learned that a crime syndicate based in New Jersey had purchased perhaps a dozen Taste of Home franchises and begun to use them as retail conduits for drugs and prostitution.

"I'll work on that now. I – Jerry can meet with the authorities. You've got nothing to hide. You might release another statement, something stronger than the fifty-word 'no comment' you put out this morning. Public apologies and vows to fix things generate interest in a stock. As strange as it seems, the best way to protect the price for Kim might be to hype this a little."

"But the Fragones themselves?" Fred persisted. "Should we meet with them?"

Kim looked at earnest Fred Fletcher, who but for his receding hairline might have been a college student. She pictured him strolling alone into a smoke-filled den of fedoras and crisp black shirts armed with nothing but his pen and his plain righteousness.

"I don't advise it. Even a secret meeting makes you seem to be allied with them. And if they come here, Kim," Lou added, giving her a wincing glance, "have Jerry hustle them out. Don't meet with them."

Kim wanted to say, "Why not have *you* hustle them out?" But then a chill realization raised brief gooseflesh. Lou was quitting. That was why everything he was saying was in the second person.

"Well. Oh, look at the time." Kim stood up, hooking her hair behind her ear. "You must be exhausted. Lou has given you your tasks. We'll meet again on Monday at two. Use all the staff you need. And – ah – check with Lou if you need help or if you've got questions." She was coming around the end of her desk to hurry their leave-taking. "Good night! Don't worry. Everything's fine. Take care of yourself, Ellie. Lou? Can I speak with you, please?"

He had been politely standing aside so the others could precede him. He glanced at Kim, then reached for one of the doors and fitted it to the other behind the final back. Kim was trying to assemble an apology so perfect it would make their relationship instantly whole, but while she was doing that he said, "I'm sorry. Every bit of this is my fault. I've been trying to . . . ."

"No!" She still didn't have the words right, so she hurried around the chairs and hugged him hard. "It's *my* fault." Her cheek was tight against the comfort of his broad tweed chest. "I didn't know what I was doing. If it weren't for you . . . !"

His arms closed around her as if he mistrusted his own strength. His cheek settled against her hair. "I'm sorry. I didn't have enough faith in you. I kept thinking I knew better."

"*No!*" She looked up at him, feeling desperate to make this right. The perfection of his dear out-of-kilter features choked off her every attempt at thinking.

"You're brilliant. You've been right all along. But I'm so damn stubborn." He took a long breath and added, "I don't know how to make it up to you. I've got some money in the bank. It's not much, but it'll buy some time. And I'd be willing to stay, but I'm sure you'd . . . ."

"You have to stay! None of this means anything without you!"

"Oh, sweet." He studied her face with a look of abstracted pain. One big hand came up to stroke her hair.

She hugged him tighter around his waist, loving the good solid bulk of him. His hand paused on her hair while he looked down at her with such tenderness that she felt at once thrilled and alarmed. She murmured, "I'm sorry. Please forgive me for what I said. I'm just so scared." But she wasn't scared. Standing there safe in Lou's arms, she wasn't afraid of anything.

For Kim to be gazing raptly up at Lou was creating a growing awkwardness. He drew her closer and kissed her hair and released her, helping her take her arms from his waist. He caught her hands as they slipped through his and said, "You really want me to stay?"

"How can you even ask the question?"

"All right. I'll stay until the end of July. We'll have it all fixed by then. You don't really need me, you know. You've always been able to fly on your own. But if you think I can help, little business wonder, then naturally I'll stay." Lou gave Kim a pained edge of a smile that seemed to be a plea that she not take any of this too seriously. She thought his new use of pet names was for the same reason, to make light of it all: he had never in six years called her anything but Kim, but now he had a different name for her every minute.

"Tell me it's going to be all right."

"Of course it is, sweet. Piece of cake."

———————

Sitting at her desk and signing letters while she waited for Bobby Sever to arrive felt so peculiar that Kim kept glancing at her watch. The pale afternoon light of mid–March made it seem to be growing dark outside, when in fact it was just after three o'clock. The thought of Bobby Sever in this room felt like a blending of past and present so messy that Kim might never be able to separate them again. She stood restlessly and went to her window to look down at the traffic striped with light where the frail sun of early springtime found thin leeway between the buildings. It was already evening where the sun didn't reach. Looking almost a hundred feet straight down made Kim feel more intensely than ever the odd, caged panic that her office sometimes raised in her. The richer and more famous she had become, the more constrained had become the limits of her world.

Each of Denton's complaints had been answered in writing before the February board meeting. Most of the directors had been met with and coddled individually. And fortunately, those out to make trouble mistrusted each other even more than they mistrusted Kim, so with Lou there to prompt Steve or Marshall to say the right things, a semblance of a normal board meeting had been held. But things hadn't looked so bad in February, when the price of the stock had stood at forty-five and there had been articles predicting that Taste of Home's frozen foods might be an even bigger success than its motel services. Kim had believed in February that the worst was over.

But then, as they were leaving the board meeting, Paul Whist had taken Kim and Lou aside and announced in his blank-eyed, mousy fashion that if the students weren't gone from the kitchens by the end of March, he couldn't rule out a strike. He wasn't threatening, mind you, but he couldn't control his workers much longer. Then Higgins & Stein had made the awful announcement that it wouldn't be carrying Taste of Home's frozen foods in any of its fifteen hundred and twenty-eight stores. Higgins & Stein was the largest chain of supermarkets in the nine Southern states, so for it to decline to carry Taste of Home's frozen foods was a blow to the frozen-food effort and might even doom the company's whole Southern expansion. The promise of frozen foods to come had been a spur to the sale of motel services, since people used to eating Taste of Home at home would be more likely to opt for it on the road. But if there wasn't going to be a frozen-food line after all . . . ?

"Miss Bonner? Mr. Sever is here."

Kim dove for her chair. She was sitting there with pen in hand when Bobby Sever walked in with careful precision. She had forgotten the prissy way he used his body.

"Bobby! Hi. Good to see you." Kim stood and extended her hand to him, but Bobby set his briefcase on one of her guest chairs and came around the end of her desk and hugged her.

"This is quite the place," he said in his soft Southern voice, smiling sadly as he stepped away. He had known from Kim's stiffness in his arms that she didn't intend this to be a meeting of familiars, so he shifted to cordiality, walking a circuit of her office while he admired her artwork and the view from her wall-sized window.

Kim said, "It's good of you to be willing to help. As I said on the phone, I'm in kind of a pickle."

Bobby had arrived at the guest chair that didn't hold his briefcase. Perhaps it was his resemblance to Timmy, or perhaps it was all the effort Kim had made to convince herself that he had been another victim, but as she looked at Bobby now she no longer saw that rapist and destroyer of a young girl's life. She didn't feel anything at all toward him beyond an ashy awareness of emotions long spent.

"My, Kimmy," he was saying, cocking his head as if that might help him make better contact with the girl inside the woman. "My, you sure have made a success of yourself. It wasn't real until I saw all this. My, my."

"You're pretty successful yourself." Kim wanted to steer this conversation as quickly as possible to the matter at hand. "Timmy brags about you all the time. What is it now? Fifteen stores?"

"Thirteen. Thanks for noticin'. We're havin' fun, but it's hardly a nationwide deal like what you're doin' here. Every time I drive by Foxy's an' see that little pink sign, I think, *That's our Kimmy.* Every time I see your TV ads . . . ."

The door opened. Lou's walk when he wasn't paying attention to walking was a loose-jointed amble, a stroll almost playful. He still had not in all this time bought much clothing for his new life, so he was wearing the same green tweed jacket he had worn to picnic with Kim on the day they met. She fixed her eyes on him as he entered the room.

"Is this about right? Am I early?"

"Just right."

He was looking at her as she was looking at him, filling his mind with the sight of her before he turned to Bobby. Kim realized he always had looked at her this way, but it was only since January that she even had noticed. So many things Kim had noticed about Lou in just the past few weeks.

"I'm J. Robert Sever. Call me Bobby." He eased his briefcase to the floor with one hand while he shook Lou's hand with the other. So then Lou sat down in the guest chair where the briefcase had been, rather than in his usual side chair. Kim could glance at him while she talked with Bobby.

"You read Higgins & Stein's announcement, Bobby, about two weeks ago?" Unconsciously Kim was slipping into Southern speech patterns. She watched Lou notice that. "Well, as I said on the phone, it took some digging but we've figured out what's going on. Too weird for words."

Lou knew about Kim's past with Colin and Faith, but still telling this story to Bobby while Lou was sitting there would be embarrassing. Even seeing Lou and Bobby together felt like an odd kind of nakedness, as if Lou could absorb by osmosis from Bobby the shame of her poor upbringing and the humiliation of her rape.

"Ah, well, I had a boyfriend in college. Sort of a boyfriend," Kim added quickly. The word "boyfriend" implied a sexual involvement. "He had a very jealous former girlfriend. And – can you believe it? – she married John David Neiquist, who's bought a controlling interest in Higgins & Stein. They've also bought stock in Taste of Home and voted her onto my board, where she tries to make all the trouble she can, although fortunately she's too suspicious to ally herself with anyone. But as strange as it seems, this woman is apparently out to break me in revenge for her old lost love."

"That sounds pretty female."

Kim snapped a look at Bobby as Lou was saying, "It's more male than female, if you've got to talk gender. I've seen more nutty revenge plays by men than I've ever seen by women. But listen to Kim. This woman has a nuttiness all her own."

"I've tried to befriend her. I didn't realize who she was at first, but at the February meeting I tried to chat with her about old times. I couldn't believe this was all about Colin, when neither of us has seen him in at least ten years. She just said God's revenge took time but it always came through. She wouldn't speak to me."

"That *is* a story," Bobby drawled, covering his thinking.

"We can't get anywhere with Higgins & Stein," Lou said to Bobby. "East Coast distribution is set for next month, and we're still shut out of eighty percent of the South."

"That's why I thought if you'd carry us in your stores . . ." Kim said.

"Hell, I'll do better than that! J.D. Neiquist an' my father, rest his soul, they go a long way back. He'll see me. We'll have a drink an' chat about the foolishness of women, then he'll pat his little wife on the head an' give you his blessin'."

Kim suffered such a bolt of mingled indignation and relief that she stiffened helplessly.

"We're grateful for whatever help you can give us," Lou said in the soft voice a half-octave higher that Kim thought of as his peacemaker's voice. "If you can get through to Neiquist that will make all the difference, but believe me, carrying us in your own stores is important, too. The trade association is telling us we're not a convenience-store product. You could help us show them otherwise."

"What, United Convenience Stores? U.C.S.? They're a bunch of biddy hens. Sure I'll carry your food, but I'm goin' to get ol' J.D. for you, too. Kimmy here an' I go a long way back," Bobby added, giving Kim a long, full look. She met his eyes, and the blush she had been suppressing for this whole meeting rose to flame in her cheeks.

"Ah, look," Lou said to Bobby, "I've got some maps in my office. We've plotted the South, showing where we are and where we need to be. Why don't I fetch those maps? You'll get a clearer sense of what we're trying to do."

Kim watched Lou leave the room, thrilling to the drape of his old jacket and the silver radiance of his cloud of hair. Even from behind, he was so richly himself that just this glimpse of him leaving made Kim need to smile. 'Love' seemed to her to be a slick and cynical word, a way to neutralize the most intense emotions by pinning them down and naming them. And then there was *making* love, God's hideous joke. So Kim wasn't thinking about loving this man. What she thought instead was that his off-kilter features and bearish shape and the cheerfully rollicking way he moved made a perfection the handsomest man couldn't touch. And his voice! Once Kim had thought Lou sounded like a cello. Now she thought all the cellos made since time was a child had tried and failed to replicate the pure music of Lou's voice.

"Kimmy?" Bobby Sever was looking back and forth between Kim's face and her closed office door.

"Oh! Sorry. So tell me, Bobby, how is your mother getting along?"

Lion's Paw Processing Plant Number Two was a white adobe building trimmed in red that looked like an old mission. It turned a beneficent face to the street, while from behind the walls that hid its pens came the muffled lowing of cattle. From the building itself came a smell of blood and a stench of putrefaction, awful smells like persistent low-frequency sounds that jarred primitive terror centers in the brain.

"Shall I go in, ma'am?"

"No. Thanks. I've got my beeper." Kim carried in her purse a panic button that activated an alarm on the dash and acted as a homing device so Tucker could find her. "These people are major investors, believe it or not," Kim went on nervously. "Why they want to see me in the middle of nowhere I've got no idea."

Sam Denton and Hicks Waverly had failed to show up for the March board meeting. They had sent no explanation. But six outside directors made a quorum, so with Lou's help Kim had rammed through two bylaw amendments that were going to make Sam Denton furious. The stated size of the board of directors had been increased from eight to twelve, and now the president couldn't be removed except by a three-quarters majority vote. Kim had been happier after the March board meeting than she had been in months. They had gone eye to eye, and Denton had blinked. But barely a week later, Lion's Paw had filed a notice of intent to buy a majority interest in Taste of Home. As simply as that. They wanted to take over her company.

Denton had refused to talk to Lou or Jerry. He had taken Kim's call only to bark that he would talk to her in person or not at all. She had dragged him across the country twice to sit in her damn useless board meetings, so if she wanted to talk to him she could damn well return the favor. So here Kim sat at two o'clock of a sunny April afternoon, screwing up her courage to go alone into that hell of a slaughterhouse and confront her worst enemies.

"Watch your step. It's pebbles." Kim thought Tucker was warning her about the footing as a way to warn her about the smell, this ghastly horror of breathing death. Kim choked. Tucker steadied her hand at shoulder height. "Are you all right, ma'am?"

Kim had read that morning's *Indianapolis Star* on the plane flying west. She had perused every bit of it to pass the time, including an article on an inside page about the discovery of a skeleton in a shallow grave by workmen digging the foundation for a new wing on the Restop Motel. Kim had tried in the hours since reading that story to convince herself it was a coincidence, but one whiff of that slaughterhouse air made her certain of what she knew was true: the men in that motel room had murdered that long-ago prostitute for stealing their fourteen thousand dollars. Now Kim had their money, and it had grown over time to more than twenty-five thousand dollars. Perhaps she ought to go to the police, but her involving herself now was going to help no one. Still, if that desperate woman had died for that money, the least Kim could do was to use it for some wonderful purpose in her memory.

"Ma'am? Do you want me to go in?"

"No. Thanks." Kim gave Tucker a little brave smile as she released his hand. She was able to look at him more easily now that she and Vic were no longer making love in the car.

"Don't be shy about buzzing, ma'am," he called after her as she started for the door.

Beyond the heavy red door that swung open with an alarming creak was nothing but an empty corridor. And a smell. The smell inside the building was even richer than the smell outside, and here the rotten strains predominated.

"Hello? Is anyone here?"

From far away came the dim clang of metal and the faint shouts of men and an awful moaning that might have been heavy wheels turning or the despairing sounds of victims. "I'll never eat meat again," Kim said under her breath. She knocked on each door as she came to it and tried to turn the knobs, but they were locked. So she squared her shoulders and lifted her chest and headed for the double doors from which the faint sounds came. Kim had expected to find carnage beyond those doors, but instead there was nothing but a red-trimmed staircase hall and a sharp amplification of the sounds and smells that made her gag.

"Why, hello there," someone said from above and behind. Kim turned her head to see the vast, satisfied bulk of Hicks Waverly standing at the red pipe railing one floor above.

"Oh! Hello."

"Nice trip, little lady?" he asked in a greasy voice on the edge of a giggle.

"Is Mr. Denton here?"

"He's in the killin' room." Hicks was frankly studying Kim's body. He kept glancing at her face to enjoy her discomfiture. Kim clutched her purse in front of her, nervously opening and closing the clasp. Lou had tried to talk her out of coming here. Now she knew that he had been right.

"Will you get Mr. Denton, please?"

"You got to go down there."

"To the *killing . . . ?*"

Kim was standing in a small, square hallway that had a closed door centered on each wall. She had the panicky sense that her beeper signal wouldn't penetrate all this masonry, and of course no one outside would hear her scream.

"Could you tell me where to go, please?"

Hicks smiled his little piggish smile. His mouth worked briefly. "I'll do better than that, little lady. I'll take you right there to him," he said as he clanked ponderously down the stairs. "Here we go. Right on through here," said Hicks, pushing ahead of her through a door with such cool unconcern that Kim blindly followed him.

Beyond the door was a metal-grid landing and a long metal staircase that led down into a vast, noisy, brightly-lit factory of death, a chaos of sounds and colors. It was a grimly diligent, efficient hell where living things entered at one side, confused and fearful. They were processed through killing and skinning and splitting into pale hanging ghosts of meat that rode a conveyor upward out of sight. Kim's stomach was heaving. She clung to the railing with both hands, swaying with the force of her nausea, staring over the edge down twenty feet at the dark cement floor below.

"Sam!" she shouted desperately. "Mr. Denton! Please!" She was mustering the strength to call for him again when Denton appeared on the floor below, looking straight up. "I'm going to be sick," she said so softly that she realized he probably couldn't hear her.

"Of all the . . . all right. Son of a . . ." Denton muttered crankily, coming around and mounting the staircase. He pushed her through the doorway ahead of him. Once past the door, he planted himself in the staircase hallway. His fists found the hips of his bloody white coveralls.

"Mr. Denton, I – do you think we could go someplace to talk?"

Kim was patting her hair into place and trying to suppress her stomach.

"We've got nothing to talk about."

"Oh, but I think we . . . ."

"You have our notice, Miss Bonner. I suggest you get yourself a good lawyer."

She did have good lawyers. On the day the notice arrived from Lion's Paw, Steve had called the best firm of securities attorneys in Chicago. But so long as Kim refused to try their poison-pill strategies, so long as Lion's Paw complied with the rules, there was little that they could do.

"We're looking for the connections, you know. You claim to own just eighteen percent, but we know for a fact you've got almost thirty. You lied on your notification! The S.E.C. won't like that."

"We didn't lie." Sam hawked and spit pleasurably on the floor before he added, "If our friends like to buy what we're buying, we can't help that."

Denton's calm confidence and Kim's own distress were stringing her temper ever tighter. She said grimly, "That's my company. You can't have it."

"It's a public company. It's up for grabs."

"But there's no way you can buy control! You know I'll never sell!"

"I'm not so sure. I figure you've got your stock all margined. When the price starts dropping, you're going to get calls and that's when you'll be selling. I give it a month, Miss B. A month at best. You're going to be out shopping for a brand-new company."

"No!" Kim looked desperately from Sam Denton's small, angry face to Hicks Waverly's greasy-fat, bland one.

"Now, me," Denton went on, "I like that fine. But Hicks here, he's got a kinder heart. He's got the hots for you in particular. It seems to me if you're friendly to him, he just might be friendly to you."

Kim looked from Denton's mirthless smirk to Hicks's piggish grin, and all the horrors of that afternoon struck her with leaden force. She choked and whirled and pushed her way out blindly through the blood-red doors.

It was a little more than a week later that Kim and Vic took their first swim in Kim's pink-and-green flower-shaped swimming pool. The new Taste of Home colors were going to be pale salmon and a rich teal blue that research had found most customers equated with low-key luxury. The new signature would be an elegant script that ended in a witty flower: it showed that Taste of Home was grown-up enough to need a more sophisticated image, yet playful enough to still kid itself. But Kim had loved those crazy, tacky drawings of a flower-shaped swimming pool. She had liked the notion of corrupting her caricature of Highgrove with this gaudy signature of the company that had built it. So when she had seen the new pool in the ground that spring she had been vaguely disappointed, in the way that failed revenge that wasn't much wanted anyway is still a little disappointing.

The pool was beautiful beyond every dream of beauty. Those five great lobes of petals on the drawings had become just an elegant abstract design. The marble surround was a rich, pale pink. The dark-green marble inlays that had been cartoonlike scribbles of stems and leaves were accents and counterpoints so exquisite that to alter them would have made the whole less perfect. Kim stood at the tall Palladian windows that opened to the terrace off her dining room and watched steam rise from her heated pool and drift off in thin gray shreds of rain.

She and Vic were getting along better on that rainy Saturday morning than they had since the night he had taken it into his head to use a whip on her. Kim's need for his support on her board had altered their relationship once again, creating a comfortable balance of equal dominance. Kim wanted badly to keep Vic with her, and not just because she needed his vote. Even more, she needed to keep him in place as an extra shield between herself and Lou.

Lou seemed to have no idea about what Kim was feeling, but she lived now in an altered world in which Louis Pointe occupied most of her mind. She had to admit what was obvious. She was falling in love with Lou. She saw the symptoms growing worse in herself as a hypochondriac takes perverse pleasure in his own dying. She was falling in love, and it was messing up the truest friendship of her life. He was scheduled to leave at the end of July, so she had to maintain this status quo long enough to negotiate an arrangement by which he would stay. She couldn't risk destabilizing their friendship, which meant she had to keep Vic in place between them. So she could watch Vic walk back from checking the temperature in the pool, naked to the waist in the chilly rain, and feel more kindly toward him than she had felt in quite some time.

"Eighty-nine," he said with satisfaction as she held the door open for him. "Let's take a swim."

"In the rain?"

"You're worried about getting wet?"

———◆———

The water in the pool was so near skin-temperature that it felt like just a denser air, buoyant and almost breathable. Kim swam as Darcy had taught her to swim, with an up-headed puppy-stroke that had Vic laughing. "What's that? The Virginia crawl?" he sputtered from the diving board as Kim made her first foray across the pool. She took a breath and dove under the water, feeling as if she were floating weightless in a substance not wet nor dry, not hot nor cold. She had a joyful sense of having been transported to a world where creatures were free of gravity and could flit and fly.

234

The pool was fifty feet wide even at the innermost points between the petals, and almost seventy feet from petal-tip to petal-tip. The designer had argued for a smaller pool, but Kim saw this pool as her gift to Timmy. After having neglected him for fifteen years, she couldn't cheat him further with a skimpy present. She squinted her eyes open below the surface, wondering where the sides might be. The water had a gray-pink caste from the gunite sides and the gloomy day that made her feel as if she were in the maw of a living oyster. Her air was giving out. She burst upward in a rush, to find herself staring in confusion at a pair of shiny black shoes.

"What?" She was shaking hair from her face, rubbing water from her eyes with one hand as she groped for the edge of the pool with the other. She looked up and up, past dark slacks losing their crease in the rain and a soaked-through businessman's trench coat to Dominick Ashton's full pink face, squinting and dripping water. "Oh! Hello!" she said as Rosalinde appeared beside him, shrinking miserably as her uniform wilted.

"I'm so sorry, ma'am! I told him you were indisposed."

"That's all right. He's a friend."

Kim understood now that Dominick Ashton was Papa Fragone's nephew, the scion of a New Jersey crime syndicate, so she had rebuffed all his attempts to arrange a private meeting. But she had been pleasant to him. She wanted to control his vote on the board. Rosalinde turned and scurried back into the house as Dominick said sulkily, "Miss Bonner, you didn't return my calls." He had the clear, uncomplicated voice of a college student.

"I'm sorry. I've had kind of a busy week."

Vic had long ago bought Kim a string bikini, and in a burst of good feeling toward him that morning she had put it on. She couldn't let Dominick see it. Somehow he seemed too young.

Vic said cheerfully, "Strip down, Nick. It's warmer in here than it is out there."

"Oh. Well, I don't really think . . ." Kim said nervously as she watched Vic arrive at the edge beside her. Hearing him call Dominick by a nickname Kim had never heard felt surreal.

"We need to talk, Miss Bonner. About the East."

"He just needs a little of your time, baby. Hey, Nick? Just a quick meeting?" Vic flung himself over the edge with an effortless grace. Water sheeted from his body as he stood from the pool.

"I really can't right now . . . ." Kim was fumbling for a reason.

"We've got to deal, Miss Bonner."

"Call me Kim," she said, bouncing a little in the water, enjoying the chilly rain on her face and the patter of drops around her. She didn't want to alienate Dominick, but she surely couldn't meet with him, either. "Ah . . . Vic? I'm not dressed for this."

"You're not *dressed?*" Dominick said in such a high voice that Kim looked up to find him staring at the tops of her breasts. She covered them with her hand demurely.

"Come on, Nick. It's not a good time. My lady needs her weekends." Vic hooked Dominick's shoulders with a friendly arm and started with him up the marble path that led around the house to the entrance loop. Kim kicked backward, watching them go, feeling a trembling internal chill. Even though Lou kept insisting to her that organized crime wasn't what it used to be, she didn't have the energy to cope with Dominick while she was fighting to keep control of her company. She didn't know what kind of deal he wanted to make. She didn't want to have to find out.

chapter Ten

May 18-25, 1988

Pieces of fruit hit Kim's limousine like soft wet bombs, thumping on the armored doors and spattering against the windows. The strikers were chanting a complicated rhyme punctuated by shouts of "... sani-TA-tion ..." and "... abomi-NA-tion ...." that sounded like something Paul Whist might have written. Kim leaned for a peek out her dark window through the globs and streaks.

"Scab! Scab!" someone shouted. The limousine, which had been creeping forward, stopped altogether.

"Mr. Tucker? I don't think it's a good idea to let them stop us," Timmy said in his easy drawl, speaking across the lowered partition. Timmy sounded calm, as he always sounded calm. Only someone who really knew him could guess how excited he was right now, and Kim was thrilled to think she knew him well enough to be able to tell what he was feeling.

Timmy had arrived last night, fresh from his junior year exams, to find that the Taste of Home National Kitchen would be on strike as of midnight over the union's opposition to the student interns that made up a fifth of the company's workforce nationwide. Now he would have to join a thin crew of management and students in replacing more than a thousand workers.

Kim resented the rotten timing of this strike. She and Timmy deserved some time alone.

"This is kind of excitin'," Timmy said as the car began to creep forward again. Kim caught a flash of dark uniforms outside her window. The police must at last be intervening. Timmy took Kim's hand into both of his, holding it flat between them in a gesture so courtly that Kim looked at him with soft surprise. He said, "There's two ways you can look at this. You can say it's a disaster an' the world is endin', or you can say, what the hell, at least it's bound to be fun. When was the last time you worked an assembly line? When was the last time you were pelted with fruit? Come on, it's happenin'. You might as well enjoy it."

"Enjoy . . . ?" she started to say. But Timmy was smiling so beatifically that she couldn't contradict him. Kim thought she would never again enjoy anything. Her hoard of cash for propping the price of the stock was almost gone. She had even handed over to her brokers that poor murdered prostitute's precious funds, and despite all her care in timing her buys she still owned less than forty-six percent. With her brokers forced now to reduce their buys until she could sell her house, the stock had opened that morning just a few points above her highest margin level. And it had taken a little more than a month. Sam Denton had been exactly right.

There was a hard thump against Tucker's door. The car shot forward. "We're clear, ma'am. They cleared the road through the gate."

Beyond the chain-link gate, an awful sense of quiet and space descended. They were leaving the very backbone and marrow of Taste of Home outside the fence: without its workers, the company was going to fall apart.

"Are you sure Merry's here? She said she'd be here?" Timmy was craning to see out Kim's window.

"Everyone's here." Kim opened her purse to hunt for a tissue.

She had awakened that morning with a grumpy stuffiness that she had been hoping might be a literal spring fever since it was in fact the middle of May, but now her throat was sore and her nose felt peppery with suppressed sneezes. And her period had arrived, with cramps and spacey nausea.

"There it is! That's her car beside Lou's. What? He's still drivin' that old Volvo?"

Kim's assistant and Timmy had discovered one another when the summer was nearly over. They had dated twice, and Kim knew from Merry that they had corresponded and talked by phone, but Timmy had spent his school vacations in Virginia.

As Tucker opened Kim's door and offered his hand to her, Kim sniffled and said, "Can you park the car and come inside and help us work? Please?"

"I'll be proud to, ma'am," he said as he handed her out of the car.

The Taste of Home National Kitchen and its warehouses and acres of paving took up every bit of what had once been a cattle pasture of respectable size. Kim had insisted on keeping the Chow Down restaurant building intact, but from the front it was only a small blue-tiled square, barely a dot in the gray-steel facade of the plant that was three hundred feet wide and two stories high.

Kim had waited to come to work until after ten. She had wanted Timmy to have the chance to wake up naturally after his two days of driving. So when they entered the original Chow Down that now functioned as offices and a foyer, everyone else was already working. They hurried to the broad observation window that overlooked the main packaging lines.

"At least they're operating." Kim looked up and down and right and left at the vast machinery of stainless steel that portioned and wrapped her food.

"There's Merry! Hey! Let's get out there!" Timmy dodged to the right through the factory door and down half a flight of steps. Kim watched through the window as he ran fifty feet to the packing end of the beverage line, where Merry and Ellie were filling cartons. She saw Merry glance up, then saw her beautiful face suffuse with joy. Timmy caught Merry in a whirling hug and kissed her there on the factory floor while Ellie looked on, smiling the satisfied smile of a new mother.

Ellie had returned to work just a week after her daughter was born, wearing little Kimberly in a corduroy Snugli. She happily went about her business, as little inconvenienced as a kangaroo, and when the baby cried she would open her blouse without a break in her conversations. She thought nothing of mothering and nursing as she worked, so nobody else was bothered by it, either; even Lou, who had never seen a baby nursed, took Ellie's periodic baring of her breast with a calm lack of surprise.

Lou must be out there, too. The realization that Lou was so nearby rocked Kim with a brief, hard wave of butterflies. She went through this every morning now, so she courted the excitement and subdued it before she risked a situation where she might see him. He was so perceptive that if she met him unexpectedly he might deduce her stupid crush.

"Ma'am? What shall I do?"

"Oh! Tucker. Ah, why don't you go find Jerry Case? They're running at half-speed, but they're running."

Tucker went out and down the steps as Kim heard a creaking behind her. She turned. Lou came walking out of a storeroom carrying a carton of packing slips. He was dressed as everyone else was dressed, in jeans and a T-shirt, ready to work, but Kim hadn't prepared herself to see him that way. Her sore throat went dry and her hand trembled toward her face. His eyes locked on hers, a soft, dark gray. He looked not into her eyes, but through them, as if he could see right into her mind.

She said, "Hi. Good morning. I see at least they're operating."

"It's Jerry's baptism under fire. He's got two hundred people doing what twelve hundred did on a regular shift. They'll never call him a lightweight again." Lou paused, looking into Kim's eyes and through them over his heavy carton. "Have you been crying?"

"It's just a cold. But I *feel* like crying." She was hunting in her purse for a scrap of tissue.

"There are some in the manager's office. I just cleaned my glasses."

"Oh. Thanks."

Kim stepped into the manager's office, which was a double room with two desks and two credenzas. The managers were identical twins named James and Jeffrey Pomeroy: one managed each of the two daily shifts, and they looked so much alike they even shared a nickname. Kim knew them both as "Jay." They liked it that way.

She was blowing her nose for the third time when Lou came into the office and closed the door behind him. The sudden sight of him surprised her eyes wider and pushed her back a step against a credenza belonging to one of the Jays. "Do you have a fever?" Lou asked in the low, soft voice he used when they were alone, the voice that sounded to Kim like the tender love-sounds a pair of cellos might make when courting. When producing baby violins.

She had had that irreverent thought last week, when she and Lou had been discussing the lawyers' latest poison-pill proposals for foiling Lion's Paw. In the middle of one of Lou's serious sentences she had erupted in a cackling giggle that still embarrassed her so much that just the thought of it now made another giggle rise in her throat. She swallowed it firmly. "I'm fine. It's just a stupid code. I'll ged over it."

"Look, go home. Don't be a hero. We're managing."

"And run the gauntlet again?"

"I've called the police. They should be out there."

"They are." Kim was pulling a supply of tissues one by one and folding them neatly. "Do you know what used to be right here?"

She smiled reminiscently as she watched her hands working. "It was the freezer. Remember that? The old walk-in freezer?"

"I know. The stove was over there." The tone of his voice made her look at him. His eyes were soft on hers.

"We've had fun, though, haven't we?" Her eyes filled. She blinked fiercely. She refused to cry in front of Lou.

"Sweet, it's going to be all right. Paul just needs a day or two to strut his union muscle. We've got a meeting set for tomorrow, and we'll be meeting every day until the strike is settled. There are concessions we can make. It's going to be fine."

"But he won't stop until we give up the students, and they need their jobs to stay in school. We've *always* had student labor! *We* were student labor! Now Paul wants the students out of here and Denton wants *me* out of here and the Neiquists are trying to put us under, and the Fragones? Heaven knows what *they* want."

"They want to sell drugs. That's what they want."

"But we stopped that. Why don't they just go *away?*"

"Oh, sweet." Lou came around the desk and turned Kim into his arms.

"I just wanted some security. For all of us. Was that so much to ask?" Self-pity swept her with the force of her illness and the discomfort of her body's monthly cleansing. She was building up to one whopping cry. Lou was stroking her hair, murmuring to her that everything was going to be fine.

"But I can't *fight* anymore! I'm just too tired. And the more I fight, the worse it gets." Kim brought up a hand and wiped her cheeks and studied her fingers for smudges of makeup. The warmth of Lou's skin through one layer of cloth and the springiness of his chest hair made an intimacy so alarming that when she realized what she was feeling she lifted her head at once.

"I've listed my house for sale, you know," she said to cover her discomfiture. "They say I'm priced out of the market at five million dollars, but the mortgage alone is one-point-three. Can you imagine that? They arbitrarily refused to lend more than a million, three-hundred thousand dollars on a house that cost me almost *five?*"

"Who, sweet? Who's selling your house?"

"John Merrill. Sotheby's. And *speaking* of Sotheby's, I gave them my Titian and it turns out it's probably by Vander-somebody. I paid a million dollars that I'd kill to have in my hands right now, and they say I should just sue the dealer. A lot of good that does me."

"You spent all that money without being sure . . . ?"

"It's a reputable dealer. And I liked the altarpiece. In fact, I still like it. I might just keep it. It's a real Titian until somebody shows me otherwise." Kim looked up at Lou defensively, but the soft intentness of his face transfixed her. She felt protected and warm standing in his arms. But now he was about to go back to Boston, the thought of which freshly stabbed her with icy panic. "Now you're even talking about *leaving!*" she wailed, blinking up into his face. "How can you leave? What's any of this worth without you?"

Lou was looking into her eyes with such intensity that Kim began to feel unbearably close to him. She was about to step away when he bent and kissed her. He hesitated, once his lips were on hers. Then he pulled her against him with a little glad moan and kissed her a long, tender, open-mouthed kiss with a sense of his whole body just beyond his mouth that was unbearably intimate. He eased off the kiss. He drew her head down against his chest with a long sigh that she could feel more than hear. He stroked her hair with his big fingers. He said, "I want him out of your house." Kim felt his words through warm skin and springy hair.

"I know. Lou, I . . . ."

They had begun to discuss this a month ago, when Lou had said playfully that a single lady shouldn't have a man living in her home. Kim had said then, as she was on the point of saying now, that Vic had problems, he needed her, and anyway they didn't share a bedroom. She was about to give Lou her standard response for what might have been the twentieth time, but even though it was literally true, the falsity of it stuck the words in her throat.

"Look at me."

She couldn't look at him. After the awful intimacy of that kiss, if he saw her face now he would be able to guess all the shames and inadequacies of her life: her poor childhood, her rape, her sexual perversion. She was naked as she had never in her life been naked.

"Kim . . . ?"

She couldn't stand this. She could never risk loving this way again.

"Sweetheart?" He stepped back so he could look at her. She hugged her arms around herself and averted her face. She sniffled.

"Kim, listen to me. You think making everybody's life perfect is your personal task, but when it's wrecking your own life that's where you draw the line. Kim? My darling? It's enough!"

"I want you to stop seeing Connie," she mumbled, not looking at him, staring at the floor.

"What?"

"Connie. I'll give up Vic if you'll give up Connie."

Lou had taken Connie to dinner as recently as last Saturday night. He had easily told Kim about it on Monday, repeating a funny story of Connie's and praising a chateaubriand they had shared. Now there was a silence so long that she glanced at him finally.

"She's my friend. I'm not living with her."

"No, but you're . . . I don't want you having friends! *I'm* your friend!"

He was studying what had to be red eyes and a shiny red nose and a grim and stubborn chin, but his face softened as if she were completely beautiful. He smiled a tender smile that made Kim recall the way his lips had felt on hers.

"You know what we're saying, don't you?"

"Nothing! We're not saying anything." Kim looked away while the floor began to slip and the walls began to ripple.

"I know. I know. Our timing stinks," Lou said as he began to pace. Kim lifted her head enough to see that he was back in his professorial mode, walking stiffly, catching his hands behind his back. She hadn't seen that in awhile.

"I feel so stupid. I've found a hundred reasons why it wouldn't work. I was too old. I wasn't your type. We were fine the way we were. A thousand reasons. Stupid." He spun to look at Kim. She snatched her eyes away.

"There's another reason." Then she paused. Her mouth felt so stiff that she could hardly form the words.

"What reason?"

"I need you too much."

He waited while she groped for words. She had to fix this now, once and for all; she had to pull them back from this edge and make him again just her dearest friend.

"I – Lou, you're my only real family. I mean, I make family all the time but having people need you doesn't make them real family. Not like they're kin. And now Ellie's gone. Jerry's gone. Even Timmy's gone." Her eyes stung hard. She pulled a tissue and dabbed at her eyes as she went on, "Vic? Don't worry about Vic. He's getting calls from an old girlfriend. He's only stayed this long because he likes being rich."

To have Vic about to leave her for Janice seemed so inevitable and so right that Kim wasn't remotely bothered by it. She didn't want Vic. She had long since outgrown him. But still, losing him felt like one more loss in a life that had held nothing but losses. She choked on such an overwhelming need to cry that she turned her back to Lou and tipped up her chin while she swallowed her tears. A less sensitive man might have comforted her in order to ease his own discomfiture, but Lou gave her the gift of privacy.

"I'm sorry," she said finally on a long exhale. "It's just – the one sure thing in my life is you. And if we, you know, did anything, I'd lose you, too."

"Of course you wouldn't lose me! Kim . . . ?"

"No. Wait." She lifted her hand for him to see. "I know more about this than you do. I know if you – ah – if anything happened, it would turn out the way it has with Vic. But I didn't love Vic, so that was okay. But you, I . . . ."

Lou turned her and drew her into his arms and held her with her cheek tight against his chest, patiently stroking her hair. She closed her eyes and nestled there, safe and protected, feeling the rhythmic rise and fall of his chest and the wonder of his heartbeat. At first he didn't say anything. Then he cleared his throat and whispered, "Kim? Listen to me. I love you. I love you."

———◆———

The sea-moist heat in Charleston made the twentieth of May feel like late July. Kim had been looking forward to seeing this lacey city that held so much of the original South, but that two-minute walk from her jet to her limousine was enough of South Carolina's heat to last a lifetime. Bobby Sever settled into the leather seat beside her. She pushed down her armrest to keep a space between them. Ever since she had picked him up in Charlottesville at nine that morning, with the buttery light and the green smells briefly making her little plane a part of Virginia, Bobby had been trying in small, polite ways to become too familiar with her.

Kim hadn't wanted to come to Charleston now. The strike was entering its third day, and when Lou had called her from Chicago after his first six hours of negotiations with Paul Whist, she had been able to tell by what he hadn't said that things weren't going very well. What she should have done today was fly to Chicago to be with Lou, but Bobby Sever was always making Kim do what she didn't want to do. Even driving his father's Mercedes on his lap that day, with her bare legs sweaty against his bare legs and the risk of a switching if they were discovered, had been all his idea. Still, Bobby was making good on his promise to sell Taste of Home's frozen food line to southern convenience stores: there were forty-two on board now, and more coming. So she had to humor him.

"Explain to me again why you think J.D. Neiquist is on the point of giving in," she said politely while she took a tissue from her purse to tidy her dripping nose. Bobby pulled a handkerchief from his pocket and wiped his brow.

"He said as much. Does this driver know where he's goin'?"

"He has the address. Believe me, the only times we've gotten lost have been when I've tried to help. Ah, would you like something to drink while we ride? A Coke or something?"

"Dewar's, if you've got it. He can't hear us?"

"No."

Kim had lowered the wooden panel as soon as they entered the car, but she had left the clear privacy shield in place. She hooked her hair behind her ear as she leaned to open the tiny liquor cabinet near her right foot.

"Is Chivas Regal good enough?"

"Fine. Just a couple of fingers, Kimmy."

"You were saying . . . ?" she prompted politely as she poured. "Any ice?" she asked.

"No ice. Ahem. Well, Kimmy, it's like this," Bobby said, squirming in his seat while he stuffed his used handkerchief into a back pants pocket. He paused to straighten his suit and align his lapels and tie with a prissy neatness that Kim found irritating. "You were right about ol' J.D. wantin' to put you out of business." Bobby nodded his thanks as he accepted his drink. "It seems he an' his wife had a deal goin'. It's, well, kind of indelicate."

"We're all grown up here," Kim said, sounding so impatient that Bobby glanced at her. She hadn't meant to sound impatient. She was trying to learn to be skillful with people, as Lou was skillful. "Look," she went on in as friendly a tone as she could muster, "I'm sorry, but there's a lot going on. We're in the middle of a strike. I just sold my house. Did I tell you about that?" She was glad of the chance to tell a diverting story. "I put it on the market on Tuesday, and some fan bought it yesterday for almost what I was asking – four million, six hundred eighty thousand. That's what the broker called him. A fan. He wants to be anonymous. But he says I can live there as long as I like. Can you believe that? Someone crazy enough and rich enough to spend all that money and tell me to go right on living there?"

"Watch out. You're goin' to find him knockin' on your door some night, lookin' to collect a little rental."

"I hardly think so!" Kim said stiffly. That possibility never had occurred to her.

"I'd move out."

"So then, what were you saying? About J.D. Neiquist?"

"He's got three grown children. The last thing he wants is more family. But this second wife, this Faith, has been at him about havin' a baby. So he said he'd keep you out of Higgins & Stein if she'd – you know – have her tubes tied," Bobby said stiffly. He took a gulp of scotch. Kim was mildly amazed to see what a prude her rapist had turned out to be.

"And he told you all this?"

"Over drinks. He told me a lot of things I could use against him, if it comes to that. You don't remember him comin' to the house when Daddy was alive?"

"What? No."

"He sure as hell remembers you. He kept askin' if that little pigtailed kid was really the famous Kimberly Bonner. So that's why

I thought havin' you here might help. It seems his wife is backin' out of their deal."

———◆———

J.D. Neiquist's office occupied a two-hundred-year-old mansion on the waterfront that had the sort of lacy verandas and ice-cream colors that Kim had imagined she would find in Charleston, together with spotty air-conditioning. He kept them waiting for almost two hours. While Bobby fidgeted through magazines and politely sweated, Kim used the time to call her stockbrokers and her real estate agent and Rodney Ralston at Indiana Commercial Bank. She was trying to arrange for an immediate swing loan against her purchase and sales agreement. The price of the stock was holding because very little was being traded, but if a large block should come on the market before her loan could be arranged or her house could pass, Kim would get margin calls and be forced to sell into a soft market. The brokers estimated she might have to sell a third or more of her stock before the price stabilized below thirty dollars. And there would be no way she could recover from that.

"Do you know what we might do?" Bobby said with the studied casualness of a preplanned speech. "It's Friday. We might spend the weekend down here."

"I can't. I . . . ."

"J.D. can be a congenial host. It wouldn't hurt to get to know him better."

"Really, I . . . ."

"I've already arranged it with my wife."

Kim glanced at Bobby grimly. He was pretending to read. So this was where his awkward cozying-up had been heading: he was hoping for an extramarital weekend with Kim in Charleston. She looked at his prissy, sweaty face and realized with a feeling of light release that whatever harm Darcy had done to him as a child, it wasn't her job to make it up to him now. She didn't have to feel apologetic about not spending the weekend with him. She didn't have to feel apologetic about anything.

It had been three weeks since Kim had last had sex with Vic, not realizing it was the final time. He would be removing the last of his things on the weekend. And Kim had just been thinking with cheerful relief that she was never going to have sex again; then on Wednesday, unexpectedly, Lou had kissed her. She could still bring on flutters of arousal just by recalling the feeling of that kiss, but her resolve to end her sex life was as firm as ever. Firmer. Her desire was all bound up in a man she loved so much that she could never take the risk of sleeping with him.

"Well, there you are. Sorry to keep you waitin'."

Kim looked up, and there standing in the room was a tall, spare man with a wrinkled white face and even whiter hair. Her first thought was that she had never seen him before. Then came unbidden a memory of ice cream cones on the hot veranda and this man, dark-haired, much younger, leaning to wipe her chin with a paper napkin. His voice saying something about "subdivision" to the grownups in their rocking chairs. Kim had the sense that she should be able to recall what had happened before and after that moment, but all that remained was a snippet out of time.

"You don't remember me, do you?"

"I do. Ice cream? On the veranda?"

Kim had thought it must have been a momentous moment for her to have remembered it for twenty-five years, but J.D. gave her a look as if she were trying to trick him. He was very tall. His body was oddly angled at the hips and shoulders as if he were fitting it into a smaller space.

"Come in. I can give you just a few minutes."

Kim and Bobby followed J.D. into an enormous room two

stories tall, where ceiling fans and heavy draperies and the absorptive power of all that space made a coolness more comfortable than air-conditioning. "Well now," he said as he seated himself behind a white marble desk while Kim and Bobby took chairs in front of it. "What brings you two all the way down here?"

Kim glanced at Bobby. He should have covered this before she arrived.

"Well, I own Taste of Home. You know that, right? The motel-food company? And we've got a line of frozen food that's been very well received. I'd like to put it in the Higgins & Stein supermarket chain."

"I see." J.D. tented his fingers gravely. His red-rimmed eyes darted from face to face. "It seems to me we've made that decision."

"Well, yes," Bobby put in. "But you said . . . ."

"Seems to me we've got a full line of frozen foods. No room left in the cases."

Bobby said, "Let me guess. She made the appointment."

"This mornin'."

———◆———

Kim spent that next Saturday afternoon companionably packing cartons with Vic and carrying them out to his pickup truck. They were kidding good-naturedly as they separated his life from hers, bickering about who really owned what and using old jibes with special relish because they would never be able to use them again.

"Hey, Vic!" Kim called from deep in his closet. "I found your gold chain."

"Keep it, babe. Something to remember me by."

"No, thanks. My next boyfriend won't wear sissy neck chains." Kim paused, coughing, looking around at the almost-empty space. "And hey, you forgot your cuffs. Doesn't Janice like to be tied up?"

"You'd better keep those, too, sugarbuns. And keep the whip. I'll give Lou some lessons in making you happy."

Kim froze in the closet doorway with the dainty leather cuffs dangling from her hand by their soft rope ties. She couldn't stand the way he kept bringing Lou up, which was probably the reason he did it: he imagined that Lou was about to move in. He assumed they must already be lovers.

But even with the little blight that Vic's mentions of Lou kept putting on her day, Kim was feeling better about Vic than she had in quite some time. She was desperately eager for him to be gone. She couldn't imagine that she would miss him. But still, he had shared six years of her life. He had been with her through the growth of Taste of Home. He had been as good to her as he was able to be, making full allowance for the person he was. At thirty-four, his blond hair was paler, his cheeks were hollowing, and he had the start of lines beside his mouth. But he was a handsome man. And he had once been hers. She felt as proud of him as if he were an outgrown house being passed along to another owner who would be able to make better use of it. It was when this odd combination of emotions was at its height that Vic turned from putting up his tailgate against the final boxes and dusted his hands together and said, "Come on, babe, I'll take you out for a farewell dinner."

"Oh, no thanks. Think of the rumors *that* would start."

"Come on. We'll go to some dive where nobody knows us. Maybe even, well, this little Italian place. Wear your black wig, babe. Have some pizza. Let's wrap it all up neatly."

———◆———

Kim had learned in her years with Vic to carry on two separate conversations. She could listen to him and respond appropriately while her mind was on something else altogether, and Vic was so preoccupied with himself that he seldom noticed her lack of attention. So she talked with herself while she talked with Vic, sitting in a dim booth of a restaurant that smelled of spices and cheap red wine, feeling strange and exotic in her Gibson wig and the leather jeans and jacket Vic had bought her so they could be a pair.

Kim had been entertaining all day one momentous thought. She could quit. It had first occurred to her yesterday on the plane trip back from her fool's errand to South Carolina that if she cashed out now, even after she repaid her considerable debts she should still have perhaps fifty million dollars. Fifty million dollars! With fifty million dollars, knowing what she knew now, she could start all over with a brand new company. She could bring along Ellie and Jerry and Timmy and do every bit of it right this time. No debt. No investors. No franchisees. She even thought she knew what her company would sell. She was toying with the idea of home deliveries of gourmet food. It would be more cumbersome than motel food, yes, but in closely-settled areas it ought to work well. She should have Ellie run some preliminary numbers.

"... so now I'm putting the farm on the market. The way you sold your house in two days was a good-luck sign."

"You're moving to New Jersey? What did you say your new job was?"

"Public relations. What I've always done."

She could quit! No more California cowboys, no more J.D. Neiquist, no more Fragones peddling illegal ideas. It seemed as liberating a thought as getting rid of all those boxes of Vic's old life: as she had outgrown the man, so perhaps she also had outgrown the company. But there was one problem. Lou had called her from Chicago again last night, sounding drawn and exhausted from his negotiations, making such an obvious effort to be cheerful for Kim that tears had started in her eyes as she listened to him. Lou blamed himself. He had said last night, as he had been saying for months, that every problem they had now was his fault. He had brought in the stockholders and the franchisees; he had talked Kim into accepting the union. If not for his shortsighted, book-foolish advice, she wouldn't have a care in the world tonight.

But that was nonsense. Without Lou, Kim would still be serving twenty-five motels from the old Chow Down. The steps he had advised had been careful risks taken to create a national company, and it had almost worked. It still might work. But if Kim gave up, Lou would never believe it was by her own choice, no matter what she said. He would blame himself. She couldn't imagine what he might do. So perhaps she was going to have to keep on fighting, but not for herself now. For Lou.

"Miss Bonner? Do you have a minute?"

Kim looked up blankly from her two conversations into the plump reddish face of Dominick Ashton, so shadowed in the dark of the restaurant that what she mostly saw was the glitter of table-candles in his eyes.

"We've got to talk," he said as he dragged a chair to the end of their booth.

"What'll you have, Nick?" Vic asked pleasantly. "We've ordered pizza with everything, but there's time to make it two. And they've got Bud on draft, you'll be glad to hear."

"*How* did you . . . ?" Kim looked from face to face as she groped past her amazement. "Vic, did you tell . . . ?"

"It's an Italian restaurant. He's half-Italian. He eats Italian every other night. That right, Nick?"

"You told . . . !"

"No, I didn't. It's a chance meeting. But I think he should join us. He's on the board." Vic added to Nick, "This is kind of a farewell dinner, but the conversation was dragging, anyway."

"Miss Bonner, you've been putting me off for months. Now you're going to listen to me." Dominick's young voice had adopted a kind of puppy-growl. His hands, fisted on the table, were trembling. Kim noticed irrelevantly that this man who had always been perfectly groomed now sported a wrinkled tie and two days' growth of beard. Then again, perhaps that wasn't so irrelevant. Perhaps he really was losing his mind.

Kim said, "Dominick, I know what you're doing. Our attorneys have been working with your family's attorneys, and they seem to understand very well we won't allow any funny business. We're going to buy back the franchises. No harm, no foul."

In truth, the negotiations with Papa Fragone were going extremely well. Without any levers he could pull on this company three states away from his New Jersey base, he seemed ready to drop his captive franchisees and devote his time to pigeons he could pluck more easily.

"We'll be more than fair. You won't lose money. But it's over."

"*It's not over!* You're trying to make a fool out of me! Do you know who I *am?*"

"Keep your voice down," Vic said under his breath.

"I'm his nephew! I'm the *heir!* This was my idea! Now *I'm* calling the shots, not you!"

Kim stared at this grim and nervous man so young his voice still cracked unpredictably. Just because he was bigger, just because he was male, he felt he had the right to push her around. Men had been making that assumption all her life. But Kim saw in a flash of insight that it was half her fault: until this moment, she had assumed that all men had a biological right to bully her.

She stood from the booth as she said, "Vic, here's dinner and a taxi. Do this jerk a favor and straighten him out." She fished in her pocketbook and tossed a fistful of bills on the table. She didn't stop to count it.

———◆———

The Kitchen Employees of America was an independent union that had been started by Paul Whist's grandfather in his own Chicago restaurant to forestall the advances of nationally-affiliated unions. By the time Paul inherited the Kitchen Employees it had grown to cover several hundred restaurants in six Midwestern states. Lou had suggested that Kim accept it for the same reason so many restaurants had accepted it: having a low-key union in place was protection against more militant national unions. The Taste of Home National Kitchen was only the third strike the Kitchen Employees had called in almost fifty years.

Kim was trying to reassure herself about all this, pacing her office and waiting for Lou and Paul to arrive, but the only thing that seemed important to her now was the fact that it had been a week since she had last seen Lou. One week today since he had kissed her. They had spoken on the phone every day, but just about business. The event that had grown to loom in Kim's mind as a climactic turning-point of her life seemed to have meant no more to Lou than another hug.

"Miss Bonner? Dr. Pointe and Mr. Whist are here."

Kim had asked Karen repeatedly to use first names. Being called "Miss Bonner" made her feel like a withered spinster at twenty-nine.

"Send them in, please. And ask Raul Mendoza to join us." Kim wanted to be sitting down, but her need to see Lou was such that she just steadied herself with a hand against the window-wall while she watched her door.

Paul came in first, looking scrawny in his three-piece suit, his flat eyes darting as he took in the room. That was so like Lou. He never went first. Then Lou came in, big and square and calm, pausing to close the double doors. He turned, and from across the room his eyes met Kim's. And she knew. He was feeling very much as she was feeling: confused and thrilled and desperate to see her. But not alarmed. This current of emotion between them didn't frighten him as it was frightening her.

Kim shook Paul's hand. They all took seats while she tried to keep from looking at Lou, who was pulling his usual chair closer to the left-hand end of her desk. She couldn't look at Lou. This meeting was important. If she had realized how the sight of Lou would rock her, she would have managed all this in some other way.

Then Mendoza burst in with a legal pad, looking brisk and earnest, his receding hairline and lovely brown eyes so familiar and so reassuring that Kim fixed on him gratefully as he dropped into the chair beside Paul's. They exchanged an awkward sideways handshake.

"Thanks for seeing us on such short notice, Kim," Lou began patiently when the room was quiet. "Now, the four-percent raise you know about, but Paul is making some other demands and I don't know how some of this will sit with you."

"Let's take a look," Kim said in a patient tone like Lou's, feeling as if she were playacting. She still couldn't look at him. She looked at Paul, whose flat slate-colored eyes seemed cheerier than she had ever seen them. Clearly he believed he had won.

"There are five points Paul is insisting on before his people will return to work. They're tough, given the condition of the company." Lou paused and took a breath. Kim glanced at him. His face was impassive; she couldn't read it.

"First, Paul has asked for five-percent profit-sharing on top of our existing 401-K. He knows we're not healthy enough yet to talk pensions, but he'll be looking for a start at pensions in the next contract.

"And second, Paul is adamant about holding union votes in the satellite kitchens. He's leaving the students alone for now. That's his one concession to us.

"Third, he insists on a no-layoff provision. Not straight. He knows we can't do that, but we've got to give them six months' notice.

"Fourth, Paul thinks it's important we give the workers more flexibility. Job-switching. Flexible hours. Things like that. And a say in how the jobs will be run.

"And fifth, well, this one's the worst. He says we're not giving enough incentives. He wants performance bonuses. Frankly, Kim, I'm not sure we can afford it."

Kim was watching Mendoza's hand taking notes. She couldn't imagine how Lou was avoiding leaping around the room for joy. *These were all his ideas!* Every item of the five was something Lou and Jerry had been planning to do, and since some of them were contrary to the dearest tenets of organized labor, their only worry had been that they wouldn't be able to convince Paul to go along. In six days Lou had managed to wean Paul from his original demands and install the company's terms in their place, while convincing Paul these were all his own ideas.

"Well," she said slowly.

Paul snapped, "That's it, Miss Bonner. Take it or leave it."

"Ah, well, can I see it written down? Raul? You've got your notes. Maybe you and Paul can work up a draft for me to study tonight. I mean, you know I really want to give in. But we're in tough shape. And it's kind of a shock. You'll have to give me at least tonight."

"Very well," Paul said impatiently as he stood up fast from his chair.

"Mr. Whist?" Mendoza called as he led the way out of Kim's office, walking backward as if he were coaxing a puppy. "My office is right here down the hallway. Would you like a cup of coffee?"

———◆———

As soon as the doors were closed and they were alone, Kim's smile began to tremble at the corners of her mouth. She said to her desk blotter, "You did it."

"I was afraid you were going to *un*-do it. You barely kept a straight face."

Kim lifted her head to look at him. "Oh, Lou, I'm starting to think we just might win. The price is at thirty-six and an eighth today and I've gotten a couple of calls from banks, but my house will close next Wednesday. They say they'll wait. And the price is going lower, but that's *good* news. With the house money, maybe I can get my majority back. And we're working things out with the Fragones. And now you've done this wonderful thing with Paul. We just might *win.*"

Lou was smiling his dear, crooked smile, the left side higher than the right. And now that Kim was looking at him, all she wanted to do was look at him, at all the perfections of his off-kilter face as ideally conceived as any painting. But Lou was standing. Before Kim realized what she was doing, she was standing, too. She rushed around the end of her desk and safely into his arms.

"Thank you, thank you," she whispered into his tweed lapel, trying to explain this precipitate hug. But he tipped up her chin with a gentle finger. And slowly, as if he were savoring the moment, he bent and kissed her.

To be kissing Lou again, when most of what she had thought about for a week had been kissing Lou, was such a sweet shock that Kim whimpered, trembling, thrilling to feelings more complex than arousal. She had tried in the intervening week to analyze that first kiss of Lou's in terms of kisses she had known before: Colin's playful necking and Jerry's efforts to please and Vic's kisses, moving, with flicks of tongue, always deliberately sexual. Lou's kissing held something of each of these kisses, but energized with a sense of power behind it as if this were the mildest kiss he could manage. Any minute now he might lose control. It was this fear that Lou was barely containing himself that made Kim resist him finally. She struggled. He lifted his lips from hers, looking into her eyes at close focus.

"Tell me you don't want this."

"I can't want it."

"Of course you can."

Kim pushed out of Lou's arms and moved away from him, into the space between her credenza and chair.

"You don't understand. I need you. And you don't *know* me, Lou. I . . . ."

Kim was on the point of telling him everything. If he knew what an emotional cripple she was, at least that would give him some kind of reason.

"Tell me you don't love me, sweet."

Kim met his eyes and softly said, "I can't."

chapter eleven

June 6-9, 1988

Rain pattered on the roof of Kim's car. Wind hit it, rocking it on its wheels, exploding in puffs against the windows. Kim liked riding alone at night with just her reading light for company. She was looking over for a final time her attorneys' latest poison-pill proposals and feeling ever better about her decision to do nothing. She had spent the ten days since the strike was settled buying a further one-point-eight percent of Taste of Home's outstanding stock while the price drifted downward toward the lower thirties. Now most of her money was gone again, and she was still fifty thousand shares short of a majority.

So today four securities lawyers had come down from Chicago, certain that now she would listen to reason. They had held a three-hour dinner meeting to press Taste of Home to take some hideous steps: incurring massive amounts of debt, voting golden parachutes for senior management, breaking itself into a nest of subsidiaries and selling off most of its primary assets. All designed to make the company so ugly that not even Lion's Paw would want it. Kim persisted in seeing this situation as a forced marriage to Hicks Waverly, with his little pig eyes. When she finally said, "Gentlemen, I'd rather be married than ugly," they thought she was being obscurely witty, but she had meant it literally.

There would be a strange euphoria in giving in. Already Kim was feeling it. Bobby Sever was calling daily now. Faith was balking again, she had scheduled the surgery, she had cancelled the surgery, she and J.D. were fighting. It seemed the whole future of Taste of Home in the South hinged on Faith Neiquist's final reproductive status. Kim could imagine how that gaunt old man was enjoying causing so much trouble. Well, enough. It would all be over very soon, perhaps within a matter of days. The price would drop below thirty, she would get more calls, and now she had nothing left to sell.

Kim had had dinner with Lou four times during the past week, not counting that marathon session with the lawyers tonight. He had taken her to private rooms in various Indianapolis restaurants and hotels, then ridden home with her in her limousine so he could walk her to her door and politely kiss her goodnight. He had sent her roses after every date, each bouquet a different shade, so tonight she had teased him that there could be no more dates because he was running out of rose colors. Kim had tried during their dinners to prepare him for the inevitable end, telling him she really didn't mind and trying to interest him in her brand-new business, but what worried her was his flat refusal to believe she was about to lose Taste of Home. And he thought her new business idea wouldn't work.

"That's what you said the last time!"

"I was wrong the last time. I can't always be wrong."

If he were Vic, Kim would have said, "Do you want to bet?" But she had learned how Lou took teasing to heart, assuming there must be some truth in it somewhere. She had learned so much about Lou in just the past few days. She had known only his business persona, but he had never until now told her where he grew up, what he worried about, how he envisioned God.

"Some Sunday School teacher told me once that God is like

the air. It makes it hard to do something you're ashamed of if you think you're breathing God with every breath."

Kim had told Lou her first secret unexpectedly, sitting in the limousine before he walked her to her door. They had been talking about the sorts of grades they had gotten in school, Kim's perfect report cards and Lou's spotty record of doing well only in what interested him. "That drove my mother up the wall. She wasn't too stable anyway. She used to drink all day while she cleaned the house, so by the time my father and I got home she was flying. He'd retreat to his study and do tax returns, which left me to spend my evenings hearing about my failings. They say you marry a woman just like your mother. My ex-wife was her absolute double."

"My mother cleaned house, too, but it was somebody else's house. And her thing wasn't drinking. It was sex. My father was some circus star. Timmy's father – you won't believe this – was Bobby Sever. He was barely fourteen at the time."

There it was. It had just slipped out. Kim realized what she was saying, but she went on to finish it, watching Lou's face in the glare of the security lights outside.

"Timmy told me," Lou said easily. "He says he envies the way you can remember your mother. And he says she was beautiful, which I can believe."

Telling that first secret had been an easy sharing. Telling the second secret had been harder. Lou was considerate about Kim's need for security, always dining in private rooms and slipping in and out through kitchens. Vic's new love affair was tabloid news, making him again briefly famous, and there was speculation that Kim must have a new love, too, but no one could imagine who it was. The *Inquisitor* had even run a picture of Kim hugging a silhouette with a question-mark in place of its face. So they had eaten their four dinners out together in the lonely splendor of party rooms, smiling across flowers and table candles, rearranging place settings so he could hold her hand. Lou liked to hold hands. That was another thing Kim had learned about him. He would place the warm weight of his hand on hers and clasp her fingers with a careful strength, as if he were afraid to crush a hand so much smaller.

"I met my ex in college," he told her on Friday over their shared platter of rack of lamb. "I didn't date in high school. I thought the girls considered me un-cute, but then I found out at our fifteenth reunion I had been a hunk and lots of them had tried to get my attention. Go figure."

"I, well, I didn't date in high school, either. I was living with Aunt Dagmar by then." This was the moment. She had been trying for days to work her rape casually into the conversation. She set down her fork. She stared at her plate "You see, ah, there's a reason I was living in Indiana. On my thirteenth birthday, Bobby Sever raped me." She took a long breath. There were a thousand wrong things Lou could say right now, and very few right things. He didn't say anything. "I guess it was some right he had. That's the way he saw it." Kim lifted her chin to gaze over the candle flame into the darkness of the empty room. "My mother was his servant. I was his servant, too."

"Kim . . . ?"

"And that's how I got the scar. He went crazy. I didn't understand it then, but I guess he was marking me. He cut me with his pocket knife."

"Oh, my love," Lou said softly, gathering her fingers tighter together.

"So that's why they sent me away. They couldn't imagine what he might do next. That's why my mother sent me away. She chose her lover over her own child." The pain of that burst in Kim unexpectedly. Her face contorted, her fingers fisted, and she wailed through tears she never had been able to cry all the agony of her long-ago abandonment.

Lou had been perfect that night. He had cradled Kim in his arms in the restaurant and later in the car, coaxing her to cry it all out now and trying to help her understand that in choosing to do what was best for herself, Darcy hadn't meant to do her daughter harm. "It's too bad I didn't get sent away, too," he even had said as the car was turning up the driveway. "Aunt Dagmar? No yelling? No drunken mother? It sounds like heaven!" Kim had smiled at that. And she had gone to bed that night feeling eerily lightened, as she had felt on the day when she had finally forgiven Bobby Sever.

So she thought she ought to tell Lou her third secret, too. She knew he wouldn't blink. He would consider her – well, say it – her sexual perversion to be just another unremarkable trait made endearing by the fact that it was hers. But she had pulled away from Lou since Friday night. She had refused his invitations for Saturday and Sunday. She had begged off on tomorrow and Wednesday, too.

It would have been nice if Kim had been baffled about why she was pulling away from Lou, but in fact she understood it very well. She had babbled things to Lou on Friday night that hadn't seemed important to him, given all the craziness she had been babbling; but Kim herself, hearing herself, had been shaken and appalled. She was suddenly seeing whole walls and rafters inside the crooked framework of her mind.

It was no wonder that Kim had hugged to herself for all these years the shame of her poor childhood and her rape and banishment. She knew now, perhaps she always had known, that none of that was really her fault. Yet she could hide behind those embarrassing secrets, telling herself they had to be secrets because if people knew the truth, they would reject her as her own mother had rejected her. She was so fearful of being turned away, so sure it always was going to happen, that she had kept those secrets as explanations that didn't really involve *her* at all. Kim saw now that

her terror of rejection had driven her to manage every relationship in her life. She had to call the shots. She had to be the boss.
And the thing she had loved most of all about Vic had been the
fact that she never had really loved him.

Kim wasn't sure why she had wanted to tell Lou her first two
secrets. She must have been testing him, while knowing he would
pass. He was going to accept her third secret, too, even though
it would be more awkward to tell because, unlike the others, it
was her own fault. But then what? The nakedness of loving a
man who could know her as completely as Darcy and Bobby had
known her and reject her as they had rejected her was such a
horror that just the thought of it now made Kim squirm on the
seat of her car. She thought she would do anything to keep Lou
from leaving at the end of next month, yet the only thing likely
to make him stay was a risk so great she couldn't bear to take it.

The car was rolling to a stop at the bottom of the driveway
loop in front of the house. Last winter the ground had frozen
so deeply that pipes to the fountain had been ruptured, so now
the circle was torn up so the pipes could be fixed before the new
owner arrived at the end of June. Kim was having some painting
done, too. She felt like a mother putting a ribbon into a daughter's
hair before she sent her away.

"I'm sorry about the rain, ma'am," Tucker said in his stoic
voice as he opened an umbrella and reached in to hand Kim out
of her car.

"That's all right. It's only water."

Kim was wearing a three-year-old silk suit in brilliant Taste
of Home pink. She hadn't worn it since the company's colors had
changed, but she had chosen it to brighten this dreary evening
and perhaps to reinforce her determination not to give in to the
securities attorneys. It was tighter now than it should have been.
Kim had been a size seven for the past ten years without ever
giving her weight a thought, but perhaps it was time to start

paying attention. Rain was falling gently, and the moist breeze was soft and warm on her cheeks. She said, "You know, it's a lovely evening."

"Very nice, ma'am," Tucker said politely as Kim started up the temporary boardwalk toward the door. Tucker followed her, reaching to hold the umbrella over her head. That was what saved his life. Before they had gone more than thirty feet, there was a shattering explosion of noise and light. Kim was thrown face-down on the muddy boards with Tucker's bulk on top of her. "Stay down!" he hissed into her ear. She twisted, desperate to understand. His arm swept above her head, holding a gun.

"Tucker? What . . . ?" The night was a riot of crackling light. A fire. But still she had no idea . . . .

"Let me up! I can't breathe!"

Tucker backed off her slowly, snapping his head around, sweeping his gun hand to follow his eyes. Kim sat up finally in her ruined suit and stared in wonder at her limousine blazing orange flames into the night sky. At first the fire involved just the engine, but then there was a flickering behind the smoked windows and the whole car roared and seethed with flames.

"Oh my," she said shakily. All she could think was that Dominick Ashton was so inept he couldn't even bomb a car properly. Kim's hands felt sticky. She looked at them one by one, sitting grace-lessly on the splintery boards. She said in wonder, "Tucker? I'm hurt. There's blood all over." She wasn't in pain, but she felt too giddy with shock to trust the judgment of her senses. "Tucker? I . . . ." Kim looked up at the length of Tucker as he stood up, menacing the night with his gun. She saw with dim amazement that blood was dripping from his hand.

"Tucker! Sit down. You're hurt." Kim scrambled to her feet, grabbing for Tucker, looking around desperately. The front door was opening. "Rosalinde! Call an ambulance! Call the fire depart-ment!"

"Call the *police!*" Tucker sat down ponderously on the muddy boards in the rain.

———◆———

Lou had spent most of the two weeks since the strike was settled helping Jerry restructure the National Kitchen. He hadn't been in the office, so Kim had seen him only at dinner; and she hadn't seen nor spoken with him since her car had been bombed two nights before. Because it had happened so late, the bombing had first been announced on Tuesday's evening news. Kim had directed her staff to hold all her calls, so she wasn't surprised when Lou came storming into her office on Wednesday morning. He stopped flat when he saw her sitting there, looking normal.

"Why didn't you *tell* me?"

"It's not important. The police are handling it." Kim had a big decision to make this morning. She didn't feel up to fighting with Lou.

"They *bombed* your *car,* and that's not *important?*"

"Look, Lou, I . . . ."

"All right. Let's start over." Lou went back out through the double doors and came in briskly, affecting a smile. "Hi, sweetheart! What's new?"

Kim smiled, loving the sight and sound of him. He had smoked a little in his agitation, and the familiar smell of his tobacco smoke made her feel the old sense he always had given her that she was being safely cared for.

"How have you been?" she asked him.

"Miserable." He dropped heavily into one of her guest chairs. "You're busy tomorrow night, too, I suppose."

"The police don't want me going out."

"There's an excuse for you. Why is that, pray tell?"

"They don't think the Fragones did it. After all, why would they bomb my car when we're about to buy their franchises back?

The police think it's some demented fan. They say I can't even move right now. I've had to ask the lawyers to contact the buyer. I gather he's some playboy from Chicago."

"Why didn't you tell me?"

"I knew you'd be upset."

"Damn right I'm upset!"

"Look, it's no big deal. The only bad part was Tucker's shoulder, but nothing's broken. He'll be back to work in a month. You should have seen him. He was bleeding all over from this *thing* sticking right out of his back, and still he was worried about protecting me. Who am I that he should risk his life for me? It's made me think, I can tell you."

"That's his job."

"And speaking of jobs, I've got a problem here . . . ."

"You're really something," Lou said under his breath. "I come storming in here as if it's some big crisis, and there you sit, doing business as usual."

"Look, Bobby Sever called me this morning. He says J.D. Neiquist just ditched his wife. Now he wants an immediate deal. I'm supposed to fly to Charleston right now. Today."

"Is it for real this time?"

"Bobby says he's doing it to spite his wife. And Bobby's got some goods on J.D., so he absolutely says the man is talking. The only problem is, I can't go. The police won't hear of it."

"Send Ellie."

"I've been sitting here thinking about sending Ellie. That's her job. But she's such a wimp! She reminds me of my mother." Then Kim realized with a stab of pain that was true. She had been protecting Ellie for all these years as she had wished she could have protected her mother.

"Think, Kim. Has there ever been anything she couldn't do?"

Kim looked at the folder open in front of her. It was a set of preliminary financials on Kim's hypothetical new business.

Even though Ellie headed administration for a half-billion-dollar corporation, she had been willing to spend an evening humoring some whim of Kim's.

"No."

"So, send her, sweet. It's time we both let go. I've spent years trying to shelter Jerry, but what he's done on his own is unbelievable. He met every delivery during a week-long strike, and once the strike was over he started back up without missing a beat. He's got students and strikers working side-by-side. He's already set up an incentive plan. I know it's hard, but sooner or later we've got to let the kids fly."

Kim looked at Lou then. He smiled his crooked smile into her eyes and said, "I've missed you."

She sat back, feeling the need for more distance. "I'm sorry. I guess I was afraid of where we were heading."

"I won't stop, my love. I'll never give up."

Her stomach constricted a little at that. She murmured, "I just need more time."

———◆———

When Vic appeared in Kim's sitting-room doorway that evening, looking wonderful in slick black leather, she had the irrational thought that he had never moved out. "Hi," she said, enjoying the sight of him. She sat up where she had been lying on her couch and folded in a dust-flap to mark her place in a novel that had been her escape from thinking. Timmy was with Merry so constantly now that effectively Kim was living alone. "How did you get past the guards?"

"We're old friends, remember?" Vic came into the room with easy grace and leaned to give her a peck on the cheek. He took her hand by its fingertips and stepped back to arm's-length, smiling his well-remembered smile. Kim looked up at him, feeling dazed by her lazy evening and then this unexpected visit. "You're beauti-ful," he said in his voice rich with remembered music.

"But fat. I've just noticed I'm getting fat."

He laughed at that, his laughter filling the deep quiet of the house. Kim was remembering what a fine companion he had been, how he had let her control all their interactions while giving her the illusion that he was in charge. She had liked the safety of that. Lou was so richly himself that she couldn't imagine calling any of the shots with him. Lou didn't care about fame or wealth or any of the levers that she had on Vic. She had no levers on Lou at all.

"Come on, babe. Come for a ride. I need to talk."

"What? Oh, I can't. I don't have a car."

That wasn't true. Tucker had found an armored straight Mercedes. Kim was being driven to work by a chatty fellow named Caleb White who drove in shirtsleeves crisscrossed by his ugly holster harness. Just the thought of Caleb White and his black Mercedes reinforced for Kim that strange new part of her personal definition of herself: Kimberly Bonner, founder of Taste of Home, blonde and pretty enough, with a facial scar; Kimberly Bonner, fatherless waif, long ago pathetically raped and aban-doned; Kimberly Bonner, straight-A student, tireless worker, loyal friend; Kimberly Bonner, a woman someone had hated enough to try to kill her. Even more than the bombing, Kim resented the fact that for the rest of her life she would have to carry that ghastly new self-definition.

"We'll take my car. Come on, when was the last time you tooled around in a Ferrari with an Indy winner?"

Kim was catching his familiar spicy scent complicated by some-thing like machine oil. As he had on the night she had first smelled his scent, Vic seemed compelling and exotic again. Kim had the fleeting sense that it was happening all over again and this time they would get it right.

"Did Dominick do it?"

"I don't think so. He's too cool for that."

"He's your friend?"

"He's kind of a drinking buddy. Come on. You can come as you are. We'll be right back."

Vic seized her hand and tugged her out of her study. He ran her down her hallway and her floating staircase and out into the flower-scented summer night.

"Vic . . . ?" There was an unexpected thrill to his familiar, playful domination. And what could it hurt? Nothing more had happened. That car-bombing must have been a random event. Yet they wanted her to spend the rest of her life cowering in panic? There was no harm in her taking a little ride with Vic. Kim waved cheerily to one of the guards as she followed Vic over the boards toward his black Ferrari. "We'll be right back!" she called.

Vic had parked near the blackened, crumbling spot on the pavement where Kim's limousine had burned. Bits of glass still crunched underfoot. "We'll be right back, right?" Kim said to him as he opened her door so she could slide into the deep black leather seat.

Vic drove for an hour, using so much care that Kim's linking this night with the night they had met began to seem like foolish fantasy. He talked a long and lazy streak, saying whatever came into his mind, telling her he was living with Janice now but the only woman he had ever loved was Kim.

"Ah, Vic? Don't you think we should be turning back?"

"In a minute. So, where was Uncle Louie tonight? I thought I'd have to wrestle him down to get to you."

"Oh. Well, we're not really going together. I've been afraid – I mean, I don't know how abnormal . . . Vic? How abnormal am I? Really? And could I be normal? Do you think I could have a normal relationship?"

"Sure you could, baby. We were just playing."

"Really? You're not just saying that? Where are we? Shouldn't we be turning back?"

It was almost eleven when Vic drove into the courtyard of an old factory building on the edge of Indianapolis. "You've got to see this." He was sliding out quickly. "The people I'm working for are turning it into condos," he added as he opened Kim's door.

"This is the middle of nowhere! What are you *doing?*"

"Come on, babe. It'll just take a minute."

When she resisted, Vic tugged her out of his car. He reached in to pry her fingers from the steering wheel, then from the gearshift, then from the door.

"What are you doing?" Fear stabbed Kim's belly, but she refused to be afraid of Vic.

"I told you. I'm showing you around." He was gripping her hand tight and dragging her through the darkness like a dog on a leash.

"Just *tell* me!" Tears smarted. "Tell me what this is about!"

"We're alone. You know I'm stronger. Do exactly what I say or I'll beat the shit out of you."

This was all so very like Vic. He really believed that he could do as he liked. For all Kim knew, he had some wonderful surprise in there; that would be like Vic, too. She numbly let him lead her through an open doorway into an inky blackness dank with stale, moist air that included, to the left, a circle of murky light.

"It's about time," Dominick's voice said coldly as Kim squinted, blinking in the confusing light of a kerosene lamp on a table. Dominick sat on the edge of the table, swinging his feet, a silhouette of bright slashes with the light beside him. As they approached him, Kim realized that there seemed to be others with him in a smallish room that was apparently an ancient office full of musty old factory smells.

"We meet again, Miss Bonner," Dominick said in a voice that was firm and calm. His face was all shadows and dancing light, but Kim could see that he had shaved. His suit and tie looked crisp and new. He was neatly, chillingly in control.

"Dominick. Hi." She stopped.

"Closer, Vic."

Vic tugged Kim to within a dozen feet of Dominick. His hand, firm and familiar, felt reassuring.

"Did you bomb my car?" Her voice quavered a little, which surprised her since she felt too confused to be afraid.

"I'll do the talking." Dominick slid from the table and dusted off his seat as he began to pace. "I've been patient with you. I gave you lots of time. I was ready to make you a reasonable offer. But you wouldn't *listen!*" he snapped through his teeth. "You made a *fool* out of me!"

"Look, you're not a gangster. You're a college graduate, for heaven's sake!"

"Hit her!" Dominick snarled.

She said to Vic, "What? *This* is who you're working for?"

"Shut up, Miss Bonner! Hear me out." Dominick was pacing that little room in easy strides. He made Kim think of a dog that had been intimidated by too much training and was overjoyed to be able to show its teeth. "You told the newspapers we botched your car. We were getting rid of your *protection.* Can't you see what a perfect job that was?"

As Kim's eyes adjusted to the dim light, she was picking out two men behind the table, just dark shapes. The room was small enough that she thought that was all there were.

"I was going to make you a reasonable proposal," Dominick went on, pacing briefly out of the circle of light. As he came back toward them, the lamplight flickered in his face and Kim recognized him freshly as that nervous boy who used to sweat and fidget. "I was going to suggest we divide the country. I'd take

everything east of Indiana. You could have the west. That seemed
fair to me. Doesn't that seem fair to you?"

"Sure," Kim mumbled as she confirmed once again that there
were just two others behind him. She was beginning to fight a
pointless panic, trying to think calmly, not really listening. Vic's
hand tightened around hers. She wanted to drop his hand altogether, enraged that he had lured her into this, but instead she
squeezed it.

Dominick was saying, "Let's suppose for a minute you were
out of the picture. What would happen then?"

What?

"I'll tell you what would happen. The price of the stock would
fall. Denton would buy up what he could, but he's tapped out, so
he'd be only too glad to split the country between us. He wants
the West. We'd take the East. And we'd get it for nothing, because
all those banks and brokers would be dumping all their margined
stock. Without you there, honey, nobody else is going to want it."

"Hey, wait a minute," Vic said nervously.

"Shut up! I'm still talking. You've got a choice. You cooperate,
and we'll make it clean. Auto accident. One quick bop on the head.
Or you give me trouble, and I promise even your own mother
won't know who you are. Now, which will it be?"

"You didn't say you were going to kill her!" Vic sputtered.

"That's not your affair. All you've got to think about now is
how you're going to wreck that car so you can walk away from it."

"*My* car?"

"You're a driver, aren't you? That's what you do?"

"No *way*, Nick! Not my *Ferrari!*"

"All right. You've got a choice to make, too. Either you do
what I say, or when they find that car it's going to contain two
bodies. Are you hearing me? Vic?"

Fear is cold. It was filling Kim's body with a chill that felt
like ice creeping along her veins, gradually making her helpless.

She was groping to think beyond it. That this guy was insane was a given. She had heard from the lawyers negotiating with the Fragones that the notion of trying to use Taste of Home for retail drug sales and prostitution had been entirely Dominick's, and his uncle was furious that a family business that had long been a low-risk drug-importing and -wholesaling racket had become clumsily involved in a venture so stupid. But, how do you deal with crazy?

"Which will it be, Miss Bonner?"

Was this how that long-ago prostitute had felt when the men in the motel room turned on her? Was this what it came down to, ultimately? Men were stronger and more ruthless, so they won?

Dominick glanced behind him. Those shadows came out around the table into the light, one on either side. Kim looked at each of them quickly, enough to see that they were as large as Tucker and armed with complicated-looking guns. Dominick was saying, "Vic won't give you any trouble, will you, Vic? It's his first time. He's a little confused." Dominick smiled a tight smile at Vic and added, "Don't worry about the car, my friend. We'll pay you for the car."

Kim was moving before she had thought it through. She dropped Vic's hand and approached Dominick, needing to be closer to him so they could talk, for heaven's sake, make some kind of deal about this. Moving made her feel less helpless. And her moving was confusing him. He backed up a step. There being no obvious place to stop, Kim lifted her arms, slipped them around his neck, stood on tiptoe, and kissed him. He tried to resist, but she kissed him harder. The way men kiss. It didn't feel really bad, and it was a way to break the ice. Then his arms were around her, surprisingly, and he was kissing her, too, and they were stumbling against the table, which made him break the kiss finally. He stood looking down into her face in close-focus. She murmured to him. "We're negotiating."

Dominick glanced to either side at his minions, perhaps an order that they back off. His arms were still around her. Truly, she had no idea what to do next, but when death is the alternative, you wing it. "If you want half the country, you've got it, baby." He was still holding her in his arms, looking down at her, his face unreadable. It seemed odd to Kim that he was allowing this. "*People* is wondering who my new boyfriend is. Somebody even better than Vic Engstrom. Won't they be surprised when it's you, Nickie?" Kim saw him glance at Vic. She knew that despite his height and bulk, Dominick was barely a year out of college, and close up he had a soft and boyish face. His eyes looked neither brutal nor crazy. Perhaps he was just confused. "Do you know what will really set you up for life, Nickie? Having a rich and famous wife. That's how the biggest gangsters did it. Who was it, um, slept with Marilyn Monroe? Who was that?" Before Kim could add, "And she was blonde, too," he was kissing again. This was amazing. Kim broke the kiss enough to murmur, "I wish you'd told me what you wanted was *me*, Nickie. The lawyers said it was the company. Silly them." And she was kissing him again.

He broke the kiss and said something that sounded like, "Are you serious?" Kim kissed him, harder. She found this to be not remotely arousing, but given the alternative, she could fake it. She was trying to frame being murdered in her mind as just an extreme form of Vic's sadomasochism in order to perhaps pump up some interest, but there did seem to be a line. Dominick, however, was getting into it now. She tried to help him along, moving against him suggestively, moaning a little. Gag. Dominick was apparently both inexperienced enough and randy enough to be diverted this way. His hands were moving, feeding his arousal, which seemed to Kim to be proof of his insanity. She broke the kiss and murmured, "I wanted you the first time I saw you, Nickie. I wanted to have you right on that boardroom table. Why I broke up with Vic? He wasn't *you*."

Vic. Kim glanced toward where he had been. He was stupidly still there. She shouted, "Get out of here! Vic! I hate you! Get out!" Then she was back to kissing, moving, whimpering, glad to hear Dominick's breathing growing huskier while his hands moved faster, even one of his hands grabbing hers and moving it toward his genitals. With every hard thing Kim ever had done, willingly touching this stranger privately was among the hardest, but with cloth between she could pretend it was something else she was touching. And she found that just her holding him there and moving her hand made him demented with arousal. He lifted her and sat her on the edge of the table and he seemed to be working on his zipper, but she was still dressed and his thugs were standing there.

"Uh, Nickie? Baby?" When she broke the kiss he was still into it, his hands moving harshly, his face in her hair. "I'm shy, honey. I don't want them here."

"They're my protection."

"Ah, can we maybe get a room, then?" His kissing interrupted what she was saying. She blurted more or less into his mouth, "They can wait outside?"

Vic had a cellphone in his car. What Kim didn't know was whether he would use it. He had been seen at her house tonight so he had to know that if she disappeared he would be the primary suspect, but she could imagine him trying to come up with an alibi. When the basis of a relationship is mutual utility, perhaps your need to save your partner is less desperate. She wanted to give it a few minutes, though, in case he had thought to call the police, so she played with Dominick's arousal for a bit. All her years of intensive necking without the intention of doing more had taught her a lot about male reactions and how to make arousal mutually entertaining, and she would periodically murmur things like, "If you've got me you've got the whole country, Nickie," to keep him focused on the thought that she was worth more to him alive.

Eventually Kim slid off the table with a show of being out of breath. She looked up and smiled at him and said sweetly, "Oh, I am so ready for this!" He was looking at her softly. He was buying it. Amazing. He was kissing her face and kissing her hair. She was less fearful now that she could focus intensely on finding her way through this, step by step. As she eased her arm around his waist and walked him toward the door, smiling up at him, feeling sad in a way that this boy was so impossibly screwed up, she was thinking that even if the police weren't out there so she actually had to sleep with him, that would be okay. His guard would let down eventually.

They walked out into a vast and desolate gray-black parking lot with crumbling asphalt underfoot and fencing lying in tangles. A chill wind was blowing. Kim's eyes were so adjusted to the lack of light that she was seeing well enough by moonlight. As she and Dominick headed for the car, arms around one another, his goons on either side of them, Kim dawdled a little, trying to give the police more time to get there if Vic had called them. If.

They had nearly reached Dominick's black Cadillac when there was a dim sound of motors, and around the building from the left came four cars with enormously bright headlights. Kim's first quick thought was that, good lord, the police were as inept as Vic, but then a lot of things happened quickly. Four sets of headlights in a row made seeing impossible; Dominick grabbed her hard while the muzzle of a handgun rang against her skull; there were shouts; he was dragging her. She heard Dominick shout, "I'll kill her!" as the shooting started, loud as those headlights. Then they fell.

From the moment early on Thursday morning when Lou first heard about Kim's adventure, she couldn't dissuade him from his determination to move in with her.

"But it's over! What do you think you can do that guards and police can't do?"

"I can keep you from taking joyrides with idiot former boyfriends, for one thing."

"But what about my reputation?"

"*What* reputation?"

That Kimberly Bonner had come through unscathed what was being called a kidnap attempt that had been heroically foiled by her former lover, Vic Engstrom, was what was making this national news. Kim had insisted that Vic take her to meet with a representative of an organized crime family in an effort to get their tentacles out of her business. Despite his reservations, he had gone with her. Then when Dominick had grabbed Kim, Vic had managed to escape and bring in the police and save her life. Kim's jaw was on the floor when she first heard this alternate version of reality, but her focus was on getting over the fear and sadness and residual creepiness of last night. The last thing she was prepared to do was dispute Vic's Hollywood story that was so easily and enjoyably believed, so she was in seclusion. She would talk to no one.

Kim had come close to dying last night. Her face had been buried in Dominick's chest by the force of the gun held against her head so she hadn't really seen what happened, but she had been told that most of the firing she had heard had come from Dominick's goons. Fortunately, Dominick had been a foot taller than Kim, so when he had briefly turned and they had thought that Kim was more or less shielded, a sniper had brought him down with a head-shot. "But what if he'd, you know, twitched or something? His gun could have killed me!" That was apparently an inconvenient question, so it never got an answer.

Kim was trying not to think about how close she had come to dying last night, but even more than that she was trying very hard not to think about Dominick Ashton. Twenty-three years old. She kept telling herself that he had been crazy, but then her mind would supply the look of his eyes, soft and young and sane. If she had kept him inside that building longer, perhaps just had sex with him on the table somehow and spent time with him afterward, could she have talked him out of his unfortunate career choice? By noontime, she had convinced herself that we are all in imminent risk of dying of an asteroid impact at any moment, so she was mostly past the shock of her close call. What remained was a queasy sense of having witnessed the last minutes of someone's life and a sadness that had her thinking about trying to get to the hospital to hold Dominick's hand and tell him she forgave him before they pulled the plug on him. Apparently his parents weren't quite ready to give him up.

By late afternoon, Kim was feeling so glum about the thought of going home to an empty house that she relented and said that Lou could move in. She had her best guest room prepared for him, the one she still thought of as Mr. Bobby's bedroom. When he arrived, his clothing was put away properly in the guest-room closets. Then they had a leisurely dinner by candlelight, talking softly under the dining-room echoes, holding hands, playfully feeding one another a bite of shrimp salad or a *petit-four*. Kim knew by the time their dinner was over that there would be no separate bedrooms.

Because the formal downstairs rooms were beyond any human scale, Kim had long since begun to make general use of the sitting room that adjoined her bedroom. Clara would turn on a couple of lamps and leave a plate of cookies, and Kim and Vic used to spend their evenings there, reading or watching television. Kim led Lou upstairs after dinner by a single index finger, feeling giddy with such a roil of emotion that she had no idea how she could broach this subject.

She might say that having watched Vic betray her had made her see how foolish she had been to be intimate with someone who didn't love her. She could add that Dominick Ashton had a bullet lodged inoperably in his brain, and perhaps there were things he should have said or done for someone he loved while it still mattered. She might even talk about her years of struggle toward a distant, dearly won normality. There were lots of things she could have said. But when she closed her sitting-room door and looked up at Lou's dear face, she choked on her inexpressible feelings. She hugged him hard around the waist and kissed him.

"Hey?" he protested when he had returned her kiss, but she went right on kissing him. "Kim?" He was being hopelessly titillated. He held the length of her body against his and kissed her rapid, eager kisses, but still Kim felt that he was holding back.

"I'm all right. I can do it now."

It was only when Lou was pretty far along that Kim knew for sure that she couldn't do it. She wasn't aroused. She was panicked. The way Lou was moving and the sounds he was making carried too many awful associations, and she loved Lou. She needed him. She couldn't bear to despise him.

"Wait!" she sputtered. One of his hands was fumbling to unbutton her dress. "Wait. I can't."

Lou hesitated with his lips on hers. He drew back, sighing raggedly, and studied her face. "Okay. Let's talk." He took her hand and led her to the sofa. He dropped there heavily, out of breath.

Kim sat down with a polite half-cushion of space between them. She had no idea what to say to him now. "I'm sorry. I really thought I could do it."

"Look, love, you can trust me," he said on a long exhale. His eyes were fixed on the pink silk flowers that stood inside her fireplace. "I won't think less of you. I won't leave you. I won't do whatever you're afraid I'll do."

"But you *are* going to leave me! In just a few weeks!"

Lou glanced at Kim as if she were fighting unfairly. They both knew this was the crux of the matter: he wouldn't go back to Boston if she gave him a reason to stay.

"Talk to me. There's more going on here. Tell me what it is." He was sitting slumped into the sofa. He crossed his legs. Kim knew that he was wishing for his pipe.

"Well, for one thing, I'm perverted."

That was so far beyond whatever Lou had expected her to say that his leg dropped and he struggled up against the cushions. A slow smile blossomed on his face.

"What? What did you say?"

"I'm perverted. You heard me."

Lou was suppressing chuckles while he studied Kim, suddenly all bright interest. "I love you. That's about the cutest thing I've ever heard."

"I mean it. Don't make this harder than it already is."

"You're not perverted, sweet. You just think you are."

"But I am." She was close to tears. "Vic used to, you know, tie me up and stuff. He had a whip. He had lots of kinky things. I could even, you know, I could have an orgasm from some of the things he did to me. The abnormal things." Kim turned away from Lou to hide what felt like furious blushing. Lou wasn't saying anything. This was it. This was when he was going to reject her.

Then he began to speak in a soft, light tone. "Me? I like to do it sitting up. Or standing in the shower. I like fellatio. I like doing it outdoors, and back seats turn me on unbelievably. Now you tell me, sweetheart. You tell me what's normal."

Kim felt touched by his confessions, and grateful, and overwhelmingly shy. She shifted her body toward his on the couch and barely glanced at his face as she said, "Thank you."

"I really meant it as a question. What's normal? I mean, I don't think getting a thrill from being naked in the grass is less weird than wanting to be tied up. But is it *more* weird? Should I be embarrassed? I'd really like to know."

"It's not weird. I think it's sweet."

Lou reached and softly stroked her hair and tucked it behind her ear while she battled flutters of surprising arousal. She had no idea what had changed her around so quickly. Had she found his confessions titillating? Had his acceptance freed her from the need to feel ashamed?

"Tell me what bothers you," he was saying gently as he watched his big fingers busy with her hair. "Is it nakedness? Is it being pinned down? What makes you afraid?"

"I don't know," Kim mumbled. She didn't.

"I'm sure if we just did it *once* . . . ."

"I can't."

"Sure you can. Listen." He was turned toward her now, his knee touching hers, both his hands on her hair. "Listen. You've been so brave. Here's one more thing to be brave about. We'll do it once. If it's a mistake, we'll pretend it never happened. And if it's not . . . ." He let his voice trail off as Kim shyly lifted her eyes to his. The earnestness of his face, the sweet innocence in his eyes made her feel unable to avoid giving in.

"We'd have to keep our clothes on," she said, feeling sulky. "Don't make sounds. Don't, like, breathe heavy. And stop if I say to stop."

"Keep your clothes on. Don't move or breathe. Fair enough."

"No, you can *move*," Kim said, feeling oddly like a child. She had the queer sense of being thirteen years old and being able at last to control the thing that Bobby Sever was about to do.

Lou leaned to kiss her. "Is kissing allowed?"

"Ah, sure. Just a little."

"Small kisses. Fine." He began to give her delicate pecks of kisses that were somehow more arousing than deeper kissing; she wanted to move closer, to keep his lips. Soon she was slipping into his arms on the sofa while she tried to kiss him beyond those patient, infuriating pecks.

"Can you take your panties off? Is that allowed?"

Kim was on the point of saying, "No!" The child she was at that moment couldn't bear to take her panties off. But she was adult enough to realize that her refusal would pose logistical problems. She stood and went behind the sofa and slipped off her pantyhose and panties.

Lou unzipped his fly while she was doing that, and when she stepped back around the sofa his naked erection was standing in his lap. There he was, wearing his old green tweed jacket, his dark-gray pants, his red-striped tie, with a tube of flesh standing out of his clothes so much larger than any Kim had ever seen that she choked at the sight of it.

"No! I can't!"

"Hush, love. We'll wait until you're ready."

"I'll never be ready! Put it away!"

"Come on, sweet. Cover it for me."

Lou didn't seem aroused. He seemed calm. He reached for her hand and drew her closer, pushing the coffee table away with his foot, and when she was standing at his knees he caught her other hand and said, "Sit on my lap, sweet. That's all we'll do. You'll be in complete control."

The adult Kim realized that was true; the child Kim quaked with terror. "You'll stop if I say so?" She was blinking back tears, keeping her face averted.

"Of course. You can just stand up."

Kim stood for minutes with her hands in his while tears coursed itchily down her cheeks. She wanted to do it. She had to do it. And she kept thinking she was about to do it, but when at last she began to do it the fact that she was doing it amazed her. She knelt over his lap and crept slowly forward on her knees. She couldn't bear to let him touch her privately, so after another minute or two of biting her lip and blinking while she stared off away from his face at nothing, she very bravely reached a hand under her skirt and guided him into place. She had thought he was too big. When he suddenly filled her, exactly right, the wonder of that made her meet his eyes.

"Put your arms around my neck." She did that. He put his hands on her hips and very gently, without making a sound, he began to move inside her. There was a surprising amount of pleasure in just his subtle moving. Kim moved a little with him, riding the feelings.

"This is fun," she murmured to encourage him. To encourage herself.

"Let me touch you."

"No!"

"I'll stop if you say so."

Kim hesitated, enjoying his gentle thrusting. Then she nodded, biting her lip. At once she felt his hand on her bottom, his fingers busy in the crack, while the fingers of his other hand began a rapid flicking at her tenderest places; and all the while he somehow maintained his gentle, insistent rhythm. She gasped, wanting to tell him to stop, but her mind was too crowded with pleasure to form words. She knew she must be embarrassing herself, gasping and moaning and grinning like a fool, but she could worry about all that later. Then Lou grunted while his hands froze, trembling. Kim felt cheated; she hadn't been paying attention. She wanted to see his orgasm, to feel and possess it in every detail. His fingers began to move with fresh urgency, commanding her to climax. "Wait!" she blurted. But it was happening. She was hugging him with her thighs, thrashing. She bit his shoulder, surprised to feel the wool grating harsh against her teeth.

chapter Twelve

June 13-15, 1988

The selloff that Kim had been dreading for months began on the following Monday morning. Faith Neiquist and thousands of smaller investors must have decided simultaneously to dump their stock: by ten the price had fallen to twenty-six and three-eighths, and by eleven it stood at twenty-three.

Kim fed in the very last of her money. It wasn't enough to buy control, but she saw it as the sort of gallant, foolish gesture every heroine has to make. She took the calls from banks when they started to come because the banks had the right to sell her margined stock even without her consent. She had nothing to say to them, no hope to offer, so all she could do was beg for one day's grace. She promised to try to fix the price. If they sold now, they were going to lose money, anyway.

Lou had left for New Jersey that morning. The police thought Dominick had acted alone, and Papa Fragone had already sworn that he had disowned the crazy kid months ago. He had his own problems. The last thing he needed was to get himself mixed up in Dominick's mess. Kim believed him, but Lou was convinced she would not be safe unless he flew to New Jersey and met with Papa Fragone personally. So Lou wasn't there to give Kim his advice. She had to manage this crisis by herself. She swiveled in her chair and gazed out restlessly at the rows of blank windows across the

ROBERTA GRIMES

street. It was nearly noon, so the sunlight in her office had been reduced to strips of carpet gilding. The opposite buildings bore sharp shapes of light where they had been shadowed a half-hour before. Soon they would claim every bit of the sun.

If it weren't for Lou, Kim wouldn't mind giving in. She would be on the phone this minute making a deal with Sam Denton and Lion's Paw. By tonight she would be utterly free: free of Taste of Home, free of her house and her staff, free of everything so she could start a simpler life and a brand-new company. But she couldn't give in. Lou would forever blame himself.

Kim and Lou had spent the weekend in bed, eating and watching television, talking and making love. The giddy, tender feeling of their weekend lingered even here in her office, so Kim imagined that anyone who entered the room would feel it, too. She could still smell Lou on her body, even though she had showered: he had a musky, metallic tang that she used to liken to pencil leads. It didn't seem like pencils now. It was utterly male and frankly erotic. Kim couldn't believe she had known Lou for seven years without realizing what a sexual man he was, so randy that he could make love for hours and days and never tire of it. She had never spent a weekend in bed with Vic. If it weren't for Lou, Kim would give in now. For his sake, she would have to fight. And there was just one thing she could think to do. She leaned and pressed her intercom button.

"Yes, Miss Bonner?"

"Karen? I'd like to call an emergency meeting of the board of directors. Tell them it's unofficial and voluntary. Skip the out-of-staters. You can skip Vic, too." She was on the point of saying Karen could also skip Connie, but Kim needed all the help she could get. "Try to get them for one o'clock. Tell them we'll be serving lunch."

Once the California cowboys had stopped attending board meetings, Kim had been able to appoint Rodney Ralston, Anne

Bilodeau, Connie Westlake, and Timmy as interim members to
fill her four newly-created board positions. Now she had a friendly
board again. She could generally assume that it would vote her
way, but what she was about to ask of her board went beyond any
rational bounds of friendship.

———◆———

Kim didn't want to be either the first or the last one into the boardroom, so she was exactly five minutes late. Marshall, Rodney, and
Steve were there. Timmy arrived as Kim did, looking so pale and
pinched beneath his tan that Kim gave him a one-armed hug in
the doorway.

"Chickie!" Marshall called to Kim as she headed for her chair.
"It's about time you got here. I had to cancel a court date. I'm
losing fees here!"

"Thank you," Kim said under her breath. She was so nervous
after having waited an hour and a half to begin this meeting that
she hardly trusted herself to speak.

"Does this have anything to do with the fact I had my shoes
shined this morning and the guy was using our stock for rags?"
Marshall went on. "Or was that a coincidence?"

Kim had to smile. She loved these people. She even loved
Marshall, brash and selfish, always fighting over what didn't
matter, but coming through fiercely when she needed him. And
now she could admit that she loved these people. The word rolled
easily off the tongue of her mind, even though she had hardly
given it mind-space at all before last Thursday night.

Connie was the final board member to arrive. She came in as
lunch was being served by workers in white coveralls who flung
motel boxes around the table and hurried out the door.

"Where's the fire?" Rodney asked, looking after them.

"They're on incentives," Kim said, feeling fluttery with nervousness. "Now they never want to leave the plant."

"Kim?" Connie murmured from right beside her.

"This is an experiment," Kim blurted to the table at large. "Fajitas. We're trying to keep the tortillas from falling apart. And watch the red sauce. It's hot."

"Kim?"

"Ah, hi," Kim said with a glance at Connie that gave her a glimpse of Connie's face, wise and friendly. Asking Connie to come had been a mistake. Now that Kim knew how Lou made love, the way he moved, the sounds he made, the way he liked to be touched, it was far too easy to imagine what she had refused to think about for so long.

"Kim? This doesn't have to be awkward."

It was embarrassing even to be seen with Connie. All these people surely knew that Lou had moved in with Kim. But they hadn't heard Lou explain, as he had explained to Kim, why it had taken him seven years to get there. Kim knew the whole world must find their situation ridiculous.

"I used to think any *second* I was going to say something," Lou had said, sweeping a gesture so the sheet fell away from his body where he sat against Kim's pink silk headboard. "The timing never seemed right. And then you met Vic. I wanted to take that bastard apart with my bare hands, sweetheart, but you were in love. I had to bide my time."

"I wasn't in love. Not with him. But maybe with you." Kim turned onto her stomach and looked at Lou, loving his body, thick with muscling and downy with hair. Vic's body had been slender and almost hairless. It seemed to Kim now that she had always known how splendid Lou would look without his clothes. It seemed there had never been a moment in her life when she hadn't completely loved him.

"But the killer was when you got pregnant. Until then I could deny what I knew was happening. But you got pregnant. That knocked the wind right out of me. I sat myself down and had a serious think."

"I'm sorry," was all Kim could say. She was. Even then, she would have insisted that Lou meant more to her than Vic ever could, but she had loved Lou with the self-obsessed love that a child has for a parent. It wouldn't have entered her mind to think of Lou as a man who had a man's emotions.

"I decided the only way to stay with you and still remain sane was to believe it never was going to happen. I had to love you like a brother. I had to get myself an independent life. So I did," Lou said lightly, hugging his knees over Kim's pink satin sheet. "You didn't like that. I knew you didn't want me dating. I even began to know *why* you didn't want me dating, but by then I also knew you had emotional problems. It was almost as if you couldn't bear to be loved."

Kim could smile at that, as a child smiles at stories of a long-ago time when she was younger and very much more foolish. That old Kim had nothing to do with her now. Lou was persistently opening her to him, straining to understand her; and when he found that playacting had been central to her sex life with Vic, he began to tease her shamelessly. Kim was appalled at first. Talking about it felt even more wanton than doing it. But soon, shyly, she was teasing him, too.

"I'm going to chase you all over the lawn in the rain and push you down and *force* you," she whispered.

"Then I'll put you over my knee and spank you so your whole staff can see what a brat you are!" Lou shot back, thrilling Kim beyond bearing. But she didn't think it would go beyond teasing. She found Lou's patient lovemaking so much more exciting than even the most titillating things Vic had done that she felt cheated now by her memories of all that passionless, emotionless, mechanical sex.

That she and Lou had been afraid to risk their friendship on the chance it might become something more made sense to Kim. To everyone else, it had to look ridiculous.

"Ah, chickadee?" Marshall called. "Is this going to be a meeting? I mean, it's nice to get the free lunch an' all, but I left a reverse-bride at the divorce altar. I'd like to have some reason to give when she sues me for malpractice and breach of promise."

"Oh. Yes. I'm sorry. Are we almost through eating?" Kim herself hadn't touched a bite.

"Have you checked the price? Should we do that first?" Steve asked.

"It was twenty-two at twelve-thirty. I doubt it'll go much lower than that. It hardly matters, anyway. The damage is done." Kim cleared her throat shakily. She didn't know how to begin to say what she was going to have to say.

"Now, ah, as Karen told you, this is unofficial. There'll be no minutes. But I've got a terrible problem here, and I didn't know where else to turn." Kim paused, swallowing. Tears started in her eyes. This was such a desperate situation that she didn't know how she was going to keep from crying. "Before we get to the crux, I just want to say one thing to you." She paused. Oh, what the heck. She meant it, so why shouldn't she say it? "What I want to say first is, well, Thank you. Most of you have been on this board from the start, and you've been terrific. You've always been there for me. And first of all I want you to know I love you. I do. Every one of you."

"That's nice, Mommy," Marshall said pleasantly. "You know we love you, too."

"And I'll love you no matter how this comes out," Kim went on, feeling her voice growing stronger. "If I lose this fight I'm going to be off the board, so this might be the last time we'll meet together, but please understand that no matter what happens, none of it will be your fault. You've done all you could. You've been wonderful. And what I'm about to ask goes far beyond what I've got any right to ask."

"*Here* it comes!" Marshall said.

"Shut up, will you?" Rodney snapped at him.

Then Kim realized with a chill of wonder that she had just made herself naked. She had told all these people she loved them, putting their relationship on a personal level, and now she was going to make a request so outrageous they surely would turn her down. She dropped her eyes to her untouched lunch, struggling for calm, groping for the strength to get past this ghastly realization that now she was utterly vulnerable. She was learning from Lou to face down her fears and grow beyond them. Come what may, she would survive this, too. She saw herself as a recovering phobic forcing herself to confront her worst terrors.

"The banks have been calling me." Kim lifted her chin and looked from face to face. "If the price isn't above twenty-eight by noon tomorrow, they're going to start selling my stock."

Marshall snorted, "Never happen! Not without major positive news."

"We're working on that," Kim told him patiently. "The strike was settled. That's good news. Now Lou is meeting with the Fragones, and Ellie's made a deal with Higgins & Stein. She says they'll sign tomorrow. I've got Fred doing some press releases. He's been in touch with Graham Harvey to get the word out immediately. There'll be enough good news within the next few days to cheer up the timidest investor. So all we need is a little time. Unfortunately, we don't have it."

"Have you bought control?" Rodney asked.

"Not quite. I'm thirty thousand short. I've completely run out of money." Kim paused, sighing, before she added, "That's where all of you come in."

"I *knew* it!" Marshall blurted.

"Marshall," Kim said to him, meeting his eyes, "there was

a time you regretted not buying at twenty. Now the stock's at twenty. Now's the time to buy. We're going into the South with all flags flying. The price will double and double again. You know that. You know it's the time to buy."

"Look, chick, I . . . ."

"All of you know where our stock is heading. The banks know, too, but they've got their rules. They don't have the time to wait me out. Now, all I need is enough buy orders tomorrow to nudge the price three or four points by noon. Then Lou should be back, and I know he'll buy. He's got lots of money. He never spends a dime. And tomorrow night the good news will hit, so by Wednesday we ought to see the public buying . . . ."

"Never happen!" Marshall said again. "You can't turn a stock that fast."

"We've got to try. And I think we can. If everyone in this room buys tomorrow, if we do our job and get the good news out, I think we can."

"You can have my medical trust," Timmy said from the far end of the table.

"Thanks, Tim." She tried to smile.

"I'll buy, too," Connie said. "I think you're right. The stock is a steal."

Kim looked at Connie fully for the first time. They sat around the corner from one another, so close that Kim could see soft smile lines beside Connie's eyes and such a look of tenderness about her face that it crossed Kim's mind to wonder whether Lou had made the right choice for himself. But stronger than that thought was a fresh delight in her new willingness to put herself at risk: sometimes, instead of rejection, she was going to find an acceptance sweeter than anything she could command or control.

"You won't lose your money. I promise. I've got, well . . . ." Kim paused, thinking. Her net worth at the moment was negative.

"You won't lose money. If you do, I'll find a way to pay you back. I promise. None of you will lose a dime."

———◆———

Kim spent Tuesday morning pacing her office while her brokers called her every half hour to announce the current price of her stock. She didn't know who was buying. She had asked her board members not to tell her what they decided to do. Outsiders may have seen the stock as a bargain, too, but whoever it was, clearly someone was buying. By ten-thirty the price was at twenty-four and three-eighths. By eleven, it was at twenty-five.

People had been coming and going all morning, so Kim's office had taken on the dignified and vaguely cheerful atmosphere of a well-run wake. Fred Fletcher wanted her to see press releases. Jerry came looking for Ellie, whose plane should have landed at ten-fifteen. Then Timmy and Merry brought a Taste of Home peach strudel and arranged it on her coffee table, for celebration or for consolation.

"When will Lou be back?" Timmy asked while Merry sliced the strudel. Timmy popped an end of it into his mouth.

"Any time. His plane was supposed to land at ten."

Lou had phoned her last night from his New Jersey hotel. They had talked for two straight hours. He had arranged with Papa Fragone for Taste of Home to buy back fourteen franchises, and he was convinced now that Dominick had acted alone. Lou had been on an ebullient high last night; he had whispered love-threats right over the phone. So Kim hadn't told him much about her crisis. There was nothing he could have done about it last night, anyway. She just had mentioned in passing that the price was down, but friends would be buying stock tomorrow. "You don't mind buying, do you? It's such a bargain?"

"We'll talk about it, sweetheart."

That evasiveness of Lou's hadn't bothered Kim at the time, but by dawn she was pulling each word apart to ferret out his hidden meanings. By eleven she was cranky with her lack of sleep and feeling outraged that Lou might deny her his money when she had been willing to give him her life. They hadn't used condoms. They had talked around it, kidded about the risk, and Kim had said finally that she was twenty-nine and it was time for her to be pregnant. She had said that, gazing into Lou's face and knowing that what she wanted most in this world was to conceive and bear his child. It seemed to be all she ever had wanted. She had gone off the pill two weeks ago as a way to reinforce her post-Vic decision never to have sex again, so by the weekend she had thought she might already be fertile. Every craving of her life had been concentrated in the yearning of her knees drawn up afterward and her mind turned inward to nurture each wiggle of each tiny sperm.

But that had been on a lusty Sunday afternoon, lying in Lou's arms and believing he would always feel about her the way she felt about him. Now, though, it was Tuesday. Now he was holding back his money, and Kim was thinking about the problems of pregnancy, the pains of childbirth, the risk of venereal disease.

"Lou! Hey! How was the trip?" Timmy called as he licked his fingers. Kim turned. Lou came striding in as a conqueror strides, grinning, filling her office with the wonder of himself. Kim froze, transfixed by him. He crossed the room rapidly and caught her in his arms, richly male and enormous, smelling of smoke and airplanes and stale New Jersey.

"I love you," he said into her hair. "I was starting to think I had only dreamed it."

"Hi," she said, hugging him, feeling shy and fretful.

"We've hit twenty-six!" Timmy called. "I'll eat to that."

"It's for guests," Kim heard Merry scolding him.

"We're at twenty-six," Kim said, standing in Lou's arms.

"We've got just an hour to get the price to twenty-eight. Call my brokers, Lou. Please. You're my only hope." There it was. She had put it right on the line. If he rejected her now . . . .

"I'm sorry, sweetheart. I don't have any money."

"You don't *have* . . . ?"

Kim had run calculations in her mind all night. Even allowing for taxes and living costs, he had to have at least three million dollars. Kim pulled away, feeling anguished by his betrayal. Her confidence was so new and so easily shaken. "But I know you'd make money," she said desperately as he drew her close again and began to give her gentle kisses all over her face. "You'd double your – stop it! What did you do with all your money?"

"I bought a house."

"You bought a . . . ?"

"I bought a house. It's time I settled down."

"*What* house?" she started to say. But already she knew. "You bought *my* house?" she asked with a giggle of disbelief. "You did, didn't you? Admit it! Tim! He bought my house!"

"It's kind of big," Timmy said.

"I know. I'm thinking of taking in boarders."

"You *did!* Why didn't you tell me?"

"I don't know. It didn't seem to be important."

"*Didn't seem* . . . !" But already Kim was past her delight and grappling with the problems of this new reality. She interrupted herself. "Do you think you can mortgage it?"

"I suppose so. But it'll take some time."

"You paid cash? He paid cash!" Kim gushed to Timmy.

It must have cost him every penny he had. Finding this proof of Lou's love completed for Kim a circle of belief. He loved her. He truly and completely loved her.

"You know you can have my medical trust, Kimmy. It's right in Rodney's bank."

"What? You haven't invested it?"

"Me? I mean it." Timmy was reaching for another piece of strudel while Merry slapped at his fingers. "You can have the money. It's yours. Just take it."

"I'll pay you back. How much is it, Tim?"

"I don't know. Four hundred thousand. Somethin' like that."

"Four *hundred* . . . ! That's control! We've got *control!*" Kim exulted as she began to dial her broker. "If we can mortgage the house . . . May we do it, Lou? Really? Do you mind? Oh. Hi. May I speak with Mr. Sheridan, please?" Kim placed her order breathlessly and then called Rodney to arrange for a transfer of Timmy's funds. "We'll buy control!" she gushed again as she hung up her receiver. "We'll own the company together. All three of us!"

"What's the price, Kim?" Lou asked.

"Twenty-six and three-eighths. He thought an order like that would push it up at least another point. We're thinly traded. That was a pretty big order. Oh, Lou! We're going to get our company back!"

Kim ran into Lou's arms with such momentum that she bowled him backward and spun him around. The thought of sharing control with Lou and Timmy was even more appealing than the thought of regaining control on her own: there was safety and comfort and a brand-new pleasure in needing people she knew would never turn her away.

Lou said, "Sweetheart? Denton doesn't know we've got the South. All these price changes just might spook him. If he sells now, you'll lose it all. It's risky, but I think you should call him. Now."

"Well, isn't this nice!" Ellie's frail voice said from the doorway with such brand-new firmness that Kim whirled to look at her. "Is this a party for us? Look, Kimsy!" she added to the corduroy lump against her chest. "They've got food for us and everything."

"How'd it go?" Timmy called heartily. He had been kissing

Merry, too. They must have presented an odd sight to Ellie, two couples locked in oblivious embraces.

"Easy as pie," Ellie said as she ducked for a slice of strudel. One hand rested softly on her baby's head to hold it in place. "What a nice old man he was. He was so taken with little Kimsy here, I was afraid he'd never let us leave."

"They signed?"

"Of course they signed. He says he loves our food."

"They *signed*," Kim repeated to Lou, stepping back into his arms. She watched Ellie chatting with Timmy and Merry, looking as cocky as Kim felt soft, laughing while her tiny daughter slept on with an infant's absolute trust.

"Call Denton." Lou brought up a hand to stroke Kim's hair. "Call him, sweet. It's not over yet."

———◆———

Taste of Home's stock-price fluctuations and the announcement that its frozen food would be carried by Higgins & Stein made the national news that night on all three networks. CBS even added the rumor that Kimberly Bonner had regained control, and it featured an interview with an analyst who asserted with a bland lack of emotion that Taste of Home finally had its act together. It could double in size by the early nineties. Kim only hoped Sam Denton had been watching CBS.

Sam had refused Kim's calls all day, until finally Karen had tracked down Hicks Waverley in their vegetable cannery. Rather than let Kim talk to Hicks, Sam had grabbed the phone. Kim had been so weary by four o'clock that she could hardly think what to say to him. "Sam. Hi," she had said, straining to hear him over the regular thumping hushes of his canning line.

"The stock is in the sewer, Miss Bonner! What the hell are you *doing?*"

"Oh. Well, I know. It's at twenty-eight and five-eighths . . . ."

It hadn't seemed to be an opportune time to gloat about the way she had survived the margin calls that Denton had been counting on. She would have control of the company again as soon as Lou could mortgage or sell her house.

"I, ah, just want to let you know we signed Higgins & Stein. That means we'll be able to finish our motel expansion into the South, and it should make a success of our frozen food, too. We're already selling well everywhere else. I thought you . . . ."

"Get to the *point*, Miss Bonner! I don't have all *day!*"

But that had been her point. Kim stopped talking in confusion.

"I'm losing *millions* on that stock! *Millions!*" That wouldn't matter if Kim were gone and Lion's Paw were the largest shareholder, but Denton was realizing he was losing his gamble. Clearly he was a terrible loser.

"I know. That's why I called. I don't want you to lose money. We've got the price up six points today, and with all the news coming out tonight, I feel sure the price is going back to where it was." Kim took a long breath. She didn't know whether to risk this next statement. She didn't want to upset him further. But she said, "I'm back in control, Mr. Denton. That's bad news for you, but you know it's great news for the stock. I'm planning to take this company private. When that gets out, the price will double. Just sit tight for a month or two. Wait me out . . . ."

"Don't bet on it!" Denton shouted before he slammed down his receiver.

So Kim was hoping he had seen the news on Tuesday night. And preferably CBS. But she spent an agonizing Wednesday morning feeling restless and desperate, expecting at any moment that Denton would dump his stock and she would get her lethal calls from bankers. She refused calls from everyone else because she didn't want to know how her stock was doing. She even

refused a call from Lou, who was off with Jerry inspecting satellite kitchens. He had to be following the price of the stock, and
she couldn't bear to hear anything awful from him.

Lou's concept of God as air was replacing Kim's concept of
God as government. Well, not as air, precisely: Lou's God was
more like a pervasive parent Who might not be willing to fix
every problem but was very willing to hug and comfort. Kim
was learning now to pray as Lou prayed. While she waited that
morning to lose her company, she found a new comfort in shyly
whispering her fervent wish that the phone wouldn't ring.

By noon she was feeling calmer. What would happen, would
happen; they still had the house. Even a few million dollars should
be enough to get them started on their brand-new business. Kim
was sitting hunched at her desk, biting her lip while she adjusted
the numbers on Ellie's spreadsheet projections for her planned
new home-delivery business. Lou would have to be a believer
when he saw these numbers! She was so lost in her planning that
when her doors burst open she looked up blankly at the noise and
confusion of a dozen laughing people crowding into her office.
"What . . . ?"

For once, Lou was at the front of the pack, so big and robust
with life that she sat back in her chair when he hurried around
her desk to sit down on its edge, nearly on top of her.

"What's the price?" he asked sharply, as if this were a class
and she were a slow student.

"I don't know. Twenty-five?"

"Thirty-one!"

"You *flunk!*" Timmy called from the coffee table, where he was
prying the cage from a bottle of champagne.

Lou leaned and said under his breath, "What, you've been
hiding? I wish I'd known that. You've missed an exciting morning.
The stock is going through the roof."

Kim had money again. Her net worth was back up to something like forty million dollars. But all she could feel was relief at seeing Lou again his old cheerful self: his advice was being proven sound after all.

"What *is* this?" She looked around blearily. There were plates of food and glasses and people everywhere.

"It's a party, sweet. I hope you don't mind. It was Merry's idea. I told her you'd love it."

"But . . . ?"

Lou drew Kim up out of her chair to hold her between his knees where he sat on her desk. He looped his arms around her waist, giving her his wonderful left-sided smile. Kim wanted to protest that it was too early to be celebrating. The price could drop again. Lots of things could happen. But her chest began to swell with joy as her own mind shouted down every doubt: they had the house; they were days away from buying control; and now they even had the South. Kim still had too much debt, but that TV analyst had underestimated Taste of Home's potential. It had to triple or quadruple in size. All its growth so far had been the barest beginning. And when she added *home deliveries* . . . .

"Sweetheart? My love?" Lou kissed her, grinning, and added, "You look like the canary who swallowed the cat."

Behind Lou, Kim's senior employees and some of her board were chatting and laughing over champagne and teal-and-salmon boxes of food as they celebrated all the final successes that Kim had been the last to appreciate. Giving in to happiness was another hard kind of yielding.

"Sweet?" Lou said under the party racket. "Can we talk for a minute?"

Kim returned her focus to Lou with some difficulty. This was her party. She should be in the thick of it. He said, "When I bought the house I thought I'd be saying you needed a place to live, so what the heck, we might as well get married." He paused to bring up a hand and watch his fingers tuck her hair behind her ear.

"Married?" Kim blurted.

The word didn't register at first. Then it did, and she looked at Lou, feeling amazed to realize that she had never had a concrete thought about marriage. When she had courted the notion of marrying Vic, she had imagined just a ceremony to legitimize their bastard child; she hadn't once considered the notion of marriage as a way of life. After all, her own mother had never been married.

"This is a special moment. Are you listening? Kim? For most of the time we've known one another, one of us has been a whole lot richer. I was. Then you were. Then for a day or two I was again." He swallowed, flicking his eyes over her face. "Now it looks as though you're back in the black, but we don't know. It's a special moment. It's the last time in our lives we'll be able to decide to get married as economic equals."

"Are you proposing?" Kim asked softly. Proposing. Kim had never thought of marriage, but as a child she had imagined some shadowy suitor's courtly proposal. Saying the word aloud triggered that memory, and with it a surge of childish joy.

"I'm proposing we talk about it." Lou smiled, reacting to the look on her face, which she imagined must be an idiot rapture. "I don't think anyone really *proposes* anymore. Not to tycoons. It tends to be more mutual."

"Propose, please. Take the risk."

Lou glanced at the celebration behind him, but no one was paying them the least attention. By the doors, Marshall was bickering with Rodney, while Ellie was gesturing amid a murmur of room-wide laughter as she described how tall and gaunt her bogeyman had been. After a brief hesitation and some tucking-up of the creases in his pants, Lou went down carefully on one knee there behind Kim's desk, looking up at her and taking her hand. His eyes were soft and his cheeks were beginning to flush as she looked at him. Kim felt a pang of guilt that she was putting him through all this, while the child within her chortled and danced with glee. He cleared his throat and said, "Kim? My love? Will you marry me?"

Kim sank to her knees, and he caught her and stroked her head down onto his shoulder, kissing and kissing her hair. She thought she was going to say something romantic, but still she didn't feel quite ready for that. She heard herself murmur, "I guess we'll have to get married. After all, you own my house."

about the author

R oberta Grimes is a business attorney and afterlife expert. She began her career as a novelist with *Almost Perfect* (Berkley 1992) and *My Thomas* (Doubleday 1993 BOMC QPB) before work and family intervened. Now her family is grown and her career is winding down, so she has reclaimed and reissued both novels. *My Thomas* is a well-researched recreation of Martha Jefferson's journal. It is now back in print without changes beyond the removal of some quaint Elizabethan words that Doubleday had wanted used. On the other hand, even the title of *Almost Perfect* had been Berkley's choice, so Roberta has had the joy of rewriting a novel that she hadn't seen in twenty years. *Rich and Famous* is a tale from a recent, simpler and more hopeful time when any American who was willing to work hard and take risks might enjoy unlimited success.

Roberta blogs and answers questions at robertagrimes.com.

My Thomas
Preview

THE FOREST OCTOBER 7, 1770

I begin to keep this journal at the suggestion of a gentleman who fears I shall lose my life unless I write it down. I think this a peculiar fear, and said so to the gentleman, whereupon he took from his pocket-book a worn Virginia Almanack and said, "For example, I can tell you where I was on Wednesday last."

I looked, and found that on Wednesday last he had paid 45 shillings to Harry Mullins and settled his accounts with Speirs and Ford and paid two shillings for an entertainment at Byrd's Ordinary. And he thought this important!

Gentlemen love to think about money and other such too abstract things, and they lose thereby the joy of the moment. I thought he could live better without his book.

"Your third of October is gone," he said. "Mine I shall recall in some detail forever."

"Mr. Jefferson, on Wednesday last I rendered a kettle of fat for soap and stuffed the sausages you ate this day and turned beds, I

think, to prepare for the ball and rocked my son for the pain in his
ears. What might I want to remember of that?"

I had spoken in jest, for I did not know the sensitive nature
of this gentleman. He felt reproved. His face went pale, and his
cheeks grew pink by the fire's light. He blinked. I had a terrible
thought of the air between us stiff as glass.

"You are right, sir!" I put my hand on his sleeve, the gray
brocade I had thought so fine when I first saw it at the ball that
night. "I know you are right. Indeed you are right. But some
lives are better recorded than others."

"Mrs. Skelton."

His voice was gone as stark as his face. He feels an awkwardness in the presence of ladies that has kept him still single at
twenty-seven, but we had coddled one another all evening until
our words flowed freely. This dance of words at first acquaintance is a very careful minuet, and there I had in a careless
moment trod with force upon his toe.

I opened my fan, for my cheeks were heating. I had made
myself believe all evening that I only entertained my Pappa's
guest, yet my own dismay made me know that I most greatly
desired Mr. Jefferson's friendship. This I must not do, for I
had resolved that I would not remarry. So my warm delight in
Mr. Jefferson's company as if he shed a radiance into the room
served for nothing. It only rose to flame on my face.

So I began to flirt. Flirting is my certain defense against any
greater intimacy. Flirting charms a gentleman while it puts him
away; it lets the lady lead. Then it was that I first understood the
shield that it had become for me. I lowered my eyes and fluttered
my fan and said the first artful thing that came to mind.

"You are right. All we may ever keep of each precious day is
its memory. So in memory of this evening, sir, I vow to begin
to keep a journal. But I shall not record in it shillings spent nor
featherbeds turned nor hog-fat rendered. What I shall record

will be all that matters. Emotions, Mr. Jefferson. I shall write what I feel."

Then I lowered my fan and smiled at him, and I saw in his face such a play of emotions that I nearly laughed aloud. He was charmed and distracted and surprised out of words.

"You may read it, Mr. Jefferson," I boldly said, and then it was my turn to feel abashed. There is a brazenness to blatant flirting that gave me not a care when I was young, but at twenty-two I feel the shame of it. "That is, you might read some part of it," I corrected myself from behind my fan.

Mr. Jefferson is such a kindly soul that my discomfiture made him forget his own. "I should like that very much," he said with the warmth of our earlier conversation. "You will read my shillings and pence, and I shall read the gentle thoughts of your soul. I should like that very well indeed."

That moment recorded and read again, I come to the conclusion that this my emotional journal might serve very well. I proposed it in play, yet the thought compelled me, so today I have begged of my Pappa this blank-book meant for his legal cases. He had it from a binder who wanted his trade but he never bought its fellows, so he gave it me now with all the ease of any valueless gift. Still he said, "Take care of it, Patty, please. Remember that books are very dear," as if I am ever to remain a child.

So many white pages! The fluttering bulk of them thrills and dismays me out of mind, for journal-keeping in a book so fine seems a duty near to sacred. Shall I search for adventures to feed my journal? Shall I move my thoughts onto a higher plane? I have a thought that I shall live more nobly, so as not to cause my journal embarrassment.

It seems amazing what I can recall when I sit with my journal to write it down. I have written my conversation with Mr. Jefferson as the cat heard it dozing on the hearth, near all of the words, and perfected by the fact that I have thought them through a second time. I did not say, "I shall write what I feel," but I said instead, "I shall write what I think." Yet now I prefer my second version, so I shall let my journal believe it true.

And I make a further discovery of journal-keeping. A few words written may stand for many. Reading our conversation brings to my mind the hours of the ball that went before, so I feel again the chill of the ballroom that thickens like ice in my bones. I hear the fiddles tuning to the harpsichord, and the rustle of gowns and the murmur of talk as my Pappa nods and the fiddlers begin *Les Petites Demoiselles* right merrily.

I had that first minuet with my Pappa. We always open the ball together. He is a gouty dancer, tender of feet, who dances in the fashion of twenty years past, while I dance in the latest fashion that is grandly fancy of step and gesture. We look, we are told, quite comical, and I smile and laugh, and so does he.

When Pappa had danced to the end of his wind, I had reels and country-dances with some few gentlemen who claim that right at every ball and will not be disheartened. I dance once with each and fly to the next with what must seem an excess of gaiety but is nothing more than a wish to be free of them. So I gaily danced with my usual spirit, freeing myself from my chain of beaux, and as I danced I noticed Mr. Jefferson standing tall and quiet by the parlor-door. I had gained my first sight of him only that morning, and had my introduction at dinner-time, yet the sight of him was so pleasing to me that I felt from the first a discomfiting connection. I feared that he thoroughly knew my mind, my rejection of my suitors and my liking for him, so I danced along faster and averted my face that he might not read my thoughts in it.

After I had flown from my last failed beau, I took my turn at the harpsichord. This I played on heartily until I had a thought of eyes on me, and I found Mr. Jefferson standing beside me, wearing a look most warm and kind. I dropped every finger onto the keys.

I recovered, but then all the dancers were off so I hastened the measure to catch them up.

"Will you dance again, Mrs. Skelton?"

My cheeks were heating despite the cold. It was indeed so cold that I could see my breath. I had chosen my gown and craped my hair with Mr. Jefferson in mind, yet there in the sight of him I was abashed. All my art in casting suitors aside seemed of a sudden mere artifice, for never had I met a gentleman since Bathurst's death these two years gone who had seemed to me anything but dim and foolish. To cast aside a beau who seemed warm and wise and who looked at me as if he had determined to love me required a more practiced skill than I possessed.

"Forgive me. Please. I must play on. Now I am behind the fiddles. Please do excuse me." This and other such things I said when I could say words between the notes.

"Here is your sister, Mrs. Skelton."

There came Tibby at what she told me was Pappa's bidding. My Pappa was nursing his gout by the fireplace while he plotted out matches for his daughters. Tibby is but sixteen, so he pulled her from the dance and directed that she replace me at the harpsichord when he saw that his eldest had set her hook into a splendid fish. So I stood and put my hand on Mr. Jefferson's fingers and curtsied deeply for his bow, and we whirled into the country-dance.

After that first dance came other dances. We had a heating, spirited reel and a country-dance of the handkerchiefs. Mr. Jefferson dances along most fine, light on his feet despite his height, and very loose of limb; there is a happy intensity to all he does, so he bows more deeply and steps more distinctly and speaks and listens with more attention than any other gentleman. Soon we were conversing in the intervals between the tunes, but it was only when the jigs began that I found a reason to slip away. I thought him too shy and dignified to want me to chase him around the room as some of the other ladies were chasing, to the great hilarity of all the gentlemen.

I stood on toes and said to him, "I am warmed too much for the chill of this room. Will you retreat with me to the parlor fire?"

We were alone in the parlor. We sat on the chairs. I tipped the firescreen to shade my face. We talked, I recall, of a mare he hopes to send this season to Partner, the fashionable English stallion from which we have had a promising filly. We talked of apples next, and then he told me he is building his home-farm on the top of a mountain. His servants have leveled the highest height, and there he has built what he assures me is a most unpretentious temporary cottage where he plans, nevertheless, to be living this winter. From there we went to talking of the swift passage of time, and from that exchange arose his thought that I should keep a journal.

So our Friday evening was happily spent. Less promising had been our morning meeting. This being late on a rainy Sunday, with Jack asleep and his ears at peace and an hour to come before candle-time, I shall tell what I can of the rest of that day. And since this venture of journal-keeping seems much like making a new acquaintance, I commence by recording my history. A story is never begun at its middle.

My Pappa is a practical man. When he saw that Providence had blessed him with four daughters to be given in marriage and a home-farm near to Williamsburg, he built to the eastern end of his house a ballroom larger than the house itself. It is, I confess, hardly more than a barn, for which it sometimes serves in summer, and the smell of curing tobacco fills it even at the moment of minuet. But it serves very well its intended purpose. Pappa offers three or four balls each year at the spring and fall sittings of the Burgesses, and whether or not these balls were the cause, he has disposed of two daughters out of four. That his first has come back seems to him no more than a passing inconvenience.

It is Pappa's keenest wish that I should remarry, and my own keenest wish that I should not. To be an aged spinster is a shameful thing, but I am no spinster; I was married at eighteen and widowed at nineteen, and my little son Jack is nearly three. I cannot face again all the trials of marriage, yet still I find a pang in putting it by, for its promise of love and nurturance persists even though I found the promise hollow. My Pappa's resolve that I must remarry has strengthened my own that I will not, for I must cultivate a solid will if I am to prevail against him.

I feel now just a more ardent version of my first reluctance to be a bride. Bathurst was the brother-in-law of Pappa's third wife. I had known him since the age of twelve, and played with him at cards and pebble-games, and we had ridden out on our pair of grays we had raised from foals to pull our chaise. He always swore that I would be his wife.

This promise of Bathurst's was a comfort to me at the callow age of twelve. Yet when I was fifteen, my Pappa began to give his balls that he might marry his daughters, so then I had my three years as a belle. Then did I dance! Then did I flirt! At seventeen I had four loving suitors all paying their addresses to me at once, and more beyond them, a whole garden of beaux that I might stroll and flirt for my own pleasure.

I had no wish to pluck a single flower when I might enjoy the garden. Yet Betsy grew fast behind me in age, and she fell much in love with Francis Eppes, so then Pappa commanded me to choose a husband that I not obstruct my sisters. Francis is the nephew of my dear dead mother, and Bathurst was related to my Pappa's third wife, which symmetry so pleased my fond Pappa that I chose out Bathurst from the rest. It seems a great foolishness that I chose my husband primarily upon my Pappa's whim, yet I sit here now and truly that seems to have been my strongest reason. I believed that gentlemen were much alike so it really mattered little.

My Bathurst was bold and dark of look, quite low of stature and thick at the waist and grim of a habitual set of his mouth, yet pleasant enough, had the angers and petulance he showed before his wedding-day been the worst that I would see of him. But they were the best. What had been just boyish sulking swelled after marriage into genuine rage, and his determination to have his stubborn will that had been the cause of childhood bickering became after marriage an iron rule. I shall not again place myself and child beneath the control of a gentleman who may delight before marriage in order to woo but will turn once we are wed into a tyrant-king.

It seems an adventure, this widowhood, if I may see it in that light. A widow controls her own property and holds her own children and chooses wherever she will make her abode, which seems a very garden of decisions. A married woman has no decisions at all. I know no other unmarried widow. Most are wed again before the grass grows on their husbands' graves, which is a sorry pity, since to marry or not is almost the only choice a woman may make, and the making of it in the negative gives her rights that she may earn in no other way.

So on Friday morning I did not dress like a lady expecting beaux for a ball. I was only very plainly attired in a jump with bedgown and apron over. I spent that morning with Betty and Ondine and Suck preparing dinner for forty people, which history said was the number we might expect to arrive by three o'clock. We had extra food by for twenty more, and a plan for a bread-and-apple pudding if even more people arrived than that.

Jack's ears were bothering him less that day, but he wanted to stay close by to me so Betty's daughter was coddling him on a corner of the kitchen floor.

"He is fussing, mistress!" little Bett called to me. She is eleven years old, and a child of no patience. I put her aside while I worked with Ondine at stuffing the quails that would wear to the table their own heads and feathers returned to them and set upon nests of their own pickled eggs.

Bett called again. I could hear Jack fussing the half-angry sound that he often makes when the pain is rising. I left Ondine to finish the quails, and I said to Betty, "He might have laudanum. It will vex my Pappa if he spoils this day."

That is why we were passing through the kitchen doorway at the moment when Mr. Dalrymple's carriage rumbled into the kitchen-yard.

This gentleman is Pappa's choice for me. His late first wife was a Carter cousin, and he has hundreds of pounds a year from England and estates above ten thousand acres, but he is a callous gentleman who cares too much for the show he makes. The thought of Mr. Dalrymple once alarmed me with the worry that I might be compelled to accept him, but now with my firming resolve not to wed I find in his pomposity much high humor. Courtship being what it is, with ladies meant to feign a lack of interest, I have been unable to persuade him that I am not merely being coy. I had worn work-clothes to discourage him so I was glad to see his carriage coming, and vastly amused when his postilion directed his horses behind the house into the kitchen-yard.

Mr. Dalrymple travels like the Governor himself in a carriage of dark-green trimmed in red with four black horses in silver-trimmed harness. He had standing at the back of it four footmen in varied livery, so I knew he carried other gentlemen within. His custom since he had bought the carriage was to carry the most honorable gentlemen he could find, and since the day promised rain he had found three companions willing to bear him for the sake of the ride.

My suitor had a new postilion. His former boy had run away,

and I knew from Pappa that he had bought a new Negro who had been in country for barely a year and was hardly past his sickness. He bought him, I could see, for the show he made, so tall and black on the blacker horse, and for the savings in cost. But I am certain he rued the savings when his new postilion knew no better than to drive a carriage full of noble gentlemen right around the house into the kitchen-yard.

"Idiot! Fool!" Mr. Dalrymple called, and he bounded out the door of his carriage. He pulled the postilion off the near leader and shook him by his handsome coat. The boy was young, I thought him still in his teens, a whole foot taller than Mr. Dalrymple, and broad and strong as the horse he rode. The gentleman seized his postilion's whip and beat the boy about the head with it while the boy could only tremble and make a sound very like Jack's painful fussing.

I reached for my son to protect him from the sight, but Betty had him first. She caught him up with his face in her bosom before we confronted that scene again.

The other gentlemen were descending. I could see they were as vexed as we, and as helpless as we to intervene. While it is not polite to beat one's slave, it is less polite to grab the whip and belabor the gentleman in his turn.

That was when I noticed Mr. Jefferson. I guessed at once who he was. My Pappa had described for me this tall young lawyer from Albemarle who went Burgess at only twenty-six and is kin to the Randolphs and heir to a respectable acreage far to the west beyond Richmond. Pappa sees him as not a bad secondary choice. I had thought Mr. Jefferson must be another of my Pappa's unfortunate marital candidates, which misapprehension made more confounding my first complete sight of him.

He seemed to me remarkably tall, the tallest man that I had ever seen, with a strong nose and chin and a look about him of sweet good humor and gentle wit. His hair was red-brown, less ruddy than mine, but I thought our coloring much the same. He wore an unadorned brown coat and a plain black ribbon on his queue. His hair above his ears was not even curled, but it played unruly on the moistening wind. I liked that lack of wig or powder. I liked the long, calm look of him as he stepped down out of the carriage door.

And I liked what came next. Mr. Jefferson looked at me with my child and my maid standing helpless at the kitchen door, and as he looked, he stumbled. I would have thought him the most ungraceful of men had his stumble not been deliberate, but I saw how with care he contrived to place himself directly beneath the whip.

"Pardon me, sir!" He caught Mr. Dalrymple's hands as if he meant to right himself. He put an arm about the gentleman's shoulders, standing as he did so far above him that he could have been a father instructing his son. I listened as we passed, and I heard Mr. Jefferson commending Mr. Dalrymple on the wisdom of his new postilion in having chosen the kitchen road for its deeper ruts and more obvious use. "The boy is learning quickly, Henry," I heard him say while he contrived to limp. "All he wants is a little instruction in custom."

That moment in the kitchen-yard changed all my plans for the afternoon. While Bett rocked Jack in my chamber-corner until the laudanum had its effect, Betty and I must find something splendid for me to wear to the ball. I had planned a brown sack-back trimmed in black to further discourage Mr. Dalrymple, but the thought of that gown and Mr. Jefferson together was a juxtaposition not to be borne.

"Your Pappa will believe you have changed your mind, mistress," Betty said as she searched with me through the press where I had folded away all my gaudy gowns at my husband's death. "If you dress yourself gaily he will think you past mourning."

"I will not marry again. You may count on that."

"Then make yourself less pretty, mistress."

Betty Hemings has all of a slave-woman's wisdom. She declares that her fortune and her bane is her face. And she is right, I know, for a gaudy gown is like a sign upon the bosom begging the attention of any gentlemen who might be in the way of a wife. That I did not want. My only wish was to show good Mr. Jefferson how grandly I am able to dress whenever I might choose to dress.

"I only refuse to be wasteful," I said for feeble explanation. "It seems a sorry pity to waste these gowns."

My poor dear mother died in childbed only days after I was born, so forever she will be for me twenty years old, as she is in the miniature my Pappa gave to me when I was near about the age of four. As a child, I found my comfort in her face when my stepmother often upbraided me, styling me most ugly and slothful and making me a servant to her own children. My miniature not even two inches long seemed greater to me than the living lady. As I grew, my mother remained twenty years old, now older sister, now equal friend, until now she begins to be my junior. I protect and comfort her in my turn.

Her miniature shows a lovely beauty, although my Pappa swears it is a pallid likeness. She had red hair that was prone to curl, and a tiny, fine-boned, wistful face, and a look she must have struggled for, as if she did no work at all but she sat on a cushion and smiled all the day. I have had some of her gowns made over for me. She was smaller than I have grown to be, but still I am able to wear them well. What I searched for on Friday was a green brocade with side-hoops and gold lace wrought in flowers. I thought it might go very well with the yellow stomacher and petticoat that my sister Tibby had given me when she passed my own height at the age of twelve.

"Will Tibby's quilted petticoat move, Betty? Do you think it might do well for dancing?"

"Will you look at that gentleman!" Betty said, sounding vexed. "How are those poor boys ever going to grow up?"

Betty was at the window, looking out at the boys who were gathering cider-apples in the orchard. I went to the window and looked out, too, and there was Mr. Jefferson in a crowd of four or five of the slaves, and two of Betty's sons among them, showing the boys how to throw an apple to knock other apples out of the trees.

"Mr. Stevens is going to switch them for sure, he sees them doing a thing like that!"

Betty could not call to Mr. Jefferson. I could not call to Mr. Jefferson. Even our overseer, Mr. Stevens, had not the position to reprimand a Burgess for throwing apples.

Mr. Jefferson told me when we talked that evening that the gentlemen were then at their cards and their pipes, and since he neither smoked nor gambled and he meant to plant apples in the spring, he had gone out to see what varieties we had and how they were doing in our ground. When I told him that our overseer would not approve of throwing apples, he said it had been an experiment. He had asked Martin Hemings if throwing would work, and since Martin had not known the answer, Mr. Jefferson had determined there and then to find out.

I needed two gowns, a simpler one for dinner and a gaudier one to wear to the ball. The green, when we found it, was wrong with the yellow, so for the ball I chose my sister Betsy's apricot lustring trimmed in fine imported Alencon lace that might well never fit her again. Betsy is great with child, and she has put on such a layer of flesh that even her stays are unlikely to help her. For the dinner, which Betty would soon have to serve – she only had time to crape my hair – I chose a pink chintz with a white linen petticoat embroidered in many-colored flowers.

The dinner table for forty people had been set up on trestles on the ballroom floor and spread with a length of homespun linen and laden with the fruits of our three days of work, our quails and sausages and squash-corn salads and kidney-mutton savories and sweet-potato biscuits and our cheese-cakes and moonshines and orange pies.

Some ladies in attendance wore homespun, too. This seems to be a coming fashion, what with the nonimportation resolutions imposed on us by the Association. The King has resolved to tax our imports to pay for business of his own, and this affront has so heated Virginia that gentlemen have been pleased to ban the import of nearly everything. When Governor Botetourt gave a holiday ball, every lady there was in a homespun gown.

For me, however, this banning of imports is taking a switch to one's own head. If gentlemen had to spin and weave, they would show a greater respect for cloth.

There was such excitement on the air! I could not help but feel it, too, even though I was grim to resist for fear that it might charm me into making one gentleman more important than the rest. My custom is to play the harpsichord as a reason for avoiding most of the dance, and I generally play it even at dinner, before and after I have my bite. Mr. Burwell's William is a fair hand at the fiddle, so we play together, he and I. We did this while the company gathered, choosing a light Italian tune that I played while William improvised a sprightly gay accompaniment. We really sounded rather well.

Betty has for long been a lady's maid, but now she is training Bett to be my maid because Ondine has slow rheumatism. More and more, Betty is compelled to assume control of the house. She likes this, I think. Her mind is restless. So even though she is breeding again and only weeks from childbed, she oversaw the dinner serving, using for waiters mostly her children. Martin and Bob came in from the orchard, and Mary, Betty's oldest, whose mind is willful, and even little Jim. Nance came in to see the dinner with baby Critta on her hip, and this occasioned one awful moment that makes me shudder even now.

My Pappa has married and buried three wives. The last of them lived for barely a year. That he turned away from marriage after that was a thing that did not surprise me at all, but that Betty's children began to come paler a year or two after his last wife's death was a phenomenon I did not understand until after my own marriage.

Our Betty's father was a sailor named Hemings who left her complexion rather pale. Her four oldest children are tall and dark, but Bob and Jim are bright mulattoes with heads of molasses-colored hair. Baby Critta is a gray-eyed towhead. In the arms of her own dark sister, Nance, she looked as white as any child.

"John!" one of the gentlemen called to Pappa from partway down the table. "John! Is this a grandchild? Who is this?"

Since he knew that a baby at a ball wearing nothing but a threadbare blanket could never be a child of the family, he said this only to tease my Pappa.

"No," Pappa said. "She is a servant's child." Pappa seemed amused by this interplay, but I felt knotted-up with rage. That every lady cast her eyes demurely and every gentleman thought it a jest was a fact I had more reason to rue than any other person there. I grimly looked the length of the table and found Mr. Jefferson sitting in what looked to be a mortified silence. I liked him still better for the look of his face that told me that he found no humor in the thought of a master bedding his slave. I resolved at that moment to make his further acquaintance.

But now it is long past candle-time. Jack is waking from his nap and fussing for milk and bread for supper. And I am tired, but I find that writing all of this down has eased my mind. I am going to like journal-keeping very well.

CPSIA information can be obtained
at www.ICGtesting.com
Printed in the USA
FFOW01n1255160414
4874FF